Originally published in Great Britain by Orion Publishing Group in 1993.

CATBIRD PRESS
16 Windsor Road, North Haven, CT 06473
800-360-2391; catbird@pipeline.com
www.catbirdpress.com

Our books are distributed to the trade
by Independent Publishers Group

This book is a work of fiction, and the characters and events in it
are fictitious. Any similarity to real persons, living or dead,
is coincidental and not intended by the author.

Library of Congress Cataloging-in-Publication

Raphael, Frederic, 1931-
A double life / by Frederic Raphael.
ISBN 0-945774-46-X (cloth : alk. paper)
I. Autobiography—Authorship—Fiction.
2. Diplomats—France—Fiction.
3. Retirees—France-Fiction. I. Title
PR6068.A6.D68 2000
823'.914—dc21   99-053507

I

One evening, when I was *en poste* in Buenos Aires, during the late 1960s, I was invited to a reception at the British Embassy. General de Gaulle was still resisting Britain's application to join the European Community; Anglo-French relations were tense, even as far away as the Argentine. Before we left the Embassy, it was agreed that my Ambassador, Pierre-Henri Mercuès, would play the hard line, while I gave off-the-record hints that a compromise was bound, in the long run, to be reached. The purpose of our duplicity was not so much to confuse the British as to leave evidence that, whatever the eventual outcome, it was a triumph for French diplomacy. Whether Mercuès or I proved to have made the correct forecast, France would maintain her reputation as a leader of the world's game.

It was a September evening at the beginning of Argentina's least amiable season. The rich had closed their villas in Punta del Este and had returned to the capital. Their faces darkened from weeks on the Uruguayan beach, the Punteños now welcomed the opportunity, even as they complained about the cold, to display their furs and their Harrods cashmere. After I had done my duty at the reception, I went into one of the downstairs anterooms in the British Embassy to recover my coat. It had been hung in the furthest recesses of the double closet. In order to reach it, I was obliged to go deep inside. When two other diplomats entered the room, they assumed no one else to be present. As often happens, they began to talk more earnestly and more candidly on the verge of parting than they had during the public part of the evening. One was Henry Capel, the British Second Secretary; the other was a Belgian called Vincent Werstricht ('*notre Flamand*' as some of his colleagues called him). Vincent and I often played tennis at the Marian college close to the suburb where we and the Werstrichts both rented houses with gardens suitable for children.

The two men were already talking about someone as they came in. There was conspiratorial glee in their dissection of his character. I gathered that he had characteristics in common with the then French foreign minister, who spoke English with a glacial competence which somehow conveyed his disdain for England. The Belgian, a gourmet who hated the fishy steaks of Argentina and whose rotundity did not interfere with smart movement around the tennis court, said that he suspected that the subject of their conversation used *vous* even when speaking to himself.

The Englishman said, 'Oh, he's such a snob that I don't find it easy to imagine him deigning to talk to himself at all!'

Such furtive malice was commonplace in the world of diplomacy. Obliged to see the same people over and over again, we were tempted to vary official effusiveness with covert spite; two faces are more entertaining than one. Even behind the scenes, what seemed to be purely personal relations were never wholly free from diplomatic considerations. If we were always nice to Africans, our off-the-record attitudes to other colleagues were often affected by what was happening thousands of miles away. Private affability could be exaggerated when our masters sought closer ties with certain countries; it might stiffen to frigidity when there was a coldness between our distant capitals. Among professionals, the cleverest blows are always struck after the bell.

As an inadvertent spy, I recognised that the Englishman and the Belgian were making a meal, or at least a snack, of the Frenchman for whom they seemed to share a common contempt. 'Don't you find it typical of the French,' Capel said, 'to consign public relations to someone with whom it would be difficult to imagine having relations of any kind?'

The Belgian laughed more heartily at this laborious epigram than it warranted, as if to prove that his country was capable of tact as well as waffles. 'What's so amusing about him,' he said, 'is that he confuses slyness with caution: if you ask him the time, he looks at you as if he wants to know whether you're buying or selling!'

Concealed among the more or less sumptuous street-wear of the diplomatic community (the poorer the country, the grander the wardrobe), I pondered on which of my colleagues at the Embassy was being discussed. I attempted to supply a name to fill the bill, just as, when first glancing at a crossword puzzle, one makes a random conjecture before giving reasoned attention to its aptness to every part of the clue. When I heard a mention of 'Florentine deviousness', I suspected that my Ambassador was being accused of it, but then Mercuès was scarcely 'as thin as the end of de Gaulle's wedge'; nor did my bachelor chief have a wife who 'drank for two and fucked for no one'.

When, as they laughed, the Belgian said, 'Oh, I quite like Guy in a way,' I continued to try, with fatuous solemnity, to think who else on our staff, apart from myself, was called Guy and hence might qualify for their derision.

After I realised that I was their subject, I was neither mortified nor even offended. So far as they knew, I had not been privy to their conversation; hence I was able, when eventually I appreciated that I was its target, to feel that it did not touch me personally. I did not even dispute the accuracy of their aspersions on the character under whose name I conducted my life; I simply discovered that I was not identical with him. If I was capable of being wounded, it was not on account of what anyone thought about Guy de Roumegouse, the *chargé d'affaires* at the French Embassy, a career diplomat whose life was, to the common eye, indistinguishable from my own.

Oddly enough, I felt a new warmth towards my colleagues as I listened to them, quite as someone else might if he had by chance overheard an unexpected compliment. If I was not pleased to be taken for a dry stick, I felt a certain pride in having carried off a successful imposture. I may even have been a little drunk with it: instead of emerging, which might have temporarily put my fellow-diplomats at a disadvantage, but would almost certainly have blighted our future relations, I luxuriated in the cosy depths of the cupboard until they had collected their things, fortunately without disturbing me. I was so exhilarated that I removed what I assumed to be my own dark coat from its hanger and strolled out into the hallway.

My wife was at a cocktail party at the Plaza Hotel; I had said that I would join her there. I ambled through the streets, relishing the solitary anonymity. Although Buenos Aires is said to be the Paris of South America, its broad avenues – flowing between tall banks of masonry – never seemed very Parisian to me. The *Sandwicherias*, with their rolled *dobles* and *triples* cut longwise from the oily loaves, were tempting, but they never offered the seductions of a good *bistrot*. One can smell the sea in BA, when the breeze blows in from the estuary, but the Seine has another flavour entirely. Only the women, in their black dresses and their coquettishness, reminded me of Paris.

It was the hour when the rich moved about the city in their cars or strolled down the Calle Florida, looking in the expensive windows as though it needed only a surge of desire for them to buy whatever happened to be on show (no one could admit that the prices would cause him to hesitate). Two couples walked ahead of me towards the Plaza. The women wore furs and diamonds, their ostentatious defencelessness advertised the potency of the men who accompanied them. Were those two tight-buttocked females the men's wives? Their

3

style was that of cocottes. When they pointed at the windows of a smart tailor's, I could hear them declaring that various articles – a vicuña coat in particular – would suit the men to perfection and that they really ought to indulge themselves. It was obvious that the women expected to be rewarded with new outfits at the same time; their encouragements were veiled demands. I was sufficiently interested in their diplomatic style to slow down and look in the window myself. The effect was quite alarming: I caught sight of a stranger, in a coat longer than mine, with velvet facings and quadruple buttons on the sleeves. The stranger was, of course, myself; in my curious state, after hearing Capel and Vincent Werstricht talking about me, I must have taken a coat adjacent to mine, and of similar cut.

I saw myself in the silvery light of the tailor's window and I wondered why I should never have acquired a coat of such elegance. It did not make me handsome, but it lent me a distinction I should never have chosen for myself. Filled with an unfamiliar, but almost irresistible sense of power and shamelessness, I told myself that, of course, I should return at once to the British Embassy, where the owner of the coat I was wearing would, no doubt, be looking with irritation – if not scorn – at the one I had left in exchange. However, I determined to postpone the moment of rectitude. Feeling in the pockets of my new coat, I discovered that there was a set of keys in a small pocket inside the main one, on the right. In the main pocket, I found two torn tickets for a cinema; there was also a piece of paper, chaffed almost to dust, with a name and a half-effaced telephone number. In the left pocket, which I now searched with eager fingers, I discovered a folded receipt for repairs to a Mercedes. From this I learnt that my name should have been Rudolph Jurgens.

Disappointed to come upon no more revealing clues to the nature of the life lived by the person whose coat fitted me so much more sumptuously than my own, I straightened my shoulders and gazed with unaccustomed directness into the reflected eyes of one of the women who was admiring the vicuña coat. She looked at me quite as if she recognised me, or at least some quality which she supposed me to possess. For a moment, I learnt what it was to be fashionable rather than correct. I might have been left temporarily at the wheel of a sports car which I scarcely knew how to drive; her eyes credited me with a brio I did not own. I was reminded of the great Juan Fangio, who had been asked, in a recent interview in *La Prensa*, why – unlike most Argentinians – he drove so discreetly off the track; he had replied that he was never sure when he might meet someone who thought he was Juan Fangio coming the other way.

4

I am a person who, should he meet himself coming the other way, would be in small danger of being swept off the road. Yet I walked on down the Calle Florida, rather than turn back to retrieve my own coat, imagining that I was Rudolph Jurgens, a person of means who was not, so far as I knew, in the diplomatic service. Was he a German? Almost certainly, but he might be a businessman or a landowner whose presence in South America owed something to his history in a Reich some of whose leaders, as I had reason to know, had been astute enough to make alternative arrangements when their good days were coming to an end.

As I reached the curve of private drive that went in under the *porte-cochère* of the Plaza Hotel, I saw the two couples had stopped in front of the windows of the jeweller and silversmith whose shop could also be reached from inside the lobby. One of the men was shaking his head at his woman who turned away from him, with a petulant shrug, and looked directly at me. She was not, I thought, the same one who had eyed me before, but her attitude was of a piece with the other. I had an inkling of what it would be to find all women equally accessible and equally amenable.

I glanced away with a haughtiness which belonged less to me than to my coat and looked into the jeweller's window. As if with borrowed eyes, I saw a woman holding up a silver brooch which had coloured panels in it. She was talking as she inspected the merchandise and the jeweller was humouring her. I thought that the customer looked rather discontented, but also rather attractive, in a slightly heavy fashion. When she took the piece of jewellery away from her face, she caught me looking at her and, still under the influence of the man I was dressed to be, I imagined a hint of cold encouragement in her manner. Then her expression changed, and so did mine: the woman was my wife and I, of course, was her husband.

When we met, in the lobby of the hotel, she remarked on the vulgarity of the coat I was wearing and advised me to return it as soon as possible. I went back to the British Embassy the following morning and informed Henry Capel of my stupidity. He took me to the closet in which I had hidden the night before and there, sure enough, was my own overcoat. Henry was apologetic about the mix-up, quite as if he had been responsible for it. Suspecting that he was embarrassed that no one had coveted my coat, I responded with forgiving geniality. As it happened, I felt a new sort of friendliness towards him; I found the memory of his disparagement endearing, not because I had mastered my resentment but because I felt none. Inadvertently, he had proved to me that I was invulnerable to a kind of affront which might

5

seriously have wounded a different sort of man. Throughout my life, in one way and another, I have noticed that I dreaded pain less than most people. Perhaps I have been spared it in its most savage forms; perhaps I feel it less keenly than others. The same may be true of pleasure.

Henry was saying that he thought it very decent of me to return so handsome a garment as the one he was hanging in the cupboard, against the day when Herr Jurgens (who owned factories near Mar del Plata) should return to claim it. He had almost certainly been driven away in his chauffeured car and had not noticed his loss. Was Capel even vaguely anxious that I might know what he and Vincent thought of me? He certainly favoured me with tenacious friendliness as we stood in the lobby of the Embassy. He was even courteous enough to ask what I thought of the international situation and whether another war was likely (confirmation that he had no faith in my capacity for small talk). Since it was a particularly sour period in East-West relations, I observed that it was always dangerous to be much stronger than one's rivals. Perhaps in order to disprove his humourless view of me, I advised him to make sure he had plenty of tins in his larder; if there was a war, it might well last a full week. He replied, without a smile, that he knew exactly where he was headed if he had to join the army again. 'I'm just waiting for the opportunity to go back to Rangoon – as a wireless operator, but I'm going to make sure I have a really decent set next time.'

As I buttoned myself into my own tight coat, I said, 'You can't beat the Japanese, can you?'

II

Although it pleased me to receive the congratulations of my family when I was accepted in the Service, I had no great ambition to be a diplomat. I am not sure that I have ever had great desires of any kind. I have had two wives, but I did not marry either of them because I could not imagine life without her, although in the case of the first one, I came very much to wish for it. Despite this, I had two children with Berthe and I should probably still be with her, had circumstances been a little different. Did I ever love her? She seemed suitable for the young man I was when I met her; I had good reasons for thinking that she was a sound choice, although I was to discover that my parents' enthusiasm for my decision was based on more factors than their concern for my happiness.

I met my present wife during my last tour of duty, when I was First Secretary at the London Embassy. I had hoped to crown my career with an ambassadorial appointment, but the promise of a 'life after death' reconciled me to modesty: I was told that, if I accepted the number two position, I should receive a lucrative, tax-free job in Brussels, after my formal retirement. It was a favour which I should as soon not have been offered, but I accepted it with every sign of loyal gratitude.

Maureen was a widow, with two daughters already on the verge of independence. She and her husband had divorced and he had then been killed in a road accident. 'I'm not sure,' she said, 'that that qualifies me to be a widow, but it sounds nicer than divorcée, doesn't it?'

I saw her first leaning over a table writing an address on a programme before a lecture at the Institut Français in South Kensington. When she straightened up rather suddenly, she seemed aware that my eyes had been on her. She was very slim and looked better from behind than full face. Although she had a pleasant expression and regular features, what she took for polite interest was, I fear, closer to disappointment. I expected more flesh on her, and a less correct manner, although had she possessed them it is very unlikely that I should have dared to make contact with her. As it was, I

7

made a professional effort to be agreeable to her, without knowing who she might be. Finding her neither particularly attractive nor particularly interesting, I was able to speak to her with a fluency which she may well have taken for enthusiasm. She sat beside me at the lecture and stayed with me most of the evening. She seemed more animated at the end than when she first looked at me; I, on the other hand, had been more intrigued by the shape of her haunches as she bent over the table than I was by all of her subsequent sociability. Her dark hair had regular grey streaks in it, either because nature had procured them or because she had it done like that; I am not a man who easily distinguishes between the natural and the contrived, so far as women are concerned. Maureen has blue eyes (an Irish characteristic, she told me) and a slightly roguish get-away-with-you briskness which may derive from her years as a nurse.

When the visiting speaker took his last solemn question from the audience, he responded by a quotation from Lord Byron about 'sermons and soda water' and their suitability for procrastination. For some reason this inspired Maureen to touch my arm, as though I had been responsible for its conclusive aptness, whereupon I asked her whether I should be seeing her again. It was a polite way of soliciting another meeting (for which I had no particular appetite), but there was something typical in the unassertive way I put the question: I might have been consulting someone who knew the future better than I, an oracle in hat and gloves (she often wears both). I could have pretended to be a different sort of man altogether; instead of which, I pretended to be myself. She said, 'That's very much up to you, isn't it?'

My wife was in Paris, where her father was dying, again. We had been on frigid terms for so long that I was unused even to the trite amiability which Maureen was displaying. I looked at her winsome, ageing mouth and the girlish blue eyes and her trim nose with its saddle of freckles and even as I concluded that I had no great wish to see her again, I was arranging to meet her at the weekend. Being committed to her would enable me to duck another, tentative invitation from which I had seemed powerless to escape, although I knew it to have been prompted only by dutiful geniality on the part of a Mahgrébin diplomat. I happened to have heard that there were races at Sandown Park, because a colleague had offered me tickets, so I said, 'Do you like the horses?'

She cocked her head and looked at me from her favourite blue eye, with the other turned aside. 'You like to go to the races!' It was as if she had made a bet with herself about my inner character which my entirely untypical invitation confirmed. 'I like them *very* much,' she said.

'I think you're a diplomat,' I said.

'No,' she said, 'it's my Irish blood. It's rather hot and it likes a gamble!' She went on watching me, as if to make sure that I drew all the necessary conclusions.

So it was that we went to Sandown, although I suspect that neither of us much wanted to do so. During the afternoon and evening which followed, I recognised that she had begun the day without any large hopes but that, as it progressed, she began to take the measure of my marital unhappiness and to fancy her chances. I felt no renewal of my first perfunctory sexual interest in her. I waited for her to find another opportunity to display herself to me as she had when she leaned over the table in the Institut. It was less that I had a fetish for that specific posture than because its repetition would indicate that her gentility was only a pretence. I liked to think that she knew all along what had excited my first, almost impersonal interest. If she repeated the posture, I should have her implicit promise that she had guessed what really attracted me to her and that she might, in due course, again make it available to me.

She found no occasion for any such promising reprise. She preferred to chatter in what she took to be a lively manner and to flatter me with questions about French foreign policy under Giscard. Although I felt no more than a certain amusement at her laborious thoughtfulness, I was unable to resist a continuation of our almost arbitrary romance, if that is the right word for it. As we drove back to London in the Renault, she told me that we were both grown-up people and we could not pretend to be children. Nevertheless, she believed in second chances.

Did I? I was too courteous to say that I had no great sense of having been offered one. Besides, I was not sure that I had ever had a first chance. My marriage with Berthe had not been arranged, in the old, formal way, but it had been so convenient that it was more a transaction than a matter of the heart. Berthe's family, the de Jardins, belonged to the *haute bourgeoisie* and had emerged with its wealth largely unscathed by the war. However, two of her cousins were on the board of an engineering company which had rather too sincerely collaborated with the Germans. I had an uncle who appeared to have been similarly unwise, although – as I shall explain – he came out of it better than Berthe's relations. In fact, he was able to give evidence of a necessarily concealed patriotism on their part which did much to retrieve the de Jardins' reputation. My uncle played a crucial part in my childhood; he was, to say the least, a man of considerable resource. The services he rendered the de Jardins did much to secure my acceptance, as a Protestant, in my fiancée's Catholic family. Condescension and gratitude were nicely blended.

Berthe seemed a quiet, handsome girl when I first met her. It was easy, and tempting, for me to believe that there was something predestined in her coming to my parents' house, towards the end of the war, in order to be safe from the fighting. Had I seen her in her own family milieu, which was much richer than mine, I should probably have been even shyer than usual in my attitude to her, but since, at first sight, she seemed almost to be a refugee, I treated her with a sort of hospitable disdain which may have given her the impression that I was of a confident, even domineering, character. I did not stay long at La Fontaine du Noyer during those dangerous months, since I was wanted by the Germans (and the Milice), which added a certain heroic lustre to the other false impression Berthe had of me.

During the negotiations which preceded our wedding, I must surely have appeared much more like my real self, but Berthe was convinced by then that I was only pretending to be the unremarkable person whose future, like hers, seemed once again to be in the hands of the older generation. She greeted my apparent willingness to do whatever our parents wanted as a clever, even satirical, masquerade which concealed from them, but not from her, the forceful character whom she would meet in the marriage bed. It is in this belated light that I interpret the brilliance in her eye during the weeks of our engagement. If I was unaggressive, in sexual matters, she almost certainly took my correctness to be a seductive hint about how different I should be when we were alone. The last thing she suspected was that I was innocent; the last thing I imagined about her was that she was not.

I was unconcerned by the stipulation that our children be raised as Catholics, since my own religion was more an excuse for spiritual indifference than the reflection of any intimate convictions. I quite liked the idea of having children with whom my disagreement could take the form of tolerance. I suspected that Berthe would never excite my keen desire (even if I was capable of it) and – rather rashly – I assumed that I should be equally exempt from jealousy. I think it is honest to say that I did not marry her for her money (to which I have had small access) or because her lack of sexual allure, for me at least, would raise no doubts about my own. I see no causal links beween what was, or was not, true of our hopes or intentions and what actually happened. Berthe had money; she did not excite me; I married her.

Maureen came from Sussex, she told me, as well as Ireland. The English seem to delight in complicated lineage. They combine disdain for other races with eagerness for a measure of alien blood. Maureen's mother, Mrs Braybrook, had a Scottish grandfather; her father (who was dead) had been an Irish Protestant civil engineer with a Norwegian grandmother. I displayed an exemplary interest in these dilutions.

Mrs Braybrook lived in a flat in a Palladian country house near Crawley Down. It had been divided into rentable sections. The tenants had access to gardens which still had an air of grandeur that the partitioned house could not match. I was invited to Copthorne Court a few weeks after I met Maureen. Mrs Braybrook was already in her eighties. Her flat had a large living room whose antique clutter reminded me of one of the rooms in my maternal grandmother's house, Le Prieuré, near Angoulême, where we were staying in June 1940, when we heard that France had requested an armistice. I did not feel any residual affection for my grandmother, but when I remarked on Mrs Braybrook's rather distant resemblance to her, I gave the impression that I had discovered an unexpected reason for liking her (and Maureen). Why should I say that it was my hostess' lipless face and knobbly, claw-like hands which most keenly recalled my mother's mother? How could I explain, even to myself, that the memory of that rather repugnant and miserly old woman seemed to make meeting Mrs Braybrook a source of secret pleasure and inspired me to redouble my attentions to her?

I was already sixty-two when I met Maureen, who was in her mid-forties, so she said. Is it typical of me that when she told me her age, I rather hoped she was lying? I do not mean that I wanted to marry a liar, only that I have always thought of lying as a form of courtesy. I should not like to have anything to do with a woman who did not take the trouble to deceive me.

Our excursion to Copthorne Court had been presented to me as a kindness to Mrs Braybrook. We had made a detour on the way home from some jumping races, to which Maureen's quite fallacious instinct told her I was partial. She had taken trouble to arrange a treat which did not, in reality, amuse me in the slightest. In consequence, I had to tell her several times how much I was enjoying myself. Curiously enough, the act of imposture was itself a pleasure, so that I did indeed enjoy the afternoon, although for no reason connected with the thunder of hooves or the few pounds which Maureen was so delighted that we won.

The old lady had evidently been primed to assume that my intentions were now serious. Were they not? Berthe had informed me, a week earlier, that she proposed to remain 'indefinitely' in France after her father's death. I had no illusions about her reluctance to return to me once she had come into her substantial inheritance. I had seen Maureen half a dozen times, without proceeding to any greater intimacy than affectionate kisses on greeting and parting. My son Patrick was living with me (he was in *terminale* at the Lycée Charles de Gaulle, on the Cromwell Road), and I hesitated to invite Maureen to Cornwall Gardens, while she seemed shy of asking me to go to her 'little place' in Earl's Court. Since I did not have the agility or the ardour to make love to her in the car, lack of opportunity gave our relationship the appearance of maturity. Our visit to Mrs Braybrook was my reward for a want of urgency which Maureen was happy to interpret as seriousness. Indifference and constancy can have much the same manners.

As we drank tea with the old lady, among her silver-topped scent jars and colonial knick-knacks, my diplomatic questions – enunciated in my always careful English – provoked tender glances from her daughter, which gave me to understand how touched she was by my considerate manner. In fact, I listened to my own stilted fluency as one might to a broadcast, hardly conscious of being its origin. I was lulled into somnolence by the vivacious drone which at least served to postpone the moment when I should be obliged once more to be alone with the woman who was at pains to show, by her grateful little smiles, how much more fond of me she was becoming every minute. Thus by the end of the afternoon, when we returned to my official Renault, something irrevocable seemed to have taken place between Maureen and me, quite as if we had consummated a passion rather than gratified an old crow. As we crossed the communal gravel, Maureen clung to my arm with keen affection. 'You're such a kind man, Guy,' she said.

Since she pronounced my name in the English style (she never tries to speak French in my presence, although she manages quite competently with our local tradespeople in the Périgord), I might have been listening to appreciative remarks offered to a third party. The earnestness of her gratitude was the more convincing since it seemed to be overheard rather than aimed directly at me. It was as if I had passed some final test in a subject which, unfortunately, did not greatly interest me. I could not say that I desired her on account of her good opinion of me, but I felt a certain impersonal urge to keep her with me, like a diploma, which is precisely what I turn out to have done.

I proposed marriage to Maureen in the stands of the Number One court at Wimbledon. The best French player was supposed to be appearing. It had been raining for an hour and a half. The man next to us was doing one crossword puzzle after another in a paperback edition with a half-finished example on the cover which he had folded back, breaking the book's spine in a way which always irritates me. From time to time he looked up, as if he were engaged in some disreputable activity (perhaps he sensed my casual revulsion). Maureen and I were sharing a tartan blanket which kept us knee to knee. The rain fell on the peaked canvas cover protecting the grass and gurgled into the drains in front of us. Maureen agreed to marry me just as they announced that, regrettably, there would be no further play that day. I had heard only that morning from Berthe that I was a free man.

III

I never supposed that Maureen regarded me as a romantic figure. I always realised that I was an approximation to what she wanted rather than someone whose specific qualities excited her. I was, after all, in my sixties. I had been a diplomat, of the second rank, for too long to imagine myself to be glamorous. Far from being offended, I thought it generous of her to be so impressed by my credentials and so interested in my small adventures. It was something of a relief to find that I was her pet rather than her love. Since I have never again contrived to turn her, even for a moment, into the seductive figure whose haunches were presented to me when I first saw her, Maureen has not been an erotic joy to me. I am not sorry, as I hope she is not. In what I assume to be a rather British way, we do not discuss our conjugal relations, or their absence. The fact that Maureen and I speak only her language together might seem to put me at a disadvantage – she can, after all, express herself more naturally than I can – but I am conscious that I am often more voluble than she, if also more formal. My English is more elegant than my wife's, but I have small knowledge of the gutter, and hence little access to the darker labyrinths in which a language acquires its double meanings and its richer reticences. I say only what I mean, which docks my speech of significant omissions. On the other hand, my simplest words, however bald or sincere, give me the pleasure of duplicity without any call for deceit: however at home I may seem to be in our common tongue, I am secretly on holiday from my native self whom I meet, like a lover, only when I am not with my wife.

My conversations with Maureen are limited by the politeness of an English vocabulary in which I am incapable of reproach or rage. I have no large wish to scold Maureen, and I am rarely angry with her, but since I do not choose to be polite, what merit can there be in my courtesy? I fear that I may deprive her of something by being so nice to her, even though she shows no sign of imagining that I could be otherwise. To be truthful, I am slightly vexed by her assumption of my unfailing good nature.

For the first three years of our marriage, my diplomatic career kept us in London. When my masters kept their word and secured me a flattering position in the Commission in Brussels, Maureen promised me that she found the city delightful, quite as if she feared that I would regard her as lacking in taste if she judged it – as I secretly did – provincial, bureaucratic and expensive.

My divorce from Berthe had gone through with all the acrimonious accountancy one might expect. Being rich, my ex-wife had no disposition to be generous. I married Maureen in a state of resigned exhilaration. She wore a black and white outfit and a straw hat with a white veil, as if in modest allusion to the lacy train which a younger or virginal bride might have chosen. Vincent Werstricht was in London, having been made Belgian Ambassador, so I asked him to be one of our witnesses. He made a charming speech which so perfectly contradicted all the things I had heard him say in Buenos Aires that I could congratulate him with unfeigned admiration, even affection. I told him that, were I his Foreign Minister, I should entrust him with the most delicate missions with absolute confidence. *'Mon très cher Guy,'* he said, *'moi aussi!'*

I had warned Maureen that I should soon be retiring, but she smiled as one does when acknowledging the inevitability of something which one does not seriously believe will ever happen, like death or baldness. If she came late to the diplomatic world, Maureen entered it with dedication. My position in Brussels was scarcely important, but it required a certain delicacy of touch in reconciling various national interests on commercial issues. Maureen arranged her little evenings as carefully as major conferences. Her flatteries appeared so artless that people whose command of English was not even as good as mine were led to think that they had become bilingual. Our Ambassador told her that she was the best servant France had among those who did not speak French. She touched him on the wrist and leaned close to him. 'I do it for you,' she said, 'and for Guy!'

She hoped that some way might be found to prolong our tour of duty in the Belgian capital. I did not tell her that I had asked my superiors to arrange for my retirement to go through as soon as possible. My pension had been handsomely enhanced and I had no wish to become involved in a negotiation over egg prices which might drag on for two or three years. Did I want to return to La Fontaine du Noyer that badly? My parents' house is very peaceful (so far our valley has escaped the improvements which are homogenising the character of so much of the Périgord) and I find it agreeable to be in the landscape of my youth, especially those wartime years when, more than at any other period of my life, I felt that I was undoubtedly alive.

Had I also been happy, I might never have recurred to the duplicity which has, ever since, been my convenient, self-denying habit.

Retirement to the familiar has, to my secret joy, proved both pleasant and disquieting. Guy de Maupassant (I could hardly have a name in common with someone whose life was less like my own) once remarked that even in the most commonplace thing there is always an element of the unknown. I walk among the scenes of my boyhood, or get into the car and drive to them, when Maureen is playing golf, as if I were waiting for that secret element to reveal itself. I think of it as popping out, as bald as a chestnut disengaged by a chance kick from its wig of deterrent spines.

At my retirement party, which was organised at the Quai d'Orsay by Pierre-Henri Mercuès, a senior politician came up to me and said that he hoped that I should now find time to write my memoirs. He was a man of ample conceit, whose figure matched that of the President of the Senate in its evidence of official banquets loyally attended. His tenure of the middle ground betokened both moderation and a resolve never to be ineligible for any coalition which might have need of a man of goodwill. He was someone whose wilful geniality was the only indication he gave of a certain bitterness; he was forever demonstrating what a good sportsman he was in not holding it against his ungrateful compatriots that they had not made him President of the Republic. His reproaches were all smiles. It was beyond his tolerant understanding to know why his humour was so often taken for condescension and his broadmindedness for lack of principle. In fact, he might have risen even higher than the plateau of subsidiary presidencies to which he had been appointed down the years, whenever a 'non-party' figurehead was required, had it not been for one thing which would certainly never appear in his own memoirs and was unlikely to be mentioned by others: his farts, which he perhaps assumed to have passed unnoticed, were of a regularity and pungency which almost asphyxiated the members of his private office. His 'gaseous inexhaustibility' (the phrase was said to come 'from very high up') inclined his governmental colleagues to entrust him with missions requiring the mastery of dossiers so complicated that their analysis would entail prolonged absences from their company.

I did not flatter myself that this distinguished Academician – he wrote aphorisms of immaculate trenchancy – was in the least interested in what I might be prudent or foolish enough to write about my unremarkable career. I recognised that when this old friend and patron of my father's told me that my 'eloquence deserved some permanent record', he was merely proving to me that he was fully aware that I had, from time to time, written speeches and articles for ministers who, lacking his facility, affected to be too busy to do more than append their names to paragraphs which I then forwarded to selected journals or sent with them to the conferences at which they would deliver them, with a few added touches of their own (which made all the difference). 'The pen,' said Monsieur le Président, 'that has self-effacingly made others wiser and wittier than nature intended or justice merited should at last be unsheathed for the sake of its owner's reputation!'

'What is more boring,' I said, 'than the full and frank revelations of those who have absolutely nothing to hide?'

He clapped me on the shoulder as if, in appreciation of my modesty, he was determined not to lose touch with me. He then gave me a winking smile, suggestive of intimate regard, and went abruptly on his way. As soon as he had departed, I was conscious that he had left behind his own sulphurous aura, like an unctuous benediction. I moved away with the tell-tale furtiveness which is typical of the innocent.

If I now seem to have embarked on a kind of memoir, it is not from any wish to advertise my part in great events nor because I conceive myself to have been unjustly passed over in the *cursus honorum*. I was, in a junior but confidential role, privy to the conference at Senlis which planned the Anglo-French collusion with Israel in 1956; I was in Venezuela during the Cuban crisis and in Damascus in 1967; by chance, I had just been sent to Santiago when Allende was overthrown and I have, in consequence, my little parcel of secrets which will, in all probability, remain *'mon petit bagage'*. I have no illusions about my own influence on great events; proximity to them often makes it difficult to realise their importance. It is only much later that one finds it remarkable to have had a long conversation with a man on the eve of his assassination, upon which one represses the embarrassing memory of the drip on the end of his nose or the nicotine tinge of his uncomely moustache which, at the time, seemed much more memorable than his political testament. It is hardly less strange, and unnerving, when a statesman who has asked one's advice on a matter of real consequence proves later to have taken it.

It is not very different with events in one's own life which one realises, years later, to have been either decisive or crucial, although at the time they seemed quite trivial. My return to the Périgord, in the expectation of cultivating my garden (which I do) or going for a little walk at five o'clock (which I do), has given me both the leisure and – to my surprise – the urge to re-examine certain events deep in my past. As a result, I find that I have indeed unsheathed my pen and that I am, almost in spite of myself, devoting several hours a day to writing about myself. My father's friend, the Academician, wrote me a note in which, with a typical flight of ingratiating astringency, he said that he looked forward to reading 'the reflections of M. de Norpois'. His allusion to Marcel Proust's archetypical diplomatic pedant – arguably the most entertaining bore in literature – was of a piece with the style of mordant flattery which he had gone out of his way to offer for so many years and which, either in his ignorance or to his satisfaction, procured him friends who might as well have been enemies wherever he went.

If I seem to have acceded to his sly solicitations, it is not because I think that he will ever want to read this manuscript. (I can imagine him saying, 'But what a snob this man is – he knew absolutely nobody!') What I find myself writing is wholly for my own satisfaction, or rather for my own dissatisfaction. I think of it as a bracing emollient which may enable me to unravel some pattern in the narrow haphazardness of my existence. I do not go so far as to crave a logic, nor am I greatly dismayed by the 'crass contingency of matter', to quote the English Platonist whom my younger, 'English' son, Patrick, citied in one of his letters from Cambridge. I have no sense of Sartrean nausea at the muddy vulgarity of life, but I should be glad – or at least amused – to have an inkling of the true shape of my character. I should also, if I may put it this way, like to like myself a little better before I part company with myself.

As I sit at my rustic table, I catch sight of myself in the little gilt mirror (hanging not quite straight) which Maureen bought at the *foire à la brocante* in Monpazier last week. In it, I have an air of urgent resignation, rather like the man with the book of crossword puzzles who frowned and pressed his lips together and looked at the tip of his busy pencil, quite as if he were engaged on some solemn and necessary business when in fact he was simply temporising by doing something which would never have been undertaken if it had not been raining on that day at Wimbledon on which I – perhaps in no very different spirit – asked Maureen if she would care to marry me. My face in the mirror looks back at me with senatorial wryness. I notice with what futile vanity the hair is brushed across the shining skull.

I am indifferent whether anyone ever reads what I may have to say here, but I am just curious enough to want to read it myself. If the manuscript turns out to be at all interesting, I may solicit some independent opinion of it, although I know that I shall probably be honoured with some tiresome editorial advice to cut out those passages which I particularly value. There is an English writer who lives in the next village whom I might ask for his estimate of its chances of publication (success does not now interest me). On the other hand, I may simply leave it in a drawer or in a recess of the attic, as peasants do with a sock of gold, perhaps for a rainy day, perhaps for the secret pleasure of imagining the surprise which its discovery will spring on future generations. Will my sons be shocked or cheered by the evidence that their father was not quite the man they thought he was?

IV

Although I am generally conscious of the principal events which I propose to rehearse for myself, I cannot say that I have any distinct idea of who the person is whose life I have lived. For as long as I can remember, there has been an aspect of imposture in my personality. It is as if I had been conscripted to fill the role of Guy de Roumegouse and had, not infrequently, been in danger of exposure as the wrong man for the part.

During the war, I had occasion to travel with false papers. I was surprised at how easily, and with what abundance of fictitious detail, I was able to bore the police. My untrue self came more easily to me than my real character; I liked him rather better than the person whose experiences I had in fact had. I was able to be so artlessly garrulous about his life that the Germans handed me back my phoney credentials before I had given them a quarter of my cover story. I easily sang the praises of a part of the Charente from which my papers said I came, although I knew it only from a few days' holiday with my mother when I was four years old. Could I have been equally plausible in giving an account of my actual existence?

At various more or less important moments of my life I have been astonished that no one questioned my right to be what I passed for. Am I inventing a scene from my earliest childhood when, on the limestone terrace where I am writing these words, I saw myself being passed from hand to hand, a bundle made substantial only by the lacy shawls in which I was lagged against the temperate climate? I have the illusion that I am – and was – watching this ritual, in which admiration and the desire to be rid of me caused me to be moved hastily along the family line, from the open window of what is now Maureen's bedroom, which I seldom enter these days. I feel as if I knew that I was supposed to be a baby, although I was, in reality, already something quite different. I was a precocious apprentice in dissembling: even at two years old, I had the knack of absenting myself from my own fleshly confinement. That something is inescapable does not, in my experience, make it any less arbitrary: although I had no choice but to be the baby I was, I have the impression that I already had a wry sense

20

that I was posing as what I could not help but be. If I have been liberated by this furtive illusion, I have made small use of my duplicity. I am rather like someone who has access to an illicit fortune but who, for fear of arousing suspicion, dips into it only for trivial indulgences which he could probably afford anyway. My secret freedom has rarely had any happier expression than a kind of aloof impotence. I once went out to buy a new suit, for a new posting. I was determined to choose what I really wanted rather than what my then wife would approve. I looked at rolls of cloth until I sneezed. After short-listing four kinds of English wool, I selected a grey chalk-stripe. When the suit had been made, I realised that the material was identical with that of one which, at Berthe's insistence, I had bought off the peg two years earlier.

One of the ways in which Maureen spices our rural life is by holding séances. Wishing that we still had to dress up for those appalling diplomatic receptions which demanded stiff collars and stiffer manners, she invites what she takes to be the Périgourdin 'gratin' to come and scratch my mother's oval table with the upturned wine glass which, moving from letter to letter around the circumference, spells out the portentous nonsense which supposedly comes from The Other Side. Does Maureen imagine that – as with horse-racing, which never entertained me in the smallest – she is doing something which pleases me? She greets each spelt out platitude as if it might solve the great metaphysical issues. Her defunct Norwegian ancestor recently spelt out that she was 'worrid' about the future of the ozone layer. Maureen wanted me to telephone a minister in Paris to press for the replacement, by the state, of all obsolete refrigerators, before it was too late. We owed it to those on The Other Side to honour the long journey they had made. I never speculate aloud on whether the afterlife can be quite as petit bourgeois as is suggested by the samples vouchsafed us by my wife's deceased relatives.

Despite my disbelief in any blissful future, I have never been able to resist quizzing those who are supposed to have knowledge of the sublime. I tend to treat priests like diplomats who might tell us more about their Master if they were authorised, or if they could be suborned. Tolerantly nettled by my usual questions, a priest once said to me that God had all the possible attributes except for Free Will; He could grant it, but He could not exercise it. Was this, I asked, because His powers necessarily included powerlessness or because, by admitting that He could have done otherwise, He would reveal Himself to be only part of what He might have been and hence, by definition, less than Almighty? It seemed, I argued, that the inability

21

of God to help the suffering child was a function of His ability to do absolutely everything: if He did anything for mankind, He could be accused of not having done as much as He might, with the result that He was constrained to do nothing at all. In that case, my priestly friend said, the advent of Jesus was an attempt to remedy the inhumanity of a God in Whom impotence and omnipotence were indistinguishable. The proof of Christianity was that it was the only conceivable means of breaching God's loneliness without compromising His singularity. 'Are you saying that,' I said, 'or am I?'

'It sounds like a still small voice to me,' my friend said.

Why do I hesitate to name him? He was called Pierre Salomon. He was a Jesuit who did not – as perhaps he could not – conceal his Jewish origins. Pierre was a classical scholar. I got to know him while I was *en poste* in Rome in the mid-1960s. Berthe always called him 'the Jew' in a tone which demanded to be overheard and challenged rebuttal. She gloried in the dandified decadence of Roman life in those easy days, when it was amusing for her to find forbidden things to say at the top of her voice. My place was to supply the embarrassed wince which promised that her outrageousness could still find someone to shock.

'What's the matter?' she said. 'Should one not call someone what he calls himself?' She stood with her feet slightly apart, as if talking from the deck of a small boat. Pierre's proximity served only to arm her boldness. 'A Jew is a Jew. He says it himself, don't you, Pierre?'

'That,' I said, 'serves only to demonstrate the extent to which he isn't one. "Once upon a time" is rarely the end of the story.'

'Do you understand him when he's like this?' Berthe turned to Pierre, as if her objectionable behaviour had made a bond between them.

Pierre said, 'Once is always once, however, isn't it?'

'Meaning?' Berthe said.

'Isn't that the principle of mortal sin? What you once did, or were, you have always done, unless God's grace can intervene.'

'Are you a Jew or aren't you?' Reaching past Pierre to the buffet for a fresh glass, Berthe stumbled and looked at him as if he had tripped her. 'What kind of a thing are you? Come clean!'

Pierre said, 'I am and I am not.'

'In the same way that Guy is a man, you mean?'

Pierre said, 'Your wife is a brave woman, Guy.'

'Is she not?' I said.

'Why can you never say what you mean?' Berthe might have welcomed some vigorous retort on my part, but she received – as so often – only an infinity of patience. I granted her the poorest possible rate of exchange for her scorn. 'It's a shame,' she said, 'that Guy couldn't be the priest instead of you, Pierre. He would have had to renounce pretty well nothing, particularly when it came to chastity.'

'It's my only vice,' I said.

Even in his belted soutane, there was a thick virility about Pierre Salomon. His incongruous black skirts served only to emphasise it. Perhaps in an effort to dissimulate his masculinity, he made no effort to keep his torso erect. His body was thrust forward over his bandy legs. The posture reminded me of the minotaur, whose hybrid origin made his beefy humanity all the more obvious. Pierre was imprisoned in his vocation like the Cretan bastard in his taurine hide. His spiritual resource fascinated me: it seemed to derive from his unmistakable manliness. I was curious about his sexual behaviour, if any, because I wanted to believe less in his God than in him. I became sceptically infatuated with the case of a man who had voluntarily decided to become what God, however perfect, had no choice but to be: a sublime being.

My infatuation was decorous and never, I think, obsessive. I craved Pierre's company because his manifest duplicity seemed a source of strength and certainty in him, whereas my own undetected division weakened and disempowered me. I sought the recipe for being reconciled to myself, while at the same time probing Pierre for signs of fracture. I was never sure what I wanted him for, but his company was always agreeable to me, whether I felt better or worse for it. My mockery of him was a kind of deference; my intimations of envy were tinged with condescension. As a consequence, our conversations were happily inconclusive and I encouraged Berthe to ask him to dine with us as often as possible. I was conscious of something approaching flirtatiousness in my nervous teasing of his faith. I particularly liked to quiz him when there were other people present; the keenness of our dialogue could then have something of the innocence of exchanges between lovers whom the rest of the company assume merely to be exchanging civilities.

Pierre was in Rome to research the relations between Jews and Christians towards the end of the Western Empire. His studies were to get him into difficulties with the ecclesiastical authorities when, years after we had left Rome, he sought official permission to publish his results. He had concluded that Christianity had been threatened more by its symbiosis with at least some Jews (especially those in Alexandria) than by any radical antagonism between the two monotheisms. A marked and irreversible cleavage had to be engineered, he argued, if the bishops and other dignitaries were to maintain their hierarchical status. His case was advanced with scholarly tact, but its implications were unpalatable to his superiors. Was he being deliberately naive when he declared his surprise at the discovery that facts could be regarded as a matter of faith? I was touched and a little alarmed when he turned to me in the crisis which the refusal of an imprimatur appeared to have occasioned in his life. If I was unashamed at the importance which he had once held for me, I was a little embarrassed to realise that he had regarded my place in his life as hardly less exceptional.

On reflection, I suppose that it was not unnatural that his double nature, and mine, gave us an affinity. In most respects, we were as different as two dogs of dissimilar size and breed who, however absurdly, quicken at each other's approach, scenting a common quality. Pierre seemed as eager for my company as I was for his. The day after one of our dinner parties, I came home to our apartment on Monte Mario and found him already installed. It happened so often, in the following weeks, that on my return from the Embassy, Berthe would stand up, drain her glass, and say, 'Here he is at last!' before going into the kitchen or her own room where, I suspected, she abandoned wine for vodka. Pierre and I would smile shyly at each other, like lovers who wonder how soon they can recover the fervour of their last meeting.

Since I come from a Protestant family, I have always regarded Catholics, especially the clergy, with more sentiment than cynicism. I learnt, as all Frenchmen do, to defer to the religion of the majority, but I could never quite share most people's almost facetious connivance with the humanity of priests. I have always had more faith in the clergy than the faithful tend to display. When my schoolfellows promised me, as we jostled between classes, that they (or their brothers) had once seen their local curé, dressed in a jacket and tie, and wearing a slouch hat, as he came out of a brothel, I did not necessarily think that they were lying, but their stories did nothing to make me look less respectfully at the next priest I happened to see.

While I was in Rome, I met a prostitute who told me that the only experience which had brought her – against her professional habit – to an unfaked climax was with a priest. She had hoped, she said, that she was pregnant with his child. Had she been delivered of it, she believed, it would have done something 'at least miraculous'. Her pimp made sure that she aborted it: he preferred cash to a Saviour. As soon as she told me about the priest, I imagined that Pierre Salomon had been her customer. I was prepared to believe that there was some insurgent force in his loins which, brought to fruition, might redeem, or at least electrify, the world. I looked at him with a suspicion which was identical with hope. A few weeks later, Berthe told me that he was her lover.

V

I am not a man of compulsive sexual appetites. If I have sometimes used prostitutes, it is more because I am irritated by the persistence of sexual desire than because I crave its satisfaction. Apart from the medical risks, against which my father warned me with particular urgency (as though being a Protestant rendered one unusually vulnerable, if not to damnation at least to embarrassment), I have always regarded whores as a greater challenge than other women. Their use has never been carefree. I have gone to them, when I have, in dread, as if to an examination. I have taken them more seriously than they could possibly guess or, I imagine, want. I have no cruel or skittish fetishes. If I can envy (and despise) the casualness with which men I have known, in various countries, repair to brothels, I have never equalled their insouciance. Although I have no sense of sin or shame, I could never approach a whore without a pounding heart, which may have been what drove me to solicit their company, despite my dread of a fiasco. However much of a hypocrite I may appear for saying so, I was excited by their humanity; their inability to refuse me made their existence seem like a manifestation of divine generosity. Had they been mere things, I should not have wanted them. Possessions have never meant anything to me. In a way that I can scarcely understand, I think that a man's contact with a prostitute can be the most honest, the most forthright, the most truly manly of all his relationships.

I recognise that this view is, in some respects, nonsense. Can I seriously claim that, during the time when Berthe and I were so unhappy together, it was the desire for an honest relationship which took me to the pavements where the women of Rome paraded? My motives were, at the best, mixed. Perhaps the most despicable was the temptation to procure for myself some sordid blemish, the better to punish Berthe for my miscalculation in marrying her. Luckily, that squalid ambition was not realised, although it very nearly was, in a manner much more alarming than any venereal infection.

My vengefulness was not excited by Berthe's telling me that she and Pierre were lovers. Nevertheless, her announcement cured me of all inclination to infect or to be infected. If her disclosure was meant to horrify me, it did nothing of the kind. I was filled with an instant emotion which I could neither deny nor identify. It announced itself by a smile.

'I don't know what you're grinning about,' Berthe said. 'Because I'm not joking, you know.'

'That's very kind of you,' I said.

'How dare you say that? What kind of a man are you?'

I said, 'You had better *not* be joking.'

She took a deep breath, which drew attention to her breasts. They seemed larger and more conical, as if having a lover had engorged them. Perhaps she had simply been to a new underwear shop (she made a positive password of '*sconto diplomatico*' in order to get the discounts which her own fortune made quite unnecessary). Her glare at my words assumed that my reaction was one of scorn or mockery. How could I have begun to make her understand that, for the first time I could remember, she had made me happy?

My happiness was not complaisant. I was neither sexually stimulated by being a cuckold nor did I fall passionately in love with the wife who had told me that she was betraying me. How could I identify my reaction or describe the thrill it produced in me? White is said to be the colour of all colours, the pure consequence of their amalgam. My emotion was white: it seemed to me that it contained a whole spectrum of feelings. By virtue of their intensity, and confusion, they blended into a kind of epiphany. I could, as the Americans say, have died and not even known it. All the problems of the universe seemed to be within my compass; I understood what it was to be spellbound. My silence was polyglot: I realised how it was that the early Christians were able, at Pentecost, to speak languages of which they had no knowledge. I saw that it was not for nothing that the Anglo-Saxons commemorated the occasion as 'Whitsun', White Sunday. My whole week was white.

When Berthe said, 'Are you all right?' I detected powerful apprehension in her voice. Did she think that I was about to die and that she was obliged to go through the motions of concern? 'What's the matter with you?'

'Nothing,' I said. 'Nothing whatever. On the contrary.'

'Typical!' she said. Relief and disappointment were as indistinguishable in her as hatred and love in me. 'Absolutely typical!'

Unlike my fellow pupils during the war, who found the sexual activity of priests a reassuring excuse for their own, I neither despised Pierre nor thought less of him on account of his seduction (if that is what it was) of my wife; I neither desired her because my friend desired her nor did I despise him for wanting a woman for whom I never felt any passionate appetite. As my feelings clarified, I discovered that one of them was that he had ennobled our marriage: he had imported a measure of grace into it. God help me, I respected what he had done. I looked at Berthe with, as they say, new eyes because of the daring she had displayed. She became an object of something like veneration or awe, not for what she was (which I still saw with unbeguiled eyes) but for what she had done and had allowed Pierre to do.

On the evening when she told me of their affair, she went into the bathroom of our flat on the Via Trionfale to wash her hair. It was a hot night and, contrary to her usual style, she left the door open. I went into the bedroom to find a pipe which I had left on my side of the bed. We slept together in the big *letto matrimoniale* which was standard in the master bedroom of furnished flats, although we rarely had sexual relations and always went to bed at different times. As I collected my pipe, I caught a glimpse of Berthe lifting her head from the basin, just before enfolding it in a towel.

The effect of the drenching water was to give the impression that she had much less hair. For a moment, seeing the bony gleam of her scalp, I thought she was almost bald. It reminded me of the women in Caillac, immediately after the Liberation, whose heads had been shaved before the eyes of a vengeful, self-righteous mob. I watched their humiliation in the Place Pasteur. I hated what I witnessed but I had to adopt an odd attitude to hide my erection.

My excitement was fatuous as well as ignominious: I could not say what it was for. Its sexual manifestation was almost accidental: I had no lust for the wretched females nor, certainly, did I have any desire for the women of the Resistance who were helping to disfigure them. I have often felt that we have symptoms, whether of love or rage, which correspond only approximately – and sometimes inappropriately – to stimuli which, were our emotions more precise or our responses less hurried and provisional, would lead us into quite other reactions to life and to each other. The physical too has its platitudes.

As I was standing in that gauche posture which adolescence made familiar (one hand in my pocket, my knee bent), I looked around like a guilty dog and saw David Poulain on the other side of the square by the temporary prison, which is now an annexe of the Hôtel La Boétie. David's tilted expression seemed to be asking me what I proposed to do about it, and to say that he expected me to do nothing. It was easier to look at the women again than to endure his cruel complicity.

The cropped women had been scrubbed blank of make-up. Their faces were terribly naked above their sacking shifts. Did I desire them? I was visited, as I stood there, by an involuntary fantasy of what it would have been to be one of the German officers who had enjoyed them. My erection owed less to the strange nakedness of those white faces than to the involuntary thrill of impersonation: I was excited not by the thought of one of those bodies under mine but by the idea of who I would have been, had I already had access to it. My desire had no object: it came from the specious memory of what it might have been to be the last thing in the world I had any overt wish to be. I had no notion of having been a hero of the Resistance (I left that to the semi-uniformed FFI who were officiating at the vile ceremony), but my personal history was wholly innocent of sympathy with the Germans or their local surrogates. How was it that I could so easily assume the jackboots and the high-peaked cap? Why did I dress the girls again in the charm which they had lost, or was its loss their charm? Something utterly unhistorical, which had nothing to do with what the Germans had actually done, clothed me, against my will, in the black elegance that, in those years of fear and shame, I detested so cordially. I watched with unwanted eyes as the crowd made up in vindictiveness for what it had lacked in courage. To be French is always to have a certain scorn for French-men.

I was wearing a collarless shirt of my father's and my trousers were too short for me. Yet I watched the bravely belted Resistance men as if I myself were a tailored dandy. I detected an irremediable vulgarity in my fellow countrymen. My disgust was wholly at odds with anything I had felt before. I had lived for this moment, since I had not, unlike others I knew, died for it. Its impact proved as dismaying as it was unexpected. I heard an unspoken commentary, in my own voice, which took no pleasure in the day which would soon be inscribed forever in the square (which is now the Place Quatorze Août). My private eye saw that public torture had replaced the secret sadism of the police in whose hands I had myself endured more than a quarter of an hour of brutality. My jackbooted self sneered at the incompetence of those who had done too little when the danger was great and were bravest against the defenceless. My career in diplomacy began that day in the Place Pasteur. I learnt abruptly, but forever, that one could make a case for, and against, anything. I discovered that no feeling, however inhumane, was alien to me. It was a relief to find that diplomacy had nothing to do with the merits of the case and that, as Talleyrand had advised, sincerity had no place in one's baggage. That afternoon, as I watched while the women were sheared, I willed myself to vigilant nonchalance. Not showing emotion became, and remains, the measure of my emotion.

When I saw David again, he was closer to me. I paraded the callousness which my quaking chest denied. His beardless face was marked by a sardonic crease, an unsmiling smile, which was less endurable than accusation. It suggested that the treatment of the women was something that belonged to my world, but not to his. It implied that my attitude to it was more significant, at least to him, than the event itself. His reading of me made me important in a way which I wished to deny. He was the only person there whose disappearance would have been a personal relief to me. Did he guess at my sexual stiffening? I felt as if it was from him alone that I was hiding it. His easy movement denied that he was experiencing anything similar. I was alone with my perversity.

The shaved women were finally released, with rough gestures, to run the gauntlet of derision. They were not so much liberated as thrown to the crowd. They stumbled with the violence of their ejection from their torturers' platform. Their hair remained in tufty drifts on the planks. They wandered among the Caillacais, wincing at blows and spittle. The real and the imaginary were one: they flinched – or were brazen – at nothing and at everything. They seemed peeled. Their skin was as pale as bones. The crowd, which had yelled and threatened them, now observed them shiftily; it wanted to be innocent of the humiliation it had encouraged. The barbers stood on their planked scaffold as if suddenly absurd. One of them had the handle of scissors stuck on her thumb, like awful evidence, and wrenched almost in panic to be free of it.

The women did not know where to go. They had the horribly easy options of the leper: wherever they strayed, the people yielded to them. The pariah and the mad dog receive the same disgusted deference. I wanted to be different. When one of the girls stumbled near me, I put out a hand and touched her arm. All her loathing spurted over me. I recoiled, less because I was offended than because I felt unworthy to help her. She looked at me like a blind person who does not know when to blink. I told myself to remember her face, and to forget it. I could imagine doing all kinds of things, including asking her to marry me. I wanted to pay her the compliment of attention, which was my only conceivable apology. Yet there was nothing fine in my wish to excuse myself: it would be my way of making sure that she never forgot what she was and what I had seen her to be. In fact, I was never conscious of seeing her again; I should almost certainly have been incapable of recognising her once she was again disguised by her normal appearance.

When Berthe straightened up from our Roman washbasin, she looked at me with wet eyes which did not register my presence. Throwing back her thinned, heavy hair, she swathed it in the white towel which she had ready. Its turbaned folds reminded me again of the shaved women, who concealed their scalps similarly while their hair grew back. It was not done to speak to them in the street. They were as good, or as bad, as prostitutes, whom it was a matter of propriety never to acknowledge. The shorn girls were divided between those who went about in defiant troops and those who, crushed by their denunciation, hardly ever appeared in public. When they did so, it was with rounded shoulders, policed by members of their own family whose cruelty to them often drove them to leave the district.

After a certain time, people ceased not to see the mutilated women. They became objects of fascination, especially those who refused to cower. There was a kind of angry gratitude on the part of the average citizen at their refusal to be crushed. Such shamelessness exempted their persecutors from undue remorse. In private at least, gestures of reconciliation began to be offered. Men murmured that some of the girls had been 'very young' and that one had to take into account that, after all, not every German was a monster. (Some of those who announced their tolerance were also, I suspect, excusing their own 'unavoidable' dealings with the enemy.) When the women removed the turbans, their new hair was as silky as a baby's. The more attractive of them were readmitted to all but the most Jacobin society. In several cases they came under the protection of men who had abused them. They seemed drawn to each other. When a woman was reluctant to be suitably 'grateful', she earned renewed reproach. Had she no sense of how lucky she was to be allowed to make amends? One girl was raped by a member of a local FFI *réseau*, who defended his action (successfully) by saying that he had been generous enough to allow her to seduce him and so pay off what remained of her debt to the community. When she proved to be pregnant, he married her. One of their grandchildren mows my grass.

Berthe's face was almost transparent without its make-up. She saw me standing there, with my silly pipe, and pursed her chalky lips. 'What do you think you're staring at,' she said, 'as if I cared?'

'Not you,' I said.

'What bothers you more,' she said, 'that he's a priest or that he's a Jew? Tell me!'

'If anything bothers me,' I said, 'it's that he's your lover and not mine.'

'That's the most disgusting thing I've ever heard in my life,' she said.

'Excellent,' I said.

'And to think that I had your sons!'

I went back into the living room. The television was showing the scene in the Italian parliament, which had once again failed to elect a President of the Republic by the absolute majority required. '*La seduta e sospesa,*' the chairman said. I watched the deputies as they scurried from the chamber and realised that I had no wish to smoke the pipe I had gone to get. I have never smoked one since.

VI

The prostitute who told me of her pleasure with the priest was a girl from Cremona. Her thrill, she assured me, was due to the intensity of his need and to the significance which he attached to what meant no more to her than a sneeze (it was through Pia that I learnt the Italian word *starnuto*). It was only afterwards, she said, when she discovered that she was pregnant, that she took his cry for an annunciation. Pia's apartment was on the sixth floor of a *palazzo* on the Via Cola di Rienzo, two floors of which comprised the Pensione Londra. One had to put a ten-lire coin in a slot by the lift in order to go up. Descent was free.

I went with sporadic constancy to see Pia, despite the fact that she was not remarkably attractive. I liked to think that she might in some way be grateful for the regularity of my custom; I made appointments with her, as one might with a dentist. If I could not go, I never telephoned (it was often difficult to get through); I simply paid her the next time. At least with me she was spared standing on the pavement. She discovered quite soon that I was unlikely to surprise her. I was neither cruel nor abusive, which she reciprocated: in this respect, it may be that I suited her better than she suited me. What I liked best about Pia was her predictability, although I sometimes went to her in hope of the unexpected. I chose to think that disappointing me was a mark of respect.

Diplomacy demanded a certain imaginative outlay which was, I suppose, no more sincere than Pia's, though it could be equally exhausting. The wooing of colleagues and foreign dignitaries might be devoid of any emotional element, but it required the same frigid attentiveness which is the mark of the competent whore. Like a diplomat, Pia knew how to ritualise routine, so raising it to the level of a courtesy or even a favour. Her style was simultaneously comforting and charged with unspoken promises that she might or might not keep.

By going exclusively to her, I was deprived of one pleasure which she could not be blamed for failing to offer: that of choice. I denied myself that selective pashadom which, I suspect, excites those who contemplate going with prostitutes quite as much their subsequent possession. If I missed the thrill of the parade, and its slow inspection, like that of a delicious menu, I resisted its temptations. I less dreaded being recognised by other diplomats, or casual friends, than I did their jocular connivance. To be regarded as doing what more or less everyone did would rob my excursions of their spice. I elected to forego observable promiscuities and preferred to enter into what became, for a while, a parody of marriage with Pia.

She dressed unostentatiously. The black skirt and serious blouse aped respectability. She wore a cross on a short gold chain at the buttoned neck. Her make-up, at least when I was due to call, was professionally blatant, but carefully applied. The exact lipstick was calculated, I daresay, to discourage kisses. It made her both brazen and prim. Had she had the right diplomas, and opportunities, she would have had to alter her appearance very little in order to pass for a school teacher. She may have been a prostitute; she was never a slut.

I was given Pia's address by a Dutchman who was leaving Rome for another embassy, in Djakarta, I think. In the practical way of his nation, he told me that she was clean, discreet and – our common language was English – 'competitive'. No Roman *puttaniere* would have been quite so practical in his recommendations.

Apart from the bathroom, she had only two rooms, one of which I was not to see until my last visit to the apartment. The bedroom contained a heavy *armoire*, a marble-topped dresser, a chapped velvet chair, with a footstool in front of it, and the usual brass bedstead. The bed was robust enough for business purposes, but some of Pia's lovers had tested its resilience. Their actions had bumped one of the brass bosses against the floral wallpaper so repeatedly that there was a shiny little hole there, which made me imagine things.

Pia kept assorted plastic flowers on her dresser. I was touched, and scornful, when I noticed – as I put my cuff links next to it – that the cut-glass vase contained two inches of water which the flowers would never need. Pia's ironing board, folded as if it had some arcane relevance to her profession, was always leaning between the *armoire* and the wall by the bed. She was careful to hang her black skirt in one otherwise empty side of the wardrobe before she unbuttoned the white blouse. She never took off her cross.

Our transactions had a decided pattern. On my arrival we always shook hands. Did she do the same with her other clients? It never occurred to me to ask her, though I did wonder. Perhaps it was a politeness she thought appropriate to Frenchmen. I would then ask her – ridiculous as it may seem – what she had been doing recently. This provoked a list of the films which she had managed to see.

34

Occasionally she would shrug and almost blush, before saying, 'I've been too busy, *sai?*' Her ideas about men, except those she had learned the hard way, came almost wholly from the cinema: she was sure that Englishman were always shy and usually homosexual, that Germans were blond and that Americans were rich. If an Englishman had proved vicious or a German as dark as a Sicilian or if an American pleaded poverty, this did not incline her to question the convention but rather to doubt whether the men could really have been what they said they were. She was as eager as any diplomat to rate received ideas above practical experience.

After we had talked about the cinema long enough for me to remove my coat and hat, I brought out my wallet and gave her the usual fee. She would continue to discuss Audrey Hepburn and Cary Grant and Marcello and Anouk while she turned her back and put my two big, dingy notes in a place which, for some reason, I was too squeamish to observe. I looked away as one might from an embarrassingly private act (I have never seen a woman on the lavatory).

When I next saw her, Pia would be standing on one leg, removing her first shoe. I took off my jacket and watched her. When the other shoe had been removed, and she was smaller and more vulnerable, she looked back at me. I nodded and then, with her back still turned to me, she undid her skirt. She never dropped it to the floor, but unwrapped it (it had black buttons, with a scoop of white in them, down the side) and revealed the black garter-belt and nylon stockings which declared her trade.

I should, I think, have liked to unhitch the garter-belt myself, but I never managed to ask if she would allow it. Not doing what I wanted made me dry-mouthed with eager frustration. Why did I wait for her to solicit what I could perfectly well have asked her to let me do? Why should it occur to her that it could be of any importance to me to strip her naked? Had she asked me, I should probably have expressed indifference. In much the same way, I have often shrugged when offered choices – for instance of an office or even of a posting – when, in fact, I felt a strong preference for one or the other. In what may have been a typically Protestant moment, my father once advised me to try and do one thing a day which I did not want to do. My mortifying habit has been not to do things which I did want to do.

My encounters with Pia hardly developed beyond our first routine. She never offered a menu of supplementary services, about which I might have asked her for further explanations, in the gastronomic style. When I was in Washington, I listened with bemusement to the 'specials' which one's 'waiter for this evening' used to enumerate.

One of my State Department hosts deglamorised the occasion by saying that – nine times out of ten – 'tonight's specials" were composed of whatever remained unsold from the previous day's printed list. Pia seemed too honest for her profession: she had no idea how to heat up old recipes. She failed to ask me for extra money by proposing a special which might tempt me to lavishness. Perhaps she had no notion of vice or of its rewards; perhaps she wanted me to like her, which was quite alien to what I wanted of her.

She leaned on one hand against the corner of the *armoire* and unclipped the black garters. Her stockings slumped down her thighs in a silky show of white flesh. Her body smelt faintly, and delightfully, of fish. On one occasion, when I was tasting her, I remembered the American menu with its 'Catch of the Day'. Once undressed, Pia was quite without shame. She made no favour of her nudity. When she took off her stockings, she raised her knees, one after the other, and gave me a first glimpse of the black clump between her legs. In the same way, a reliable waiter will put a basket of bread on the table as soon as you have given your order.

There was a brisk generosity in Pia's lack of haste. By keeping her back to me, she postponed what she assumed to be the best part, my front view of her. She also proved that, within the limits of our contract, she trusted me. The fact that I always felt a twinge of disappointment at her actual appearance was something that I concealed from her, as one might an infidelity or a distaste for ginger. The trouble which I took to hide something from her was possibly a sign that, in my usual way, I was growing fond of her even as I discovered her not to be exactly what I wanted. Had I found a woman who was, I should most certainly have had to give her up. Otherwise she would, in no time at all, have dominated me so completely that my life would have been ruined.

Pia's buttocks always proved less plump and more creased than I hoped. It was absurd to hope that they would have improved in texture and firmness between one visit and the next, but I looked at them, on each occasion, as if they might have become as smooth and delectable as my imagination wished. It may be that I could have found another pair, on another street, but something deterred me from their pursuit. Was it that her shortcomings domesticated Pia and thus rendered her agreeable to me?

As if to alleviate my disappointment, Pia would bend down to retrieve her stockings from the floor. Her movement, extending the flesh, would restore her behind, for a few seconds, to its elastic youth. Her inclination, as she leaned forward to gather the stockings, gave me a glimpse of the furred bracket of her sex. Did she stay bent over for a little longer than tidiness demanded? In fish restaurants, they will show you what is available and then, once your appetite is primed, they remove it for preparation.

Pia would finally straighten up, discard the garter belt and turn to me with an air of honesty, like a typist on time for work. Her unpouting style threatened to lame my desire. She smiled slightly at my sullenness and canted her hips, tilting her curly black heart towards me. As I caught the fishy whiff, she was reaching behind her to undo her brassière. Her breasts were her treasures. She babied them in her hands before letting them bob free in front of me. That moment, when she had nothing else to take off, released a coarseness in her face for which I was grateful: there she was.

I sat on the bed and she came and stood in front of me. Her mouth was thick now, as if she had been struck. When I looked at her, I could sight its red pout between the lank cones of her breasts. The gold cross was loose between them. I sometimes used it to tease a nipple. She preferred me not to. After I had looked at her for a while and felt her flesh against my cheek and mouth, she would allow me to site her directly in front of me (my hands on her warm waist). Then she raised one foot – with its cherry-coloured toenails – and placed it on the edge of the bed beside me. She leaned one elbow on the knee and rested her chin in her palm; she knew that she might be there for some time. I steadied her with one hand under her buttock. That was how we always started.

VII

I was almost fifteen when war was declared. My parents had an apartment in a solemn building overlooking the Luxembourg Gardens. I went to the nearby *Lycée* Montaigne. We spent the academic year in Paris, but as soon as the *grandes vacances* began, my mother, my sister Louise and I returned to La Fontaine du Noyer. My father would join us when the Ministry of Finance, in which I was told that he held a high but unspecified position, more or less closed down at the beginning of August. Since we always went to my grand-mother's house at Easter, only a small fraction of the year was in fact spent at La Fontaine, but I have never thought of anywhere else – least of all Paris – as my home.

My accent was, of course, indistinguishable from that of the Parisian children with whom I went to school. However, to entertain them I would sometimes mimic the harsh consonants of our Périgourdin gardener, Roque, and of his even more grotesque bastard son, Baptiste, who was my age but was already as powerful as his father. When I mocked the provincials who would never know of my treachery, I did so with a greater feeling of affection for them than for the Parisians whose applause I was seeking. My mimicry was a sort of furtive audition for the peasant society from which I was debarred. My mother considered Roque and his family little better – and certainly more dangerous – than domestic animals. My identification with them long preceded the experiences, during the war, which brought me into unexpected contact with the peasants. It was as if I was rehearsing how to be at home with them. How much more natural was the aptitude I showed in reproducing the elegant tones of our Parisian friends?

I had no notion of my parents' wealth. I knew only that we had whatever we needed to render us unmistakably of our class. It came as an unstartling surprise to discover that the apartment, which I had always assumed we owned, did not actually belong to my father. It was rented to him, at an advantageous price, as the result of some ministerial finesse. It was handsome, but not harmonious: it con-tained two huge living rooms, with shuttered windows looking over the chestnut alleys of the Luxembourg, but its dining room was hardly bigger than a railway compartment. Its constriction either deterred my mother from entertaining or gave her an easy excuse not to do so. If my parents dined with friends, they went to restaurants (Lapérouse was a favourite).

My father's rank might be unclear to me, but his financial independence and his qualifications from the Polytechnic gave him the aloofness which money and membership of the 'X' network were likely to merit. His punctilious subservience to temporary political masters conveyed the degree to which he despised them. He never openly disparaged the ministers with whose mimicry less discreet friends would seek to amuse my mother. (Her silvery laugh was always a joy to hear, although quite a rare one.) Just as my father's loyalty did not entail respect for his masters, so his reticence in no way implied faith in the system to which he gave his long working hours. His dedication was a function of his awareness of the unworthiness of the institutions, or at least the men, to whom he offered it. Was his courtesy to my mother of a piece with this deferential haughtiness? The only hint of secret feelings came when he delivered one of his sudden, apparently unmotivated remarks. I remember once when we were waiting for a train at the Gare d'Austerlitz and he said, not so much to me as simply in my presence, 'Faith always contains its grain of vulgar expectation. Unlike cruelty.'

He then looked at me, almost shyly, as if uncertain whether he had or should have spoken aloud. I can see his grey eyes (the pearly colour of my favourite suit) and his thin, unwavering lips. He seemed to license a question which he doubted my courage to ask. He looked at his watch – it had been his father's – and then back at me. I wanted to ask him what he meant, but I did not take the second chance any better than the first. Was he going as close as he chose to reminding me of his hereditary disdain for the Catholic heaven and for its hellish alternative? It was as near as we came to discussing religion.

I had no alarmed sense of difference from those who went to Mass. Few of my friends were as fervent as my sister. To my maternal grandmother's delight, Louise converted to Catholicism at the time of her first menstruation. My father's remark on the platform may have been an almost involuntary reaction to thinking about his daughter's secession from a Protestantism which, in his case, had no pious expression. He was a man against whom only a fool or a fanatic could conceivably wish to discriminate, yet he was always on his guard, always disposed to wariness and to assumptions of ingratitude. In consequence, he was a difficult man to thank and an even more difficult one to please. Just as emotion excited his irony, so sincerity struck him as tantamount to immodesty.

For such a man, to be vulgar was not a matter of social origin but of spiritual crassness: it amounted to something as fatuous as having hopes. One of the few occasions when I remember him laughing out loud was when he received notice of promotion in the Ministry of Finance. The congratulations were in the handwriting of a right-wing politician in a shortlived coalition (as most of them were). This particular man had gained office by advocating 'vigilance' in the Civil Service, by which he meant the summary dismissal of unreliable elements. He could hardly have insulted anyone more neatly than by expressing his faith in him. My father held the letter between finger and thumb, like a ridiculous fish. 'France,' he said, 'is impossible.'

During the *drôle de guerre*, when the war had started but both sides hesitated to do anything irrevocable, I continued to go to school in Paris. Having retreated to my grandmother's for Easter, as usual, we stayed on in Charente when the news worsened. 1940 was a famous summer; the countryside was thick, almost curdled, with its heat. The harvest was soon golden, like Louise's hair. My little sister ripened that year: it was as if she overtook me in age. Her new piety, no less than her beauty, set her apart from me. She became a woman; I remained an awkward boy. I was thin; my hair was browny-grey; I wore the charmless spectacles of my generation. I even had spots; they were only on my throat, but they made me feel like the red-necked chickens who scrabbled in the unevenly gravelled courtyard of Le Prieuré, unconscious of their imminent execution.

The sagging roofs and prolapsed stairways of the old house suggested my grandmother's penury, but their decrepitude was more probably a function of her willpower. She could have afforded to renovate the place, but it entertained her more to ask the local artisans for their proposals than to proceed to practical conclusions. She was a patron who never did more than was essential to her comfort. For the rest, she preferred to recruit hopeful solicitude; estimates were more amusing than bills.

The land beyond my grandmother's unpointed brick walls was rented to local farmers with whom she was demandingly un-accommodating when it came to the accounts. Pitilessness was a morality with her: to forgive was – 'In two words,' my father would joke – 'un – pardonable.' As a small boy, I had the illusion that the old lady – whose husband had died at Verdun, of dysentery – was my father's rather than my mother's mother. She and her son-in-law exchanged unsmiling drolleries which one might have sworn derived from the same stem. There was something flirtatious between them; it aged him and made a wrinkled girl of her.

The collapse of the French armies, concealed and proclaimed by the vague communiqués, was declared by increasingly crackly voices on the wireless. It was as if the airwaves themselves were suffering from emotional turmoil. At Le Prieuré, shame took on the lineaments of indifference. My father's mouth tightened until he seemed to have no lips at all. Having warned against the follies of recent policy, he had too much pride to derive any satisfaction from having been right: what virtue could there be in having advised fools of their folly? His presence at Le Prieuré, during those disorganised days, was itself evidence of his resignation to disaster.

My mother's brother, Jean-Claude, owned factories near Poitiers. He had all the petrol he needed to visit his mother and he arrived one lunchtime in his open *torpédo*. The snarl of its chromium pipes and the leather belt across the bonnet gave him the allure of someone who, in the midst of confused torpor, was full of virile competence. He ate with a good appetite, while denouncing all the appropriate scape-goats. Crapulous politicians, venal Jew Communists and financiers, conspiratorial Freemasons (did he suspect my father of belonging to their fraternity?) and duplicitous Anglo-Saxons had, exactly as he predicted, sold France to the highest bidder. This was not a time for mourning or for hanging one's head but for saying aloud what everyone knew to be the case. As his voice blared in the heat of that beautiful, calamitous June afternoon, he challenged anyone to disagree with the broad outlines of his thesis. My father said, 'Is that the telephone?'

It was. He left that evening in order to go to a destination which was either secret or, more probably, so frequently changed that he was not sure where it would next be. The effort to find his dossiers took him back and forth across the disintegrating country on a series of journeys which were as pointless as he considered them, for that very reason, obligatory.

My uncle displayed no inclination to board sinking ships. He assumed my father's place, facing my grandmother at the far end of her long, hand-sawn walnut dining table, and sniffed the wine as if he suspected that her servants were cheating her. (His glance at me warned me to take my cues from him while I had the chance.) I looked away down the table, with its puddles of light and shade: the hand-planed surface canted the plates at odd angles. Marité was bringing round the heavy soup, in a Limoges tureen. Although she may well have been older than my grandmother, she was treated by her, after a mere forty-seven years' service, like some recalcitrant probationer. I knew that my uncle was glaring at me. Being the only other male present, I was the privileged target of his suspicion that his analysis was falling on sceptical ears. 'And what,' he wanted to know, 'are you proposing to do now?' He seemed to be implying that the first part of some surreptitious plan of mine had now succeeded and that he was curious to discover how much further I proposed to venture in cowardice and villainy.

I said, 'I suppose I shall go on with my studies.'

His eyes swept the room in appeal to a jury which alas, was not fully empanelled. The gummy pictures of my grandmother's ancestors (and mine, come to think of it) had to stand in for my peers. 'Has it occurred to you,' he said, 'that it is precisely those studies – and the men who determine, for their own ends, what they should be (and what they should *not* be) – that have brought us to our present pass?'

My mother wiped her lips in order, I thought, to be busy when I sought her support. 'To tell the truth,' I said, glad to be able to turn aside and deal with Marité's tureen, 'I haven't thought about it.'

My uncle held his napkin in the air as though he wanted to throw it down, but had too good an appetite. 'There we are,' he said, 'he hasn't thought about it!' He was giving my mother a chance to say something. She worked at a smile, which he took for permission to continue. 'How can you consider continuing with your literary studies without taking into account that the triumph of Germany – because triumph it is, however you look at it – is a triumph of attitudes quite as much as of crushing military competence? Excuse me, Miki, but I'm afraid I'm right.' My mother's name was Mireille, but she was known familiarly as Miki. My uncle treated her silence as a brave but misguided objection to his remarks, which prompted him to elaborate. 'It is, I'm sorry to say, a fact – though not a welcome one – that we outnumbered the Germans in both tanks and aeroplanes. It so happens that this is something about which I know a great deal (and I weigh my words). Where we were – and are and, I fear always will be – outgunned is, if I dare say so, morally. When I speak of morals, I speak of cohesion, of national ambition and national, yes, virility. Because now what is going to happen? What is going to happen?' He scowled at Marité who had stopped beside him, the big tureen resting on the napkin she had folded across its base. He seemed disconcerted or criticised by the sound of the breath coming and going in her old nostrils. He helped himself, but she remained near him, until he began to drink his soup. 'Defeat,' he began again as her slippered feet slurred on the grey flagstones, 'defeat comes to some people as a relief. It seems to mean an end to choices and to begin a period of mere endurance, when we shall have the luxury of submission and none of the pain of choice.' How old was my uncle when he spoke like this? No more than thirty-eight or nine! 'I disagree. I disagree profoundly and completely. We shall have to choose more than ever in the years ahead. Are you relieved not to have to go into the army?'

My mother dared to say, 'He's only just sixteen years old.'

'Now you mention it,' I said, primed by what I took to be her support, 'I suppose I am. Who wouldn't be?'

His face was ripened by the wine which, from the downturn of his mouth, might have turned sour. 'Don't be too sure,' he said, 'that nothing further will be demanded of you. Dare to imagine that even – I might say particularly – in the present circumstances something possibly heroic, even perverse, may be necessary for the future of our country.'

'I'm not sure that Guy wants to be a hero,' my mother said.

'Or perverse,' I said, scarcely knowing what that meant but hoping to rally my mother to my side.

'Is it a matter of desire, Miki? Isn't it a matter rather of belief? Desire and belief, two utterly different things whose confusion lies at the root of the disaster! Your teachers – men who have contributed markedly to our decline – disdain belief and promote desire. Who said that it is the duty of an intellectual to do something every day to impede the state? I foresee – I *hope* I foresee – a fundamental change in what the young are taught and in those who are trusted to teach them. The heroic and the intelligent will have to come together: what was unthinkable yesterday must now be thought, for the sake of tomorrow.'

My mother said, 'More soup?'

'It must,' Jean-Claude said. 'Full stop, that's it.'

My uncle had been too young to fight in the Great War and he was, he informed us, unfortunately too important to have been recalled for the one which was now ending. He had performed some of his military service, between the wars, in the Rhineland, during the period immediately preceding our withdrawal from it. This experience of having been in an army of occupation may have disposed him to respect the 'correctness' of the Germans when, during that great blue summer, they installed themselves in France. He still had his *torpédo* and he continued to arrive at Le Prieuré, as though he had just left the war zone, with an air of windswept bravado. In fact, he was continuing to oversee the factories which were increasingly devoted to the service of the occupying power. He said that he judged the Germans by purely professional standards: one had to be realistic and admit that they knew what they were doing and how to do it. 'Full stop, that's it.' Did it occur to him that realism and treason might speak the same language?

I write as though I was immediately revolted by my uncle's 'honesty'. In fact, I judged him with the timid rigour of an adolescent, at a time when to be a sixteen-year-old boy was to belong to no happy club. I had no notion, as today's young people have, that I was a member of a generation whose moment was due. Had I continued my studies in Paris, I might have had a greater sense of solidarity with my comrades. I can still remember the veneration I felt for the eighteen-year-olds in *terminale*, with their loitering, waistcoated elegance and their unquestionable intellectual refinement. I now had small prospect of such election.

I had a sorry complexion and a suddenly, incontestably beautiful sister. Even at fourteen, and in the midst of our national disgrace, Louise had a quality so sublime that I could not believe that her destiny had anything in common with mine. The breasts which now filled her blouses with uncreased roundness, her ripe hair, her grey-blue glaucous eyes, all her natural qualities seemed like moral attributes. She displayed a dynamic repose about whose physical reality I was, and wanted to be, largely ignorant. Not only did I not see her naked after she was eleven or twelve years old, but I purposely refrained from catching sight of her in the bathroom and from watching her dress or undress. I even averted my eyes from the armholes of her summer dresses, although I was intrigued by the glimpse of her friends' breasts to be gained through theirs.

I remained alone with my own unappealing self. The involuntary eruptions of my sexuality embarrassed and isolated me, although the resulting stains on the sheets were never overtly remarked by Gertrud, the Viennese refugee who served as our *bonne* and whose duties included making my bed in Paris. She was a small, black-haired woman with stocky legs. Her eyes shone with memories which her resigned shoulders could treat only as a burden. Did I imagine that she looked at me with hungry pity if I came into my bedroom while she was changing the sheets? If so, apprehension quashed opportunity: I flinched from her heat.

My uncle's accusing attitude to me was both a reproach and a compliment. As I was indeed glad to be spared joining the colours, my unavoidable reprieve became less ignominious when it could be regarded as a crime. Jean-Claude's arrival came to fill me with delicious dread of what he might say next. Since unfair accusations can always trawl some vestige of evidence to support them, I was almost gratefully surprised by the gravity of his charges; they seemed to make me more interesting, and certainly more iniquitous, than I could have been without him. My uncle turned into a malign oracle whose predictions seemed to determine what lay ahead for me. During the months after June, he alone of the whole family dared to use the future tense with proprietorial conviction. To disagree with him was like disagreeing with the clock.

On his rare returns from Vichy, my father had no confident diagnosis to offer. He seemed to have decided to replace judgment with pedantry. Politeness and irony, like loyalty and dissidence, shared premises and amenities. His pinched person resembled his ministry, whose departments had been driven to cramped cohabitation in one of the grand hotels in Vichy. He offered no account of life in that parody of a capital city. He said only, 'It was never a water I cared for.'

My uncle continued to live in Paris. He moved freely, at the wheel of his *torpédo* between the occupied and the unoccupied zones. He had a new apartment in the Rue Lincoln, whose previous owners were said to be grateful for his tenancy. We, on the other hand, had been evicted from the flat overlooking the Luxembourg Gardens. A German administrative officer to whom it was allotted wrote several letters to my mother, during the first year of his residence there, in which he reassured her about the health of our cat (Eugénie) and apologised for a broken piece of Sèvres china. He spoke of replacing it, when he went home on leave, with an equivalent item of Dresden.

VIII

It would be pleasant to claim that the numbness with which I continued my studies, during the two years after the defeat, had some tincture of nobility. Unable to return to the *lycée* Montaigne, transformed into offices over which the German flag now flew, I was obliged to transfer my schooling to Caillac. I found myself among the sons of local shopkeepers and peasants. In Paris, I had had the illusion that I should be happier in the Périgord; in Caillac, I dreamed furtively of Paris. My scholastic diligence was less an attempt to ignore France's humiliation than a sort of emigration from the yokel company which I was now constrained to accept.

The timelessness of the curriculum promised that the war was a negligible contingency. The excision of non-Aryan authors scarcely altered the anatomy of the course. The pretence that nothing fundamental had changed recruited my teachers to inflexibility. What had been forced upon them had to be presented as if it were desirable: the philosophy of the Marshal, whose photograph hung beside the blackboard, enjoined penitence and unquestioning labour. I worked diligently, but without enthusiasm (which might have smacked of light-heartedness). My industry was as unprincipled as the idleness of my comrades Martegoutte or Despinasse whose laziness, Monsieur Chantal said, was of the kind which led directly to national degeneration.

At the beginning of the war, when it was assumed that both sides would face each other along more or less the same lines as on the previous occasion, civilians from the border regions were evacuated inland. Trainloads arrived in Périgueux from Alsace. They were received with scant grace. Most of them spoke a patois indistinguishable, to local ears, from German. When the evacuated families were dispersed among the communes of the region, all but the least favoured of the newcomers found it difficult to hide their dismay: they felt that they had been sent to live among savages.

After the defeat, they assumed that they would be able to return to the homes they had left. They were disappointed: the Germans were happy to leave them as an administrative embarrassment to the

French authorities who lacked the will or the resources to repatriate them. Through no fault of their own, the Alsatians became the abiding evidence of a defeat which, but for their presence, it might have been easier to forget. We had three of these 'guests' in my class: Magnac ('the maniac'), Loubet ('the lout') and Altschuler, who was dark and clever and was known, unsurprisingly, as 'le Fritz'.

The Marshal encouraged the French to revert to a way of life from which the Périgord had, in fact, scarcely deviated during the now derided years of the Popular Front. Paid holidays and workers' insurance – now equated with Bolshevism – were almost irrelevant in the countryside. How should peasants abandon their animals and go bicycling to the seaside? At best, they might leave their farms for a midsummer *fête champêtre*, a wedding or a funeral. When the Marshal declared that rural values were now needed for the salvation of France, the peasants were as puzzled as they were flattered to hear that they were the moral exemplars of an, alas, remote national resurgence. Their dedication was now said to offer lessons in stewardship to cynical metropolitans. In due course, they took this as a licence to demand fat prices for the eggs, chickens and other produce which foraging Bordelais came to seek.

Life scarcely changed at La Fontaine du Noyer. I saw seasons there I had never seen before. The tranquillity of the countryside put a happy cushion between us and the outside world. Gertrud had been able to escape from Paris, thanks to my father's connections, so that we were not even deprived of the middle European dishes at which she was so deliciously skilled. Simone, our gardener's wife, never lacked ingredients for her local recipes. We were, in some respects, more comfortable than ever. Although our movements were restricted, the donkey-cart was as good a way of negotiating the rutted winter roads (few of them asphalted) as the Renault, which was jacked on bricks in one of the *granges*. Roque had veiled it with a sheet, weighted by a stone at each corner. The tall car looked like some corpulent bride awaiting a husband.

My own virginity was without any dream of curtailment. In those days, only girls were called virgins; my own unprimed state was without the delicate passivity which I took to be natural to the female condition. More messy than innocent, I had no private hopes of its alleviation. Our removal from Paris deprived me less of opportunity than of the imminent shame of inexperience. I had been mortified and intrigued in particular by one of my contemporaries in Paris, Lucien Paoli, who smoked Turkish cigarettes after school and was gloatingly explicit about the amenities of a brothel in Alexandria which, so he said, his father had arranged for him to visit, *en prince*, as a fifteenth birthday present. I elected to regard his *dépucelage de luxe* as a depravity typical of mercenary types who came from the Levant. I was relieved to hear Paoli *père* described by a friend of my father's as a 'fruit and vegetable man'. In fact, he was a wholesale importer of dates, sultanas and pistachios, with offices in Djibouti and Algiers, as well as Smyrna and (I believe) Baghdad. When my father's friend – whose servants were advised to call him Monsieur le Marquis – mocked the Paolis' pretentiousness in running a Rolls Royce, with a uniformed chauffeur, I scorned his snobbery before being infected by it. How convenient it was to believe in the vulgarity of all ostentation except one's own!

Lucien Paoli was fat and strong. The fat was as intimidating as the strength; it made a pasha of him, even when he was sixteen. The chauffeur (Marc-Antoine) drove him each morning to the *lycée*. Marc-Antoine sat in the open cab, whatever the weather, so it seemed, while Lucien rode in the back, with a lap-robe across his knees. A great leather hood, like that of a giant perambulator, mounted on pliable arms, was opened over him if there was a risk of rain. He had the allure both of a potentate and of a victim. Some of my comrades would have been happy to bully him, had he not been so powerful. Instead, they – perhaps I mean we – accepted his favours as if they were offered in appeasement: our greed for the treats he dispensed at the café, after school, contained less gratitude than a kind of furtive savagery. His generosity made us vulturous doves.

Paoli (I never thought of him as Lucien) had an unfailing, unamused smile on the neat lips which seemed too small for the cheeks which bulged above them. I am sure that he could have dealt very easily with those who imagined that they had chosen to spare him their persecutions. He patronised them in a way which they elected to find ridiculous and even craven, but I suspect that he did so because it pleased him, not because he feared their malice. When Paoli tried to befriend me, by asking me to ride home with him, I declined with spiteful politeness (echoing the tones of my father's disdainful friend). I wanted to go but I thought that Paoli would assume all kinds of low things about me which, alas, would be true. I wanted to hear more about *l'Éthiopienne* who, with another girl *'plutôt maline que câline'*, had initiated him in pleasures which were harder to find in Paris. I was more amazed by the complicity of his father than by the caresses he had enjoyed at his expense.

Soon after the outbreak of war, he told us that he was leaving for America. Somehow I had the impression that the Rolls would drive directly across the Atlantic, with Paoli ensconced in the back with a hamper, and that his own decision was responsible for his departure. Accusations of cowardice were inevitable, but they were tinged with envy. Paoli's imperturbable indifference to our view of him transformed him, very soon, into a legend. He said goodbye without offering the slightest indication that he would miss us. He bought us our final round of favours without seeming either to be glad to be spared further exactions or obliged to sentimental regrets. He smiled as blandly at our requests that he let us know what New York was like as he had at occasional barbed remarks about Marc-Antoine's frogged livery and brilliant leggings. Only as he got into the Rolls for the last visible time did I realise that I was going to miss someone who was going to be perfectly happy without me. I said, 'You will write, won't you?' He smiled, or rather he continued to smile. I knew that I should wait in vain for a letter, but I still waited. I remember wishing that I had gone with him to America, although I should never have dared to do so, if he had made the offer. Paoli appeared immune to the common fate which seemed to hang over us, in imprecise menace, well before the 1940 débâcle; he resembled an outsize dandy for whom even his daily routine had been specially tailored.

My father worked in Vichy for some months, perhaps as long as a year, but he never suggested that we join him there. It was as if he were honouring a penance and preferred to endure it in solitude. His sense of duty required him to perform whatever labours were demanded of him. 'I am,' he said, 'an unheroic Herakles.'

My uncle came rarely to the Périgord. When he did, it was not because he was short of provisions or because he wanted to escape from Paris; he brought Paris with him, in the strenuousness of his speech, the refusal to abandon what he called 'the topic of the century'. When my father had, as he put it, 'been resigned' from the ministry, Jean-Claude demanded that he not cease to think about 'the New Europe'. There was a measure of vindictiveness in his refusal to allow his brother-in-law to lapse into rustication. He demanded to know why precisely my father had provoked his own dismissal. He would not allow sourness to replace lucidity. When my father alluded to his late masters as 'these gentlemen', Jean-Claude said, 'No, no. Let us call them what we know them to be – temporising trimmers. Eunuchs who are happy to watch what they are not capable of doing! (Forgive me, Miki!) You are too cautious, my dear friend. This is not a time at which brave men can afford to be cautious.'

My father said, 'I leave bravery to you, my friend.' The omission of a reciprocal endearment was the nearest he came to overt antagonism.

Jean-Claude let his hand fall to the table and smiled, while closing his eyes in brief disappointment.

Something in Jean-Claude's energetic opportunism was as enviable as his ideas were suspect. His refusal to wait on events made him attractive to me, even as an opponent, whereas my father, whose actions I approved, seemed too austere to excite emulation. His stoicism was like that which enabled citizens of the ancient world both to endure tyranny and, in some cases, to derive a perverse pleasure from its injustice. The Stoic's ability to rise above injustice made him, in some sense, its sponsor. My father recoiled from those who practised and profited from autocracy, but he refrained from what he would have regarded as vulgar protest. For whatever motive, my uncle always seemed to go literally out of his way to provoke my father to a less passive attitude. Soon after his arrival at La Fontaine, while still in his luxurious leather, I would hear him ask his brother-in-law whether he could 'spare a minute or two from what you're doing,' quite as though my father were still engaged on affairs of state. I was torn between them. If my uncle seemed brash, even bullying, he had a seductive vitality, whereas my father's fastidiousness was at once refined and insipid. I could guess what he was repudiating, but I had no idea what he might embrace; he would rather die than compromise with what he despised, but he gave no hint as to the kind of cause for which he might be inspired to live.

IX

'Fritz' Altschuler was a good chess player who lacked opponents. His marks in class were nearly always the best; when they were not, I had the impression that he had contrived for me – or occasionally Pistolozzi – to share the odium of primacy. Fritz's parents had found lodgings in a narrow house behind the Chapel of the White Penitents. In those days, Caillac was a secretive place. Not a single road was straight except for the traverse, which had been driven through the congeries of streets by some provincial Haussmann for the sake of a presidential visit which lasted only an hour or two. Photographs of the laurelled arch erected in Poincaré's honour are still hanging in the Mairie.

The streets to the left of the traverse, on the far side from the Cathedral and the market square, were alleged to be rougher than those in the *beau quartier*, though they were probably only poorer. Caillac was a small and peaceful town, but its inhabitants had a tradition of wariness. It had been held by the Protestants for a while, during the Wars of Religion, and resisted the great Turenne during a long siege. There was some pride in this gallant episode, although almost no Protestants remained in the population. The place seemed nostalgic for those brave days; the walls were thick and the windows of the adjacent buildings were narrowed as if in suspicion of outsiders. The steep, buttressed houses were enjambed against each other. A jagged path, veering left and right, went up from the traverse to where the Altschulers lived. Hooded stairways were visible through tight doorways; there were blind alleys and sudden spaces which could not be guessed at from a few feet away.

The Altschulers had three rooms. None was bigger than our pinched dining room in the Rue de Monsieur. Fritz's father made and repaired clocks; his mother, who had been an expert at tapestry restoration in Strasbourg, did sewing for anyone who would give her work. The punctiliousness of her stitches embarrassed the clients who underpaid her. Someone warned her that if she wanted to continue, she should try to be less perfect.

Fritz and I played chess, with red and white bone pieces, in the window of the smallest of the three small rooms. We were hunched against Cyclopean slabs of limestone, below a slit of a window. Fritz reminded me somehow of Paoli; or was it that my attitude to him resembled the one I had taken to Lucien (as I now dared to think of him)? Fritz too seemed to be waiting for a fate which I was to be spared, or denied. He was not as large as Paoli, but he too resembled a man who had agreed to pretend to be my contemporary. The beard which already stippled his hot cheeks announced that he lived by a different clock.

He began to teach me chess on summer evenings in 1941. After our sessions, I would catch the last 'little train' which ran from Caillac, in a lazy loop, to the villages along the valley of the Dordogne. At his father's suggestion, he lent me a little book on chess tactics. I remember only the phrase 'A pinned piece is a paralysed piece'.

I had a two-mile walk from the Port du Noyer, where the train stopped, to La Fontaine. The little station was a concrete hut, built on the site of the quay where, in my grandfather's day, timber barges were lashed together before being floated down the river to Bordeaux to be broken up. Sometimes, if the weather was bad, I would find Roque waiting for me with the trap. I was glad, but I scowled. My mother did not welcome my staying in Caillac; Roque deputised for her displeasure. I wondered what harm she imagined could come to me, or of what pleasure she thought she ought to be depriving me. Chess seemed a lame wickedness.

I am sure that Fritz could have found a worthwhile opponent without having to train me for the office, but he became determined to make me his equal. It would be a proud day for him, he said, when I could beat him playing his best. I appreciated his earnestness, which was not without irony, but I cannot say that I liked him. He had a rather rectangular face, with moist red lips and lustrous black eyes, not unlike those of Pierre Salomon, but smaller and more intense. I admired his intelligence and I was flattered by his opinion of mine, but he recruited me with a more peremptory confidence than his refugee status seemed to warrant. I felt that he was doing me favours when it should have been I who accorded them. We talked with great animation and I was always glad when he proposed that we 'pass an hour', yet at the same time I was astounded, and almost annoyed, by his assumption that he was my equal. Should he not have been more timid and more conscious of the hostility which his presence excited? I feared his fearlessness and I resented having to feel for him what he failed to feel for himself. My apprehension on his behalf could scarcely be distinguished from a grudge.

When my mother asked my why I wanted to stay so late in Caillac, I would say, 'I told you: chess!' I said it, however, in a tone which made it sound like an excuse, if not a lie. I did not specify with whom I played; my abrupt courtesy defied her to press me. Perhaps I wanted her to believe that I was having a love affair, or at least a *rendezvous galant*, with an unsuitable girl – what girl would not have been unsuitable in her eyes? – or even that I was going to the brothel. My deliberate, if artless, mystification gave my time with Fritz an allure it might not otherwise have possessed. Although there was nothing illicit in our meetings over the chessboard, they became glamorous by virtue of what my mother suspected them to be. In silly consequence, my heart would pound, as though my emotions were engaged, as I pressed my hands on my knees in order to climb the sapping steps to the little courtyard which gave access, with a certain devious charm, to the Altschulers' apartment.

The war hardly touched us in the period before the Allies invaded North Africa. The licensed newspapers were thin and advisedly parochial. Fritz pointed out that they were interesting only for what they did not say. 'Negative inferences,' he declared, 'are our best grounds for hope.' One could gauge how badly the Germans were doing not by any account of their reverses (which were still rare and never reported), but from noticing, for instance, that they were still successfully attacking a Russian city which they had attacked success-fully several weeks before. When the Russians began to strike back, Fritz would observe, 'Our friends the Germans have taken queen-sacrifice to unprecedented lengths, my dear Goose! Because look, they are now being irresistible fifty miles further from Kiev than the last time they swept the board!' Why did his glee not wholly please me?

As I began to improve, our chess games became exercises in constructive enmity. He disliked my incompetence more than he enjoyed his regular victories. In an access of impatience, he would sometimes accelerate the situation by moving first his pieces, then mine, in order to illustrate the logic of battle which my folly had made irreversible. He would weigh my dead pieces in front of my eyes, like offal, until he had conclusively demonstrated how, in effect, I had defeated myself. Then, having reconstituted the board as it had been before my bone-headed 'discord' wrecked the beauty of the game, he would show me the other logic, which the right move on my part would have set in train and which he would prove, with another show of acceleration, would have led to my victory rather than his. 'And this way you are the winner, not me! *Hein? Hein?*' he would say, in a

Germanic way which made me a bad loser even when I had, in a sense and thanks only to him, theoretically prevailed.

Fritz's omnipotence was devastating, but it was frail. I knew how easily he could be swept away, like my pawns, if the authorities chose to arm their malice. That sullen knowledge, which had nothing to do with intelligence, put me in a class to which Fritz, for all his skill, could never obtain entry. I wished for no practical dividend from my unearned superiority, but I could not renounce its furtive comfort.

One winter's day, at the end of 1942, I was sitting on the clammy wooden bench of the little train when I noticed three or four men in uniform standing in a field. A hedge was being burnt out behind them. The flames made hot commas along the text of blackened branches. I was by now a pupil in the *classe de première* and we had been doing Virgil's *Georgics*; I found myself wondering whether he ever described such a landscape. The uniformed men were a grey anachronism which imported a new present into a scene that, without them, would have belonged to no specific time. They wore boots and forage caps. Thick belts flared their tunics into curt, pleated skirts. They were the first German soliders I had seen.

I was not incredulous exactly, but I had to make a conscious effort to understand their presence. At first I thought they had come to help on the land or to set fire to it, as if they alone were entitled to use matches. I had heard, of course, that the Germans had crossed the demarcation line and abrogated the treaty they had signed with Vichy, but the reality of their invasion only now came home to me. I was not shocked; my little smile might have been seen as a sign of amusement, but it was more an acknowledgement that the next step had been taken towards some dreadful but not wholly undesired test. The inoffensive attitude of the soldiers was almost endearing; they stood about like lost boys. They had no obvious weapons. We rolled past their truck at a level crossing. Perhaps they had stopped to take a leak or buy some white wine. Why did I twist to look at them again? They were a kind of tasteless treat.

We rarely saw Germans in Caillac. Périgueux, well to our north, was their garrison town. La Fontaine du Noyer, being remote from Caillac, was even less threatened by the *Fridolins*. The wild boars which frequented the forests on each side of our valley were a greater menace than the Germans, who would scarcely see our unequal towers, behind their screen of pine and walnut trees, even if they did have occasion to pass along the dirt road which headed on south towards the Lot.

My mother was annoyed by the arrival of the Germans in the 'Free

Zone', not because she resented the breach of faith but because it obliged her to recognise that the war was still in progress. She had convinced herself in 1940 that the matter was closed. My father's decided reticence on political matters was, I suspect, a concession as much as a form of self-denial. If he made any comment on the policies of Pétain's government, my mother would say, 'It's too late now,' rather as if someone had suggested a game of bezique (which she liked) too near bedtime. She was permanently out of temper with the world in which she was now forced to live. She dressed with reproachful formality for the meals to which outside company was rarely invited. She gave the impression of entertaining private ghosts before whom certain standards had to be maintained.

My sister's beauty began to attract young men to the house, but her cavaliers – who did often come on horseback – were not encouraged to stay. My mother's only criterion of worth was now one of 'blood': pedigree was alone reliable as a measure of quality. When I reminded her that, before the war, she had spoken disparagingly of dinner parties where there was no wit but a plethora of *particules*, she said, without a trace of humour, that it was her business to make sure that Louise did not do something unworthy of the family. I suspect that she had become a snob out of moral confusion, just as some women who have led racy lives revert, in later years, to a religion which, in their happier days, they found ridiculous. Louise attended St Joseph, the Jesuit school in Caillac, where the supervision was notoriously rigorous.

From time to time inspectors came to the *lycée*. Perhaps they were supposed to check on the 'patriotism' of the staff but, so far as the pupils could tell, their visits were without consequence. Early in 1943, however, a *traction-avant* – one of the black Citroëns which were now reserved for the use of the authorities – drove into the schoolyard. The men who got out wore shiny raincoats and black hats, as if they had been warned of a coming storm and had the unrationed means to dress appropriately. We watched them heading for the *proviseur's* office. I could not help looking at Fritz. I saw in his flushed face – he seemed to shave even the unbearded part of his cheeks – something which was less like alarm than embarrassment: it was as though someone might be taking more trouble over him than he deserved. One would have thought he was about to receive an unwanted distinction.

After a few minutes, the men came out of the tall, frosted glass doors of Monsieur Chantal's office and one of them had some difficulty in closing it again. His courtesy was a demonstration. The other men looked at the buildings and at each other. When the door was shut, they all returned to the black car whose cowled wheels and rounded shoulders gave it the appearance of being dressed as they were.

Fritz was studying me as one might a picture in a gallery. I was an object to him. Monsieur Picpus, my *prof principal*, was talking about the Sullan constitution. He had coloured chalks with which it was his annual habit, and pleasure, to depict on the blackboard the elaborate measures by which the Roman dictator proposed to protect the state against demagogues. Monsieur Picpus' chalks were like an unobtainable delicacy left over from before the war. He handled them with jealous tenderness. The colourful freckles of their green and rose and purple dust were the last vestiges of peace. He watched us, as he used them, to be sure that we appreciated his generosity. He had drawn the plan of Sulla's system so often that he hardly needed to look at the blackboard.

Monsieur Picpus had a drooping, unkempt moustache, like a *poilu* from the Great War. His eyes were of uneven size; a drooping lid gave the left one a baleful, unblinking sadness, while the right, being normally lidded, appeared more skittish and more keenly lit, as if it had not seen the terrible things which blighted its fellow. Monsieur Picpus wore a salt-and-pepper cotton coat, which reached below his knees, and a long scarf which, on cold days, he kept on throughout the class. He made no overt connection between Sulla and the Marshal, whose photograph was now slightly tinted by the chalk dust, but when he spoke of the 'old soldier who, by a heroic effort of will, put Rome's clock back to a time when the common people had no control over their destiny', it was impossible to distinguish sarcasm from endorsement.

Monsieur Picpus did not make himself available to us after class. He came from 'the North' and was not known to have either relatives or friends in Caillac. He could not be goaded or charmed into personal declarations. When Pistolozzi, with a grinning slip of the tongue, called Sulla 'the Marshal', Picpus wrapped his long dark scarf around his throat and said, 'This is the first century before Jesus Christ, *hein*?' His baleful eye looked reproachfully at us; the other gleamed. The bell sounded. Monsieur Picpus loaded his still-long coloured chalks into their black felt holster and sloped towards the door.

As we jostled after him through the narrow door into the corridor (Magnac was trying to trip Martegoutte, as usual), I said, 'What do you think they wanted this time?'

Fritz said, 'To be important, didn't they?'

'Is that what you want?' I said.

'I don't want anything,' Fritz said.

'That's because you already have it, isn't it?'

'What?' Fritz said.

'Anyway,' I said, 'there *are* things you want. I know there are.'

He said, 'Not yet.'

'Then you may not get them at all,' I said.

Fritz said, 'Do you not want to play today?'

'It's all the same to me,' I said.

We passed the unmarked Citroën in front of the Hotel Madeleine. The shutters of the hotel were all closed except for a pair on the ground floor which hung at right angles to the façade, as if they had been pushed open petulantly by someone who could not be bothered to lean out and fasten them correctly. I could see men in suits inside, together with a woman in a hat with a feather in it. Her blonde hair hung in a pageboy style.

'Tourists,' Fritz said.

I said, 'You know what you should do, don't you? Come to my house.'

Fritz said, 'It's late.'

'There's plenty of time,' I said. 'We can catch the train I always catch.'

'Do you really want me to?' he said.

I said, 'You can if you want to.'

He said, 'We may as well get the pieces, don't you think so?'

'We've probably got a set,' I said.

'Anyway,' he said.

I did not like the feelings I had now that I knew that Fritz was planning to come with me to La Fontaine. I had not liked the feelings, which were not the same, that had prompted me to issue the invitation. I walked beside him up the steps to the house behind the Chapel of the White Penitents. The name of Judas kept going through my head.

Madame Altschuler was sitting at the table where Fritz and I usually played chess. She must have been using the last of the vanished daylight. Although the lamp was now burning, her work was still tilted towards the dark window.

Fritz said, 'Guy has asked me to his house.'

She said, 'Is that all right?'

I said, 'Naturally, madame.'

She did not look up. 'Do you have clocks?' she said. I knew that the question was intended for me, but I looked at Fritz, as if she had addressed him or had spoken in a language I did not follow. My silence raised her eyes from her sewing. 'At your house,' she said.

I said, 'Oh, yes. A few. Some.'

'My husband repairs clocks,' she said. 'He is a clockmaker.'

I said, 'I know, madame.'

She said, 'Are you sure you have room?'

'Plenty,' I said.

'The times are very bad,' she said.

'Indeed,' I said.

'Tell your parents. Please.'

'They know,' I said.

'About the clocks.'

'I will,' I said.

'You're very kind to do this,' she said.

'Not at all,' I said. 'Not at all.'

'Be careful,' she said, as she embraced her son.

I think I heard him say, 'How?'

X

A few days after Berthe told me that Pierre Salomon was her lover, he telephoned me at the Embassy. I admired the calmness of his voice. Its bass timbre was uninflected by any sign of anxiety. He had called, he said, to tell me that he was planning an excursion to Cerveteri to see the Etruscan tombs. A cousin from Nice was in Rome and had lent him a 'machine' (he made a car sound like an outlandish article).

I said, 'I'm not sure that I should.'

Pierre said, 'Can this be a moral matter?'

I said, 'I have a lot of work to do.'

'Then do it quickly. Have you seen them? The tombs?'

'I don't believe I have.'

'My dear Guy, can belief be relevant? Either you have or you haven't! And since you evidently haven't and clearly should . . .'

'All right,' I said. 'All right.'

The car was a Citroën *traction-avant*. It was a grey post war model which had already been superseded by the aerodynamic version which my Ambassador used. I hesitated over telling Berthe of my outing. It was not that I doubted whether she would know of it (I assumed she did), but I wished the whole responsibility for the occasion to rest with Pierre. Clearly, he wanted to confess or to boast or to secure my complicity. If I failed to tell Berthe, she would be inhibited from questioning me, even though she was aware of the expedition. It amused me to dress for a rural ride on a Thursday morning (my Ambassador had raised no objection to my day off) and to observe my wife's affectations of puzzlement as I took an English tweed hat from my cupboard instead of my usual snap-brim. I kissed her rather perkily, in genuine admiration of her performance, as I went to the door.

The *traction-avant* had been modified after the war, but it still had a chromium bar along the top of the front seats, which gave it the style of a public conveyance. Although the back seats were unoccupied, we seemed to be on our way to collect other passengers. Despite the Roman sun, Pierre was wearing a dark blue mackintosh, crackly and voluminous enough to contain his deep-chested body without any tightness. I found his rainwear less incongruous than suggestive of privileged access to meteorological information unavailable to laymen. Were my cream trousers and linen jacket (over a 'graph-paper' shirt and brown tie) going to get soaked before the day was out? Was I mistaken to carry the brown cardigan which Berthe had bought me (the *sconto diplomatico* had been an irresistible seventy per cent)?

We drove out along the Via Cassia. Pierre asked me to watch for the junction which would take us to the Aurelia. He was not an experienced driver. The car seemed unnaturally loud, almost insubordinate, like a horse uncertain of its master. Pierre's nose and lips – whose edges were fretted, I now noticed, with tucks and tiny lines – were luminous with sweat. He looked at me from time to time like someone making sure that a child whom he has undertaken to amuse is not yet conscious of his nervousness. His anxiety both amused and disturbed me. The last thing I wanted from him was any kind of entreaty. I was relying on his mastery of all the skills necessary to procure for himself whatever outcome he desired.

It was nearly lunchtime before we were approaching Civitavecchia, where Pierre proposed to eat. Like many priests, he paid considerable attention to his food. Just before the city limits, he pulled in to consult his Michelin guide. He seemed to expect me to find his gastronomic fetish rather endearing. Although I felt neither anger nor resentment at his being my wife's lover, I elected – almost coquettishly – to deny him any easy favours. Noticing that I was observing his bookish greed with a distinctly secular humour, he said, 'I don't see why we shouldn't have a decent meal, do you, Guy?'

I said, 'It's all the same to me.'

'Is it?' he said. 'Why is it?'

I felt a sudden prick of tears in my eyes and hardened my expression accordingly. 'I eat sparingly at midday,' I said. 'Do you want to know why that is?'

'Guy, Guy, Guy!' he said.

He selected a *trattoria* across from the black beach. The sand must have been of volcanic origin. Although copious, it seemed less an amenity than a blight. The few people who were sitting on it were fully dressed. Some children ran without enthusiasm; they appeared to be playing at pleasure rather than enjoying themselves. The sea had a soupy listlessness. A few small waves slouched along the tideline. The air itself was tainted with greyness; one took it like medicine.

Pierre made a rustling, crackling sound as he shucked his raincoat. I glanced apprehensively at what he might have underneath it. Which did I dread more – some jaunty boldness, or ecclesiastic severity? I hoped he would be wearing something clever, which might encapsulate his role as demon and divine. He had on a double-breasted blue blazer with black buttons, a turtle-necked grey cotton Ascot (as the Roman shops called them) and very dark grey trousers. I had already seen his grey socks and thick-thonged sandals on the pedals of the Citroën. The sandals had buckles big enough for a gate; their bulky intricacy looked as though it might have been contrived by a blind man in order to astonish the sighted.

Pierre straightened his jacket as if he expected congratulation on his wardrobe. I withheld it; I was beginning to enjoy withholding encouragement of any kind. It was not that I expected to emerge as the day's improbable victor but rather that, as with Fritz Altschuler, I wanted to give the master a run for his money. All my subdued aggression was in preparation for a defeat which I hoped only would be elegantly contrived. My secret weapon was my unsuspected indifference with regard to Berthe; she was a prize I was not unwilling to have Pierre win. If he had some notion that I did not love her, he might well imagine that I would be indignant at his doing so.

'Rigatoni, Guy,' Pierre said. 'The prawn cocktail, then the rigatoni fatti a casa, a bottle of Valpolicella, plus some San Pellegrino – e poi avanti, what do you say?'

I do not like prawns; rigatoni remind me of boiled drain pipes; Valpolicella gives me a headache. 'Perfect,' I said.

Pierre actually rubbed his hands. 'Oh, I do like outings,' he said. 'That sense of wrongdoing without doing anything wrong, it's one of the prime rewards of the cloth!'

I said, 'The people on the beach are going through the motions of being on the beach.'

He swivelled to look through the window as if this must be something worth seeing. 'Very noble of them,' he said. 'I've always watched the people at the back of films with particular respect and admiration – the diners who speak and are not heard, the soldiers who fall and do not cry out, the meek who are not necessarily mild!' He tipped this last phrase almost roguishly towards the handsome, hirsute young waiter who was sniffing the cork of the Valpolicella. 'I like backgrounds,' Pierre went on, 'unresolved diversity which lacks the self-consciousness of the particular. Communion! Communion!'

I said, 'To be candid, I rarely go that far.'

Pierre snorted as if I had said something both amusing and disreputable. He could, he implied, acknowledge my dissidence as a man, but not as a priest. His sparkling, disapproving eyes reminded me that he was both. The better I liked – almost venerated – Pierre, the more scandalous the motives and purposes which I found myself attributing to him.

The prawns had not been peeled before being coated in a glutinous sauce resembling diluted toothpaste. They were so awkward to handle that I suspected that Pierre had chosen them because their manipulation was likely to embarrass me. My pale clothes were vulnerable to the smallest spot. Part of my respect for my priestly companion was due to an almost skittish dread that he had miraculous, virtually Protean abilities. Why should the transformation of food into a form of weapon be beyond him?

The truth was, I rather revelled in the illusion of being in someone else's power. My delight in it derived from the potency which I could in this way attribute to him. I had no desire to be helpless in the hands of someone who had no idea of what to do with me. Pierre's genius could make something of me, I fancied, which I could not otherwise be.

I worked carefully to avoid marking my clothes with the dressing from the prawns. Pierre seemed incautiously competent. He peeled his prawns in his mouth, with energetic agility, and ejected the transparent detritus into the discreet vessel he made by curling his forefinger inside his thumb. 'Dining in the Vatican,' he told me, 'teaches one resource. Does it ever occur to you that the Christian diet – the diet which happens, in many countries, especially in the Mediterranean basin, to be happily cheap (I'm thinking in particular of shellfish and pork) – is what one might call inadvertently designed to be an affront to the Jews?'

'No,' I said.

'You're very decisive there, Guy, for once. Are you therefore in doubt?'

'I've never considered the matter,' I said.

'Surely,' he said, 'surely! Haven't we licensed people – haven't we conspired in some sense – to make the world by all available means an affront to the Jews?'

'Berthe is right,' I said.

'*Berthe*?' He might have been enunciating the name of an obscure Swiss theologian. My wife's name, on his surprised lips, sounded like that of a man. 'Right? In what respect?'

'She says you really are a Jew.'

'And I really am and she really is right. Have you heard differently? Never from me!'

I hoped and feared that the mention of Berthe's name might induce

Pierre to broach the issue which I took to be central to our improbable excursion. It was, as it were, the Sicilian opening which might impel him to make a move on the invisible board which my preconception of the day's purpose had unfolded between us. I looked forward to the appearance in his eyes of the equivalent of the double exclamation marks with which chess writers applaud a brilliant subterfuge.

'What I mean . . .' He had to stop to accommodate the steaming heap of semolina tripes which the waiter was putting in front of him. The reek of the *rigatoni* struck me like the raw breath of the cabhorses who stood twitching in the Piazza di Spagna, near the flower stalls. It did not encourage my appetite. 'What I mean,' Pierre said, 'is that the vast majority is, even now, even *now*, in dread of some revanchist stroke – heaven knows of what kind – which will put the Jews in a postion to exact compensation. It's that fear which requires us – you, me, everyone – to compose a history of iniquity, of barbarism even, which will make such a comeback impossible. We must by all means dishearten, disqualify, discompose those whose God we have usurped and whose morality we parody. Thus the unfaithful spouse honours marriage in the breach!'

I said, 'You schematise.'

'I am a traitor,' he said. 'I may be right to betray what I betray, but can that mitigate my treachery? Isn't this bacon in our *rigatoni*? Has there ever been any sentence but death in cases of treason? We are dealing not with justice here but with taboo. Is there something wrong with that?'

'It's excellent,' I said. 'First you schematise, then you dramatise.'

'I'm also a Platonist,' he said. 'I meant the food.'

'Your treason will remain unpunished,' I said, 'whatever its supposed penalty. Unpunished and, in all probability, applauded, as you very well know. You toy with the final pleasure, which would be victimisation, but you have ensured that it will be denied you.'

'Perhaps that *is* the final pleasure, my dear Guy. Denial. Have you thought of that?'

'Of course,' I said.

'And have you pushed your plate away because you're displeased with it or with me?'

'Let's just say that I've had enough.'

'Then may I?' He took my plate and tilted it over his own. My lunch slid into the remains of his, leaving a residue of sauce across the edge of the plate which he replaced in front of me. 'I come across this kind of thing constantly.'

'And what kind of thing is this?' I said.

63

He said, 'Is something wrong?'

'Is it not?' I said.

He frowned. He might have been trying to place a quotation. He said, 'We've got plenty of time, if that's what's worrying you. The day is long; only art is short!' My failure to smile made him serious again; he took it for a prompt. 'I come across it in the concern, even among my more intelligent colleagues, over what is left of the Jew in me. Their gentle inquisitions cannot let the matter rest. In theory I am a Catholic like any other, but there remains something about me which fascinates and – yes – dismays them. Because it puts them at a piquant disadvantage, they will not suffer me to deny it, or take my denial without suffering. One of them – a Dutchman, if you please, Van Breuckelen (whose family, he says, founded Brooklyn) – he said to me the other day, "Do you think that we shall find the same thing with Him that we find with you?" At first I was puzzled, but he thought I was pretending. What he wanted to know was whether Jesus, on His return, will be more at home with me than with them! They think He will repair to the Jews and not to the Church fathers. They suspect him of being no better than a *converso*, if you know what that is.'

'I can imagine,' I said.

'I have even heard circumcision – or rather its lack – discussed as something which might make them distasteful to Him. They hate the practice and they wonder, secretly, whether they should not submit to it. They fear being improperly dressed, so to say, at the final inspection. You see what a threat I am, what a challenge to their geniality? Is something wrong with your watch?'

'I don't think so,' I said.

I paid for the lunch and we walked along the promenade. There was a cobbled access to the beach between us and where Pierre had parked the Citroën. As we approached, a Vespa with a wooden wagonette attached to it was being driven along the front. It swerved, just in front of us, and lurched down the cobbles. We were not in danger but there was a certain insolence in the driver's manoeuvre. He resembled the hairy waiter who had just served us in the *trattoria*. Another young man, with curly fair hair and wearing a sort of white uniform, was sitting in the wagonette, with his legs over its back fence. He had a rumpled, sunless face. I imagined him with a husky voice.

The Vespa slewed onto the beach. As its tyres were snubbed by the black sand, the wagonette tilted and its passenger half-fell, half-vaulted from his container. There was an air of wilful urgency about the whole operation, as if the two young men had been summoned to repair a broken main or rescue a dog. And yet, at the same time, it was obvious that they had not. Pierre and I proceeded to the car, but we went on watching the pair of them. We might have been awaiting an apology or an assault, but with no large expectation of either.

The driver stood away from his machine and zipped the key into his denim jacket. He and his friend walked down the steep part of the beach and stood side by side looking at the sloppy sea. Pierre and I were in the car by now. The key was in the ignition, but Pierre seemed disinclined to turn it. He was enlarged and sated by the lunch. There was an amiable, lazy gloss on him. He treated the two young men like a show which had been mounted for our digestive amusement.

After a certain time, as if they had been counting the seconds, the two of them simultaneously slapped each other with the backs of their hands. They remained side by side and struck each other with a flicking motion, less a blow than a signal. A moment later, the curly-headed one, in the white uniform, began to chase the other.

I said, 'Is that our waiter or not?'

Pierre said, 'Should I know?'

The dark youth ran and dodged, dodged and ran. There appeared to be some agreement about the scope of the area in which the pursuit took place. When the unmarked limit was reached, the dark young man had to check, face and evade his pursuer in order to stay within bounds. This led to a series of moments, more and more frequent and prolonged as the two of them grew breathless, during which they stood quite close, facing each other, panting and feinting before they were ready to run again. Their tennis shoes churned and worked the sand.

Pierre finally made a shrugging face and reached to turn the ignition key. The young men were once again grinning humourlessly in each other's faces. On this occasion, however, when the fair one grabbed at his friend's lapel, the dark youth – instead of evading him – snaked out a hand and clipped the other one quite smartly on the ear. It was as though he had sensed our boredom and was promising a new development.

His friend grabbed him round the waist and they heaved on each other for several seconds before toppling onto the black ground. At the beginning, their fight seemed as stylised as the pursuit which preceded it. They rolled and scuffled, with first one and then the other on top. They fell apart from time to time, whereupon one would scramble away, not too hurriedly, only to be caught by the ankle or the wrist and twisted into new contortions. Some kind of convention seemed to govern their exercise. Perhaps they were fellow-workers in some frustrating enterprise and this was their daily way of working off repressed energy.

The darker of them was also larger; the other was more compact and more cunning. The latter demonstrated his tricks like a cruel teacher; he smiled hurtfully and posed little questions (inaudible to us), as he worked an arm or pinned a leg. Once his opponent, nodding and wincing, indicated that he had taken the point, the rumpled one would release him, pending a riposte whose naiveté he would demonstrate by again tying the other one into a fleshy knot before bouncing him, like an idle motor, until he came to life with new, flailing vigour.

'Does this interest you, Guy?'

I said, 'I feel that something's going to happen, don't you?'

'Then we'll wait,' Pierre said.

The dark boy broke free and palmed himself to his feet. Targets of blood shone on his cheeks. He went up and down, pumping air into his lungs. Finally, he stayed with his knees bent, a spread of fingers leaning on the sand. The fair youth was less out of breath, but he put his hands on his hips, miming equal exhaustion. Tact and derision played on his face. He seemed to have aged in the few minutes we had been watching: he was now a man baiting a boy who happened to be bigger than he.

The fair one held out his hand and snapped his fingers for the keys to the Vespa. The other shook his head. The fair one looked at his watch (on a silver strap) and became businesslike: he brushed sand from himself and turned away, mounting the beach with the perky, trim-buttocked style of a bullfighter who is leaving a cowed beast behind him. In his confident disdain, the possibility of another furious charge does not even occur to him.

The dark boy looked down, as if he were consulting some secret text. Once he had the recipe, as it were, he looked down once more and then launched himself at the back of the other. It was a last, merciless throw. His opponent seemed to divide into two halves; his face had time to register both surprise and a kind of amusement, while his back buckled from a kick to the kidneys which was followed, almost instantaneously, by an arm which locked itself across his throat and put an end to the moment of divorce. Even as he was struck down he seemed to remain in command.

Could he really be as defenceless as he now seemed? The humiliations which he had forced so magisterially on the other became the warrant for revenge. I wanted to believe its savagery to be a pretence. Even as the fair boy – whose maturity seemed all spent now – was thrown down, throttled, dragged, turned over, kicked, spat upon, I was waiting for his witty response, his check and mate.

Did the dark youth not have similar expectations? He stopped occasionally to stand over the ragged figure on the floor and prodded an unspoken question with his toe. Deadness and playing dead were too close for satisfaction. As for Pierre, I glimpsed the hint of activity in his shifts of expression: he was reading the boys' conflict in some personal way, but I could not tell what. I could see only that his mind was busy in his face.

The dark boy walked backwards, dragging his victim by the heels, face down, towards the sea. I realised now that the fair one's uniform was that of a house-painter. A white cap spilled from his blouse pocket and lay in the trench left by the trailing trunk. The dark boy took a new breath and turned his back on the other before hitching one heel under each armpit and continuing his trudge to the water. He shuffled into the sea with his inert litter behind him.

'My God,' I said, 'he's going to drown him!'

Pierre put a hand on my sleeve. I smelt the ghost of the prawns which he had shucked into the whorl of forefinger and thumb. He was not placating me; he was encouraging me to endure whatever might be in store. I turned to get out of the car. The door handle was at a strange angle, almost vertical. I did not know which way to push or pull it. As I hesitated, Pierre opened his door – he was adjacent to the promenade – and stood up into the air.

The victor seemed conscious of the big, dark figure against his horizon. He turned again, ankled in water, and looked up towards us. As if to do us a favour, or deprive us of a satisfaction, he relinquished the plimsolled heels from under his arms and let them plop. This release seemed to end the drama. The fair youth came to life; he shook his head and, in his turn, looked up at us. His chin was bearded with brackish froth from the tideline. I was leaning on the car roof by now, having succeeded in opening my door. The prone boy pressed his hands on the black sand and got to his knees. He shook himself like a dog and rose to his feet.

I said, 'Do you think he was going to piss on him? I thought he was going to piss on him.'

'No,' Pierre said.

The dark boy tried to slap some of the blackness from the other. He seemed less sympathetic than eager to destroy the evidence before someone in authority came along. The fair hair was darkened by the water, and less curly; the rumpled face had lost its wisdom. Its owner sought no reconciliation; he walked on up the beach without the earlier strut. He grabbed his hat as he stepped over it and thrashed it white against his thigh. He came up the cobbled incline and walked right past us. He said something to Pierre under his breath.

Pierre said, 'Funny type!'

I said, 'What did he say?'

'What they always say.'

'Who are "they"? And what?'

'I don't always get their slang,' Pierre said. 'Is your Italian good?'

'*Così*,' I said.

He said, "Cerveteri! Shall we go? Before it's too late!"

The dark youth was calling from the beach: 'Tonio, Tonio!' He was astride the Vespa now, dangling the key towards his late opponent. Tonio shook a loose hand, goodbye and forget it, without looking back.

Pierre said, 'Guy, are you all right?'

I said, 'I think so. I have a slight headache, that's all.'

'Because if you'd sooner go home . . .'

I should have liked nothing better. I said, 'Go home? Of course not. Good heavens!'

XI

I seemed to be Fritz as we quit the little train at Port du Noyer. The lettered board is still there on the concrete hut by the overgrown line. Normally, the deep-shadowed stands of chestnut and pine which mounted on each side of the valley hung there like reassuring landscapes along a familiar corridor. That autumn evening, however, the valley appeared both immense and enclosing, as if we were walking without issue.

Looking about me with Fritz's eyes, conscious of the stiff shoes which were a vestige of the world he had left behind, I felt nervous for him. How would my mother respond to an uninvited guest? I could imagine her electing to be disappointed at the palpable evidence that I had indeed been playing chess all those afternoons in Caillac, when she liked and hated to think of me doing something disreputable.

The road was firm, but unmetalled. Its rutted surface was studded with pebbles and chunks of crushed limestone. The valley seemed deserted but I knew that there were farms and hamlets, some with as many as sixty 'fires' (the peasants counted hearths, not houses), behind the camouflage of pines and oak trees. Under one arm, Fritz carried a cardboard box with the chess pieces in it; his satchel with his pyjamas was in the other. On his head was a flat brown corduroy cap with a button on the crown.

At a point which I always thought of as halfway, the track forked and we had to veer right and then left again. In fact, this fork was considerably nearer Port du Noyer than to La Fontaine, but it was the only obvious punctuation on the road. I explained to Fritz how I deceived myself with this false division of the journey. He listened politely, as one might to a stranger who excuses himself at length for a fault which no one would otherwise have remarked. I listened with him, wondering – as I imagined he might be – what more important considerations the speaker was concealing.

I feared for Fritz and I feared Fritz. I did not think that he personally would hurt me, but I feared the hurt that was coming to him and which, in my powerlessness to prevent it, I somehow desired. My interest in him was a kind of curse. Even if he were to disappear, he would remain a charge on me; he dignified and irritated me. Did it occur to me, as we started the two-kilometre stretch of walnut orchards along the valley floor, that it would be best, for him, if Fritz stayed permanently at La Fontaine du Noyer? There had been no manifest sequel to the visit of the men in shiny coats and black hats, but I was sure that something sinister was imminent. I also knew that Fritz was made strangely important by it. If I saved him from his fate, I felt that I should be depriving him (or was it myself?) of something enviable. I was not sure whether I wanted to help Fritz or whether, since my help was a kind of contempt, I hoped that he would be spared it. At the same time, I was wondering whether we should play chess before dinner or after it and whether Gertrud would have made one of her *apfelstrudels*.

The cultivated walnut trees, bracketed under the wild forests on both sides of the valley, seemed like tethered victims. They were more valuable and, in some way, finer than the spruces and oaks and chestnuts in the wild army on their flanks, but they lacked the useless freedom of the uncounted and unaccountable. Their pollarded regularity tamed them. The ground beneath them was ploughed so that their nuts could be gathered easily. The valley was their camp.

'We go up here,' I said. We had reached the two stone pillars at the end of the chestnut alley which went up to La Fontaine. Two gryphons crouched on stone balls. Their claws had weathered to mere toes; their beaks had dwindled to wise old noses. The drive was felted, as if for a funeral, with wadded leaves, gold and yielding brown; the pressure of our feet squeezed wet prints in them. A recent cart had ruled parallel, veering grooves between which Fritz and I agreed to walk. The field to the right of the alley belonged to us; that on the left did not. Its owner, Monsieur Cabanne, and my father did not speak, although the quarrel which began the sullen feud was between Cabanne, who was a local peasant, and Roque, our gardener who had seduced the other man's daughter.

At the end of the alley, our arcaded terrace glimmered in the yellowish light which still seemed to be stored in its heavy stones. As we neared the house, there was a brief, violent flurry of some laurel bushes; suddenly, something was standing in the open ahead of us. Fritz looked at me, not at it. The hare seemed almost as tall as ourselves. Stalked on its high hind legs, it was vivid with some luminous force, quite as if some part of the lost day remained lodged in it. The darkness which was closing on us did not threaten it. It looked at us without either trust or rancour. It was perfectly foreign.

Fritz said, 'Do you eat them?'

70

'You can,' I said.

'But do you?' he said.

'Sometimes, I think. Simone does the cooking. I don't always like to know what things are, but I think it's quite good. In a *civet*, if you know what that is.'

The hare moved its head first as we approached him, then I saw his two rear hooves peck the leaves and he rattled in among Cabanne's laurels. After he had gone, I seemed to see his head more clearly than I had when he was tensed in front of us.

Roque and his son, Baptiste, had stacked wood under the arcades. Bundles of vine cuttings, for kindling, lay on top of them. A flight of naked steps led up to the terrace at each end. Another flight, with stone balustrades, had been inserted in the centre of the long terrace at my mother's instructions. It had a split halfway up, where you could choose to go left or right. Either way, you came to the same last four steps which took you up to the flagstones where I remember being passed around as a baby. When I asked my mother why she had bothered with a third way up, she said, 'I can't expect my friends to come up unguarded steps, like peasants, can I?'

Baptiste had closed the tall, unplaned shutters. A stripe of warped light showed where my father was working in his study. I had no clear notion of what he was doing since he left the Ministry of Finance. Once, when I met him carrying old dossiers from the attic, he muttered that he was interesting himself in local history. He seemed like someone who, while working diligently, was striving, at the same time, to give an impression of diligence. In those days, we seemed to need to pretend to be what we were.

My mother said, 'The chess player!'

Fritz said, 'I hope I'm not intruding, madame.'

'You said I might bring him,' I said.

'And bring him you have!' My mother spoke pleasantly, but in my anxiety – or was it Fritz's? – I detected a hint that it had been something of a liberty to take her at her word. 'Where is he going to sleep?'

'Louise's room?' My sister stayed, *en pension*, in Caillac during the week, so her bed was empty. 'Or . . .'

'Simone will make up a room.' My mother glanced at me as though Fritz, rather than I, had made the impertinent suggestion that he use Louise's room; her barely tolerant eyes warned me to advise my friend to honour the proprieties.

La Fontaine is a long house with two main floors. It seems taller on account of the steeply pitched roof in which there is a series of attics, with mansard windows. Most of the attics were uninhabitable; they connected to form a long *grenier* divided only by oak beams whose solid cross-ties came at knee level. Wooden pegs stuck out like arrows fired into them by some archaic bow. The roof, like many in our region, was built three or four hundred years ago by the shipwrights who spent the winter doing *charpenterie* and the easier months constructing the timber rafts which they launched at Port du Noyer.

I led Fritz up the rustic stairway which climbed from the top landing into what I always thought of as the no man's land of the attic. Although never forbidden to go there, as a child I always had a sense of trespass in that unfinished region, with its splintery floors, its heaps of cloudy bottles and abandoned boxes. In the summer, the rough rows of *lauzes* – the stone 'tiles' of the Périgord – admitted dots and dashes of sharp light. I would pretend that their brilliant scribble conveyed a message I could decode. There was something delight-fully alarming in this 'cellar in the sky' with its hint of secrets and its scuttle of furtive inhabitants. Forgetfulness and disorder were per-mitted here as they were frowned upon downstairs. My mother deplored the attic; she sneezed in its dust and its roughness snagged her dresses. Her distaste spiced my appetite.

Respectability was bracketed between this jaggedly illumined dark-ness and the hellish dungeons, in the basement, where Roque's *barrique* gave off its hot pungency when the new wine was seething in it. Down in the cellar I would come across the cold, heavy remnants of ancient agriculture. The rusting implements seemed too heavy for mortal hands. Their tortuous screws and grappling irons, their branding plates and curved blades recalled an old war between man and nature.

Fritz said, 'It's very big, your house.'

'It's *quite* big,' I said, impersonating my mother; fear that Fritz might ask for something which it was not in my power to accord put skirts on my words. 'But it's . . . deceptive.' That was her sort of term all right.

Fritz said, 'I meant to keep up.'

'Roque and Simone can manage it between them. And Baptiste helps. Roque's son. He's very strong – stupid, but strong.'

'Useful,' Fritz said.

It suited me to act as though Fritz had said the wrong thing, although I did nothing more offensive than to show him how polite I could be. My urge to protect him was excited by a feeling that there was some hidden aspect of him whose explosion would be worth seeing. In the manner of a knowing character in a myth, I was being agreeable to a god whose favourite I hoped to become; my attentive-ness was less innocent than I should have liked, if I wanted to like myself for it.

'Useful?' I said.

'Extra hands,' Fritz said.

We were in my domain now, under the *lauzes* whose peak was so far above us, in the darkness, that we might have been in a cathedral. I snapped a match against the side of the box and enjoyed Fritz's startled eyes. 'Roque made him on a peasant girl,' I said. 'When Simone couldn't give him a son. Coldly. Like that.' I held the match to the paraffin lamp which was always left at the top of the steps. 'And that's why we have a sort of a feud on our hands.'

I held up the lamp and invited Fritz to inspect the shady heaven of my childhood memories. I led the way along the *grenier*, stepping with nervous authority over the tie-beams which had once seemed much higher from the floor than they did now. We advanced as though some monster might live at the end of the attic. We were too old to admit to this fantasy, but the illusion of danger sweetened the adventure.

'What sort of a feud?'

I said, 'Oh . . . it's about this field . . . and this family . . . it doesn't bother us; it's not worth talking about. They daren't do anything, because Roque . . . Roque isn't someone you do things to.'

I fell deliberately silent, as though Fritz had raised a tactless subject. Then I heard the rustle of voices through the unsealed floorboards. It is a curiosity of La Fontaine that sounds travel – or are baffled – in unforeseeable ways. No conversation is safely secret and no shout necessarily carries to its desired recipient, even when he is in plain view.

The voices I now heard were not audible syllable by syllable; I could not distinguish the words, only their murmurous intonation. My parents were discussing something. I had, of course, heard such spasmodic exchanges before and I was always struck by their formality. I was reassured and disappointed at the same time by the discovery that, even when they were alone, my parents practised such articulate rectitude. My vanity was sufficient for me to imagine that their performance was mounted for my sake, even though I was too young to guess what they might be concealing, or encoding, in order to spare or intrigue me. They offered a long and habitual 'No' to something which I was powerless to imagine and which, had they been more generous with each other, would have entailed an inadvertent generosity to me. Had they been less cautious, I should have been the smallest of their concerns. Fritz became the witness of my regular disappointment as I listened to what I could not hear and yet heard very clearly: the evidence of my parents' intimate propriety. How differently Roque had got his son!

We left the attic and went downstairs. I led Fritz along the flagged passageway to where smells of supper dispelled all memories except those of appetite. Simone and Gertrud stood at different ends of the long, scrubbed table. It was as if the two women, obliged to proximity, literally could not face each other: the aproned, ample Simone stood, in plain slippers and thick brown stockings, at the short end, by the cast-iron range, while Gertrud – in black shoes, dress and stockings – was at the extreme end of a long side. Not only were they working as far as possible from each other, but they also arranged not to see each other if they looked up. At the same time, the pair of them seemed quite at ease; they exchanged routine words concerning the meal they were preparing, quite as if they had chosen to be the colleagues which circumstance had forced them to be. Imposture salted routine.

Gertrud was rolling pastry. Her hands continued to work, but her eyes fastened on Fritz as if he were some delicacy which, on account of the war, she had never hoped to see again. She and Fritz were exiles who did not dare to acknowledge each other. He awakened a happy pain from which she had supposed herself exempt, while her effect on him was to rekindle the fire in his cheeks. He seemed to blush with the same hungry shame I felt in the days when Gertrud made my Parisian bed and I knew that the stiff stains on the sheets told her of my spent desires.

Formality at table was my father's way of dressing for dinner. He behaved as though Fritz were some kind of an ambassador. My friend matched his dry courtesies with questions about the 'researches' which I had mentioned to him. My father was at one end of the narrow oak table, while Fritz was nearer the other, next to my mother. Good manners required my friend to address some of his remarks to his hostess but, leaving it to my father to respond, she limited herself to smiles and frowns and a few whispered words to me, weighted to be overheard, concerning the room in which Fritz should sleep. Gertrud had been told to make up the bed which my uncle occupied when he came to see us.

Fritz's polite prompting led my father to reveal that he had been investigating a strange case from the last century. Suddenly quite animated, he glared at me and my mother with an air almost of accusation, as if it had taken a stranger to ask the right questions. The case concerned a local aristocrat, distantly related to our family. 'Incidentally,' my father said, 'and before I go on, most of our aristocracy has an entirely false idea of its own importance. You know the story about the devil creating the French nobility. . . ?'

'Oh, Jean-Marie, Jean-Marie,' my mother said.

'He took the prize specimens and scattered them in the rest of France and when he got to the Périgord he only had a few crumbs left and that is what our local *gratin* comes from – the bottom of the bag! Hence their present attitudes, which are not, on the whole, to be admired.'

'Jean-Marie,' my mother said. She might have been warning him of spies in our midst. 'What was this man's name?'

Called to order, my father proceeded with the story. Our ancestor, Rodolphe de Tourian, had been set upon at a country fair soon after the outbreak of the Franco-Prussian war. So far as my father could discover, he was of genial character, a young landowner in his thirties who might not be universally loved by his tenants but who had no need to fear their enmity. He was the younger brother of a more dynamic character, Émile, who had radical political opinions and who had caused an outcry in Caillac on account of his loud hostility to the Emperor, Louis-Napoléon. (My father addressed himself in an explanatory style to Fritz, as if he were alien to French history.)

The country fair was held twice a year, on a piece of common land some eight kilometres from Caillac, near a hamlet called St Amand-en-Caillacois. Its few ancient houses were on the edge of a district of marshes and scrubland, interspersed with pine forests, known as 'The Double'. Wild boar and deer were hunted there; people said that they had seen wolves. The common was roughly fenced for the fair; there were hurdled enclosures for the animals on sale and booths at which food, drink, tools and harness were available. Business and pleasure were one.

'It's difficult to detect exactly what happened, or why,' my father said. 'Our cousin went to the sales, it seems, more out of duty than appetite. He thought it right for the local landlord to take an interest, but he was not himself involved in buying or selling. A promenade was all it was. And at first, apparently, his visit was seen as something of an honour; he attracted attention only because he was what passed for a gentleman on a peasant occasion . . .'

'Jean-Marie!' my mother said.

'But if his arrival was – in a way – flattering, it was also . . . disturbing. It required a response which was not quite, let's say, natural. Rodolphe was an outsider; he obliged the peasants to a certain self-consciousness – they had to behave themselves, which meant being false to their inclinations, as it does, I daresay, for all of us. Such . . . distortions of our natural urges happen all the time, don't they? They rarely lead to anything as dramatic as on this occasion, happily. It was a time in French history when people were both excited and confused.' My father paused and looked balefully at my mother. Did he need her permission to go on or was he making sure that she saw the relevance of his words to our present condition? Her nod was both meek and peremptory, answering both possibilities. 'The Emperor had, let us be candid, launched France into war in an almost frivolous, certainly an unreflective spirit. By the time of the events I'm describing, it was on the way to being a calamity. If their loyalty to Louis-Napoléon was still beyond doubt, the peasants must have sensed, as simple people do, that they were being faithful to a man of straw.'

My mother rang the bell. Fritz refused Simone's cheese, as I did, but my father took a sliver of the home-made *chèvre*. I would have to wait to see what dessert we were to be offered.

'From the examining magistrate's report,' my father said, frowning at a fallen flake of his cheese, 'our cousin's ordeal began with mere badinage. Some of the peasants were out to prove that it was indeed a holiday by adopting an intimate, not to say insolent, tone with their superior. They wanted to know if it was true, as had been reported, that Rodolphe's brother had gone so far, at the meeting of a political club, as to shout, "Long live the Republic!" '

'What was wrong with that?' I said.

'What was wrong with that? What was wrong with that was its implication – that the Republic was better than the Empire, which was now France's official constitution. It was a cry that might have been banal, even patriotic, at another time but which amounted to treason on young Émile's lips.'

Gertrud had come in. She carried exactly what I hoped: a long, flattened *apfelstrudel*, its pastry lightly browned and crinkled on top. My mother's eyes were bright with warning; they advised my father to abate his narrative until Gertrud was safely out of the way. 'You must know this dessert,' my mother said.

'Not at all, madame,' Fritz said. At the same time, he looked up at Gertrud with a smile, as if to show that his ignorance did not imply that he doubted the quality of what he was about to taste. My mother pressed her lips together. Did she suspect some complicity between my friend and the Austrian woman who, quite mistakenly, she took to be of the same stock as Fritz?

'What happened next, Father?'

'With regard to Émile? No action seems to have been taken, but there were many rumours and many exaggerations. In short, a petty scandal, but without a resolution. Which is why Rodolphe was so keenly quizzed. What had really happened? What was going to happen? Was his brother a revolutionary or what was he? I have a suspicion – this is very good – that the peasants who seemed aggressive very nearly – but *only* very nearly – relished Émile's impertinence and wished, by their own, to hint at a modicum of sympathy with it. Who knows? At all events, something which was never central to the fair, which had no political aspect whatsoever, began to infect it and alter its character. How? It seems that some of those on the fringe of the crowd around Rodolphe, who probably couldn't hear what was being said by those privileged to be near him, got the impression, or passed the word, that he, not his brother, had pronounced the forbidden phrase, and what's more that he had just done so. The allegation seems then to have passed back into the centre, so that those who could have denied it received it as if it were something that had just been confirmed. Thus the crowd which, a moment or two before, had been escorting Rodolphe as though he were their patron, from whom benefits could be expected, began to adopt a more strident, though apparently still light-hearted, attitude.'

'Where on earth do you get all this from, Jean-Marie?'

'I have only to unsettle the dust and there it is, in the files, and the newspapers, and the court reports. The movement of the crowd seems to have stopped. Rodolphe was wedged in among his inquisitors. They demanded, rather formally it seems, whether he endorsed his brother's treasonous slogan. With a smile, which may have been a little nervous, he said that he had no interest in the restoration of the Republic. When this appeared to appease the hotheads, he added, "Or of the monarchy". Doubtless, he was hoping to disperse what tension remained with a little jest. It was not well received. To be hostile, or even indifferent, to the monarchy – by which he almost certainly meant the Old Régime – sounded to the quarter-educated rabble around him like a repudiation of the Emperor himself. The crowd jostled to get nearer to him, but it was impacted on itself. It began to rock. Those at the back said that "the traitor" was being protected by the outside "Jacobins". Rodolphe and his brother became one and the same person. Even now, it might have been possible – and it certainly would have been prudent – for our cousin to excuse himself with a few diplomatic words and insist on getting away, if only to buy a pig or stand drinks to the company. How do you like the dessert?'

'Excellent,' Fritz said. 'One of the best I've ever tasted.'

'Well!' my mother said. 'And he said he'd never had it before!'

'One of the best desserts, madame.'

I said, 'Mama, my friend comes from Alsace, not from Vienna.'

'Alsace!' my mother said. The whole province might have been some implausible fabrication. 'You may as well go on with your story, Jean-Marie, though I don't really know why it takes up so much of your time.'

'Penelope had her tapestry,' my father said. 'I have this. So . . . he could have got away, he preferred to stay. Or at least he stayed. He stayed and he became the focus of a mob which was confused in its purpose, if it had one, and its sentiments. Its unity derived only from the fact that it had, very soon, a single and undoubted victim. It was confusedly convinced of just one thing – that someone had urged them to cry "Long live the Republic!" They now insisted, with chanting urgency, and a measure of laughter, that he should "Say it again!" You see the horror and the beauty of our cousin's dilemma? How should he say again what he denied having said before? And if he said it once, might he not just as well have said it before? He could not possibly do what was wanted of him, nor could he refuse to do anything without depriving the crowd of its sport. How wrong, one realises, to separate comedy and tragedy! How utterly ignorant of clever men not to see that, as in this case, tragedy can be rooted in comedy, derived from laughter and its infectious inhumanity! Do you not agree with me?'

Fritz said, 'We think that laughter can save us, but it's the tinder than primes the fire.'

My father said, 'Who said that?'

Fritz said, 'Did they hurt him?'

'Did they hurt him! They taunted him; they made way for him and then they pursued him; they beat him and they let him go again. Some played his protectors and others his persecutors. They did not hurt him until he was hurt; he was the game which had to be finished. When he was hurt, like Cyrano, by a bolt of wood that came somehow from nowhere, the local dignitaries, such as they were, became alarmed, more for their reputation than his safety. They took him into their angry custody, proving their loyalty to the crowd by handling him as roughly as those who had been attacking him. The mayor and his deputy locked him in a cellar, but they did not put a guard on it nor did they interfere when the rabble vented their rage on the locks they had turned. They made a day of it all right, all of them, in that outlandish spot, between the fenced and the unfenced, the neat and the wild.'

'We have no coffee,' my mother said.

'A surprise to none of us,' my father said.

'Some people do; we do not.'

78

I said, 'I thought my uncle brought us some.'

My mother said, 'Guy! In front of a stranger!'

'Is the truth not true in front of strangers?'

My father said, 'And are manners not manners?'

'What did they do to him?' Fritz said.

'They killed him. They killed him very slowly. Was that evidence of their cruelty or of their lack of clear intention? They wounded him, abandoned him and then came back and wounded him again. They pushed him more and more towards the point where it was a brutal kindness to finish him off. They wanted him to admit that they were right; they wanted him to agree what good fellows they were. They laughed at his bewilderment and thought that it proved him a fraud, since they knew very well, by now, what they considered him to be and what, therefore, he *had* to be. They killed and killed and killed him.'

Fritz said, 'Comedy dies hard!'

My father said, 'I think perhaps we should help this young man, don't you? What do you say, Miki?'

My mother frowned. He might as well have touched her breast in front of other people (something I had never seen him do). The open use of her pet name was a public intimacy which she elected to take as an affront. 'If he needs help,' she said. 'And if he wants it.'

My father said, 'Have we finished?'

'I'll leave you,' my mother said. Fritz stood as she did. My father stayed in his seat; so did I. My mother made a placating gesture, a flutter of ringed fingers. 'I must have a word with Simone. And I'll tell Gertrud that you approved of her dessert.'

'Very much,' Fritz said.

What remained of my mother's disapproval was bent on her husband as she went past him to the door. She signalled to him on no account to bother to open it for her. He rose and did so.

As he returned to the table, he said: 'They beat and hacked him to death while he pleaded with them to take their joke no further. Here again, my young friend, is something for you to think about. He accused them – as he lay in the straw of some outhouse, terribly wounded and without even the feeble defence of "official" voices raised against the savagery – he accused them of not being serious, of not meaning him the harm, the agony, they were inflicting on him, and that accusation, which might have been true at the outset, goaded them to even more barbarous acts.'

'Even Jesus could not believe that people knew what they were doing, could he?'

'They beat this innocent cousin of ours to death and then – is this the worst of it? I don't know – then they built a fire and tried to burn him. To put it crudely, they wanted to barbecue him. Even this unforgivable act had a double motive: there were those who wanted only to destroy the evidence, to pretend that he had not even been there that afternoon, and others – others who gloried in his roasting and – really, I can hardly endure to say it – who wanted to put him on the menu, who wanted to make a picnic of him. There were rumours, and they're not necessarily false, that parts of him were actually skewered and eaten, that they dipped their bread in his fat . . . and forced it on those who recoiled.'

'Papa!'

'Silence denies nothing.'

I said, 'And this was only a hundred years ago.'

'Less,' my father said. 'Considerably less. I could easily have known some of those people in my youth. I probably did. I often went hunting in The Double. It was quite the best place for game in the whole corner. So . . .'

'Didn't anything happen, sir, to the people who . . . who did those things?'

'To some of them, my friend. Once France was completely defeated and the Emperor had been deposed. There was a judicial inquiry – its papers supply me with most of my information, naturally enough – and eventually four of the so-called ringleaders were brought to trial. Shame winnowed them from the others, but it also meant that they were regarded as innocent by those whose guilt was visited on them. You can imagine the process. They were there but, they said, they did nothing that others did not do, and the exemption of those others implied that they had done nothing. It was a crime which, since they had all committed it, might as well not have been committed. Its victim became revictimised, since if it had not been for him they would all have been the blameless people they still insisted that they were.'

'So they were found not guilty, were they?'

'They were convicted, and executed. The authorities, who still had no power to control France itself, brought a portable guillotine across the country in a closed carriage. The jury, who were from another district, consisted of good men who, since the defeat of Louis-Napoléon, found it incomprehensible that anyone should attack, let alone murder, a man who – as one of them remarked in a cutting I have from the *Dépêche de Caillac* – "supported the Republic, as we all do!" Rodolphe had a republican club named after him, although there's no evidence he cared a fig for the Republic one way or the other.'

'And what about his brother, sir?'

'Émile? Oh, Émile went on to become a minister until a financial scandal in connection with the colonies obliged him to resign. He had made a good deal of money by then and he became a local snob down here, like some many of his kind. He called himself the Count of Castelnaud.'

When I woke in the night, I had the illusion that I had fallen from wakefulness into a dream. I heard voices filtering from somewhere, like mice creeping along the beams. My parents were talking in the dark; their voices sounded unlit. I could sense their meaning, but not the words themselves. My father was accepting an objection raised by my mother, yet every syllable of his acquiescence was freighted with contradiction. Their voices were not raised; black spaces came between them. Their silences were bleakly appetising, though I could not say to what appetite they appealed. How did I guess, unless I did indeed hear some actual phrases, that Fritz was the subject of their dark debate? My father's suggestion that we do something for my friend chimed uncomfortably with my own fear that I had brought him to La Fontaine du Noyer not only to challenge my parents – to 'show them something', as they say – but also in order to have done something. In the guise of a friendly act, I was preparing a defence. Doing something and doing nothing were blended, like loyalty and treachery.

There was something passionate in my mother's determination not to have Fritz in the house. In that trenchant mildness of hers there was an implacable element which spoke tacitly of motives which I could not begin to fathom. I caught no more than the blurred cadences of my father's arguments in Fritz's favour. I feared that he was going through the motions of righteousness without having the will to realise them. To my shame, I discovered that even as I conceded Fritz's perilous situation to be more dramatic than my own I could not hold it to be more poignant; this attitude had nothing to do with anything more terrible than the balance of power between my parents, and between them and me. I had an impression of rage on my mother's side, an animosity which made Fritz something to do with her husband rather than a young man in mortal danger. I was drawn into a similar fierce indifference to Fritz's own fate: I wanted them to reject him, not because I wished Fritz ill but because it meant that they would be responsible for whatever happened to him. Personally, I could never have done what I connived at their doing.

Lying in bed I thought of Louise, whose beauty, being natural, was immune to political contingency. She was beyond criticism; I *was* criticism. I was an ugly young man with ugly habits who had brought dissension to the house, a suitor who, unlike Louise's cavaliers, could not be turned away at my parents' discretion. I needed to be labelled a rebel before I was able to become one.

I fell asleep into a new spasm of wakefulness. I hardly knew, and I scarcely know now, whether imagination preceded reality or whether it was sponsored by it. Gertrud came into my mind, I think, because I was contrasting her usefulness, and the ease with which my parents had included her, like a piece of baggage, in their retreat from Paris, with their reluctance to take Fritz under their protection. I was playing with Gertrud in my sleep, reviewing her glittering tolerance as she made my bed, when I seemed to hear and then certainly did hear her voice. I had been bolder in my vision of her than ever before, not because I desired her but because I felt that she owed me something, of which her nakedness was only an initial payment. Her voice, now that I knew that I could indeed hear it, had a hoarse caution which immediately promised that she was where she should not be. Why did I get up? Why did I walk so carefully along the cold corridor to the door of the room where my uncle habitually slept? I had no experience of the meaning of what I heard, but I seemed to have heard it before. The origin of its chaffing regularity was as clear to me as the cause of that declivity at the head of Pia's bed in Rome. I could hear the conspiracy behind the heavy door. It made me second my mother's wish to secure Fritz's eviction, even though I had no feeling of moral outrage. I did not visualise the scene, although I knew the words for what was happening in Fritz's bed; I was aware only of how achingly I was excluded from it and how much I resented the pleasure which neither of the participants wished to deny me. Fritz and Gertrud became the guilty parents of whom I felt myself to have been deprived.

There was no conclusive scene at breakfast. Fritz and I would, of course, return to school in Caillac. Roque was asked to get the trap ready to take us to the station in order to be in good time for the little train I always took. My mother did not come down for the brown drink we agreed to call coffee. My father spoke warmly to Fritz in her absence. As he shook hands, he said that my friend's remarks about our cousin had been highly intelligent and had given him insights for which he deserved credit. He hoped that they would have an opportunity for further discussion, which implied that they would not.

Fritz and I set out in a pearly mist. The unshaven Roque sat on the box of the donkey-cart under a sack which he had unpicked to make into a blanket. One seam remained fastened and formed a peak over his knees. The valley was old with frost.

Fritz said: 'Your parents are not very happy, I think.'

'What gives you that idea?'

'Your father wishes he were different.'

'And what does my mother wish?'

'She wishes that she did not wish that he was.'

When I rehearse that morning's lurching ride, I can believe that Fritz was being almost ostentatiously generous in affording me a reason not to like him. It was a masterly, self-effacing coup – not so much a queen-sacrifice as, impossible though it may be, a king-sacrifice, a deliberately contrived and refined resignation which sanctioned our divorce.

Roque sat in front of us, muffled and lagged against the chill and damp. I was reminded of the executioner who crossed France with the portable guillotine, plodding with a good conscience towards the fulfilment of his contract with death. Fritz observed the landscape with urbane attention; he turned on his seat to notice the mist rising from a man-made pond on which a decoy duck floated at an implausible angle. He held the box with the unused red and white chess pieces in his lap, like an émigré's petty treasure.

The men who came to the *lycée* a few days later allowed Monsieur Chantal, the *proviseur*, to lead them to the room where Monsieur Picpus was comparing the relationship between Sulla and Julius Caesar ('the divine Julius') with that between Pericles and Alcibiades. Swinging the long ends of his scarf, he continued the lesson, as if he had not noticed the intruders, until Monsieur Chantal was obliged to excuse himself and say that certain 'guests' would now be leaving us, for administrative reasons. I knew at once that Fritz was doomed. I had not expected Magnac to be named as well; I should not have called him the maniac all those months if I had.

I knew and I did not know (no, I did not know) what would happen to Fritz. It seemed to me then that merely leaving Room 17 with the hatted men was itself the terrible thing. When their names were announced, Fritz and Magnac stood up. Loubet made no move to join them. The *proviseur* stood under the freckly portrait of the Marshal and watched us. I saw intimidating entreaty in his stance: his authority was on its knees to us not to make a disturbance.

Monsieur Picpus, in his salt and pepper coat, put the ends of his scarf across his chin and threw them over his shoulders, one in each direction. Fritz opened his desk and took out the box of chess-men. I hoped that he was taking them with him. He came by my desk and, without looking at me, he left the box on it. Unseen, they shifted together in their cardboard hutch.

As the hatted men followed our comrades from the classroom, I stood up. If it was not too late for them to see me, it was late enough for them to ignore what I did. I had, after all, only stood up. I stood there as they marched away down the passageway. I stood there as we watched them cross the playground. I stood there as the Citroën doors slammed and the car drove away. The *proviseur*, who had stayed in the room, glared at me, but he found it prudent to leave Monsieur Picpus to continue the lesson. It was convenient to assume that I had got to my feet because I had been 'put on' just before the interruption.

Monsieur Picpus paid no attention to me. My standing there, and its purpose, if any, did not concern him. I had no idea of why I had stood up nor of how long, or for what reason, I should remain there. I felt that something had happened to me, not that I had done anything. Having stood up, I stayed standing up. I had no intentions, no hopes, no plans. Nothing was in my head, but it was there with a white obstinacy which blanked me of all emotion. My standing *was* my emotion; that was all there was to it.

When the class ended, and the school day with it, I assumed that I should be prompted by something, if only habit, to move out with the rest of the room. The bell rang. Desks banged. People jostled to the door. Martegoutte tried to trip Despinasse. I stayed where I was. A great stiff frost was on me. I was white to the bone.

Monsieur Picpus was left along with me. He said, 'Come, come, little one.' It was not characteristic and it was not the right thing to say. 'I know, and I agree, and now I'm going to lock up. *Hein*? *Hein*?'

He left the room, but he did not lock the door. The lights went out. I heard Monsieur Chantal lock the outside doors and then the gates. I was alone in the school. I stood there all night. I did not think that I was doing anything. I felt in no danger. I felt nothing. It did not occur to me that there might be punitive consequences for my action. I did not feel that I had acted. I wished that something forceful would move me from where I stood. Nothing did.

Monsieur Picpus came in the morning. He was carrying a stack of our *cahiers de brouillon* for correction. Did he always come and work at his desk so early? He saw me and he said, 'All night, eh? Well, well! We must get someone to come, I suppose, mustn't we?' It was not a threat; it was as though I had broken some record which needed to be ratified by independent witnesses. Monsieur Picpus went out. He returned with a mug of hot liquid and a piece of bread. He held them out to me. I did not move. He did not disagree with my immobility. He put the steaming mug on his desk and went to work.

Monsieur Chantal arrived at nine o'clock with the *censeur*, Monsieur Bougival, and another member of staff, Monsieur Rougier, whom I knew to be a keen advocate of the *chantiers de la jeunesse*, a Vichy institution which was supposedly dedicated to initiating young men in manly labour. They went to camps and sawed logs or broke stone while singing patriotic songs in honour of the Marshal.

Monsieur Chantal came up to where I stood and said, 'Now what is all this about?'

I stood there. Had I been waiting for this moment? I was incapable of responding to it. I had locked myself up and thrown away the key. My classmates were coming in. My presence, and that of the professors, prevented them from acting normally, as they had the previous evening. They were more embarrassed than solid with me.

The *proviseur* said, 'This is serious, Roumegouse. You will now explain yourself.'

The bell rang. The door closed. My class was all there, except for the two who were not. Monsieur Rougier said, 'Your father is a respectable man, a responsible man. He will hear of this.' Rougier was freshly shaved; his chin shone. 'What do you say? You will say something, do you hear me? You will say it now. Or else.'

I said, 'Long live the Republic!'

XII

There were two cars already at the site when Pierre and I arrived at the necropolis of Cerveteri. One was a Borgward, the other a beige Simca with international plates. The Etruscan tumuli were half-buried, like fortifications. They were capped with thick crusts of earth and grass. Archaeologists had gouged a system of trenches in order to reach the black mouths of the tombs. One might have been at the site of some ancient war between man and mortality.

Pierre said, 'Shall we start at the best? Let's start at the best!'

I said, 'You've been here before.'

Pierre said, 'I read, Guy. What else do I do? I read and that gives people – including myself – the impression that I've been in places, not to mention situations, which are in fact quite outside my experience. I go again where I have never been before!'

I followed his perky lead without enthusiasm. I was beginning to be impatient for the moment of truth. The massive arrangements with which the Etruscans confronted the housing of the dead were impressive but without much interest for me. I decided, as we trudged down the long staircase to the first musty sepulchre, that I should not only throw away my pipe but also grow a moustache. I was not in a mood to play the pupil.

'So,' Pierre said, 'here we are, Guy! The domestication of death. What do you make of it? Something of the Pompeian brothel in its cubicular practicality, wouldn't you say?'

'I am here to be instructed,' I said.

'The bas-relief interests me, as a mode, doesn't it you? Egyptian overtones as well, by the way. The relief is halfway between the three- and the two-dimensional, quite as if the sculpted was melting into the decorative. Why does man tend to do this – reduce, or promote, the functional into the decorative, quite as if use were something . . . unworthy?'

I said, 'We do it with women as well as with things, don't we? Or are women things?'

Pierre said, 'Is something bothering you, Guy?'

'Not in the least,' I said. Frustration was scorching me like a match which one lights, only to find that the fire has not been properly laid or the gas is switched off and there is no useful place to apply the flame. 'Perhaps I could do with some air.'

The sharp light branded me. I felt that Pierre had tricked me into being his audience. I recalled how he had sometimes been at the apartment when I returned from the Embassy and how I had believed Berthe's story that he had called to see me. I tried to feel indignation at what, in truth, only slightly amused me.

I ambled along the path under the bulbous umbrella-pines, while the cicadas made rusty noises in the branches. I heard American voices and saw a little girl of three or four running along a path which converged with mine. A woman was calling, 'Lucille, Lucille,' while the child ran chuckling along, working her busy arms. As she approached me, I saw that she was naked from the waist down. She stopped and cuffed flaxen hair from her eyes. She turned, in the hope of pursuit, and I could see a tuck of pink tissue in the cleft of her behind. A second later, her mother appeared, still holding the plastic pot from which the child had evidently escaped. The little girl glared at me and said, 'I don't like that man.'

The mother was bespectacled and had a gap between her large front teeth. She wore a floral dress and had painful-looking red arms. She was probably embarrassed by her daughter's fugue and by her nakedness, but her eyes seconded the child's accusation. It was as if I had done something.

I said, 'I shall not hurt you, Lucille.'

The little girl's face rumpled and she showed her gums. 'What did you say?'

'I won't hurt you, Lucille.' I spoke as distinctly as I could, thinking that my French accent had confused her. 'So don't worry.'

'He looked at me,' she said.

'Lucille!' The mother's tone startled me. What made her call so loudly and impatiently when her daughter was within her grasp? I turned away and then saw another girl, perhaps twelve years old, scrambling across the tussocks from where the Simca was parked. She was waving a clean nappy like a flag of surrender. I heard her mother say, 'Where was it, Loose?'

'Where you said – but could I see it?'

'This is a very good one,' Pierre said. 'This one you really shouldn't miss, if you're up to it.'

I did not want to go into the tomb, but I went. Pierre pushed on to examine a street of identical, bourgeois stalls of scant distinction. All alone, I went through the motions of interest in the grey and ponderous redoubt which reeked more of urine than of the sublime. I frowned; I loitered here and went briskly there. But what did I care for the past?

Pierre's archaic head, with its imperial nose, came through the door. 'Enigmatic, do you find them? I can't say that I do.'

'Did I say they were?'

'They do – the pundits. Can you take a bit of a walk?'

'There's nothing wrong with me, Pierre. Please stop being so considerate.'

'What intrigues me is what we can never know. For instance . . .' He held the hiatus until we were inside the next tomb. 'For instance, was this really the last resting place of a bride, as we're promised, or was it a metaphorical rendering of man's relationship with death?'

I said, 'Does any society spend time and treasure hacking out metaphorical representations of abstract topics?'

'Don't they *all*?' Pierre frowned at what might have been alarming symptoms of mental incompetence on my part. 'Or are you joking? Every society of any interest to us spends most of its time and treasure in advisedly – not to say ostentatiously – futile exercises, doesn't it?'

I said, 'Oh all right.'

'But Guy . . .'

'Why isn't it ever enough to agree with you?'

'Think about it: for every utilitarian Roman aqueduct weren't there a dozen useless temples? In the midst of catastrophic battles, the Germans proceeded with an unproductive massacre which involved converting the machinery of war into that of murder. Chartres! The Incas! The Mayans . . . Egypt! Unless we see that perhaps even the simplest, the most practical action is indelible with purposes beyond our sensible calculation, we have no eyes at all. What this place brings home to me is that everything is everything. One goes from here to there and there to here without realising – perhaps in order not to realise – that ubiquity consists of going nowhere. You don't like me, do you, Guy?' He turned, bulky and monstrous in the dated gloom of the burial chamber, and grinned at me. His torso was pushed forward by the angle of the wall, his head lowered like a bull's. I saw the Minotaur in him, cooped and ferocious in his baffling stall. 'If you don't, say you don't. I shan't eat you.'

I said, 'Every confession that one dislikes someone else suggests that one has reservations about oneself. I'll tell you what I don't like, and that's the Etruscans.'

'The best stuff's in the Villa Giulia, you know.'

'Meaning you think I don't. A society should be judged by its second-best stuff in my opinion. I don't like the silly smiles and I hate these railway stations on the way to Hades, or wherever they thought they were going.'

'Good. Excellent.'

'I haven't come here to be marked,' I said.

'The smile is certainly overrated; it may well not have been a smile, but we can let that pass.'

'Then let us,' I said.

'We can get out of here, Guy, whenever you say the word.'

I said, 'I'm sorry if I'm depriving you of something. I'm afraid I very badly want to piss. This reduces my small appetite to be kept in after school.'

'Piss,' he said. 'Others have, why shouldn't you?'

'Probably that very fact. Let me ask you something.'

'I have time, if you do. What?'

'Why is Berthe not here?'

'Berthe?'

'Why did you not ask her to join our expedition?'

'Does she like this sort of thing?'

'Do *I*?' I was infuriated by the glossy ease of his imposture. His whole body was posed in a question mark. He was courteous inquiry incarnate, while all the time I was sure that he knew exactly why I had mentioned Berthe's name. 'She should be here because this is all about her, isn't it?'

'My dear Guy,' Pierre said, 'something seems seriously to be troubling you. What?'

I heard a muted rushing sound and then the bright silence of the child standing under the lintel. She now wore a quite long, pleated blue skirt with white dots on it and little blue pumps. She gazed at Pierre and me as if she had confirmed a suspicion.

'Aleesha? Aleesha?' Her mother's anxiety ran, a little breathlessly, to catch up with the child. 'Don't go in those places without Mommy.'

Pierre said, 'Would you please excuse us?' Even his simple English seemed a form of condescension. Alicia narrowed her eyes and yielded reluctantly to the hand which he put on her head. The little girl whose nakedness had been presented to me a few minutes earlier acted as though she had not seen me before; I was reminded of a prostitute who makes it a matter of honour not to give any hint of recognition – thus recognising you – when she crosses you in the street. Alicia's mother, on the other hand, cringed against the wall of the pathway, in apparent dread of my touch.

Pierre loped on and then waited for me. The air was busy with all kinds of tiny things. It was like an often projected negative, dotted and dashed with meaningless excitements which, because they are unpredictable, can seem more dramatic than the film itself. I could not be sure whether the cottony fronds, drifting in the soupy atmosphere, were natural or man-made. A sneeze humped my back as the older girl, who had earlier gone to find a nappy, came towards the tomb, rather as though she were her mother's patient keeper.

'Hello, Lucille,' I said.

'Are they in there?'

'They sure are,' I said, playing a small American trump on Pierre's English trick.

Pierre said, 'Now let's have this out, shall we?'

'In a minute.' His remark made relieving myself a more leisurely luxury than it would have been. As I ambled back, buttoning my cream trousers, I adopted a tone of conciliatory disdain. 'I want to make something clear at the outset,' I said, 'that what you are is of no consequence to me. I don't blame you and I can't congratulate you. I am neither shocked nor intrigued.'

'What are you, Guy?'

'Curious,' I said. 'Curious, that I must admit. I want to hear from you.'

All sorts of rippling wrinkles and sketchy smiles crowded onto his face. He cocked his head to look quizzically at me. I observed these activities without sympathy. 'I too,' he said, 'am curious, and more than curious. With the best will in the world, you puzzle me. You want something from me – that I can see clearly enough – but I cannot divine what. Are you please going to tell me?'

'Look,' I said, 'I have nothing to tell. I have done nothing; you have done something. I can't give you an account of nothing.'

'You're so angry,' he said. 'So *angry!*'

'No,' I said, 'but I resent being incited to anger in order to be put in the wrong.'

'Guy, can you believe me to be seriously in the dark here? Because please try.' The faltering sun haloed his taurine head and flared on my own burning face. Pierre's shadow climbed me as I approached him until, against my will, I was taking him for shelter from the heat. 'Guy, what the hell is this all about? Shit!'

'I admire your indignation,' I said. In his shadow, I was able to open my eyes fully and give him the measure of my unblinking reproach. 'I admire it because it elevates humbug into a species of art. Berthe was not asked because, if she were here, we couldn't discuss her. You know that; I know that; and that is what the hell all this is about.'

Pierre said, 'Good God. Good God!'

I said, 'Did she tell you she wouldn't ever tell me?'

He said, 'I think perhaps we should go back to the car.'

I said, 'The car will be fine. The guardian is there; I tipped him. Or is there something in the car you want to show me?'

He said, 'I'm afraid there's been a misunderstanding.'

'Courage!' I said. 'You can rely on my discretion. I'm not a man to make a scandal. I too have a career, though mine does not, I admit, depend on celibacy, though if it did . . . I simply want to know how you see this matter developing.'

Pierre said, 'How can I convince you of my perplexity, followed swiftly by my astonishment? If I've offended you or your wife . . .'

'Berthe,' I said.

'It was wholly inadvertent. I imagined that she would be busy, Berthe.'

'In what business did you suppose her to be?'

'Guy, this is unworthy. I'm pained by this.'

'You begin at least to recognise what it is, I take it?'

'I had some notion of friendship between us – a just balance.'

'Shit,' I said. 'Tell me something, where did you grow up?'

'I spent the war in Syria,' he said. 'I returned to France in forty-seven.'

'I had a friend in Paris, before the war, who was born in Egypt. His father sent him to a brothel when he was fifteen, as a birthday present. Did yours do as much for you at any point?'

'This is quite enough,' he said. 'What is this about? I'm ceasing to be amused.'

'You know perfectly well. I know; you know. Yet *we* are not permitted to know. What's the point of that? Do you hope that He doesn't know?'

'I know that you're in distress of some kind. I know no more than that, I swear to you.'

I looked at him as if he were a breathing artefact. He was certainly much more interesting than any bas-relief of ancient Etruria. Warped by its contradictions, his body appeared to be strengthened by the clash of ancient forces. The joints resembled the knuckled locks and hinges on which castle doors depended. (I thought of Roque's dungeon.) His face was at once sublime – the skin tensed across the temples and delicately veined next to the dark, Persian eyes – and compromised with sensuality. The mouth was mobile and pulpy within a ridged circumference of almost white skin. It shaped his words with censorious accuracy, licking them into his chosen language, it seemed, at the last moment (he was, I knew, fluent in Italian, Greek, Spanish and German), so that when he spoke it was as if he had kept back some of his intended meaning, issuing only a pale simulacrum of it. His true language would be an amalgam, the language of all languages. Any tongue he used seemed to have been selected patronisingly. Only my sense of disgust liberated this sudden awareness of his genius. And yet the more I looked at him, the less I felt any emotion. He seemed to siphon my feelings from me. 'My dear friend,' he said, 'because you are indeed that, I am powerless to help you unless you help me to do so.'

I said, 'Be damned to help. I simply want to hear what you propose to do.'

The more I stared at him, and he at me, the more extraordinary and diverse he seemed. He might have been composed of separate sections, riveted by the blood which, here and there, rouged his priestly pallor. His body was a federation of parts with distinct aptitudes and constitutions. He bent forward and looked at me with eyes that seemed positively wrinkled with scrutinising effort. 'Guy,' he said, 'I'm lost. *Lost.*'

'Through your own act,' I said. 'Or are you going to blame Berthe? I can't believe that you're seriously going to accuse her, are you?'

I now watched a clever man attempting to understand something very simple. The complications of his mind turning on a single issue were almost touching in their grinding convolution. His mouth went bulbous; the lower lip shifted towards the left. Finally, he said, 'Guy, this is . . . not true.' His index finger went to his brow, directly above his narrow prong of a nose. 'It is not true.'

I said, 'Repetition confirms nothing.'

'I think you had better tell me what she said.'

'I've known for some time,' I said.

'Persistent error is still erroneous,' he said. 'Because let me put this very clearly, very very clearly: your wife, whom I like – *like* – very much, is evidently a very unfortunate and misguided woman. Because, and I weigh my words here, there is no truth whatsoever in what I take to be her allegations. None. Categorically.' He snapped shut the invisible dossier with a swing of his shoulders and lumbered down the path towards the car. I stood there while his shadow peeled from me and was supplanted by the waning heat of the red-faced sun. I was furiously immobile, like an engine in neutral.

'Guy? Are you coming?'

I stood there.

A voice at my elbow said, '*Si chiude, signore!*' I could almost believe that Pierre had split his forces and encircled me with his tricks. The voice belonged, in fact, to the guardian. He wore rumpled fawn trousers, with an excess of belt around them, and a peaked cap.

Pierre was leaning on the car. He seemed almost to have it under his arm. It was hard to believe that he was going to fit his towering bulk behind the steering wheel. He said, 'Are you feeling better now?'

'Better?' I felt like someone whose savings had just been declared worthless. 'Yes, of course.'

'Guy, if you can bear to, I want you to tell me exactly what Berthe said. This has to be cleared up.'

'For whose benefit? And can it be? If it doesn't concern you, isn't it best if we say no more about it?'

'She's accused me of seducing her?'

'I'm not sure that seduction was mentioned. She said that you were her lover.'

'I'm a priest,' Pierre said, folding himself down to get into the Citroën. 'I'm a priest.'

'And a Jew,' I said.

'Is that worthy?'

'You're many things.'

'She said that we were physical lovers, she and I?'

'Is there any other kind?'

'Come, come,' he said. 'Come, come.'

'You deny it?'

'You still suspect it?'

'I never suspected it,' I said. 'At one moment it was unthinkable, at the next, having been told it, I assumed it to be true. Without transition.'

'You're still angry with me.'

'I was never angry with you. Now shall we go? You wanted to get back to the car. Here we are; let's go.'

'First I must find the key. This explains a great deal, of course.'

'Then explain it,' I said.

'We've spent the whole day under a misapprehension. You imagined that I asked you to come out here with some dark purpose – you thought that I had done something . . . unforgiveable . . .'

'Not really,' I said. 'In fact, I feel more unforgiving now than I did before.'

'There you are: you're angry. Because she lied to you?'

'If she did.'

'I swear it, Guy. I swear it by everything I hold sacred.'

'All right,' I said, 'all right. I believe you.'

'I'm your friend, Guy. I asked you to come with me today because I sensed that you were under strain.'

'Perhaps I'm only under strain when I'm with you. Have you, in your chaste way, given Berthe to understand that, if things were different, you would want to make love to her?'

'I suppose, with ingenuity, I could contrive an answer which would speak to your fears, or hopes, but the truth is that, in any practical sense, I have done no more than drink a glass of wine with your wife, while waiting for you, on one or two occasions, during which we have discussed the cost of living in Rome, the churches with the best Gregorian chant and the prospects of global destruction. Chitchat of that kind!' As he spoke, Pierre was heaving and squirming in search of his keys. It was as if some eruption were taking place underneath him. 'Does she have any history of psychological problems?'

'Isn't that something of an abdication?'

'From what? Key! At last!'

'She claims you are her lover and you want to find an explanation in mental disorder. As if she were a case and you were a nobody. As you can indeed pretend to be, like Odysseus, who knew he wasn't one, when he needed to escape from the Cyclops' cave.'

'And you . . .' Pierre peered through the windscreen into a suddenly darker landscape. 'You are once again alone with her. Is that your grievance?'

I said, 'I owe you no confession.'

'And I owe you for lunch,' he said.

'Lunch was my pleasure.'

'False pleasure,' he said. 'It pleased you for reasons which were wholly spurious.'

'You believe in God,' I said. 'Let us leave the great issues there, shall we?'

'And you don't?' His forehead was almost against the windscreen. He seemed to be talking to the purple world beyond it.

I said, 'I cannot even understand what it would be to do so.'

'Shall I tell you? It would be to speak a language which was fully authentic. A language charged, as yours will never be, with sublime conviction.'

I said, 'My life has been lived in the wrong order.'

He found a moment to look at me. I had the strange sensation that I could see him both full face and in profile at the same time. He then hunched forward to peer once more at the spooling road ahead of us.

When we reached the intersection with the Via Aurelia, we had to wait for a break in the evening traffic. Pierre's eye was pinched in a vigilant wink as he looked past me at the headlights streaming away from Civitavecchia. When the cars slowed, he edged forward. He was immediately hooted, with wheezy urgency, by a vehicle which must have been charging along the rough shoulder of the road, inside the traffic. It was a Vespa which swerved around me, avoiding the wing of the Citroën with its front wheel. The wagonette it was towing clipped the bumper. Its white-uniformed passenger was bounced into view and then fell back again. The Vespa stuttered and then accelerated on down the Via Aurelia. Our windscreen seemed dusted with the images of a dark and a fair face, suspended between apology and accusation.

I said, 'It wasn't our waiter, you know, we saw on the beach.'

'You take it that the two just now were the same couple we saw before?'

'One was certainly the same,' I said. 'If my wife lied to me, does that make me a fool?'

'The most interesting fool,' Pierre said, 'is the one that one makes of oneself. Am I clear on your side?'

XIII

I was told that I had committed a serious breach of discipline. I was relieved to hear it: the accusation dignified a gesture into a crime. Monsieur Rougier took me into his room. The dark morning required a light in the half-glassed cubicle which he used as an office. He wore a buttoned woollen top, which was neither a jacket nor a blouse, and uncreased black trousers. His black belt was punitively tight. Round, shell-rimmed spectacles seemed to mark him as some kind of a specialist: they might have been for seeing through things. Although Rougier and I were alone within the grey glass walls, he conducted himself in a public way: the occasion, as it were, outnumbered us.

'It cannot pass unremarked.' With a lift of eyes and chin, he checked whether I had dared to sneer at his parody of the Marshal's famous dictum 'They shall not pass'. Cheated of insolence, he braced his shoulders. 'Your father has been informed.'

I said, 'Thank you.'

'You have already gone too far, little one. Go no further. For the moment, you had better go home. That is an order.'

I said, 'Has Altschuler gone home?'

'He has been sent where he will be most useful. That is all.'

I stood there.

Rougier said, 'The dossier is formally out of my hands, or the *proviseur*'s. That is something you should have reckoned with before you did what you did.'

'What did I do?' My tone suggested that I had been unavoidably absent from some interesting event.

'I shall not flatter you with attempts to interpret your action. You know; I know.'

'Do I come to school tomorrow?'

'That is assuming that tomorrow will come. Await instructions. You will receive them.'

'By telephone? Because it doesn't always work.'

Rougier came and breathed on me. 'It will work,' he said, 'when it needs to work. You are free to go.'

'Free?' I said.

He wanted to do something to me; I felt the heat of his shapeless desire. 'To go,' he said. 'To do as you're told. Do it.'

As I walked across the yard, lights were burning in Monsieur Picpus' classroom. I watched the silent film of my comrades as they copied the diagram of the imperial organisation decreed by Caesar Augustus. Using his coloured chalks, Monsieur Picpus gave the impression that he was devising the boxed format for the first time, although we all knew that he reproduced it year after year.

When he turned to the class and put a question, it was answered by someone – Pascal Delmas – sitting next to the empty place recently occupied by Fritz. I looked at my own absence and recognised myself to be both lucky and unlucky. I breathed the uneasy knowledge like fresh life. I reached the gate ('GARÇONS' was inscribed on the yellow lintel) and went through it to where the black *traction-avant* had been parked. Whose part was I re-enacting, that of the victim or his escort?

As I walked through Caillac, Delmas' father was unloading fish. The crates were stencilled with the name of a wholesaler from Arcachon. The scaly corpses, braided with ice, slipped and slithered as the box was tilted. Monsieur Delmas wore gauntlets. When a few crabs took the chance to sidle into the gutter, he picked them up and threw them with the usual curse into a seething mass of their more docile fellows.

I did not expect to find the Altschulers in their rooms. Why then did I head for them? Fritz's chess-men were still in my desk; there was no reason to climb the steep path to the little yard behind the Chapel of the White Penitents. Did I hope that the door would be locked? It was open. I climbed the steps which always reminded me of stacked Cantal cheeses and went into the apartment.

In the narrow room where Fritz and I played chess, the table was branded with a bar of silvery winter light. I sat in my usual place and paddled my hands in the rectangle of warmth in front of me. Dismayed by my lack of emotion, I tried to excite myself with visions of Fritz's ordeal. I sat on the edge of the bench, exactly as I had when I watched my king harried by the instructively pitiless Fritz, and I waited for my penis to thicken and lift.

I heard the slur of feet on the steps. I sat looking at the tidy room like a pupil awaiting his master. The Altschulers were people whose description I should already have been unable to supply; I seemed to have prepared myself not to remember the couple who came into the room. Monsieur Altschuler (with whom I had, of course, shaken hands and exchanged courtesies) was a squat man, with a squarish, trim beard. He wore a belted blue coat and a blue-black felt hat. His wife was carrying a paper parcel, strung as tightly as a boned joint at the butcher's. She wore a maroon coat, heavy shoes and a rakish hat with a brave feather in it. Her husband said, 'You should not be here, please.' The words fell from his lips like fragments of a civility which would never recur. I thought of the teeth of some ugly villain whom Popeye, fortified with spinach, had hit in the face. I saw my silly, past self laughing at what I should never again find funny. 'Go back to school now, please.'

I said, 'I can't. I've been ordered home.'

'Then go home.'

I said, 'You should leave here, shouldn't you?'

'We are leaving,' he said.

'Who sent you here, Guy?'

'I was not sent, Madame. I came. To say goodbye.'

'Goodbye then, Guy. It was kind of you to come.'

'Where is Fritz? Do you know? You all ought to come with me.'

'It would also be kind of you to go.'

I was a green crab thrust back into the heap. I had gone to the Altschulers' apartment like a free man; they made me a child again. I walked down to the traverse aching for misfortune. No precise symptoms corresponded to my fever; I neither flushed nor paled, I could contrive neither cramp nor faintness. My imagination was in a panic of incompetence. I gazed with scornful amazement at the routines of the Caillacais as they went through the motions of the ordinary. Their daily round furnished each of them with an alibi which left them exactly where they had always been. Their buying and selling, their lighting of cigarettes and drinking of 'coffee' (with the bitter face the bitter stuff deserved), their handshakes and their embraces denied –and so implied – their responsibility for what they so believably were not doing. In the most active possible way, they were giving a performance of impotence. I was mortified and reassured; I was different and I was the same. If my own survival.did not appear to be at stake, at least I was not quite the kind of liar they were: in my case, the pretence to normality was a pose, not a fraud. However inelegantly, I was playing the dandy; my freedom was a function of a condemnation which I had deliberately incurred, whereas they were locked into the pretence of choosing to be what they lacked the nerve not to be. I revelled in the temporary immunity of a marked man: what doomed prisoner ever thinks that he might die before the date fixed for his execution? Neither germs nor accidents alarm him. Although I had no sense of being under sentence of death,

I was almost skittish in the knowledge of my place in Rougier's bad books.

I learned at the station that the Altschulers, and others in their situation, had been ordered to catch a train at a quarter past noon. They could take one suitcase per person. The failure to appear would mean that they would never again see their children, who had been rounded up separately. They all arrived in time for the train. I do not think of them as sheep.

As for me, I caught the little train to Port du Noyer. The events of the last two days had robbed the year of its seasons. I cannot remember whether the landscape which wheeled past me as I looked at it with Fritz's eyes was dressed for spring or summer, winter or autumn. I remember only that I played with the belief that I had smuggled Fritz into my own skinny frame, like contraband. We breathed in tandem.

One of the other passengers resembled the kind of black marketeer depicted in official cartoons: he had thick, juicy lips and a bulging raincoat; it looked as if every crevice of him were fat with goods or cash. He contemplated the landscape like a butcher who has the right knife for any throat; beauty was weighed by the kilo with him. When he saw me looking at him, there was a flare of kindled suspicion in his eyes, before he concluded that I was not the contact he was seeking. I stared out at what I knew – the 'English' castle, stilted on its slice of cliff over the river, and the mill where a dripping wheel turned, hesitated and fell on into the green pulse beneath it – and I could believe that I was seeing it all for the last time. Duplicity gave me life; fear armed my courage. I promised the Fritz in me that our expulsion was a deliverance.

The plump man put a cigarette between his teeth and held it there while he snapped a flame to it. When the train stopped at Port du Noyer, he and I were the only passengers to descend. Had he possibly been sent to arrest me? I felt a surge of vanity and a kind of coquettishness: so far from wanting to escape, I tried to accommodate myself to his pace as I led the way along the valley. Being unfamiliar with the mushy track seemed to make it into a hill for him. I had not gone far when he coughed and called out, '*Monsieur . . .*'

I might have been wise to bolt into the trees. If he had a gun, could he get it out before I reached the screen of pines? Could he sprint after me in his skiddy city shoes? I stopped and waited for him, frowning with a show of polite surprise. 'Can I help you?'

He said, 'Saint Amand.'

I said, 'Guy de Roumegouse.'

His thick brows made a problem of me. 'A place so called.'

'Saint Amand!' I emended his pronunciation in the peasant style. 'You want Saint Amand?'

'They said to get off at Port du Noyer and it wasn't far.'

I looked at his pointed shoes. 'Follow me, and I'll indicate the path.' Cheated of a policeman, I became one myself. 'Have you come a long way?'

'Périgueux.'

'Really?' It was enjoyable to induce a man to fear. 'Many Germans there?'

'Some,' he said.

'Be careful,' I said, 'in Saint Amand.' I pointed to the track through the forest to our left. Corded wood was stacked along the ditch in a long, metrical palisade. 'People are jumpy there.'

Adjusting his hat, he said, 'Do the woodmen always cut regular lengths?'

I said, 'Yes, usually.'

He sighed like someone who has put his last coin in a machine which again fails to disgorge what he hoped it might yield. Although I had never heard a password before, I recognised the bait as one does a diplomatic hint or a sexual overture. He set off without saying anything else. I missed him; he seemed gross and ignoble on the train, but I had now redressed him with a certain glamour which he took away with him through the trees. I suppose it must have been the autumn of 1943; I can see squashed chestnuts in the drive, some of them still wigged with their green, spiky coverings.

A Renault two-seater with a corrugated bonnet was parked near the arches where Baptiste was sawing wood. The wipers had cleared twin crescents from the muddy glass so that the car appeared to watch me with arched eyes. Baptiste was wearing overalls and clogs. He continued sawing with unabated vigour even when the end of a log lolled from the main stem; as it fell, he managed another empty stroke, as if part of his task were to cut the air itself into lengths.

'Guy, you had better come up here.' My uncle was leaning over what I always thought of as my mother's balustrade, at the top of the central steps. He wore an off-white raincoat with many panels and buttons. For some reason I had the feeling that it had belonged to someone else first. I chose to go to the left side of the terrace and climb the unguarded steps. It was a kind of docile disobedience to take the long way to get to my uncle. I met Roque coming around the house in clogs and gaiters. He was nudging Pierrot, the annual pig he was fattening for January, with a pointed stick. He let the stick ride the pig's flank when he was not using it as a goad.

Jean-Claude was growing a moustache; it was thick and dark, trim but not narrow. Yellow pigskin gloves were tucked under his epaulettes. I said, 'New car, Uncle? You seem to be privileged. Where have you come from?'

'Périgueux. Why are you smiling? I don't think you have much to smile about. You've grown.'

'You too,' I said. 'Is my father at home?'

'They're inside. Waiting for you. You've done something very foolish, Guy.'

I said, 'Were you sent for? Or were you sent?'

'Insolence between us is a luxury.'

'One of the few,' I said.

'Mere gestures are the last things we need. You've drawn attention at a time when discretion alone can produce results.'

'And motorcars?' I thought he was going to strike me; he nodded as if he had had some bad news. 'They took my friend away,' I said. 'I wish they'd taken me.'

Without any softening of his expression, my uncle said, 'I understand.' I looked at him with something like disappointment and sidled between the half-open shutters, through the tall doors with their leaded Murano glass and into the vestibule between the living room and my father's bureau.

'Guy? Will you come in here, please?'

Pale light laid steely blades across the burnished furniture and the chintzy canapés. Simone had lit the fire. My mother was writing at her table, under the solemn, laughable portrait of my great-grandfather in the robes of a peer of France. She wore a blue silk dress with long sleeves, as if she expected to go out soon. There was a white silk shawl around her shoulders. My father held a fat old book level with his eyes. The formality of their poses flattered me.

They allowed me to stand there while they went on doing, or pretending to do, their chosen things. Did they suppose me to be suffering? The silence was spicy with freedom; I scented it to my pleasure and surprise (as sometimes, after a gale, we smell salt from the Atlantic, a hundred miles to the west). It surprised me with its blandness; I was not so much exhilarated as indifferent. Liberty consisted in the discovery that the disapproving scene had no power to intimidate me. This freedom from emotion enabled me to play a kind of game. Some men, I am told, are capable of sexual excitement without sexual urgency; the symptoms of desire are hot, but they remain inwardly cold. They can thus achieve successes beyond the

101

competence of sincerity, which always carries its quota of gaucheness and its risk of impatience. I knew what I might have been expected to feel, but I was dispensed, by that very knowledge, from feeling it. My parents had always been more indulgent than severe, but my new coldness now saw them as going through motions of indulgence while hoping that I should generate my own severity. I refused to judge myself on their behalf. I was ashamed only that I had contrived a scandal so empty of manifest outrage: I had not sabotaged property or published subversive pamphlets. Still less had I used physical violence against the authorities. I waited to hear what allegations had been formally made and how my father could contrive to dissent from the general censure of my behaviour while at the same time, but for more elegant reasons, finding it deplorable.

He finished reading his paragraph and sighed, as if enduring the pertinence of the text, and put the plump little volume face down on the arm of the sofa. Leaning to look into the fire, he said, 'Long live the Republic?'

When he looked over at me, his mouth had contracted; his upper lip had replaced the question mark in his tone with a circumflex. His brows came together in a parody of reproof. I felt a flutter of dismay, as one does when an opponent makes a sacrificial move which suggests that he may have a plan outside one's menu of response. Freedom seemed to evaporate; I was pulled back into a familiar prison. I said, 'I'm sorry if you were worried by my not coming home last night.' My apology was the only provocation I could offer. 'There was nothing I could do.'

'And you did it, it seems,' my father said.

My mother, having no part in this, stood up in her rustling blue. She drew the white shawl quite tightly across her breasts in both directions. The movement had the style of a caress, at once self-protective and primly wanton. She walked between us on her way to the door, as if offering something which she was sure that neither of us would want.

I said, 'Did you telephone the police? Last night?'

My father said, 'Let's say that I telephoned someone I know. *In* the police. You made a stand, it seems.'

'Was I wrong?'

'Do you hope that I shall justify your action by condemning it? I shall not. I ask only if it was effective. Was it?'

'Effective!' I tasted the word like a new flavour. 'Yes,' I said, 'I believe so.'

'Your mother and I have quarrelled about it. She thinks your action . . . tactless. Selfish. Perhaps pernicious.'

'And how do you find it? You've quarrelled you say, but you show every sign of being in agreement.'

'Those are the most intractable quarrels. Perhaps she thinks me responsible. Perhaps I am: had I not told you of our cousin's misfortune, you might not have . . . appropriated his phrase.'

'They took my friend away. The one who was here two nights ago.'

'Clever boy,' my father said. 'Did you like him very much?'

'No,' I said. 'But I should very much have liked to. Does that matter?'

'Not in the smallest. Your gesture . . .'

'– was neither brave nor useful,' I said. 'You are quite right.'

'To be right is often to be wrong,' my father said, 'in times like these. What would you say it was, what you did? Would "quixotic" be fair?'

'Perfectly,' I said.

'Finally,' my father said, 'no one noticed Quixote, except himself and perhaps Sancho, who had to get him out of his scrapes as best he could. Jean-Claude is here; did you see him?'

'Didn't you hear us talking just before I came in?'

'I was reading Montaigne, on friendship.'

'Montaigne!' I said. 'Hardly a recommended text these days!'

'You will remember what he experienced with La Boétie: that sense of total and immediate sympathy. You felt something similar, perhaps, with . . .'

'On the contrary,' I said. Yet I felt the wince of something alien to me within my own frame, a hint of Fritz. 'Why is my uncle not married?'

'That's quite a different matter.' My father's tone implied some link between the topics, so prompt was he to deny it. 'People don't have to be married, although it can be convenient if they are.'

'Louise, for instance.'

'Louise is too young to think of marriage.'

'But not too young to have it thought of for her?'

'Our information is that the Germans are looking for any opportunity to deport people of your age for forced labour. That, no doubt, is why they took your friend.'

'His parents have been taken too. They are not of my age.'

'They may come for you at any time. It's a matter of transport.'

'You're well informed,' I said. 'I met someone just now. On the little train. He said he'd come from Périgueux. He smelled of somewhere else. As cops do.'

'He spoke to you?'

'He asked me a silly question. I told him how to get to Saint Amand, which doesn't mean that he wanted to go there necessarily.'

'What you did, in school, was in some ways admirable; in others, it was – regrettable. Not for moral, but for tactical reasons. It was, however, worthy.' My father seemed to summarise conclusions at which he would have arrived in the light of excuses which there was no time for me to offer. 'Be that as it may, you cannot now remain in this house. What question did this man ask?'

'Whether the woodmen always cut regular lengths.'

'That damnable Cabanne,' my father said. 'If it weren't for him, we might take the risk. Anything else?'

'What does Cabanne have to do with it? He only wanted to know where Saint Amand was.'

'You have to leave here. Wait a minute. I shan't be long.' He went to one of the tall embrasures and unlatched the window and stepped through onto the terrace. My sense of liberation returned at once. Their having plans for me was the proof that my escapade had gone beyond easy treatment. I was to go and they were to stay. I felt neither resentment nor gratitude. If my future was being plotted, it was in an unforeseeable dimension. I was clean of emotion, unless curiosity is an emotion. I *was* curious; I was determined to stay on my own trail, wherever it led, quite as if there was an alternative.

My father and uncle stepped back into the room. Jean-Claude said, 'Why did you not mention this man to me?'

I said, 'He was of no importance.'

'You go too far. It seems to be a habit. We'd better leave right away. Get your things.' He might have been rebuking my father through me. 'I'll be back soon. I'm now in a hurry.'

He went out, grabbing his shoulder for his gloves. I heard the wheeze of the little car. I said, 'Is this wise?'

My father said, 'A small case. You don't want to be too heavily burdened.'

I said, 'Are you sure I shouldn't just run into the woods before he knows where I've gone? Do you really trust him?'

My father said, 'He's your mother's brother. And he's the only one who knows where you can go and how to get you there.'

I said, 'Roque can bring me food. And keep me hidden.'

'You have to go somewhere we don't know about, whatever happens. Here, take this.' He took the thick little volume from the arm of the canape and closed it, reluctantly, as if he were losing more than his place. I looked at the spine and saw that it contained both La

104

Boétie's *Discours sur la servitude volontaire* and Montaigne's essay on friendship. My father had tears in his eyes and hated me for them.

XIV

'What will you say to her?'

'I may say nothing.'

'Is that honest?'

'Is it honest to have told me that you and she were lovers?'

'Should she not know that you've been disabused?'

'I believed her; and I was wrong, you say. Now I am to believe you. Are there to be no limits to my credulity?'

'I understand.'

I said, 'Syria! I never knew that. Were you in any danger while you were there?'

'It was less exotic than it sounds. And much hotter. I was never in any danger that I was aware of, at least until today!'

'You flatter me,' I said. 'And excite yourself perhaps. You find it amusing anyway.'

'Ironic.'

'Irony is comedy without resolution. I suppose its chastity appeals to you.'

'Chastity never appealed to me.'

'I'm less amused than you are by what's happened. Or rather by what hasn't.'

'But you do believe me?'

'Belief tells us nothing about the truth.'

'That's a matter of opinion.'

'And mine is that belief is not a kind of personal knowledge; it is the denial of it. Isn't that the sweet irony of Thomas? He remained dubious even when his doubts were dispelled.'

'You have a text, *Monsieur*?'

'His title was never abrogated, was it?'

Pierre said, 'I trust you're going to forgive her.'

I said, 'No amount of forgiveness can exempt us from what we have failed to do, can it?'

He said, 'You can't forgive me, is that it?'

I said, 'Have no fears on that account.'

106

'Why the rage?' Pierre said. 'Why do I have this impression of undischarged fury?'

'I'm wondering the same thing,' I said. 'Do you think we should open a window?'

'Can you really have supposed that my vows meant so little to me that I should enter on a love affair with a friend's wife?'

'So little? No. But perhaps enough. Do you go to prostitutes?'

'My dear Guy, your flatteries know no bounds!'

I said, 'Are you going to forgive her?'

He said, 'It hardly matters, does it? I don't have to live with her.'

'Nothing at all happened between you?'

'Nothing whatsoever.'

I said, 'You make that sound like a description.'

'You hear it like one,' he said. 'Your wife and I exchanged some decorous conversation while I was waiting for you. She was principally curious to know how things had changed since she was a regular communicant.'

'The decision not to go to Mass was hers. I neither influenced nor commented on it.'

'There are cruelties of omission, are there not?'

'I refuse to be judged because I've been deceived.'

'You seem to be deeply grieved. I've never heard you petulant before. I was simply wondering, as a friend, whether your failure to react to her – let's say – provocations might not have prompted her to the present, well, melodramatic fabrication.'

I said, 'Are you flattered at all?'

'You could say that I was touched, and saddened.'

'I don't think I should want to say that, or anything like it.'

'Guy, I realise that it is not easy for you to take, but I am innocent. Completely innocent. I can search my conscience and state categorically that I have done nothing to enchant your wife. Not even spiritually have I flirted with her in the smallest degree.'

'You don't find her attractive?'

'No,' he said. 'No.'

'Some women, but not Berthe?'

'Some women are so strikingly beautiful . . . one is a man, after all. This can't come as a surprise to you, surely?'

'Is beauty particularly attractive? That hasn't always been my experience.'

'These Italians,' Pierre said, 'they drive like – like conquerors! Has it occurred to you that she might be jealous of the friendship between you and me?'

107

I said, 'Friendship?'

Pierre said, 'Jealousy rarely weighs with accurate scales. Are we not friends? Of course we are!'

'You reminded me of somebody,' I said. 'Whom you do not resemble in the least, and whom I did not particularly like.'

'That's rather a fervent declaration.'

'Damn you to hell,' I said.

Pierre said, 'Shall we stop and have something to drink?' He pulled off the road into a new development. An Alemagna café had been finished and its lights shone across an unfinished pavement. Parked cars were tipped at odd angles on the potholed surface.

'Ah, temptations!' Pierre observed at the sight of the display case under the gleaming bar. 'One has a mortal duty not to resist them all, don't you agree?' He pointed to a couple of *suppli*, one dark, one pale. I ordered a *capuccino*; he said he wanted a *strega*. I did not quite believe the urgency of his appetites; mine were not for the things available to us. I disliked the dottle of chocolate which I knew would be sprinkled, as if it were a favour, on my scummy coffee.

We sat on black, pseudo-cane chairs at a little white table. Pierre was already biting into his rice-ball, which he held in a paper napkin, sideways. There seemed to be a spot of particular succulence he wished to taste first. With his head tilted, he said, 'Good! Good!' His eyes solicited me, one above the other. 'You're missing something. Think again!'

I watched the grains of sugar sink into the creamy bubbles in my cup. I said, 'Presumably we shan't be seeing each other again.'

'Wish? Command? Prediction? Fear – which? And, if you like, why?' He held up the remains of a rice-ball, swallowed and then raised his little glass as though its yellow contents could quench a great thirst. 'It might be best if I refrained from coming to your apartment.' He put a new napkin around the second of his *suppli*. 'But for the rest . . .'

'Are you proposing that we meet secretly?'

'Discreetly,' he said. 'If we make an abrupt break, it will turn this into something more dramatic than it is. Why not let it languish gradually? Boredom is an amiable solvent.'

I said, 'You're a bit of an Italian yourself, aren't you?'

'I'm a bit of everything,' Pierre said. 'My colleagues . . .'

'You told me,' I said. 'And I remember. In the sense that you're a bit of a conqueror, aren't you? Your innocence tips your lance, but it makes you no less of a lancer. You're thinking of Berthe more than of me, aren't you?'

'I'm thinking, if you must know, of you *and* Berthe. The two of you.'

'And your part in us,' I said.

'I like you, Guy . . .'

'But you have the malice to make that sound like a concession, or an improbability. I don't doubt your generosity, but I am not, I have to admit, touched by it.'

'I do like you, Guy. Not least when you're at your most pompous and preposterous, as you are at this moment. I recognise, as you do, that this conversation is a fraud, because what is sincere between us is the fact that we are sitting here, in a kind of inexpressible passion which draws us together for no good reason and with no prospect of resolution.'

I said, 'That pair on the beach, do you think they were lovers?'

'Exhibitionists we may be sure.'

'You think it was only a show? He might have killed him.'

'He may still,' Pierre said. 'Can killing not be part of a show? Why else, very often, does it take place?'

I said, 'The truth is, nothing I can think of can express how I feel towards you.'

'And you suspect that it was the same with them?'

'One played and one was in earnest, that was my impression, but I'm not sure which. One did what he wanted; the other had it done to him.'

'The dark one, he had the last word, didn't he?'

'But to leave someone with the last word, isn't that to do something to him? I keep seeing the other one, the fair one, as he turned away, before his friend attacked him, and I wonder if the sweetest moment wasn't the one in which he could hear the other at his back. Victimisation and mastery, can't they go together? He procured his own helplessness and made a triumph of it. Isn't there something sublime in making innocence into a vice of which not even God could find any evidence?'

Pierre said, 'You wish it were true.'

'I fear so,' I said. 'A confession without content! But then again, if it were true, would I wish it to be?'

He said, 'I'm sorry.'

'You're embarrassed. So am I. You find me ridiculous? Don't shake your head; I do too. Even if I were to kill you – throw you on the floor and manage to damage you with some of this disgusting plastic cutlery – even if I were to do that, there would not be the smallest element of dignity in it. It would simply be a comedy with blood. Tragedy is not on my menu, is it? Only its parody. Why?'

XV

While I was squeezing clothes and toiletries into the soft suitcase which my mother had found for me, Gertrud came into my room with some clean handkerchiefs. They were like fresh pastries; I could smell their warmth from the iron. Gertrud wore her black uniform with a white, bibbed apron. Fritz was between us as she helped me. I looked at her bold black legs and the pout of her breasts inside their white hammock and I assumed my friend's desire, without sharing it. The permission in her eyes made my head hum with violent thoughts. I wanted to hurt her, not because I should derive pleasure from it but because striking her naked flesh would be an act of physical contact without physical dividend.

She said, 'I shan't see you again, Monsieur Guy.'

'They'll look after you,' I said. 'You're useful to them.'

'They're less strong than you think,' she said. 'You can be saved, but I can't, any more than he could, your friend.'

I said, 'He may come back to you. He's clever. It's not finished yet.'

She said, 'You do not wish him to come back.'

I said, 'Isn't that why I hope he does?' She was standing beside me as we pressed down the lid of the case. Each of us clicked one of the locks home. I turned the key. What I wanted to do to her was terrible because I could not say what it was. 'I'll see you again, Gertrud. You see if I don't.'

'They will give me away,' she said. 'Like a dog.'

I went down to the terrace to wait for my uncle to return from wherever he had gone in such a hurry. I could hear the invisible Pierrot snorting and snuffling among his kitchen scraps like some pompous statesman on whom a local Circe had worked her just malice. My father came out and stood next to me. He put a roll of banknotes on the lichened parapet. I was surprised that he had so much money at his disposal. It seemed to me, as I put it in my pocket, that he was not so much helping me out as paying me for some service. He said, 'You had better not write, or telephone. At least for some time. I can't believe that they'll be interested in your case for very long, but for a month or so, we had best be prudent. Very. After all, we are never – or not for very long – only what we are. All freedom is on a leash, is it not?'

'A mortal coil,' I said, like a good student meeting his examiner with a reference he might admire. He offered neither consolation nor encouragement as we looked down the chestnut alley for the little Renault. Did he suspect that I had contrived my exile rather than having it imposed upon me? The apprehension which he seemed to be showing was, I gathered, more my mother's than his. My wantonness was not as disagreeable to him as I might have liked.

The money in my pocket made it seem that I was already on my way. Quite as if the whole episode were now a subject for retrospection, I heard myself say, 'How is it that you trusted my uncle over this? Is he not a *collabo* and someone with no scruples of any known kind? You wouldn't trust him over anything except my life, would you?'

My father said, 'You know nothing about these things. And this is scarcely the time for them.'

'What things?'

He said, 'I don't ask you to be a coward, but I do ask you to be sensible from now on. Survival is not a disgrace and it may be . . . instructive. No one forbids you to be a hero; I ask only that you not be one for my sake, or his. Endurance is not a sign of weakness. Show courage, if you absolutely must; folly, never.'

'I shan't be doing anything for his sake,' I said, 'if you mean my uncle.'

'Don't be so sure. Denial is a powerful motive.' He seemed to be hurrying to tell me all the things he might have taught me earlier. At the same time, I sensed the urgency with which he scanned the trees for the car. I could almost hear him listening for it. If he loved me, he hated me too. 'He has contacts which are quite beyond me. Without him . . .'

'You wouldn't be able to be rid of me. I quite understand. They're going to lose now, whatever we do or don't do, is that your view? Which makes resistance a luxury, I suppose.'

He said, 'We may all lose. Never rely on history for balanced accountancy. If patience seems dull to you as a virtue, allow me to recommend it as a vice.' He might have been quoting an author whose work was especially delicious to him, less on its merits than because it was unknown to others. 'Obvious minds see only loud events as history; they hurry their children to parades and violent scenes, but for me history – like love? – is rarest when it seems, to the easy eye, that nothing is happening. Listen, is it raining? Is that the car? Take the weeks that lie ahead, however many of them there are, as that kind of rarity.' He seemed to be conveying to me something that was precious to him in as offhand a manner as he could. I remembered how I had once wrapped one of my favourite models, a red Amilcar (with doors that actually opened), and given it to Louise for her name day. Having previously forbidden her, rather roughly, to play with it, I anticipated her excitement as she took off the paper. She displayed only symptoms of embarrassed disappointment, after which she held it out to me.

'It's yours,' I said.

She shook her curls. I was immediately angry, and tearful. I went to bed early, saying that I had a headache. My mother came, after a while, and told me that while it was generous to give away something I treasured, I had been wrong not to give my sister something new as well.

I said, 'She said she wanted it more than anything in the world.'

'Women always want something else as well as that!' my mother said. It was a spring evening in the Rue de Monsieur. My parents were about to go to the opera (Rameau's *Les Indes galantes*, I think). My mother wore pearl earrings and roped pearls braided in her hair. When she bent to kiss me, I saw the weight of her breasts and I smelled her silky heat. She was like someone I did not know, and the more precious for it. Her advice came from a store of wisdom which, like her perfume, was seldom disclosed to me. She touched my head, and I guessed that she guessed that it did not really ache. I loved her for seeing through me and not saying so except with her eyes. 'Goodnight, little man.'

There was movement among the trees along the valley road, but it was the donkey-cart, not the Renault. Roque was bringing Louise from the station; it was Friday evening and she was coming home for the weekend. I caught an eastern smell on the air and looked up to see my mother leaning in the half-open window of her bedroom smoking an exotic cigarette. I knew at once she had been given it by her brother; such things came from Paris, and from circles in which it was impossible to move without compromise. I was not sure whether my memories of the evening before she went to the opera had been prompted by the cigarette or whether the thought of Paris, rising to her from me, had somehow been responsible for her lighting it. She still had the silk shawl around her shoulder. She looked down at me as I waited with my suitcase and I sensed the wry envy of someone who thought she could make much better use of another's good fortune than its guileless recipient.

By the time the donkey-cart was squeezing moist tracks in the

112

chestnut leaves along the drive, the headlights of the Renault were blinking between the walnut trees along the valley road. My mother pressed her cigarette against the sill and went back into her room as Louise rolled in below us. I ran down the central steps and took my sister's hand, like a footman, as she put her neat boot on the trap's running board.

She said, 'Are they talking about you!'

I said, 'Louise, I'm going away. You're lucky to see me.'

'I'm glad,' she said.

'I want you to do something for me.'

'Anything,' she said. 'As long as it's dangerous.'

I said, 'Don't get married until I get back. If I do.'

She said, 'Beast! I thought it would be something interesting at least. Why should I marry? I'm not going to marry.'

I said, 'Because she'll want you to.'

'There's no question of it,' she said, as if I had proposed that she should do what I was seeking to prevent. 'Where are you going?'

'When the war ends,' I said, 'you can do as you please. I don't know where. And you're not supposed to.'

The Renault was coming up the alley, its headlights sulphurous in the evening mist.

Louise said, 'Why did you do it?'

I said, 'Probably because I didn't know how to be brave.'

'I want to come with you,' she said.

'Out of the question,' I said.

'Suppose I were pregnant,' she said.

'You don't know what you're saying.'

'Oh yes, I do,' she said. 'It's just that you don't know the me who's saying it.'

I said, 'Well, whatever you do, don't do that, will you?'

'You see?' she said. 'You're one of them really!'

'We've had all these years,' I said, 'and now there's no time. I want to be with you; I want to talk to you.'

She said, 'I'll marry if I want to – or even if I don't, if I do! I can only be myself, I mean, if I agree to things which I don't want. That's the only way a girl can make room for herself.' She spoke in a hot whisper as we stood by the black hoops of the arcade near the wooden horse on which Baptiste had earlier been sawing. 'Tell me some other things you don't think I ought to do and I'll tell you all the things you should. Such as the landlord's daughter!'

'I shan't be doing anything like that,' I said. 'When I come back, we'll go away, shall we? When the war ends, we'll go somewhere together.'

'They did that, didn't they?' she said.

I said, 'They? Who?'

'And that's why we never shall.' It seemed more like a promise than a refusal. Her radiance, in that darkening moment, appeared supernatural; she was glowing. Had we ever been close companions? Had we ever liked each other very much? Nothing reliable was sealed between us, but I felt the pulse of an unattainable passion. I remember the millwheel tipping, tipping towards the seemingly still surface of the thick, powerful stream. I saw it as she had seen it earlier that evening as the train clacked along under the lee of Castelnaud. My uncle was coming up to us. I ignored him like a predator. When finally I turned and looked at him, he could have been a different man. Was it only the moustache? There was an expression on his face which I should have wished to see on my father's. I was shocked by his air of tender ruthlessness. I loved him, or it.

He said, 'We must move. I'm sorry. No time left.'

I kissed Louise three times, holding her hand in its green and red woollen glove. She pulled away and the last of her kisses was like that of someone leaning forward on a quayside as a boat falls away from it. She brushed past my uncle and scampered into the house. He was looking up towards my mother's lighted window. Did I see the movement of her silk shawl? I heard the breath in Jean-Claude's nostrils and felt, rather than saw, some stifled movement of his arm, like that of someone who has almost forgotten that he is not in uniform and is about to salute in the wrong circumstances. He converted the motion into an invitation to get into the car.

'So,' he said, as he manipulated the plunger-like gear lever, 'you've made your decision, by which the rest of them must live. I hope you're pleased with yourself.'

'Not in the least,' I said. 'But if it offends you, I can easily make my own arrangements. I can hide in the woods.'

'And get everyone shot. Of course you can. What you did was something you did to everyone. Your parents must now claim that you have disappeared and it's a matter of life and death that it be true. There must be a cleavage between you and them, all of them, which holds. It has to be real. You don't come back here under any circumstances until I say so.'

'*You* say so?'

'They're very methodical, our friends. You must neither weaken nor be brazen, do you follow me? Do what you want, in secret, but do nothing to attract or deserve attention. By brazen, I mean don't do anything which is conceived as a gesture, not an act.' The car lights beat boldly on the tree trunks and then spilled thinly into the fields. We appeared to be going at a hectic speed as we bucketed along the valley. 'If you're bored, that will be evidence that you're behaving exactly as you should.'

I said, 'How is it that you manage still to have a car?'

He said, 'I have a permit. Your suspicions are true, but so are things you do not suspect. You happen to be my sister's child.' He was crouched behind the wheel as though it needed some energy of his own to keep the car moving. 'You know nothing of me or of what I'm doing. That is not only an instruction, it is also a fact. I will tell you this, however, for your comfort, even though you deserve little of it: you cannot betray me. You can try, but you won't do it.'

'Why is that a comfort?'

'For reasons which I hope you will never discover.'

'Why do you make such an effort to tell me things you don't want me to know?'

He looked at me with encouraging disgust. 'You've chosen a bad moment in which to grow up, or to pretend to do so. You wish me to know of your contempt? I am perfectly indifferent to it. You think that you can dispense with me? You can.' We had reached the false halfway point on the way to Port du Noyer. He stopped the car and leaned across me to unlatch the door. 'Go on. Get out.'

I said, 'I'm quite willing.'

'Then why do you find it so difficult to say? Do it then.'

I turned and reached for my suitcase which was on the bench behind us. He threw my hand back into my lap and pushed me towards the door. 'Come on,' I said. 'Shit!'

'You want to be an animal? You want to be lost in the wild? Go and be one. Alone. And see your parents taken away after you've crawled home to have your nose wiped. Shit! Don't you ever say shit until you know what shit is.' He leaned across me again and slammed the door against my thigh. 'In normal times, you'd be in the army. You'd have a sergeant. As it is, you have to be your own. What you did was nothing. A nonsense. What you're about to do – which is another nothing – will be the measure of what you are, or aren't.'

'And you're the one who's arranged it all, are you?'

He said, 'Do you think it was your father?'

XVI

'Do you want me to come upstairs with you?'

'Very much,' I said. 'But of course not.'

'You were wrong not to have one of those rice-balls. They were *extra!*' Pierre had to raise his voice as the rain, for which he had been prepared all day, began to boom on the roof of the Citroën just as we reached the Via Trionfale. 'I'm willing to come up, not because I have any appetite for the occasion – quite the contrary! – but because the truth is easier between three.'

'Frankly, I'm not of a mind to re-enact the Trinity.'

Pierre said, 'Your idea of what will vex is almost identical with what entertains me. Don't imagine you can scandalise – or bribe – me with theological small change.'

'You doubt whether she'll have the nerve to accuse you to your face, is that it? You think your presence will guarantee the truth being spoken, or that everything which is spoken will be true. You confuse witness with insolence.'

'You're right,' he said. 'We'll say goodbye now. Definitively.' He had pulled up adjacent to a wide puddle between me and the kerb. His eyes gleamed as if in anticipation of the very friendship to which his outstretched hand was putting an end. 'Do you want to borrow my coat to get into your building? You can let me have it back another time.'

'There won't be one,' I said, stepping nonchalantly into the puddle I had been determined to avoid. I scurried, with one foot wet to the ankle, across the pavement to the green marble portico of the apartment house, making an odd arm movement – a sort of apotropaic salute – as I thrust towards the heavy glass door. I seemed to have forgotten that it opened automatically.

The lift was at the ground floor, but I still pressed the red button, at the same time slapping raindrops from my shoulders. I hate having wet knees and I had them. The lift flashed '*al piano*', but before I could open the door, it started up.

I tried to imagine exactly where Berthe would be in the flat when I entered it. If I could be sure of her pose and manner, as I always was of

116

Pia's, I could see myself handling the scene with the same competence that I contrived with the prostitute. Since the boys would be there, a sexual resolution would be difficult, indeed impossible, so I decided on a routine of courtesy. I would conceal my knowledge of Berthe's fabrication and savour her efforts to sustain it until the moment was ripe to spring my surprise. I should approach the matter as Fritz had once taught me, with that alert sense of 'having been there before' which mates the future with the past. By an opening which gave the impression that I had not discussed the matter with Pierre, Berthe would be lulled into compounding her falsehood. In a calm delirium I saw Pierre as a new kind of piece on my board, a cross between a bishop and a knight blessed with cryptic powers. Perhaps I was catching cold. My trousers were almost transparent over my knees.

I began to be impatient to see my wife. I saw myself appearing to be devastated by a situation which I was capable, at any moment I chose, of turning to my sweet and undeniable advantage. 'Perpetual mate,' Fritz used to say, 'is the unending ending.' I pressed the button again and again, knowing that it would have no effect on whoever was getting into the lift. It had stopped at a high floor. Through the glass aperture in the door (its wired pattern echoed that of my shirt), I saw cables dangling in the void and then the greased surge of the counterweight. The car was coming down.

As the lift sank to my level, a little green light flashed in the 'al piano' slot. I opened the door with a courtly flourish, and in the urgent desire to take possession of the car as quickly as possible. My mental bladder was full.

To my dismay, the passenger was Berthe. Having pulled the door open, I was standing to one side as she swept past me. She walked towards the street without even noticing who the doorman was. I heard my surprise express itself in an almost plaintive wail, which I should not have authorised if I had had time to think. 'Where do you think you're going?'

My wife was wearing a white shower-coat, quite loose, and slingback white shoes, which I considered ill-advised. She carried a green silk umbrella, of a very slim design which was fashionable at the time. It was as if she expected wet weather and a dry pavement. After I had spoken, she took another step, like those cartoon characters who walk tranquilly out onto the void, before falling or scrambling impossibly back to the edge of the precipice.

'Oh,' she said. 'It's you. I'm walking up to the Medaglie d'Oro for some supplies.'

I said, 'Come upstairs. It's raining.'

'I shan't be a moment. I didn't expect you yet. I have an umbrella.'

'I'm actually later than we said, not earlier. He's rather an erratic driver. You'll still get wet. It's falling down.'

She said, 'The girl's prepared some food. The boys have eaten. It's only a shower.'

I said, 'I know exactly what you're going out for. I want to talk to you.'

'Then come with me,' she said. 'Guy, has something happened to you?'

'Because I want to talk to you?'

'It's probably better if you do it somewhere else. Knowing what you want to say.'

'You have no idea what I want to say.'

'Guy, have you been drinking?'

'That's a good question coming from you. I have not been drinking.'

'So I now see,' she said. 'You know your trouble, Guy? You're drunk on abstinence. You're dried out, completely.'

I said, 'Don't walk away from me. I want you to come upstairs. We have things we must talk about.' My anger was due more to the ruin of my expectations than to her response to my presence. If she did come upstairs, what could I say to her to match the weight of my demand that she hear it? Only by disobedience could she now do what I wanted of her.

To my enraged relief, she turned away and went on towards the street. At that moment, one of our neighbours, Miguel O'Higgins, a Peruvian consular official, and his four daughters scurried through the sliding doors. They were carrying musical instrument cases of varied cumbrousness. I found that I was still holding the lift door. They thanked me and packed themselves ingeniously inside. I let the door sigh shut. A moment later, their feet flew up past my eyes and the little window went dark.

Berthe was standing in front of the sliding doors, not quite breaking the circuit which would trigger their opening. They faltered, but did not quite have the impulse to let her out. 'By the way,' she said, 'in case you're interested, it's not true. About Pierre Salomon, if that's what all the fuss is about.'

I said, 'I don't want to discuss that here.'

She said, 'Since it's not true, what is there to discuss?'

The doors gave way to her now, but I took three fast strides and caught her coat. I said, 'You can't say something and then not say it and expect everything to be as it was before. What exactly isn't true?'

118

'You know perfectly well. And now I want to get to the pharmacy before they close.'

'Pharmacies don't sell what you want,' I said.

'Will you please let go of me before somebody comes?'

Her sleeve was voluminous. I had grabbed emptiness at first and now I groped for the flesh of her arm quite as if she might not be there at all. Her hair had a reddish hue that evening. Had it always been that colour? I was not sure whether I should be foolish or observant to comment on it. In a film which Pia had described to me recently, the heroine proved the degree to which her husband took her for granted by wearing a blue wig and blacking out one of her front teeth. The woman whose sleeve I was holding was the mother of my sons. She said, 'Have you finished?'

I said, 'As far as you're concerned, that's it, is it?'

'Look,' she said, 'you forget and I forget. Is that fair?'

'And what are you proposing to forget exactly?'

'You're going to tear my coat in a minute. You forget what I said and I forget what you did. Will you please let go of me?'

'And we go on as before, do we?'

'What else?'

'You lied to me. I didn't lie to you.'

'I made something up,' she said. 'Like a joke. If you know what a joke is.'

'I know what our marriage is,' I said.

'Is it a marriage? That's already more than I know about it.'

I said, 'How do I know that you're not bluffing? You could have said something false in order to distract attention from what was true.'

'I'm not a diplomat,' she said.

I said, 'I should like to kill you, are you aware of that?'

She said, 'It's just about the only interesting thing about you, as far as I'm concerned.'

XVII

It was too late to catch a train from Port du Noyer. My uncle drove over the bridge and on to Caillac. I found myself on the same platform from which Fritz and his parents had left for Paris. I was to go in the other direction, first to Agen and then to the smaller town of Rodecin where I would be met by a man whom I was to obey without question. I rather looked forward to that.

Meanwhile, we waited for the train which I could almost believe had been summoned from the void by my uncle's special powers. That he had influence with the authorities might, in the circumstances, have been expected to fuel my scorn and warrant my ingratitude: it would have been convenient to be able to take whatever he offered and still find it inadequate to excuse his venality. In the event, I found that it gave him a certain glamour. He was like a surgeon, unalarmed by blood. His warning against questioning whatever might now be asked of me seemed to recruit me to a rough fraternity in which he was always a reliable elder. He was asking not only that I endure but that I do so for his sake. He disowned and appropriated me at the same time; I was both disgraced and elect.

My father had confessed that he depended on Jean-Claude. His own scruples had rendered him impotent; Jean-Claude's worldliness was my one practical resource. My petty rebellion had pitched me into reliance on the only close member of the family whose behaviour I strongly suspected had been dishonourable. That my uncle was despicable was not, I began to feel, a reason to dislike him. No, it was worse than that: it was a reason to love him or, at the very least, no reason not to. As we stood on that bleak platform, I felt my parents – especially my father – receding from me as if I were already pulling away in some smooth, wild acceleration. I no longer owed my father any account of myself. As for my mother, although her snobbish caution made her unworthy of conscious respect, she seemed to have a new hold on me. The flash of that silk shawl of hers, the look which Jean-Claude gave her as he opened the door of the little Renault, both intrigued and recruited me to something I could neither specify nor resist.

The lights of the train scarcely showed as it clanked into the station. The engine was a veteran, whiskered with steam. Three or four men swung down from the train, almost before its brakes snatched it, squeakily, to a halt. I shook hands with Jean-Claude and climbed aboard as two other men, in dark coats and broad-brimmed hats, walked onto the platform from the buffet. They stood there, still with menace, but did not board the train. Were they watching for me, or people like me, or were they watching over me?

My uncle did not wave as the engine snorted and the train lurched forward. Although our connection was obvious, we rehearsed ignorance of each other. I sat on the slatted bench and was drawn out of the world I knew like a cork from a bottle. Did the two men go up to my uncle as the station slid away from my sight?

I had only my genuine identity card with me. I had no right to be travelling so late without a special permit. Having assumed the night hours to be a dead zone, in which any movement was likely to be questioned, I was almost disappointed to discover that its inhabitants went about their business with something like impudence. The restrictions against unauthorised activity seemed to immunise those who were bold enough to act without hesitation.

As we stopped at some intermediate station on the way to Agen, I saw money pass between an untroubled man smoking a cigar and two plain-clothes men who chatted and checked his count at the same time. The war professionalised the night. If what was done was illicit, as much of it was, the police could be lubricated in the usual way; the unusual thing was that the underworld was now everywhere. The regulations made life easier for those with the wit or nerve to deal with them. Only the innocent were at a loss.

Most of my fellow-passengers appeared to know each other. There were swaying handshakes as they passed up and down the train, quite as though they were in their regular office. Two prostitutes sat across from me. One was fat and blonde, the other had a dark, haunted voluptuousness. I seemed already to know, though the experience of it must have come later, that she was of the type known in brothels as 'the Jewess'. The women sat with their feet in each other's laps. They had removed their shoes and set them toe to toe against the back of their seats, behind their legs, and were chaffing each other's toes and insteps. I had a silly hope that their air of rapt concern and the energy of their friction was some kind of a demonstration, or tease, for my benefit.

When they were warmer, the women tucked their feet under them so that their silky knees shone, and opened a little wicker box. Now it seemed only that they had been postponing the pleasure they knew to be in store for them. They had oranges and a small *terrine* of what looked to be *foie gras frais* and a wedge of blue cheese and a bar of Swiss chocolate. Occasionally, they fed each other. They might have been one creature with two mouths.

Were they the first prostitutes I ever saw? They were undoubtedly the first I ever heard. Their barely audible conversation seemed to have been turned down, like the volume of an illicit radio. Something enviably untamed transformed their reticence into a conspiracy to which I wished that I could be privy. The 'Jewess' took a slip of paper from the bottom of the hinged basket, where it had been hidden by the delicacies, and read it with the help of a pair of spectacles which she passed, with the note, to the other. As the blonde finished reading, they both wanted to laugh, but forbade each other with fingers on each other's lips. I had the desire to do quite different things to each of them.

I felt bereaved when they walked briskly away from me across the platform at Agen without even saying goodnight. They were approaching the exit when a young girl with pale lips, who had been sitting on a bench, with a bundle in her lap, called out to them. They stopped and tilted their heads in tender surprise: the girl had grown since last they saw her. She met their levity with unsmiling lips. The whores became her soldiers. She marched them out of the station.

I had been told by my uncle to take the first train to Rodecin. There was a delay. I waited with odd apprehension. I hoped that I should not be questioned; I was piqued to think that I might be. I thrashed my imagination for a story plausible with undeniable details. The joy of deception excited me almost more than the shining tarts and their off-duty knees. I sat and waited. No one paid me the smallest attention, even when I walked up and down the platform like a man with a password on the tip of his tongue.

The train, when at last it pulled in, had several goods wagons attached to a single passenger carriage. Its main purpose was to collect farm produce, a business better undertaken at night, when allied fighter-bombers were unlikely to strafe it. At the next stop, somewhere among the orchards of the district, a uniformed gendarme took the seat opposite me. I had been shivering, either from the cold or from loneliness, when he joined me. His corpulent presence revived my vitality. I acted indifference while preparing myself for his interrogation. The severe girl on Agen station became my sister. The whores became our aunts, whom I had escorted to her care after they had been bombed out in Cherbourg. When I was confident of boring him with my saga, I looked directly at him. He had closed his eyes and was sound asleep.

Rodecin was in a department without the familiar history of the Périgord. Instead of our local stone – ochrous or rubicund, according to the quarry – Rodecin was made of brick. Dawn put a rouged glaze on the station and the terraced houses beside it. I saw unforested hills in the background, some with big, four-square houses on them.

When I got out of the train, the gendarme moved behind me. Was he on my trail? He simply changed seats, taking my warm place for some reason, and went back to sleep. I am not sure that he even opened his eyes at my departure. The stationmaster was standing, in his important cap, near the exit. He was a small, fair man with glittering blue eyes. As I passed him, he said, 'Are you the little package?'

I was taller than he. I said, 'Perhaps I am.'

He indicated the station yard. Something in the neatness of his manner suggested a rugby player. In the yard, I saw a perky man, darker but of similar build. He stood astride a bicycle with a wagonette attached to it. A tarpaulin half covered some lengths of cut wood which protruded at an angle. The driver held up the tarpaulin and invited me aboard. I climbed in awkwardly and smelt the mildew on the inside of the material as he tied its corners. I arranged myself sideways, knees under my chin. I felt more humiliated than hidden. Anyone could have seen me getting into the wagonette.

I saw nothing of Rodecin as my driver pedalled sedately through it. I had no vision of it, but it seemed to be rather long. Finally we turned and I felt that we were going up an incline which became steeper. Our wheels were on a less smooth surface and then we stopped. When the tarpaulin was peeled back, there was the smiling but not altogether genial face of my driver. His flat cap was tilted on the back of his head. He wore a collarless woollen shirt and a leather waistcoat. Behind him, I could see lengths of timber leaning against the mossy wooden wall of an *atelier* whose windows were crusted with sawdust. My driver watched, but did not help, as I scrambled awkwardly from the wagonette. I was in a cobbled yard with rusty gates onto a side street. It had high walls. There was a glazed door into the kitchen of the main house, which was at right angles to both the street and the *atelier*. My driver raised his chin for me to go in there.

'Am I staying here?'

'Doesn't it suit you?'

'Perfectly, if I am.'

'Lonchat,' he said. 'Robert. You are.'

His wife was in the kitchen. She was larger than her husband. She had hennaed curls, as heavy as sausages, and a wide, doughy face with bulging, wet eyes. She shook my hand correctly; she seemed to want to make it clear that our relations would be, if not brief, certainly without warmth. However closely we were to live, I was to keep my distance. My meals would not be with my hosts: I could collect my 'soup', if there was no one in the house, but I was to eat it in my room. The lavatory was on the landing. I should be discreet in its use. There was a tap outside the door for water. She would now show me the room. Lonchat grinned at me as his wife led us up the stairs. I now knew what I was up against and – his look suggested – I also knew that he had been up against it for years.

'What will you do,' he said, 'with your time?'

'Are there a lot of Germans around?' I said.

'Not many. But you can't go out. They pay people to keep an eye on things.'

I said, 'About the rent . . .'

'All taken care of.'

The room was under the roof. Slats of *lambris*, made of cheap pine strips, went right to the peak of the house and formed a tall circumflex above the mahogany double bed. It had solid foot- and head-boards bracketing the lumpy mattress. The bed, although not large, scarcely left room for a small chest and a bedside table with a pot on the lower shelf. There was no carpet. A mansard window looked over the yard. I could see rooftops, but none with windows in them. There was an unshaded bulb over the washstand, with the usual bowl and jug. There was a candlestick by the bed. The wind rattled the ill-fitting window. A small unpainted metal stove had a few sticks of wood piled beside it on a box of shavings which would serve for kindling.

'All right?'

'Ideal,' I said. 'What are you going to tell people about me?'

'Enough,' Lonchat said. 'And no more than that.'

I said, 'Excuse me, but I have to know, in case . . .'

'Don't worry,' he said. 'Hardly anyone comes here. I work alone. My wife . . . has very few visitors.' If his grin solicited my agreement that there were advantages to being married to a shrew, Madame Lonchat seemed to find this a quite satisfactory reference. She took a deep breath and went out of the room. 'I shall say you're a distant relative – of my wife's! – from the north. You're here for your health.' He coughed rather seriously for a moment and then smiled again. 'Your lungs! Why not? But have no fear, no one is going to bother you here.'

124

I said, 'Lille?'

'Lille!' he said. 'Why not? Do you know it?'

'No,' I said.

'That makes two of us,' he said. 'Lille! Why not?'

'Excuse me,' I said. 'But what do you do? Are you a carpenter?'

'Good guess,' he said.

'Because if there's anything useful I can do, I should be very happy.'

'You stay where you are,' he said, 'until you hear different.'

He shut the door. The catch was not reliable, but the care he took resembled that of a jailer. I saw that there was a lock inside the door. I went and twisted it, for no good reason, and then I sat on the musty eiderdown and tried to imagine the future. I was disconcerted to learn that my rent was already paid. What was I to do with my money if I could not use it to buy attention? I was deprived of a relationship with the Lonchats which being the paymaster might have given me. If it became known that I was rich, I should now simply be in danger; my security made me insecure.

I inspected the chilly room for a hiding place. If I had a secret, I should feel rich again. I chanced on some loose slats in the *lambris* above my candlestick. The strips had narrow tongues which could easily be separated. The quality of my landlord's craftsmanship indicated why he took lodgers.

I inserted nearly all of my money behind the slats, on a solid beam which ran along behind them, and refixed them with more care than had been taken in their installation. What else could I do? My solitude was my company: never before having lived alone, I was a stranger whom I regarded with curiosity and suspicion.

The failure of my hosts to show any interest in me made them more intriguing to me than they would have been, had they pampered me. During the days that followed, I grew vigilantly inquisitive about their mundane habits. I watched Madame Lonchat as she punished her wash at the concrete slab under the pump in the corner of the yard. I wondered where exactly she went in the unknown town when she left with her basket, wearing a hat brimming with false fruit. I guessed at a long main street behind my roof and hidden from my view. In my vanity, I liked to think that Madame's absences were part of a routine of regularity which had now become a wilful imposture; what had been normal for the Lonchats was transformed, by my simple presence, into duplicity. Lonchat himself was more an odd-jobman than a *menuisier* in regular demand. His main activity seemed to be the construction of cages. He used pieces of old *grillage* which he detached, with cheerful curses, from rotten or derelict frames that he had collected on his rounds with the wagonette. When he had made the new cages, he loaded them and pedalled off, his cap on the back of his head, his knees spread in a leisurely, foolish way. He had, it seemed to me, contrived his puckish manner in order both to amuse himself and to gull others, much as I, in my loneliness, was disposed to create a patient and tolerant persona who would supervise and contain my more volatile side.

I became avid for news. So far as I could hear, my hosts listened only to official bulletins on their capricious wireless. I would creep down the stairs in order to overhear the announcer's increasingly sibilant assertions. I teased myself into taking an extra step each day, until I could actually see the set through the glass panel of the sitting room door. It stood on a lace runner on the dresser, among the brassy mementos of a family without achievements.

Listening to what I knew to be distortions and half-truths, I was reminded of Fritz, who had instructed me always to take note of what was not being said or admitted. Cases of 'terrorism' or Bolshevik outrage were denounced with particular disgust, just as the taking, or execution, of hostages excited hypocritical regret. I was now at an age when, in other circumstances, I should have been in the forces which I could guess to be poised to invade the mainland. I felt neither old nor young. I both dreaded and desired the victory which now loomed. I looked forward, but without partisan enthusiasm, to the division of Frenchmen against each other. I knew which side I should be on, if given the chance, but I had no pugnacious wish to be given it. I had no scores to settle. If I felt any animosity, it was directed against my father; I felt strangely grateful to him for giving my hostility such a conveniently undangerous target. Looking back, I decided that I had made my literal stand against Fritz's deportation in order, as I thought, to be worthy of him. The story of our ancestor had been an inspiration which I now considered a mere cover story on my father's part to excuse his months of passivity. Having agreed, on my honour, to abide by my family's injunction to stay where I was, I was free to wish that I had made my escape, while I could, to 'The Double'. The Resistance had its local bastion in the district where our ancestor had been roasted.

I chewed over the same sour cud, day after day. I set myself to read my father's copy of La Boétie and Montaigne's essay, which was bound up with it. Remembering my father's well-intended remarks about my friendship with Fritz, I almost blamed him for its lack of that reciprocity of which Montaigne was so proud: no, I was not Fritz and, no, Fritz was not me. I was bereaved by his loss, but I was not wounded. Was I not somehow made stronger? His absence was dearer to me than his presence had been. My memory of him was unencumbered by his sometimes abrasive voice; my mind's eye was blind to his hirsute jaw and those alien cheeks.

I surveyed my narrow room for clues to its past use or tenants. A few days after my arrival, I saw that there were flat handles on the band of vertical panelling below where the *lambris* inclined towards the apex of my roof. The doors of the little cupboard were so tightly warped together that the crack in the stained wood had been invisible. Opening them would be my first luxury. I was not in a hurry to succeed. I told myself that I must leave no sign of my intrusion. The wood had not to be split and no loud noise should be made. The cupboard bore all the signs of my landlord's handiwork: the hinges were rusty and the edges of the wood unplaned. A splinter slid under my thumbnail and I howled silently as I drew it out with my teeth, having carefully nibbled the nail to the blood.

When I opened the doors, I found only a few mildewed books and a box of unpainted and unsanded wooden trains with solid wheels. Did my hosts have a child? Was he a prisoner of war, or had he been killed in some accident? I was not moved by pity at their fancied loss; I made it an excuse for despising them for treating me no better than a prisoner myself. Yet I drew a certain satisfaction from my confinement. Rodecin became an unknown territory which honour rather than timidity barred me from exploring. It was not the Lonchats who were my harshest jailers; I capped their indifference with my own inflexible régime.

Since it was beneath my dignity to play with the toys which I had found (and now had the pleasure of concealing when Madame Lonchat had occasion to come to my room), I removed the bent nails which pinned the wheels to the chassis of the little train and set about refashioning the components into a chess set. I crept downstairs, while Madame was pounding her laundry in the yard, and stole a black-handled paring knife from the kitchen. With chastening clumsiness, I then hacked out a set of pawns and their noble companions sufficiently distinct for me to be able to play against myself.

My endeavours were not made easier by my poisoned thumb. The splinter had probably not been entirely removed by my efforts. I sucked the place as pink as it could be, but the nail swelled and I watched the pus thicken and spread under it until the merest touch caused a gasp of agony. I was considerably diverted by my medical attentions to myself. I did not expel the pus until I was sure that enough of what I thought of as *crème anglaise* had been stored for a great spurt of it to be released. The sweet pain of its ejaculation was an operation I prolonged and to which I looked forward with such keen dread that when the wound ceased to pulse and showed every sign of having healed, I felt deprived of a pleasure.

The books in Lonchat's cupboard were nearly all published in the last century. Their pages were moist and gummy and held little allure. I preferred to read the squares of old newspaper on the peg by the lavatory, which stank so regularly that I suspected that my host had had a hand in its plumbing.

Perhaps I made Madame Lonchat into more of a dragon than she need have been, had I myself tried to be more amiable. When I asked her for a piece of old wrapping paper, she gave me a big brown sheet on which I was able to square a chessboard. I concealed its use, lest my theft of the knife and dismemberment of the toy train be discovered at the same time. When I tried, belatedly, to play the grateful lodger, by praising her *soupe de fèves*, my diplomacy paid no noticeable dividend; it sounded, even to my ears, that I was implying that other dishes she had cooked were little to my taste.

My failure to charm Madame Lonchat began to earn her my increased attention. Although she was no beauty, I observed that she moved with a certain gliding elegance. Perhaps she had been a dancer in her youth. The length and monotony of my days, and nights, turned her from an object of scrutiny to one of – dare I say it? – reverie. One sunny afternoon, when the sky was a blue reminder of that summer of 1940 when we were at Le Prieuré with my grandmother, Madame Lonchat set herself to do a big wash. She came out in a sleeveless bodice and went to work. The vigour of her movements tilted her forward over the concrete slab. She leaned the heels of her hands into the thick sheets and punched out the airy blisters. Her breasts fell forward too. She must have been over fifty, and her arms and neck were unattractively mottled, but her breasts were immaculately white, surprisingly firm and appetising as they squeezed together under the low bodice. I took care to stay invisible by the mansard window as I gazed at their pneumatic succulence. How could she be unaware of their almost independent beauty? Why should I be indifferent to it? Nothing about her excited me except those uncreased globes and the dark valley, squeezed like the exclamation mark they deserved, between them. The memory of those glowing, apparently nippleless spheres, and the hope of seeing them again, kindled an interest in Madame Lonchat which never extended to the rest of her person or character. She became the cruel keeper of what, in my imagination and my dreams, evolved into a pair of hairless pets of elastic complicity.

Having been in my hosts' house for a while, I assumed that I knew the limits of their lives. Their only regular visitor was Lonchat's brother, Riri, a smallholder who lived outside the town and brought occasional supplies of eggs and chicken. He was almost twice the size of Robert and had a loud voice which came up the stairs to visit me, even though, so far as I knew, its owner was unaware of my existence. His artless gossip reminded me of the perennial feuds and malice of the countryside. His habit was first to decline food and drink and then to stay for whatever was available, not leaving until no further bottle was opened. My own portion of food was delayed, and often diminished, by his arrival.

Late one afternoon, when I was playing chess on the floor beside the humped bed, I heard muffled voices in the yard. I was vain (and anxious) enough to think that the newcomer might have something to do with me. I was greedy for incident, even if it were to be disagreeable, or at least until it was. It was unlikely to be the end of me if I were deported from a room where freedom was growing more and more burdensome.

The voices, of which one was my host's, went through the kitchen door and lost their caution, though they did not become properly audible. I heard the rattle of dishes before steps sounded on my stair. My hosts would hardly have fed a policeman or a German, so I was exempt from all but curiosity. I slid the chessmen under the bed, on their crinkly board, and opened a history of the *Tour de France*. The yellowing volume had been part of the secret library in the cupboard. I had been puzzled by an opening chapter dealing with apprenticeship in the Middle Ages. What connection was about to be established between *menuiserie* and the famous bicycle race? The question prompted a wholly spurious enthusiasm for the text. In fact, there was no connection: the '*tour*' about which I was reading was the name given to the last stage in the graduation of an apprentice, when he went from one part of the country to another, learning the styles peculiar to each.

When I heard the knock at my door, I waited for a moment, to suggest that I was in no hurry to breach my solitude. I went and untwisted the lock and then I said, 'Yes?'

Lonchat came in, followed by a young man who was carrying a suitcase more ample than the one I had brought. I sensed at once that my host was about to ask me a favour. His smile could have been borrowed from his brother; it was now false and purposeful where it was commonly artless. He saw my dishes on the floor and picked them up as though it were his habit. 'Have you had enough? There's always more.'

'Quite enough,' I said.

The young man was about my age. He was fair and clean-shaven, with pale blue eyes. He was not tall, but he was well-proportioned. There was a strange candour about him. Looked at directly, his outline seemed a bright blur. He resembled an angel in a devotional print which Simone's mother once brought home from a drenching pilgrimage to Lourdes, after which she caught a fever and very nearly died.

Lonchat said, 'Someone to give you some company at last!' He moved the newcomer's suitcase further into the room and then backed out. 'I'll leave you to get acquainted.'

I said, 'Guy de Roumegouse.'

'Forgeau, Félix.' He spoke quietly, allowing me to sample his accent. We shook hands. I thought of boxers before a bout, and of my poor preparation for one. He was neat and mild and gave no sign of anything more hostile than wary respect. There were freckles across his short nose and on his downy upper cheeks. The blue eyes had very black irises.

I said, 'You're from Paris.'

'The eleventh,' he said. 'But I worked in the eighth.'

'What work?'

'In a hotel. The Royal-Concorde.'

'I never stayed in hotels in Paris,' I said. 'We lived near the Luxembourg. What're you going to do in Rodecin?'

'Stay here,' he said. He had his weight evenly on both feet, hands by his sides. He was really very neat.

'In this house?'

'In this house. In this room.'

I said, 'They're never going to get another bed in here.'

'That's why we're going to have to share this one,' he said.

'Says who?'

His head indicated the people downstairs. 'It seems quite big.'

I said, 'This is supposed to be my room.'

'I don't imagine it'll be for very long.'

'Are they relations of yours?'

'Not at all,' he said. 'What are they like?'

I said, 'Why are you here?'

'They said they'd get me out, and they did. This is where they told · me to come. Here I am.'

'You're not willing to talk about it.'

'I'll talk about anything,' he said. He lifted his damson-coloured case onto the bed. He had a gold ring on his left little finger. 'What would you like to talk about? You? Me?'

'Who arranged for you to come here exactly?'

'You're a trusting type, aren't you? Telling me your name! But then I told you mine, so I must be one too. The same people arranged for me as arranged for you, I expect, don't you? We have to hope so.'

I said, 'What did you do at the Royal-Concorde?'

He said, 'Room service.' He appeared to be in excellent humour, which shortened my temper. 'How do we wash?'

'There's cold water on the landing. If you want hot, you have to ask her, or heat it on the range when she's not there.'

'Why when she's not there?'

'She doesn't know I go down,' I said.

'You just sit in this room all day?'

'I read,' I said. 'I play chess . . .'

'By yourself?'

'It's perfectly possible. Do you play?'

'Chess? I'm the world champion.' He was rinsing his face and hands. 'No, I don't.'

'I can teach you,' I said.

He dried himself on my towel. 'We can teach each other all sorts of things, can't we?' he said. 'After all, why not?'

XVIII

Félix moved delicately around the room as he took articles from his damson suitcase and disposed them in the little cupboard under the washstand or stacked them between the bed and the wall with the window in it, which he had taken to be his side. He seemed to find more space in the attic than had been available to me. Although his appearance was barely adolescent, his competence made him older than me.

I said, 'I have to be honest: I've never shared a bed with anyone before.'

He said, 'I won't bother you. You won't even notice me, if you don't want to. Never?'

'Have you?'

'Have I? Yes, I have. You've never slept with anyone?'

I shook my head. 'So you see,' I said, 'I wish we had, at the least, two beds in here.'

'I can assure you,' he said, 'it's not of any importance.'

'I'm going to talk to the Lonchats. Perhaps they can find you somewhere else. Or perhaps I can find another room myself.'

'You prefer to be alone? Do you snore?'

'Not to my knowledge. Do you?'

'I knew someone who snored so loudly he woke himself and then he accused me of snoring! Good God, do you sleep with only one sheet?'

I said, 'That's all they gave me.'

He said, 'You're very accepting. Do you always accept things?' He reached into the bottom of his suitcase and brought out a large white sheet and held it out for my approval. 'Do you like me better now?'

I said, 'That's a bit lucky!'

'You want to be lucky, you've got to be bright.' He could have been quoting from some text, like my father when he came out with one of his unattributed aphorisms. 'If they don't pay you anything, you have to pay yourself.'

My dismay at Félix's presence was increased by his good humour. To him, we were conscripts to proximity; he had been in worse

132

situations, hence this was a tolerable one. He made me aware of my social class: his deference had been too immediate to be founded on my personal qualities. His dexterity pampered and disarmed me, he became my organiser. He remade the bed; he swept the floor; he stopped the window from rattling. By doing so much, he made me both privileged and helpless.

When he saw the grey sheet in which I had been sleeping for more than two weeks, he said, 'And when's Madame proposing to change this little number?'

'Who can say?'

'I know who can ask. There are going to have to be some changes around here, Julien!'

I said, 'Guy.'

He said, 'I know. I know.' He rummaged again in his apparently inexhaustible case and brought out a large buff envelope. 'Would you like to see some photographs?' The way he spoke recalled the man who had trailed the pass-phrase at me. 'They won't bite you, but never mind!'

I took the envelope and sat with my back half to him as I slid the photographs from it. There were about a dozen of them. I had never seen anything of the kind before. Yet I recognised them to be in some way typical. I recalled Fritz's expression during an endgame: 'We've been here before, haven't we?'

A man in shirtsleeves sat on a bed with one foot on a stool beside it. Although partly naked, he seemed rather respectable. A slim naked back was toward the camera at the bottom of the picture. Its head was between the legs of the man, who rested one hand on the fair hair. I did not look at Félix. His breath seemed to be smiling somewhere near me.

Did the naked back and the fair hair belong to a woman? If so, she was very slim and had unusually short hair. The following photograph was less ambiguous. A black-haired woman wearing only a straw hat was standing by the same bed with one foot on the counterpane. Her bush bearded the man sitting below her, on the bed, in a dark, unbuttoned, chalk-stripe suit. Another girl, young and slim, lay on her stomach on the bed attending to the man. Her eyes rolled up to look at the other woman. The man was holding a cigarette.

I stared at this scene as one might at a holiday snap whose owner one does not wish to offend by too cursory an appreciation. Then I put it behind the previous one. Next, a young man was kneeling in front of a tall, military-looking man with cropped hair and a gouged scar under his ribs. The black-haired woman was in front of the young man, smiling at the other one. She was wearing only an open waistcoat.

As I looked at one picture after another, Félix moved from my side and stood by the window. He might have been waiting to learn whether he had been successful in applying for a job. As for me, how honest can I be about the effect the photographs had on me? I was not directly stimulated, but my vision was blurred by the confusion of my response. If I hurried to get to the end, I could not help wondering what the end would be. My imagination both flinched and raced. My mouth flooded with a strange saliva; excitement and revulsion used the same means.

I tried to look only at the females. Yet the cropped man engaged my interest: his scar announced a life outside the room. The air of command in the tight mouth and of scorn in his posture denied that he was merely a subject for a photographer; he was someone one might meet, and fear.

In another shot, the young fair girl was kneeling on the bed with her head on the bolster, her eyes looking back up and over her shoulder at the cropped man whose hands were opening her. The dark woman sat in the background in a languid pose like that of the woman in Degas' *Déjeuner sur l'Herbe*. I could not help imagining more things that were going to happen. But when I went on to the next photograph, there were no females in it. There were no more females in any of the remaining pictures, all of which came from a more professional, posed collection. The young men were oiled and slick. Their lovers were older. One had a spade-shaped beard. The all-male photographs appealed to me so little that I paid another visit to the earlier pictures, whose participants now seemed almost to be friends.

I noticed details which had eluded my quick scan: a curl of hair, a deeper shadow, a gleam in a watchful eye, a missing button. The dark woman was friendlier on second view. Something in her eyes reminded me of Gertrud. Her air of succulent tolerance redressed my memory of our little Austrian *bonne*. I had wondered, naively, what signal, what affinity, led Gertrud to Fritz's room during the night he spent at La Fontaine du Noyer. Now I saw that she needed no larger lure than instigating and witnessing his pleasure. Kindness could sponsor lust as well as pity. I had never desired heavy little Gertrud and I did not do so now, except in connection with Fritz. My lost friend, whom I had not liked all that much, was essential to what I could only now imagine Gertrud to be – a complaisant woman who would be ardent but not solemn, shameless but undemanding.

Despite the bright demonstrations in Félix's brochure, I flinched, even in my fantasies, from getting into bed with the couple from whom I wanted nothing more than not to be counted an irrelevance. Gertrud-and-Fritz, neither of whom I desired separately, became a single item which I lacked the wit to embrace but with whom, in some unspecific way, I longed to be associated.

Can those photographs have been merely pornographic when they made me aware not only of what I was missing, and might loathe or enjoy, but also, and more devastatingly, of my spiritual destitution? Not until that evening had I feared that there was something in me which inclined me both to long for and to back away from what was at once humane, transcendent and savage. I was reminded of a visit with my mother to the Jardin des Plantes. She had promised that we were going to see the wild animals. I observed the caged bears, and their dancing response to raisin buns, and the lions, with their mangy torpor, and the pumas, parading like mannequins, the elephants with their wrinkled resignation, and then it was suggested that we go to a café. I asked when we were going to see the wild animals. I was told that I had seen them. Now, at last, I felt that I had.

I saw that Gertrud had given herself to Fritz because she alone of all our household had the candour to see his future. I had pretended to concern, but there had been an element of gloating in it: I showed him a world which would be there when he was not and which was perfectly indifferent to him. She gave him more than a spasm of pleasure; she also gave him its memory. She lodged a sliver of eternity in his mortal baggage. My cry of 'Long live the Republic' served no such humane purpose. My expulsion from the *lycée* and my consignment to my present temporary oblivion proved that I was in a quite different category from Fritz, to whom I had fancied myself reconciled by them.

The photographs prompted me to an epiphany which was quite distinct from the accompanying revulsion (and its thrill). I was shocked in more ways than I could specify. I shuffled through the whole stack, set the edges straight and put them back in the envelope, which I held out to Félix. 'I'm afraid I don't like these pictures,' I said.

'I expect you've seen better.'

'Not at all,' I said.

He took them back like a salesman to whom rejection is all in a day's work. He was neither offended nor insinuating. When he was not speaking, my new companion had the hermetic scruples of a pet who can avert aggression with a snarl of docility. His trimness appealed to the eye; it seemed to make him smaller than he really was. It would be heartless not to offer him a scrap of indulgence. I was ashamed of my scowl and of the urge to infect him with a sense of shame which was alien to him, yet I persisted in my wordless reproach.

I dreaded the moment when we should have to get into the double bed together. Even as I told myself that it was only part of that uncomplaining obedience I had promised my uncle, I craved a grievance against Félix. Although I loathed him less than my own want of robustness, I wished that he would commit some misdemeanour to justify his ejection. He ignored or was unaware of my mood. Having offered to let me wash first, he undressed neatly, while I pretended to read a ludicrously royalist account of the anti-Jacobin rising in La Vendée.

In the corner of my eye, I was conscious of him using a bar of white soap of a luxurious kind we had not seen in years. With a little of the water from my roseate jug, he made a ration of lather on his pink chest, from which he culled suds for the rest of his all but hairless body. The curls in his groin were reddish and quite sparse. I did not look; I saw. My vision of him was overlaid by after-images of the photographs which he had replaced in his suitcase. My view of life suffered from double exposure.

He said, 'You're welcome to it if you like.'

'Oh, no thank you. We may as well each use our own.' I implied that the tallowy knob of kitchen soap which I had brought from La Fontaine was too precious to be shared. 'If that's all right with you.'

'Up to you,' he said.

He put his soap in a black Bakelite container which he handled with a certain pride. I undressed and stood in the corner by the door, in my underpants, in order to wash. Félix covered his nakedness unhurriedly, despite the chill in the room, with a pair of off-white cotton pyjamas rather too large for him. He slipped under the covers and lay down in a third of the narrow space we were to share. He could hardly have been more tactful, yet his head was on the bolster which I should also be obliged to use.

I postponed joining him, although I did not wash as thoroughly as he had. I explained that I washed all over only in the morning. When I turned towards the bed, he was not looking at me. I crouched along the wall and climbed in my side. His clean sheet was a delight, but my flesh flinched from any inadvertent contact with his body.

Lying next to him in the darkness, I elected to think that I had only pretended to be shocked by Félix's photographs. I had wanted to make it clear that I was interested neither in his merchandise nor in him. Relieved by his unobtrusiveness, I now told myself that I had been very lonely and that I should welcome his company. His resourcefulness would complement my lack of it. Why had I neither questioned Lonchat's right to forbid me even the most discreet excursion into Rodecin nor asked for the smallest additional service? Why had I not used the money hidden in the *lambris* to procure me some modest diversions to alleviate the monotony? I wanted nothing more than a few books of a less dusty flavour than the history I was reading and whose partiality so infuriated me that it was, in fact, the only thing I really enjoyed about it.

It occurred to me now that the silent figure breathing next to me contained a volume of experiences and abilities which I might explore with profit. During my solitude, I had been more interested in general, outside events than in my own prospects. I was keener to guess what was happening on the war fronts than to speculate on whom I might marry, or kiss. I did not dwell on the circumstances whereby I might lose the virginity which irked but did not plague me. Since I had no comrades whose initiation might draw attention to my puerility, I felt no urgency to be done with it. Madame Lonchat's bosom provided a supple target for fantasies which, on account of her general lack of attraction, excited no more sticky urges.

I was more anxious about the interruption of my schooling than about anything else. I had sought to retain what I learnt from Monsieur Picpus by attempting to reproduce his plan of the Sullan constitution, which I did with some ease. I now had the fantasy of educating Félix by adopting the magisterial role which would require me to revise all the lessons I feared I might forget. Having already lost most of one year, it seemed that I should be into my twenties before I went to university. Should I ever have time for one of the *grandes écoles* without which it would be difficult to get into the public service? My apprehensions savoured of hypocrisy, since – even to myself – I was pretending to a greater disappointment than, in some department of my heart, I genuinely felt. Yet it would be an alarming liberation to be left behind in the race for postwar preferment in a Paris which, I suspected, would be largely similar, in its formal structures, to the one in which my father had made his career. The freedom to be something else led me to wonder what else I could possibly be. When I tried to imagine a braver new world, in which radical revisions, if not a wholesale revolution, had taken place, I could only wonder how I might survive in some new system which was not favourable to my class and did not disqualify those with ruder gifts than mine.

Why had I shuffled Félix's photographs together so hastily and handed them back to him? On reflection, the participants were like fellow travellers whose invitation to join them had been too haughtily rejected (I thought of my two tarts, even though they had lacked *Boule de Suif*'s open-handedness). When I ran the photographic images past my mind's eye, they seemed to flicker to life. For some reason, I fastened my desire on the woman in the straw hat. She was unimaginable as a virgin; her pout had never been a stranger to sex. Her easy flesh made her both fascinating and disturbing. She might not think of other, more capable men when she was under me, but I suspected that I should. The dread of such comparisons would inhibit my desire for her, yet it was the lure of them which made her desirable.

I then thought of the blonde. I saw the lick of wetted hair which stood for the forbidden way the cropped man had ridden her. In one case, she was straddled over the black-haired woman, and yet seemed to be her victim. Even the desire I could see excited in her was a tax she paid. Of course, I imagined being her generous redeemer; my wad of money gave me rights which I should never exercise without her sincere agreement. This noble version was overprinted with a darker one, of greater piquancy, in which only when she was riding me, and so became my exacting judge, could I conceive her being the woman of my life. There was a relentless greed in my projections. I seemed to be galloping through my life in a way which I wanted to restrain! I was eating the menu rather than the food it advertised.

I tried to deny the link I forged between the blonde girl and my sister. Having always recoiled from Louise's sexual maturity, I could not now help retrieving whatever buried snapshots of her my memory could provide. Their sly accuracy promised an interest I had always scorned: a new breast gleamed through the armhole of a summer dress; her dressing gown fell aside to reveal the sheen of her plumping thighs; the pollen on her forearms, even the pinkness of an eyelid and the blue-whiteness of her eye as I tried to dab out a fleck of straw with a corner of my handkerchief, all these things came back to me, coloured and enlarged by some process I was powerless to interrupt.

When I tried to think of other things, I turned back again to my vision of Louise at our last meeting. I saw that it was her desires, not social convention or daughterly duty, which made her tease me, and herself, with the idea of marriage. Until Félix arrived, I had been baffled by her almost playful attitude to my slightly heroic gesture. I realised now how much she envied my facile, male exit. I could see her as we drove along the N10 towards Angoulême, the summer before the war, and I knew that she was watching and not watching men relieving themselves by the side of the road, while their women waited in the cars and did patient things. The escape from domesticity which I had achieved through one act of wanton display, she could manage only through submission to domesticity itself. Unless she wanted to be a whore, she would have to be a wife. Her threat of marriage, to someone whom she did not yet know, was her only means of matching my showier, but shallow, defiance. She would be a bride as I was an exile; she could go too far only at the same time as going nowhere at all. Convention could serve desires, even as desires subverted convention. Oh Louise, Louise!

The rhythm of Félix's puppy breath made me aware of his whole body. Like other effects of his arrival, it was more enlightening than he could possibly have intended. No one could have been less intrusive; he seemed to sip the air for fear of taking too much of it. The sound of him recalled the way sounds travelled along the beams of La Fontaine: Fritz and Gertrud came alive in my ears. I heard her muted encouragements and Fritz's yelp of rapture. And then, with involuntary curiosity, I rehearsed the silences of my childhood. How was it that the house never telegraphed a hint of my parents' connubial activity? Until that night, I had rejoiced in my exemption from unwanted knowledge. If I was not so naive as to suppose that they had renounced sexual relations, I had certainly been naive enough to presume that they must still have them. Félix's photographs robbed my family of their privileged clothing. They stripped and pitched them into a common pool where nothing they did was unthinkable. Layer after layer of protection drifted or was torn away from them. Was I dreaming? My dreams were ideas, not visions. After thinking of Louise, whose heat made her embrace the idea of a husband, as if he were already worth having, whoever he might turn out to be, I began to consider my mother. Had she too found marriage a quick cloak for desires so reckless that only decorum could assuage them? I seemed to be swallowed into her and to lie, like some minuscule spy, in her unsprung womb, conscious even in the secret years before my conception. Had she had a lover? (My God, had Louise?) Did I care? Had he been my father? I could not imagine what I imagined.

XIX

Have I given the impression that I am a man without genuine human warmth and that I am trying to excuse my lack of ordinary affection? The truth is that I am in many ways, so far as I can judge, an affectionate father and, in the right circumstances, a considerate lover. I am not complaining when I say that, for all sorts of reasons, my circumstances have been unusual and that my character has, presumably, been influenced by them. In writing this account of myself, I have no notion of giving a full picture of my life. The nicest parts do not trouble my memory as others do. Happiness is not a subject which excites my pen.

In another sort of book, I should speak more freely of my sons. My neglect of them here has nothing to do with indifference; I prefer to think that it derives from my respect for them and, perhaps, my fear of what they will think when they read what I have written, if they ever do. Patrick, my 'English' son, went to Cambridge; David, his senior, followed the French *cursus honorum*: first *Sciences Po'* and then *l'É.N.A.* They are both good tennis players and Patrick, in particular, has a social confidence and an easy manner which will, I am sure, make him a success in the diplomatic service. David is rather more solemn; he is unmarried and still a communicating Catholic.

As a father, I have been as assiduous as I believe I have been fond, but if I have given them as much of my time as I could, I cannot say that I was ever unguarded with my children. From very early on, my marriage revealed itself to be not at all what I had expected or Berthe had wanted. Our only recourse was to imposture; for the purposes of my career and her family, we pretended to mutual esteem. We did so with such courteous irony, at least in the presence of other people, that it created quite a bond between us. We were like actors in a play who, although they are personally indifferent to each other, are constrained by the theatre to display all the symptoms of passion without being encumbered by its emotions and who, as the run continues, begin to enjoy at least the success with which they deceive everyone except themselves. Occasionally Berthe and I so far forgot ourselves as to act as though impulse rather than imposture was keeping us together.

I can give an instance of the perverse thoughtfulness which could transform apathy into complicity. In the late 1960s I had reason to hope that I might be sent to Athens as Ambassador. It was the critical moment in my career, when I should switch ladders, so to speak, and have access to the highest levels of the service. Until then, I had been given interesting and sometimes delicate assignments, but I was never more than second or third in command. Having been un-officially advised of my imminent transfer to Athens, I was actually taking lessons in modern Greek, when the Colonels mounted their coup. This turn of events could not, of course, be attributed to any act of mine, but it blighted my prospects and, in the end, was probably responsible for my failure to achieve the highest positions. My mentor, Pierre-Henri Mercuès, explained to me that the reason for Gaston Ribette receiving the appointment reflected great credit on me. Ribette had been in the Middle East during the war and had rallied to de Gaulle only at the last minute, whereas I had been in the Resistance and had been decorated in the field, which hardly made me the right emissary to a group of Neo-Fascist collaborators (it is typical of diplomats that, off the record, we use extremely undiplo-matic language). Had I had a less good war, I should no doubt have been confirmed as Ambassador to Greece and would have progressed from there to Rome, London or Washington. I tried to convince Mercuès that I could dissemble as well as the next man, but he patted me on the shoulder and said, 'As well as Ribette? A little modesty, little one, please!'

The Colonels lasted long enough for Gaston to make a success of his posting. I am flattered that he continued, during his subsequently flourishing career, to do whatever he could, from time to time, to put in a bad word for me. Perhaps it was not entirely due to him that I was regarded as lacking in flexibility. If the Colonels had fallen swiftly and democracy had been restored, I might still have gone to Athens, but their tenacity established the shrewdness of Ribette's posting and somehow confirmed that mine would have been unfortunate. Although the Greek case was a particular one, the fact that I should have been a bad choice for Athens seemed to disqualify me elsewhere; I was never offered a major embassy. When, a few years later, I was told that Helsinki was available, if I wanted it, I did not feel the vocation. As a result, I passed my career in the shadow of men who were sometimes smaller than myself. I was not disgraced but my record was marked by an ineradicable 'touch of oil'.

I was disappointed not to go to Athens; the prospect of going there had rekindled my interest in the ancient world. David was then ten years old; I thought it unlikely that we would have another child and I had the sentimental idea that, if he were exposed to the Greek light, he might be interested in what I remembered of Monsieur Picpus' comparison between Pericles and Julius Caesar. The isles of Greece had a romantic hold on Berthe's imagination, which was also the repository of her grievances. She accused me of being secretly delighted that she was not going to get to see Naxos and Santorini and Mykonos. She had heard that there was a man in Mykonos who was known as 'the king of trousers'. What chance was there now of his ever making her a pair?

With a certain vindictiveness, I decided to take her to Greece for a holiday. David would have his experience of Hellas and she would get the trousers which would almost certainly not suit her. I should have the satisfaction of getting nothing that I wanted for myself.

Routine demanded that I tell my Ambassador in Damascus of our excursion; courtesy required that I call the Embassy in Athens on our arrival. The city was quiet, which was not its usual condition, so young Stanislaus Girard told us when he called at the hotel to make sure that there was nothing he could do for us. The tranquillity which seemed orderly to those who favoured the Colonels was against nature to those who despised them. For the moment, the majority seemed at least to accept the new régime, which had supposedly eliminated the old corruption (if only to instal the new) and had succeeded in tidying the streets. The absence of tourists gave us uncluttered access to the ruins and to the shops. Just as my mother would have, Berthe ignored the causes – and practices – of the 'National Revolution' and commented only on its effects, which she found admirable.

She discovered a dress shop in Ermou Street which made attractive and – in those days – innovatory use of pieces of old material 'from the islands'. Since it was expensive, Berthe had herself measured for a brocaded dress and a raw silk trouser suit with an antique waistcoat from Spetsai, which would have to be taken in. While a pretty girl with ancient eyes pinned her in the upstairs workroom and the proprietress unfurled further temptations, I waited downstairs. The proprietor was behind the till. When an American woman came in and pointed to a dress pinned on the wall, he pretended not to understand her inquiry. Finally she had to ask him in so many words. He said, 'The price is on the article, madam.'

'I just saw the same thing down the street,' she said. 'A third cheaper.'

He said, 'In that case, madam, go back down the street. It was not the same item, because this item is handmade. If you can't see the difference, I congratulate you.'

The woman said, 'Oh listen, how about coming down a little bit? Don't you want to make a sale?'

He said, 'The price is on the article, madam.'

He was quite tall for a Greek, but short in the leg. He looked too strong, in physique and character, for a shopkeeper. His eyes were narrowed as he spoke; his mouth was defined by the scorn which barbed his courtesy; his nose was lifted as if he could smell the unpleasantness to come. The woman looked around the shop for something to dislike, an excuse to be gone of her own accord. At the same time, she could tease the owner by seeming still to be in the market.

There was a display of icons and amber 'worry-beads' in an alcove. One of the icons was hardly bigger than a playing card, but it was subtly painted with the face of a haughty, ascetic saint who resembled the proprietor with his air of intangible aloofness. The woman picked it up and turned it over. 'Well, how much is this then, since it doesn't have a price?'

'That is not for sale, madam.'

'Then why is it in the shop?'

He said, 'Why are you in the shop, madam?'

She said, 'Did you say what you just said?'

'Of course.'

She wanted to do something more than walk out, but what was there? She looked to me to be her champion; I declined the honour. When she had gone, I picked up the little icon with the proud, remote face on it. 'It is a very nice one, though, isn't it?' I said.

He said, 'Do you like it? Take it!'

'Oh,' I said, 'I couldn't possibly do that.'

He said, 'That is the best possible reason for doing it.'

I said, 'Will you and your wife join us for dinner?'

He said, 'There is no need for that.'

'Isn't that the best possible reason for doing it?'

He held out his hand. 'Nikos Karavas.'

He had been a sea-captain before he met his wife, Ourania. She was trim and clever and she bore him four children, after which she was still clever, but no longer trim. He had given up the sea to make a home for her and the children, but he could not renounce his hunger for it; there was salt in his blood. Although I do not share my compatriots' obsession with boats, I sensed an affinity with Nikos so sudden and so surprising that I actually blushed when Berthe came down the stairs from the workroom and I had to explain that I had invited our new friends to dine with us. She and Ourania agreed to be amused by what had been arranged behind their backs; Nikos and I might have been children.

I asked him to select a restaurant. He gave me the address of a *taverna* in Kiphissia. We should have no difficulty in getting a taxi. We went back to the hotel and arranged for someone to listen for David, who was happy to go on reconstructing the walls of Mycenae from a 'push-out' book we had bought that afternoon. The *taverna* was rather smarter than I expected. Nikos was wearing a browny-grey suit and a dove-grey tie; Ourania was in a black and red suit of her own creation. I guessed that Nikos had chosen the restaurant to please Berthe; it seemed rather proper.

He was unsmilingly gratified by the praise with which we greeted the little dishes of *mezes* before the meal: 'You say they are good as if you assumed they would not be.' I was slightly distressed that our rapport had not been fully sustained; I felt that I was now being suspected of the condescension which Nikos' American customer had displayed. The two women, on the other hand, were whispering together with every sign of renewed intimacy. Ourania spoke French (her mother was from Alexandria), whereas Nikos and I had only our stilted English in common.

Nikos drank several glasses of ouzo and called for retsina with the moussaka, which was a speciality of the place. I made no attempt to match him drink for drink; I left that to Berthe. The drink and the money which she was spending in our guests' shop made her provocative. Having clinked a new glass with him, she demanded to know what Nikos thought of the Colonels. Ourania looked imploringly at me, as though we had suddenly become old friends. Was she afraid that the drink was stronger than Berthe knew?

'Ah,' Nikos said, 'you want to talk politics. *Ta politika.*' He said the Greek words loudly, less to instruct us than to alert the people at the next table.

Ourania said, 'Nikolaki . . .'

He talked politics. He talked politics loudly. Although he did so in English, the weight of his words fell with unmistakable insolence on the ears of the army officer at the next table. The officer's companions wore rightist moustaches and new suits, which suggested that they might only recently have been promoted to civilian importance. Their warning glances merely encouraged Nikos to render his sentiments into Greek. He spoke, in a soft, educational tone of treason and of shame. He paused only to translate for Berthe's benefit before he resumed his lisping derision. He ironised about the aesthetic finesse of censors who had banned plays which had been the glory of Athens for two and a half thousand years. He denounced the putsch not in the name of any political faction but in the name of 'something as contemptible as common decency'. The whole restaurant began to hear him, not because his voice was raised but because others fell silent.

It was as if Nikos had elected to cross above the diners on a high wire. They were torn between the hope that he would do so without falling (at least on them) and the sly wish to witness a catastrophe. He announced that he understood the sudden need for people to hide their faces in their napkins; such concern for their families was an honourable cowardice. People began to sweat; a few smiled, un-prettily. Nikos congratulated the army officers on their new uniforms. Had they been at Thermopylae? How was Leonidas and why had they not died there with him? Years ago Greeks were not promoted for enslaving other Greeks.

Finally, Ourania pushed her plate away. She felt ill; might we leave?

'Before our friends have had some *loukoumia*? Is this Greek hospitality, Ourania? And then coffee! We must have some Turkish coffee, mustn't we, to celebrate our new *entente* with our new friends across the Aegean? Did you not see the photograph of one of our highly intelligent leaders shaking hands with a sentry from across the frontier? It was in one of our newspapers, which is at last free to print what is really good for us. Such an improvement on the truth!'

Berthe was flushed with a sense of Nikos' hectic daring, although she could not fully understand what it involved. She took her cue, like the rhythm of her drinking, from him. She drank to Christian Greece and to the new airport; she drank to the army and its honour and to the King and his wisdom. I covered my glass; it was the only way that I could sympathise with Ourania, whose face had blanched to marble.

Nikos said many things. No policeman came. No one ordered him to be silent. The rightists tried to start a conversation, but were quenched by a low, almost inaudible hissing that came from mouths which dared not open; the sound was of the most timid imaginable bravado. I admired Nikos' performance with wholehearted uneasi-ness. I suspected that he had planned it from the beginning; he had chosen the restaurant because it would contain people whom he despised. How serious a risk did he run? And why did he run it? Ourania was the only person in the room who appeared seriously distressed. For the rest of them, Nikos had gone so far that his improvisation was a kind of jazz, a solo turn so superb and so individual that there was nothing to be done but to leave him alone. He was a new Prometheus whose anguish and pride were indistinguishable and to whom no one need do anything more than leave him to his suffering.

When he had punished his wife almost to the point of suffocation, Nikos called for the bill. I objected; I was the host. Nikos was cold and drunk; he would not have a foreigner buy his dinner in Greece. As I insisted, a man in a dark suit, with the rosette of the *Légion d'Honneur* in his lapel, came across the restaurant and put his hand on my sleeve. He heaped banknotes on the bill, shook my hand and that of Nikos, bowed to our women, and went back to his corner. Nikos said, 'You are a lucky man, my friend.'

We said goodbye on the pavement without thanks, since none were due. Ourania told my wife that the clothes would be ready in the morning: 'In Greece, we work at night.' In the taxi, Berthe began to cry. She recovered by the time we reached the Hotel Grande Bretagne.

As we went into the lobby, where a string orchestra was playing cosy music, I said, 'Interesting man.'

She said, 'You should have married him.'

Nikos was not in the shop when we went for Berthe's final fitting before taking the boat to Mykonos. Ourania saw that the new clothes were properly packed with tissue paper and serious knots and we went straight to Piraeus.

Once we were on Mykonos, Berthe soon found the 'king of trousers'. She preferred to drink coffee in his bright workshop rather than to come to Delos with me and David. She also declined to come to the beach, after the first time, saying that it seemed to be reserved for men. When I asked her if she wanted to leave, she said that she was happy to stay for a month. I tried to be flattered by the care she was taking to make me uneasy.

David and I went swimming. Between swims, we kicked a ball until we were too hot not to go back into the water. It was tepid and rather shallow and one had to be careful of spine-fish. It was difficult to be carefree. I tried to tell David about ancient Athens and the Delian league, but he decided that he would sooner go back to the hotel. Did I mind?

As we sauntered along the sand, a tall man, thick-chested and handsomely grizzled, was approaching us. He was toting an inflated mattress over his shoulder along the shoreline. He was followed by a fair-haired boy so tanned that his hair looked like a linen cap. The man must have been in his late fifties (he seemed old to me then); his strut boasted that he owned the slim boy who followed literally – and a little naughtily perhaps – in his footsteps. As the man strolled past me, I could see that he had a deep scar in his side, just below the ribs.

David said, 'Are you all right, Dad?'

I said, 'I'm hot, that's all.'

'We'll soon be home,' he said.

Why did I tell Berthe about the man and his slim slave? The mattress which he was carrying somehow reminded me of Herakles with some prize over his shoulder. Perhaps I had no more malicious motive than to amuse my wife. To make her smile was the kind of uphill work which amounted almost to taking exercise; I felt good after it. I needed to display a little cunning in order to convey to Berthe what the man was, without saying so in words which would offend our son's innocence.

That evening after dinner, Berthe wanted to try on her new trousers, which had been delivered while we were eating our *pilaffi*. She said they fitted perfectly; I thought them very tight. Perhaps it was the same thing. The material carried black and white stripes. 'He calls them Buchenwalds,' Berthe said. Since I was not amused, I smiled.

We walked from the hotel enclosure along the quay to the steamer office, in order to check the times of the sailings to Santorini, even though we knew them. The big, grizzled man came out of a taverna and ambled towards us, accompanied by a vivacious old woman who should have been a headmistress. He was wearing a blazer with gilt buttons and white trousers. She was complaining, in English, about the way this dreadful little man had been sticking something into his donkey. The man nodded to me.

Berthe said, 'He recognised you.'

I said, 'His mother, do you suppose? Do you think she knows?'

Berthe said, 'Women usually do. *I* do.'

'And what exactly do you know?'

She said, 'How to make you angry. Don't I?'

I said, 'I'm not in the least angry.'

'How to make you tell lies,' she said.

We looked in the window of the office, which confirmed what we did not doubt, and then Berthe said she wanted a drink. She wanted several. She drank them in the face of my patient displeasure; I knew it would please her. After she had crossed her new striped legs, in a way which made me fear for the seams, she said, 'What do they do to them, those men, to their creatures?'

I said, 'You know very well.'

'Do I?' she said. 'Well, I want you to tell me.'

I said, 'You don't need me to do that.'

She let her leg ride up and down. 'Guy,' she said, 'these may be the isles of Greece, but I'm not sure that you're the man for them.'

I said, 'I'm going to take you back to the hotel now.'

She said, 'To do what?'

I said, 'I'll tell you when we get there.'

I put money on the table and then I walked ahead of her along the quay with my jacket over my shoulder. I hardly know how to express what I felt or intended. It was one of my rare moments of possession, when I both knew what I wanted and was determined to have it. Berthe was the sole object of my desire and at the same time quite incidental to it.

I collected the key and walked up the single flight of stairs to our room. I went through the door first. She said, 'Guy, I want to see that David's all right.'

'All right.' I was quite polite. When she came back to our room, I said, 'Was he?'

'Of course.'

I said, 'Now I want you to kneel on the bed.'

She said, 'Oh Guy, what do you mean?'

I showed her. 'With your head on the pillow.'

She said, 'And then what happens?'

I said, 'You'll find out, won't you?'

She said, 'At least be careful of my trousers. Don't you want me to take them off?'

I said, 'That's the whole point, if you must know.'

She said, 'They're brand new, you maniac.'

I said, 'The seam was going anyway. And you can always get him to make you another pair, can't you?'

'I shall have to,' she said. 'You are disgusting, aren't you? You're going to hurt me.'

'Not if you're a help,' I said. 'You can decide.'

'There's one thing you're not going to do, I hope you know that.'

'I'm glad you know what it is,' I said.

And that was how we made our 'English' son.

XX

'Are you awake?'

'I've been awake most of the night,' I said, 'and now you've woken me up.'

Félix said, 'I've brought the breakfast.' He put the unpolished wooden tray on the bed. My usual diet was scorched stale bread. On Sundays, Madame Lonchat gave me thin, sour rhubarb jam to go with it. I saw that there was a saucer of it between the bowls of 'coffee', although it was only Thursday. 'I thought it looked a bit dry.'

I said, 'Who arranged for you to come here?'

'That'd be telling, wouldn't it? Would you like to see something?' His long pyjama trousers covered his feet, except for the big toes. 'Something someone gave me before I left Paris?'

'Not more pictures, I hope?'

'I'll never show them to you again. I thought perhaps having been alone all this time, you might like a bit of fun. Now I know better, don't I?' He was lifting the damson-coloured suitcase onto the bed. After extracting a show of sweaters and shirts, he found what he was looking for, wrapped in layers of newspaper. I was skimming flecks of skin from my bowl with the back of my spoon. 'Not bad, eh?' He held up a pair of silk underpants, with an elasticated waist. 'Not bad at all for wartime?' The newspaper that fell from them to the floor was German. 'I've got three pairs!'

'Pansy pants, I'd say.' Did I mean to hurt him? Did I really believe that there existed a category of person corresponding to the term I used? Perhaps it was a measure of my innocence that I could be so merciless. Or did the German newspaper prime my cruelty?

Félix said, 'I don't like that way of talking.'

I spread jam. 'Who gave you that stuff?'

'Do you really want to know?'

'Why else would I ask?'

'Because you think I want to tell you. A German officer. A major.'

'A lot of Germans use the Royal-Concorde these days, I imagine.'

'Nothing but,' he said. 'Do you masturbate?'

I had my bowl to my lips. It was hot. I said, 'Rarely before breakfast. Never during it.'

'Do things happen in your sleep?'

I said, 'How come you had to leave Paris so fast?'

'I suppose they happen in everybody's. Unless they happen before. Why did he give them to me?'

'I didn't ask you that.'

'You assume things. You shouldn't. Personally, I distinguish between the man and the uniform. Rudi was very . . .' Félix was a schoolboy seeking the right word from a meagre store. 'He was very *correct*. Once someone isn't what he is in public, I don't think about it any more. Am I wrong?'

I said, 'Who knows?'

He said, 'I thought you might.' He enjoyed his dry bread and rhubarb jam. He liked the coffee. He gave me a lesson in simple pleasures. 'A lot of people think we're disgusting. I expect you do too.'

I said, 'Would you like me to teach you chess?'

'And what shall I teach you in return?'

'You could always tell me a bit more about yourself. I expect that would be an education in itself.'

Félix said, 'Have you ever had a woman?'

'Unfortunately not.'

'If you haven't had it,' he said, 'you probably miss it, don't you?'

I drew the sheet of squared paper from under the bed and set out the chess pieces I had made. 'How did you come to work in a hotel?'

'I had an uncle, didn't I?' He might have been having a joke with a third party who was invisible to me. 'Chess! You seem to be in a big hurry. Is it that much of a thrill?'

As I started to explain the purpose of the game and the forms of mobility peculiar to the various pieces, I could hear the thinness of my patience turning to pedantry. I recognised how unlikeable I was making myself. Félix listened with good humour, as if he believed that my long preamble must lead to something worth knowing. The more he smiled, the less I did. 'As you can see,' I said, 'it's a game of almost limitless possibilities, once you get the hang of it.'

'Those photographs,' he said, while I was reminding him what castles could do, 'they came as news to you, did they?'

'I thought we'd agreed to let that subject drop.'

'Is it at all amusing, this game?'

'It's the game of games,' I said. 'There's no end to its subtlety.'

'But is there any beginning to its fun?'

'Look,' I said, 'we're stuck in this room together. We may as well find something we can do together.'

'This is the queen, right?'

'This is the king; that's the queen. She's more powerful than he is. Much. You don't want to lose your queen, or you're likely to be done for. On the other hand, the king is crucial: if he gets trapped – checkmated – that's the end of the game. You can lose as many pieces as you like, you're not beaten until your king is cornered.'

Félix said, 'Imagine if I was a girl, would you be teaching her chess?'

I said, 'That would depend on the girl.'

'I think you probably would.' He seemed again to share the joke with the invisible third person with whose complicity I felt myself to be outnumbered, even though there were only two of us in the room. 'That's the king and that's the queen. And that's the bishop going slantwise.'

I said, 'What made you come to this particular house? That's the thing I'd like to know.'

'And the knight goes . . . is that right? I was sent. They said this was where to come till things cooled down a bit.' He moved the chesspieces in a way which showed both what he remembered and what he could not be bothered to learn. I waited for his silly solitary game to end, but he managed to continue. His brow was contracted in a parody of concentration. He looked at me and jumped one piece over another and landed on a third, with a clack, before removing it. He made chess into draughts and my lesson into an excuse for foolery which he took to be entertaining. I fought not to smile. I was seriously angry, but he was droll.

I went to the window and surveyed Lonchat as he tramped in and out of the *atelier*. I craved my life with Fritz and wounded myself with the idea that he had tired of my company. At the same time, I took painful pleasure in the fear that I had betrayed him. I had not only failed to keep him at La Fontaine, I had also gloried in an immunity he could never share. Gazing through the uneven lens of Lonchat's window (the little *menuisier* was now a giant, now a dwarf, according to the pane I saw him through), I wanted Fritz and me to have been the agents of our own divorce. While I recognised that he had been swept away by something neither of us could have resisted, severally or together, my vanity shaped a past for us in which my vindictiveness and his infidelity were cardinal. I created a lost love for myself, while Félix played games behind my back.

I reflected that Félix was never going to suffer Fritz's fate. He was a swimmer who would always emerge from any tide with a cheerful shake of those saleable curls. My mental menu of his sexual services proved how specifically his photographs had instructed my imagination. Although the participants in them were not necessarily his personal acquaintances, my fancy recruited them to a life continuous with his. The cropped man and Félix's 'correct' major became identical; the blonde girl was his sister, unless she was Félix himself in some elastic revision.

Our landlord was loading his wagonette with finished work. From the dry shape of his lips I guessed that he was whistling without enthusiasm, in order to give the impression that he was carefree. At the same time, he would glance around him with perky apprehension. I was reminded of the chickens at Le Prieuré, when they strutted and pecked and then went into panicky flurries, as if Marité's baleful glance had reminded them of their unreliable lease on mortality.

A man in a black beret leaned his bicycle against the rusty gate. He came into the yard quite as if the place were empty and he was considering its value; he had eyes which added things up. As Lonchat emerged again from the *atelier*, carrying a slatted dish-dryer nailed onto long legs, the man called out a question I could not hear. Lonchat's feet stammered; I fancied that he was uncertain whether to make ground towards the stranger (and seem anxious) or whether, by failing to do so, he ran the risk of appearing surly. His hesitation was touching; I could see that he was a man who weighed and then took risks. I had no notion that he was not venal, but I could still admire the quality of his bluff as he temporised with a scratch of his head and an answer which did its best but did not quite meet the question, whatever it was. If the man in the beret was a policeman, as I assumed, he seemed satisfied. Before leaving, he felt obliged to come across the yard and shake Lonchat's hand. My landlord grinned and shrugged, apparently apologising for being only as helpful as limited knowledge permitted.

When the man in the beret had wheeled his bicycle out of the gate, Lonchat tilted his face towards the pale disc of the sun as it thinned the morning mist and borrowed a little of its radiance. I admired him without gratitude; for some fatuous reason, I took the view that he had saved Félix from discovery rather than me. I had been preserved only from guilt. He put his leg over his bicycle and went, in his unhurried, wide-kneed way, out towards the street, with the same dry whistle between his chapped lips.

'Come on then,' Félix said. 'Teach me this game of yours, if you have to. And then maybe I can teach you one of mine.'

He became a surprisingly docile pupil. His bright response to my tuition made me wonder why I had remained so aloof from Louise. I began to feel ashamed of what I had always taken to be my tact in not trying to help my sister with her lessons. Her beauty had contrasted so favourably with my uncomely adolescence that I had been happy to think that my mind at least was better shaped than hers.

My initial displeasure with Félix made it easier to be at home with him. I was the master; he was my class. My mission was to complete his education. To conceal my aversion became my sweet and secret duty. That I did not want him in my life was part of what made his presence strangely delightful. Was I sincere when, after several days, I announced that he was making real progress? When he nodded, did it mean that he believed me? We victimised each other, I daresay, with more resourceful tenderness (and malice) than could have been contrived between equals.

I continued to dread the nights, however, when – after his invariably thorough wash – Félix would put on his outsize pyjamas and get into our bed. I always allowed him to do so first. I had the idea that a woman waited in bed for a man and that it was then up to him to decide whether or not to make advances to her. Having contrived, apparently through courtesy, that Félix never join me, but that I always joined him, I was protected from what I dreaded – not so much the assertion of his desires, if he had them, as the denial of my right to resist them.

Was he unaware of my determination to play the part of the indifferent husband? He neither adopted coquettish poses nor did he sigh, even faintly, when I took my place beside him and, leaving the maximum distance between us, turned my back and fell asleep as quickly as possible. His show of matching indifference was not entirely pleasing. If I dreaded the touch of his manicured fingers (his suitcase proved to contain matching scissors and clippers in a pigskin case whose loan I refused), his steady respect for my chastity denied me repeated opportunities to reject him.

By becoming his teacher, I was able to assume a dominance which became more demanding as the days passed. I tried to infect him with an appetite for the game more enthusiastic than mine; it amused me to play Fritz while Félix played me. My wish for him to catch the infection was sharpened by the power I should then have of being able to disappoint him, if I chose, by withholding further tuition.

In this way, Fritz became part of our games. If I suspected Félix of having his secret companion (to whom, when scolded for a feeble or inattentive move, he would address little shrugs and *moues*), I could counter him with mine, whom he did not suspect at all. Am I complicating those days in confinement with Félix and Brute (as I designated his invisible minder)? How real at the time were those imaginary presences? More real than the embarrassed memory cares to confess! Were it not so, I might have been able to shuck the long influence of my time in Rodecin. If the fear of an understanding between Brute and Fritz had not haunted my seclusion, should I ever have become the doubly wary person I am?

The impalpable nature of my dread was both my shame and my consolation. I recognised the absurdity of being more dismayed by the intimacy between Fritz's phantom and the invisible Brute than by the actual fate of my deported friend. How much would Fritz ever have meant to me, even when I was actually playing chess with him in the little room behind the Chapel of the White Penitents, had there not been something daring in my association with a marked man? The kind of friendship of which Félix's talk, and his photographs, had made me conscious did not, I was sure, have any relevance to what I had felt for Fritz. His absence filled me with an emotion which could have had no practical expression, if those dark jowls and flaring cheeks had come to share my quarters. My love, such as it was, was limited to what was reliably beyond my grasp.

One afternoon, when I had been teaching Félix a slightly more ambitious endgame (bishop, knight, pawn and rook against three pawns and two bishops), he made a move which varied my prescription. I invited him to think again. He raised his choirboy eyes to mine and the black irises gleamed with impudent contentment. He pointed a manicured finger at the board. 'All yours, maestro!'

I considered the position and squirmed and smiled; he appeared to have me, but I wanted him to think that it was by my design. I gazed at the position with waning confidence that I could escape. I imagined Brute smirking at Fritz and Fritz shaking his head in connivance at my defeat rather than supplying me with the neat trick I needed. My desperate situation pleased him; he joined Brute in contempt not only for me but even for chess itself. The treacherous swine had accepted membership of a club which was defined by my exclusion.

I searched the empty pockets of my mind for a solution which would make fools of all three of my adversaries. Chess is a devilish sport; everything is patent and yet there are bluffs and deceptions, traps and tricks. My bishop had been cornered by Félix's fluky wit. Now, although it was only a postponement of what should have been inevitable, I staved off its loss by checking his king with my knight. He had only to make a simple withdrawal, but he was guileless enough to capture my knight with a pawn, whose capture in turn retrieved my position and made his hopeless. Within a few moves, I was in command of the board.

He said, 'I had you, didn't I?'

'You had me and you let me go. After supper, if you like, I'll show what you should have done. You could've had me in four.'

He said, 'I'm thinking of maybe going out. I've had an invitation.'

'How?' I said. 'And how can you go out?'

'Don't you ever want to do anything except play chess?'

'What else is there?'

'What about wrestling? Don't you ever want to do something physical?'

'I don't know anything about wrestling,' I said.

'No? I know a bit. Get down on the floor.'

I said, 'Isn't it noisy?'

'Put the blanket down. It might come in useful. So what's the idea? The idea is to pin the other guy to the mat. All methods are good! Like for instance . . .' He had turned me over abruptly and slammed me gently onto the blanket, his weight across my chest. 'There are good moves and bad moves and fluky moves and clever moves. Chess with bodies is all it is!'

I said, 'I don't want the Lonchats up here, that's all.' Did he let me flip him over or did I surprise us both by the strength with which I unhorsed him against the washstand and had my knee on his biceps? 'Who taught you? The major?'

'I've come up the hard way. Get off me, will you?' As soon as I let him up, Félix reached for the comb he kept beside our washbasin. 'You have to learn how to defend yourself if the system doesn't do it for you.'

'This major,' I said, 'what did you do with him?'

'What he wanted.'

I said, 'You're not really thinking of going out, are you? Because that could land both of us in it.'

He said, 'I wouldn't do that to you, would I? I can stay at home though, if you like. I was thinking I might make a few useful contacts.'

I said, 'That's your real game, isn't it?'

He said, 'You want me to say it, don't you? The thing you don't want me to say: what my real game is. Which you know very well. Making you what? Apart from a hippopotamus?'

'The major,' I said. 'He's what it's all about, isn't he, you being here. Did he pay for you to come? Or did something else happen?'

Félix said, 'Don't think I couldn't have defended myself!'

I said, 'Did you rob him or did you betray him, or did you do both?'

He said, 'And I was just beginning to like you!'

'Isn't that always what precedes betraying people?'

He said, 'Is that what you want?'

I said, 'How are you aiming to get past the Lonchats?'

'What do they care? You want to make jailers out of them because that excuses you being a coward. I've got friends, even if you haven't. How come? Because I trust people even if you don't. Are you afraid I'll split on you? I won't. But worry about it if it keeps you warm! I'll tell you what, when I do go out – I'll see if I can find a proper chessboard. That paper of yours isn't exactly classy, is it? Anything else Mother would like?'

'I wouldn't mind a good book,' I said, 'if you get as far as the library.'

'You're not such a bad type.' He flexed his fingers. 'I'll see what I can subtilise, shall I?'

'Are you a thief?'

'Have I ever stolen anything? Sure. What about you?'

'I don't think I have. What did you steal?'

'Nothing I've got here, if that's what you're hoping. Unless you include the sheet we're sleeping on. But that was part of my wages really. I sometimes took things people left behind. You'd be amazed what they do. You can find people that way as well as objects of value. I once discovered this old auntie, sitting in the bathroom with a towel around his shoulders. She'd gone; he'd stayed. You dry their tears, you pull their whatsits. Do you think it's wrong to make people happy and maybe get tipped for it?'

I said, 'Did you know any of the people in those photographs?'

'Rudi bought them for me. Rue Grégoire de Tours.'

'Rudi being the major?'

'When in uniform. He bought them for himself and then he gave them to me. Anything else you want to know before I bugger off?'

'A great deal,' I said. 'Like, does he know where you are?'

'He doesn't know anything,' Félix said. 'Have you got any money?'

I said, 'What do you need money for?'

'The books, possibly. Are you afraid I'm going to steal it, is that it, and you don't want me to know where you keep it? Do you ever wonder why you have such a low opinion of other people? Because I've got the answer: you don't think much of yourself finally, do you? What happened was, they asked my help because I was the only person who could do what they wanted.' He was a boy soldier all of a sudden, standing at attention but with his chin puckering with unexpressed tears. 'I was thanked personally by someone on the

Central Committee. Now tell me what you think I did. You won't even come close.'

'Presumably you gave them Rudi.'

'And that's what you think of me, is it? No wonder I'm going out.' He licked a finger and smoothed his eyebrows, daring me not to be amused. 'If you were any fun, I wouldn't do it, would I?'

I said, 'Fun isn't everything.'

He said, 'In your case, sweetheart, I have to tell you – fun is strictly nonexistent.'

XXI

After Berthe had detached herself from me and walked on out through the automatic glass doors of the Roman apartment house, I neither pursued her nor did I press the button for the lift. I stood in the greenish marble lobby in a frenzy of inertia. My mind raced to catch and abuse her; my hands were ready to rip the white showercoat from her shoulders and do something hurtful to her. I could imagine how she would realise, as I threw her into the gutter, how thoroughly she had misjudged me. She might be impressed by the ruthlessness of my assault.

As I waited for her to come back, a camouflaged door opened in the back wall and Nando, our squat Neapolitan concierge, stepped into the lobby. He wore the peaked cap and brass-buttoned livery which he donned for night duty. He must have switched on the wall-lights behind the scenes; they flickered and then steadied in their sconces as if saluting his advent. My face must have flickered and steadied with them; Nando looked at me as if I might be having some kind of an attack, although he had supplied the symptoms. 'Are you all right, Excellency?'

'Perfectly, Nando, thank you.' He flattered me with his ambassadorial apostrophe more to inflate his own importance than in deference to mine. 'I'm just waiting for my wife.'

'I think she just went out,' he said.

'That's precisely why I'm waiting for her.'

He looked away and dropped his jaw. He might have been sharing his bewilderment with a concealed confederate. 'I understand, Excellency.'

Nando's puzzlement confirmed me in my patient posture. He had granted me a motive for it, by being its witness. I was like a woman who, once she is confident of an observer's attention, can ignore his presence with every sign of conviction. My performance rendered Nando manifestly invisible, which inspired me to think again of Félix, whom I wished to forget, and of my uncle, whom I could not.

I married Berthe with a sense of relief and even of gratitude, not so much to her personally as to the seemingly providential circumstances under which she was presented to me. Was it not a happy fate which contrived that she should be at La Fontaine du Noyer on both occasions when I returned there? Her family were cousins of cousins and they had sent her for safekeeping to my mother. She was, in a sense, under our patronage. Although her parents were richer and grander than mine, she had the rudiments of an orphan in a fairy tale, with whom it was both romantic and (in this instance) rewarding to fall in love. Having come in haste from Rouen, where she was in danger from allied bombers, she arrived in a state of attractive – because temporary – destitution. When I first saw her, she was wearing one of my mother's old dresses.

I agreed to play the lover's part without remarking the want of those emotions which might have been required to add ardour to my case, had things been less easy to arrange. Politeness was assumed to mask a passion which, for the present, did not need to show its face. As for Berthe, because she was quiet, I took her to be shy; because she was not beautiful, I knew that she must be intelligent. Since she had lived through the war without being touched by it, I took her innocence for granted. What better partner could there be for a young man who had endured heroic days without himself being a hero? (As I shall explain, I was given more credit for bravery than my actions warranted.)

For the moment, it is enough to say that our marriage came at the right time. So opportune was it that I accepted the arrangments with a yawn that was indistinguishable from eagerness. 'Whenever you like, Mama,' I could hear myself saying, with the implication that the substance was infinitely more desirable to me than the ceremony. In fact, the alacrity with which I went to the altar with Berthe was the measure of my indifference to her. It did not occur to me that my dissimulation could conceivably be matched by hers; she was a well brought up young girl, with money and a name, on whose unmarked wax I was certain that no impression had yet been scored.

The ghost of freedom stayed alive in me precisely on account of the relief I felt that I was about to marry a girl for whom I had no precise feelings at all. I observed her with a tender facsimile of impatience; I deceived her without lies. She pleased me because I seemed to please her, which perhaps reciprocated the deception, though I never suspected it. Her style was amenable and eager at the same time; she was happy to ride, she was happy to walk. Strange as it may seem, I did not pay great attention to her body; there was nothing displeasing about it, but I did not speculate about her legs or her breasts. My lack of desire made a gentleman of me.

When my father asked me whether I really wanted to marry Berthe, he did so in a quizzical way which led me to assure him that I wanted nothing more. I offered this assurance in a surly tone, quite as if it were an act of rebelliousness. My acquiescence in the family's plans felt like the betrayal of an allegiance which I had not sufficiently proclaimed. The war was being wiped too promptly from the board, leaving only a faintly coloured smudge, more nostalgic than terrible. I was reminded of the dusty stain of the Sullan constitution when the time came for it to be replaced on Monsieur Picpus' blackboard by the more durable reforms of Augustus.

My father had been asked, early in 1945, to return to Paris as head of the private office of the minister, later to be my friend the Academician, who had rallied to de Gaulle's appeal at the first hour, when few others had even heard it. 'He seemed an unlikely man to burn his boats,' my father observed, 'but I daresay he had found that they were not seaworthy. He had a Jewish mistress, you know. One can get rid of wives, but not of mistresses; they, after all, indicate a choice rather than a transaction. Should I have gone to London, I wonder?'

I said, 'Your reputation seems to be safe.'

'Your mother would like the apartment back. I gather it was the scene of quite interesting activities. We may find it better furnished than when we left it.'

I said, 'There's nothing like stolen property to make one feel that one has done something worthwhile, is there?'

He said, 'So . . . our young cousin . . . you think she's the right girl, do you?'

I said that I thought she was just the girl I needed in postwar France. I meant my parody of his own manner to indicate that I was conscious of the social trap into which I was walking. In this way, I convinced him, and myself, that I was not in reality about to be trapped by it.

We were walking in the shade of the chestnut alley. The leaves were still sticky, like the *dragées* which Simone was again licensed to make. My father turned off, between the trees, halfway down the drive and went deliberately into the big field which had belonged to Cabanne. His deviation seemed both casual and callous; it was harmless and it made me see him in a new, cold light. It asked me to endorse the official view of an affair so petty that, in view of the great events which were now drawing to a close, it would be finicky to dwell on it. The field had not been ours and now was; I was being advised to accept the dividends of war without squeamishness. In a way, Berthe was among them.

As we reached the earthen track at the bottom of the valley, my father said, 'In the last analysis, it doesn't matter whom one marries, does it? As long as it's the right person.'

Until that day, his aphorisms had always seemed the very stuff of maturity. His civilised ruefulness had marked him, more than office or title, as a grown man. His latest remark sounded like one of the expected series, but all of a sudden it smacked of pleading, not stoicism. He wanted me to promise that he had missed nothing by marrying my mother and that what he hoped had been good enough for him was as good as anyone could hope. He seemed, quite abruptly, to ask me to look on my mother's nakedness, and perhaps on his, and to sympathise with something I was still unwilling to acknowledge. I had always taken his wit as a specific against the sentimental; now it was like alum on the tongue, both tasteless and shrivelling. I said, 'I have no doubt you are right.'

He said, 'My marriage with your mother has given me more than I had any right to expect, which is, of course, quite what I expected of it.'

He dressed his anguish elegantly enough, but my glimpse of it in disarray was unnerving; the dandy's coat had sprung a tiny but irreparable hole. Without malice, I wished that he was dead. At the very moment when I looked to him for confirmation that it was possible to be a man by accepting that happiness was an illusion, he chose to admit that he could not quite endure its absence. If I had set a higher standard for him than I cared to observe myself, what else made him my father? I saw him now as someone who had been imposed upon rather than as a man who had deliberately constructed his life on the aristocratic disdain for personal gratification. The tiebeams of my life softened and yielded as if, all this time, termites had been gorging on them. There was no blinding light, but I winced at the garish sky. Down towards the Lot, I heard thunder mimicking the guns which we should not hear again. I said, 'I'm not doing what you did, am I?'

He said, 'Good heavens, no.' He need hardly have confirmed it quite so strongly, whatever it was. 'Besides, Berthe's family is a long way from your mother's.'

'And she doesn't have a brother, does she?'

'There's also that, not that I'd thought about it.'

'She looks good in her clothes,' I said.

My father did not make the obvious retort, but he made it obvious that he did not, which once again blemished him in my eyes. His warning, if that was what it was, hardened my resolve. I was like the alcoholic's child who deliberately drinks in front of his parent. He imagines he does so in scorn, not in emulation, but he still takes the same poison.

Was my marriage an act of pure perversity? I was enough of an intellectual to assume wilfulness to be synonymous with liberty. As I chose to see it, my conformity was no conformity at all; deliberately to do as my class and circumstances would have dictated, if I had not thought about it, was to parody what I appeared to honour. Docility and dissidence kept perfect step as Berthe and I walked down the aisle in the spring of 1947.

Her parents gave a reception for two hundred guests at their manor house near Pontoise (it has now disappeared under a motorway). Baron Bertrand de Jardin spoke with conspicuous lack of condescension of his cousins and their generosity in giving sanctuary to his daughter during the recent *'règlement de comptes'*, which was perhaps a too tactful term for the battle which had proved the unwisdom, never mind the treason, of the once flagrant collaboration which my uncle had had to work so hard to render forgettable: his evidence of my father-in-law's furtive patriotism was decisive in retrieving the family's factories and property from sequestration. Jean-Claude had revealed how willingly the Baron had arranged for his own production lines to be sabotaged and with what thoroughness even the finished work had been primed to disintegrate in battle. It was not surprising that my uncle made the speech on behalf of the guests. He spoke with especial warmth of my good fortune and asked me to take good care of the car which he was lending us for our honeymoon.

Berthe and I spent our first night together at the Grand Monarque in Chartres. It was then a cavernous old post house which offered a combination of luxury and discretion. Although my mother-in-law had reserved the bridal suite, she was determined that her daughter should not be embarrassed by vulgar connivance. We were greeted as if we were not young lovers, but regular and staid visitors. Our plush, unaired suite had two mansard windows and no view of the Cathedral.

Taking our evening meal in an almost empty dining room, we attracted the attention only of one particular patron, who wore a dark suit protected by a napkin tucked in at his loosened collar. He frequently dabbed his concentric chins with clinical gravity. He looked at Berthe whenever a new dish was put before him, quite as though his hunger had to be verified by hers. He suggested some court official to whom the *jus primae noctis* was traditionally deputed. His appreciation of Berthe was so ceremonious that I began to imagine him coming to our table, without a shred of shame, and announcing that it was time that she and he went about their bedtime business. Is it possible that I was faintly disappointed when he rose, after wiping a gleam of coffee from his bulbous lips, and left the dining room without a single insolent step in our direction?

I said, 'Did you see that man?'

'What man?'

'He never stopped looking at you.'

'Which proves that you did!'

I said, 'Is there anything else you'd like?'

She touched her napkin to her mouth and shook her head. She was wearing a blue silk suit. There was a white scarf around her throat. Her pearl-chokered neck was rather short. She said, 'Shall we go up or what?'

'I had the feeling he was a retired executioner,' I said.

After she had undressed, she spent some time in the big, white marble bathroom. By the time she joined me in the bedroom, I was standing in my dressing gown by the window, looking out at the moon which was leaning on the housetops. It made me think of Félix. I kept my back to Berthe's hesitations, which seemed to put her in my power. Finally, I heard the rustle of the covers and turned to look at her.

She was leaning back against the velvet headboard, which was of a damson colour. Her fine brown hair was flattened up against it like a pale halo. She wore a short-sleeved jacket over a white, lacy nightgown. As she watched me come towards the bed, her jaw slid slightly to one side, as if she were confirming a measurement of some kind. I wondered whether she loved me, and what it would mean if she did, or did not.

As I got into bed, Berthe said, 'Can I ask you a question?'

I said, 'You're my wife, aren't you?'

She said, 'What is the single most important event of your life so far?'

I said, 'The truth?'

'Will it hurt that much?'

'What is most important to me,' I said, 'is not strictly a part of my life at all. A man I – admired – of my age is dead and I am alive and that is the most important thing I can tell you about myself. What about you?'

She said, 'Nothing is important to me now except for you.'

I said, 'Poor Berthe!'

She rolled her head on the velvet, not entirely in disagreement. The crepitation of her hair touched me. I kissed her lips from which, for some reason, she had cleaned the lipstick she had worn during the day. Had she taken advice? In later years, my only erotically stimulating memory of her came to be of that natural mouth. Of course I discovered, when I began to visit prostitutes, that one of their common graces, on receiving payment, was to wipe the make-up from their lips.

After I had kissed Berthe, she gave a little smile, almost a shrug, which indicated that I was now welcome to whatever I wanted. I was reminded of that smile the other day, in Caillac, when I had gone to market for Maureen. The shops were just opening and I saw a woman crouched down inside the glass door of a new shoe shop in the Place de la Libération. She looked up, with a sort of insolent humility, supposing that I was to be her first customer, and her expression recalled the young Berthe so keenly that I went straight in and bought a pair of espadrilles.

Berthe did not pretend to any experience of desire, nor did she affect coyness. She left everything to me, rather like a good wife who prepares a full meal in the oven, lays the table with every sign of thoughtfulness but elects not to be present in person. I eased the little jacket from her shoulders and tried to free her breasts. The neckline was too tight; she was obliged to lift herself in the bed and raise the white gown over her head. Her face stayed veiled in the lace so long that I suspected that she wanted me to caress her without her having to witness it. When I did so, I was startled by a muffled cry. Did it imply licence or disapproval? Its faceless immediacy recalled other things which I had heard and which I assumed she had not.

I seemed scarcely to be present myself. I turned back the bedclothes and enjoyed what I could see. The curly brown thicket was slightly powdered, as if someone had attended to it and then gone away. The talc came sweetly to my nostrils as I brushed my lips against her belly and used the flat of my hand to warn her where I was and wanted to be. Testing her voice a little nervously, as she emerged from the nightgown, like someone who checks it after laryngitis to be sure it still has the same range, she said, 'Take me?'

Wondering what lurid novel she had read as a primer for her wedding night, I kissed her and, while not ceasing to caress her, whispered, 'Tomorrow.' I made postponement both a favour and a vice.

What did that girl I slept with at the Grand Monarque have in common with the woman for whom I waited in furious patience in the greenish Roman hallway? What right had I to anger in view of the long fraudulence of our marriage? I had wronged Berthe by being so scrupulous in my first seduction; my tact deprived her of the occasion to see how little I cared for her. The promptness of her pregnancy was a welcome excuse for me to become considerate, rather than cold-blooded, in my treatment of her. My own performance was, of course, of more concern to me than her deception; she thought that my stratagems were devised for her pleasure, when they were, in truth, the means of my own excitement.

I saw the white coat flash under the Roman street lamps and went out into the street to confront my wife with a helping hand. She crooked her elbow and spun away to keep me from taking her basket; I might have been an incompetent thief, to whom she could react with more impatience than fear.

I said, 'Why did you lie to me?'

She said, 'Oh for God's sake – am I to have no pleasures?'

I said, 'Why this particular lie?' My voice was loud against the traffic on the Via Trionfale. 'Why Pierre? Answer me!'

She said, 'Must we do this here?'

I said, 'I know where you'd sooner be.'

'Then let's go there,' she said. 'There's one just down the road.'

'Come on then.' I took the basket. There was a little bar called the Giaconda a block down the street. It had a blue neon smile over the entrance. My indignation did not last through the ordering of the drinks – scotch for her, Cinzano soda (which I detest) for me. Once we were left alone by the garrulous waiter, I could only say, 'I've had a very embarrassing day, thanks to you.'

'You're lucky,' she said. 'And if you're expecting excuses, you're wasting your time.'

I said, 'Why did you marry me?'

'For the same reason you married me,' she said. 'My money. Slavery was my only way to freedom. Pretend to be shocked. Pretend to be yourself; God knows you've had enough practice.'

I said, 'When did I ever try to get money out of you?'

'You're the kind of murderer,' she said, 'who hasn't got the nerve to kill and the kind of thief who hasn't got the nerve to steal. You open the door for your victims instead.'

I said, 'Whatever may or may not be true, I never meant to hurt you.'

'You never cared enough for that! Do I now congratulate you?'

'You're a rich woman,' I said. 'Why don't you leave me?'

She said, 'Do you remember the first time you ever saw me?'

I said, 'Yes, you were standing by the old walnut press at La Fontaine du Noyer. You were with Roque. I thought at first you were something to do with him. Nineteen forty-three, the late summer, wasn't it? I was confused because you seemed too . . . substantial – '

'Not as substantial as I am now.'

'You were wearing a blue marine skirt, quite full, gathered in a band at the waist and a cotton blouse and you had a blue kerchief round your head that hid your hair. I thought you might be married, though I couldn't say why. You seemed older than you were the next time I saw you. Why?'

'Why married?' she said.

'The way you were standing. You seemed – well, I thought you were some kind of a peasant. I thought perhaps you had something to do with Baptiste. You remember Baptiste – I thought you might be something to do with him. Or did I? Perhaps I'm only saying that now, to amuse you.'

'Oh Guy,' she said, 'what a fool you are! You get everything right and everything wrong and all at the same time.'

I said, 'Were you jealous of me and Pierre, is that it?'

'I don't give a jump about you and Pierre. Who cares about a stone once it's been thrown? What is there to be jealous about? Have you been holding hands again?'

I said, 'How many drinks have you had already today? Jealous of our friendship. Which is now at an end, thanks to you.'

'He disgusts me,' she said. 'All that flesh, all that passion, all that scholarship, all the Jew all over them all. He's like some filthy Alsatian cheese rotting in its silver paper. Do I get another scotch?'

I said, 'Passion isn't exactly your sort of thing at the best of times, is it?'

Berthe said, 'What do you know about it?'

I said, 'We may as well get back to the flat. I want to say goodnight to the boys.'

She said, 'You really thought I was a virgin when I married you, didn't you?'

166

XXII

Félix put on a clean shirt and a dark brown wind-cheater. After tucking his grey trousers into his socks, he opened the window and climbed out into the night. I was miserable and I hated him, but I was not miserable because I hated him. I mourned his absence no less than I had regretted his presence. I recognised the primness of my lethargy, but what could I do about it? Even as I tried to imagine doing to Félix what his correct major had done, I was dreaming of an escape, not a pleasure. I wanted a way out of his contempt rather than a way into his affections or his body. I desired desire as if it were undesirable. I was full of emotion, yet empty of passion, unless disgust qualified as a passion. Because I hated my dependence on what I did not want more than I hated Félix personally, I was denied the wholehearted directness of enmity. In his absence, I found him quite charming. Indeed, I waited up for him like a parent afraid that his child is coming to a bad end. What could have been more comic than my sitting there worrying about Félix's virtue? He had known very well how to take care of himself in Paris; it was absurd to suppose that he needed my tutelage in Rodecin. Might he have been lured into a trap? Even in my innocence, I was pretty sure that he had somehow advertised his availability to those who shared his disposition. It even occurred to me that the bicyclist in the beret might have passed some coded message to him via our landlord. I had few illusions about Félix, but I clung to them; I could imagine him victimised, physically overwhelmed and taken advantage of. How much did my own memory of rolling him under the washstand supplement, and spice, my fears? I both hoped that he would learn some bruising lesson from his truancy and that he would not be too badly hurt.

Sitting with my father's volume of La Boétie on my knees, in sight of the damson suitcase, I regretted my first moves with Félix. I had been too candid and too supercilious. Nor had my middle game been much more elegant; I had started too many gambits and then abandoned them. I had assumed that he would be glad of any favours I granted him. His outburst of free will gave me an inkling of God's relations with man: no sooner had I become aware of Félix's irresponsibility than I had an involuntary sense of what it would be to love him. There was something infuriatingly seductive in his defiance. As I sat on that narrow double bed like a stunned widower, I could conceive of a God who, by granting free will, contrived a previously unimaginable emotional life for Himself. By licensing an impertinence which He never guessed that man might dare to display, He discovered bereavement. Félix had made a painful fool of me. I hated him as fondly as perhaps God had come to hate man, who could believe anything of Him except small-mindedness.

Had Félix any notion of the suffering his absence inflicted? I had shown scant signs of delight when he was with me. How easy it was now to understand God's leniency towards the sinner who returned to the fold! In the meanwhile, His anguish necessarily lacked any practical embodiment; God's love for the sinner was identical with his inability to express it. Hence human suffering was the evidence, less of God's nonexistence than of His hapless envy. When we were away from Him, He could only wait for us to want to come back.

I concluded that the Incarnation was God's first and last attempt to enter the world of the one creature who had had the nerve to escape Him. In the event, His divine son suffered like a man, but could not forget Himself long enough to find pleasure like one; He wept, but He did not laugh. Not being of mortal stock, He could only be an impostor among men. Debarred from the joys of the transitory (which are enjoyable because they do not endure), eternal life was His inescapable fate and His only promise to the men whose brief passions meant nothing to Him. Heaven was God's attic; man had to do His sinning for Him and then report for His covetous judgement.

My effort to philosophise myself into patience became a crazy attempt to compose a metaphysic which would prove that, while Félix was playing billiards or whatever he was doing, I had been involved in something more serious than chewing my fingers. There was an earnestness in my considerations which I often repeat in my dreams. Others may envision lubricious liberties in their sleep; I frequently engage in disputations with well-known intellectuals, who almost invariably laugh at my careful phrases and ignore my ironies. 'Eternity is very long,' I said recently to a leading savant, 'especially at the end.' He declined to publish this.

Early in our marriage, Berthe asked me what kind of dreams I had. I told her that I could never remember. It did not occur to me that she was trying to find some clue as to the hidden character of the man with whom she had agreed to live. Why did I not take the opportunity to report an entertaining scene in which my desires and her reluctance (as I interpreted it) were both liberally burlesqued? I could have pretended to be puzzled by what it meant to see us both in a hotel bed in which we were joined by a cropped man and a blonde girl who said that she was a friend of my sister. Again and again in my life, I have constituted myself the guardian of secrets which were not worth keeping. Recently, I discovered my old stamp collection in the attic at La Fontaine du Noyer. I am not eager for money, but I took it, with a measure of excitement, to a dealer in Cahors, imagining that time might have gilded it behind my back. He advised me to give it to my grandchildren to amuse themselves with.

I kept setting times by which it would be reasonable, or understandable, or not wholly unforgivable, for Félix to come home. I veered from the determination to be tolerant, even complicitous, to the decision to punish him as he deserved. The strap securing his damson suitcase put me in mind of Roque's belt, which I remembered seeing – or rather hearing – him use on Baptiste when his son was younger and not so strong. As I sat in my room, the fall of the strap on the boy's flesh and the simultaneous grunt of the father flushed and excited me in a way which I should have preferred to be spared. I walked around the house afterwards in a morbid search for the place of punishment. I think Roque must have bent the boy over the wooden horse where he sawed wood for our fires. Even today I am drawn and repelled by the now ruined buildings where Roque and the others cornered Cabanne and his wife.

I almost – but only almost – envied Baptiste his beating. I knew that I could never belong to such an unsubtle world, but as Baptiste grew in strength, I had half a notion that his muscles were the result of his father's floggings. My own father would never do such a thing. I might have sought to exasperate him, but I preferred, by my scholastic diligence and social propriety, to give him no hint of the want of force which I attributed to him. Even as I found myself imitating his style, I could have wished for a bolder model; the brutality I almost craved was a brutality which I should then have been licensed to exemplify. My uncle Jean-Claude was a convenient contrast to my father. I may have been horrified by his enthusiasm for the New Europe, in the weeks immediately after the defeat, but his robustness, even in a bad cause, was enviable. Now that he seemed to be in command of my destiny, I was aware of being enmeshed in a design too complicated for a mere pawn to understand, but I was somehow flattered even by my punitive sequestration in the Lonchats' attic room. Whatever happened to me, provided I could endure it, would gain me honour in Jean-Claude's eyes. By the same token, it was a criticism of my father, who had done absolutely nothing wrong but for whom there was nothing I could do. As I thought about my uncle, I thought I could understand why my mother was always so pleased to see him. Had he sent me to Rodecin to prove to her that he could always do for her what my father could not?

It came to my mind that the damson suitcase, with its suggestive strap, must still contain the photographs. I wondered whether a second view, in private, might appal me less and so lead me to see Félix in a different light. I had no notion of apology, nor yet of (as I saw it) descending to his level, but I did think that I might find subtler ways of dealing with him. Perhaps I could arm my secret self, while maintaining my bourgeois exterior, so that he would continue to take me for the prude I could teach myself not to be. I might not escape my predicament, but the bars of my cage might become more elastic, like the waistband on his pansy pants.

As if it were an act of resistance, I lifted the suitcase onto the bed (next to the volume including Montaigne's essay on friendship) and pressed the silvered catches. The unlocked tongues sprang free, proving that there was a guileless aspect to Félix, unless there was also a wicked one. Some officious part of my being claimed that I was conducting a legitimate search, but I knew very well that I was entering forbidden territory because it was forbidden. However, my curiosity was less urgent than my determination to prove myself other than Félix thought. I meant to leave his case exactly as it had been before my intrusion. There would be divine satisfaction in such an invisible visitation.

Was I capable of such neatness? I waited for the first signs of my typical clumsiness. I was sceptical of my competence even as I crossed the start-line. I came to the correct major's envelope under the first layer of silk. Félix had no cause to hide the photographs from himself, did he? I trembled as I handled the envelope; I wanted to look again at what I had not wanted to see the first time, but I was conscious that I was leaving fingerprints, quite as if Félix disposed of a forensic laboratory in which to confirm his suspicions. My apprehensions were absurd but they could not fail to furnish me with a new and somehow more resourceful and dangerous image of Félix.

As I peeked under the neat layers of his belongings, my ears were alert for the smallest sound indicating his return. Since he had left by the window, I assumed he would return by it, but I could not be sure. Was the step on the stair that of the Lonchats' thick-bodied, short-legged cat, or did it belong to the feline Félix, about to spring a surprise? I hoped, in one way, that I should have ample time to slake my careful curiosity and return my roommate's things to their apparently untouched state, but at the same time I was inclined to recklessness: I wanted to fling his things onto the bed and plumb the depths, whatever the danger. The greater my sense of the risk of being caught in the act, the more disposed I was to take it. If I unpacked his stuff in such a way that it could not quickly be restored to its place when I heard him coming, the more likely it seemed that he would return almost immediately, which was my overwhelming desire. I craved the very scene which I continued to do everything possible to avoid.

When I looked again at the photographs, they were naturally less surprising, but they also seemed less repugnant. I was astonished to find how clearly I remembered them. On second view, however, the collection taken in the hotel bedroom had a rather forlorn appearance, as if they had been waiting for someone to release them from their strained poses. Expecting to be stiffened by lust, I was embarrassed by my sympathy for these unsleeping beauties. They were an education, but not a treat.

The glossy male set was different. I did them the honour of hardly looking at them. Their contortions were boastful; their inhumanity was unwilting. There was no sign of their clothes in the bare arena where they sported. Their heartlessness came down on me like a truncheon. I was bruised by the fantasy of a separate domain in which affection never mitigated desire. It was a place in which no one needed to pretend to be at home. Its savage glamour was repellent and irresistible.

For some reason, I am reminded of something that happened when I was *en poste* in Syria. We were a quite small diplomatic community in a state whose attitudes to the West varied from malevolence to indignation. France's quasi-alliance with Israel, until the Six Day War, made us a frequent target for the latter. The Soviet bloc was, of course, much more popular with the Syrians. I remarked to a Czech diplomat, with what was supposed to be sporting facetiousness, that I envied him his amiable reception, which took him to the best tennis courts in Damascus and, for all I knew, to other less advertised social activities. Istvan was a dark-haired, dark-eyed man with a certain Slavic vivacity; we had played tennis together with two Italian consular officials, who were remarkably adept in their changes of position. Istvan responded to my remarks by saying that each of us always tended to be jealous of the other; for his part – and he would thank me for not making it generally known – he rather envied Westerners their enforced lack of contact with the Arabs, who were demanding, ungrateful and incapable of reading the instructions on what was given to them. His comments were at once outspoken and guarded; I took it that he was implying something more than disillusionment with Damascus.

My impression appeared to be confirmed when he telephoned me at home (as if to prove how friendly and how well-informed he was) and invited me to play some singles. I agreed, although the weather was particularly hot and I had no strong wish for single combat. Then he called again and said that he would like to see me anyway. He had enjoyed our conversation and would like to renew it. Did I know Moroccan Ali's? He gave me instructions on how to find it.

I immediately suspected that Istvan, who held a quite senior postion in the intelligence service, was interested in coming over to us. He was willing, I assumed, to earn his fare by giving us information from inside the Czech Embassy until we were ready to make the necessary arrangements. It was, of course, essential to gain his confidence and not to hurry matters, but the opening, trusting moves were clearly being made.

Moroccan Ali's had a narrow frontage in one of the maze of streets adjacent to the souks in the centre of the old quarter. There were several rooms behind the one on the street. All were tiled to shoulder level and all contained wooden tables and benches on which more or less comatose Arabs were sitting or lying. Istvan was waiting for me. I ordered tea.

He said, 'Are you sure?'

I said, 'Better safe than sorry.'

He said, 'Safe can be sorry, can't it?'

We seemed already to be exchanging passwords. He ordered tea too. We talked about the scandals of the day and about our chances of defeating Marco and Peppino at our next meeting. I was convinced that a more dangerous subject loitered behind the screen of our banalities. This presentiment made the commonplace into something exotic, though I was not yet sure how far Istvan wanted to go. In short, the meeting had the allure of a flirtation. I was intensely aware of his physical presence (that beard-stippled chin), of the movement of his dark eyes whenever someone came in, of the discreet urgency of his address when he leaned in to speak to me over the steam from our tall glasses.

The secrecy of our rendezvous was somewhat spurious. We were scarcely more inconspicuous there than at some diplomatic gathering where we could have had the same conversation without arousing any suspicion. The truth is, the diplomatic life was so repetitious that any clandestinity was a kind of sport. Some people found their diversion in adultery, some in other forms of deception, whether it was espionage, falsified expenses or enterprising use of the diplomatic bag. My meetings with Istvan, in which he took the initiative during the next few weeks, were charged with an air of undisclosed purpose which gave them a tincture of the erotic, even though we never did anything more physical than lose in three sets to Marco and Peppino and discussed nothing more emotionally charged than the improbability of Syria and Egypt maintaining a unity which had never, in fact, been underwritten by any sort of common purpose, except the destruction of Israel. I admired Istvan's liveliness and his lack of cant; I also respected the leisurely way in which he delayed the approach for which I was waiting.

When he telephoned me, I always hoped that Berthe would be out of the house. If she was not, I spoke in unrevealing phrase. Our next rendezvous at Moroccan Ali's was always proposed by him and agreed to by me in such a way that no one could have known where we were agreeing to do again what we had done before. Who knew whether the Syrians (using French technical staff) were tapping our lines and whether they would report their findings to Istvan's Embassy – or mine? I made an excuse to Berthe, lest she call my office in the Rue Ata Ayoubi, and went off to the souk.

On the crucial occasion, Istvan was already at a table in the second room at Moroccan Ali's. His mood seemed less relaxed. Fearing that I might be playing my fish too casually, I decided on more abrupt tactics and suggested that we come to the point. He appeared relieved and asked me, with sudden sharpness, whether I knew what I was getting into and whether I had the stomach for it. My mind sought to make sense of the conflicting signals while I did my best to conceal my confusion. He had taken me for something which I was not, whatever it was. It was alarming and a little flattering; I was disappointed to disappoint him, though I was determined to do so as promptly as might be.

Our embarrassment, being mutual, was quickly and gratefully dissipated. We had each of us been misled by some kind of availability which we sensed in the other. I took him to be about to defect to us; he read me for someone anxious for a secret life. Our preliminaries demanded evidence of tact from both of us, which had served to fortify the impression of an imminent intrigue. In consequence, we set out to prove to each other that we were worldly, uncensorious (even of the treason which each expected of the other) and able to manage our 'affair' with entertaining facility even in front of such an intuitive pair as Marco and Peppino. Thus we had courted each other without having any substance to our intimacy or a correct expectation of what might follow from it. We had mimicked friendship and trust in the interests of a transaction which never had any reality at all.

When we both realised how we had taken pains over as complete a misapprehension as we could imagine, we enjoyed a few minutes of such pure rapport that it seemed to yield a glimpse of the sublime. All sorts of shameless confidences seemed briefly possible, before we became conscious of our nakedness once more and, after shaking hands, agreed to go our separate ways.

Alone in the souks, I wondered what signal could have emanated from me to suggest that I was venal or duplicitous. To clothe my excursion with plausibility, I bought Berthe a set of 'local' brass coasters, enamelled with Arabic slogans which were doubtless more interesting for being unintelligible. Only after I had made the bargain and had them wrapped in screws of newspaper did I stop to examine one closely. I discovered, on turning it over, that it had been 'Made in India'. Could it be that Istvan had misinterpreted my hitherto unvoiced wish to break away from my wife as a desire to be divorced from my country? Only as I tried to analyse how our misunderstanding could have occurred did I face the fact that my marriage was disposable.

My dismay at misreading Istvan gave way to elation. We had parted without rancour; perhaps I could achieve as much with Berthe. The Syrian capital, with its many symptoms of French tutelage, which the authorities were lazily eager to disavow, seemed evidence that one could live civilly with those with whom one had once been closely linked. Walking through a city at once free of colonial occupation and indelibly marked by it, I had an inkling of life on the far side of Berthe.

There is an intriguing moment when a feeling, previously impalpable, takes on words. Some agitation of the body presages the transition from a physical to a mental state. How do we settle on the terms which express our sentiments? They swarm, almost without summons, and give shape to our ideas. Sometimes our sensations require more colourful plumage than easy words supply; they flutter in them, as it might be in an off-the-peg costume, fretful that they can have no more elegant expression. I wanted to have a more exhilarating notion in my head than divorce; I wanted to celebrate something which, in the form it now came, lacked the brave possibilities of which Istvan and I had seemed to have a common, disparate view. We had laughed at the prismatic radiance of our misreading of each other and

I was sorry that, alone, carrying the Indian coasters to a wife from whom I should like to have parted with an equal sense of colourful prospects, I began to rehearse my overtures to her in such grey and hesitant terms. Only when Aeneas stammered, Monsieur Picpus used to tell us, did he reveal himself for what he really was. Nevertheless, he went on to kill Turnus and found Rome.

Our house in Damascus was a clean white cube. It had a neat garden with a chain-link fence around it. I had found a larger, more interesting one when we first arrived in Syria. The rent fell within my stipulated allowance but the First Secretary at the Embassy protested to the Ambassador that the house, in an old section of the city, was too grand for a Second Secretary. He did not want the place himself but it irked him that I had found a treasure so promptly (we had actually spotted it while driving in from the airport). I argued and then I gave way; since my arguments displeased my colleague and my concession lacked grace, I made an enemy without the compensation of getting what I wanted.

Every time I went home, I was reminded of the nicer house we might have lived in, even though there was nothing wrong with the one we had. On this occasion, I returned in a state of anxious elation; I wanted to see Berthe, quite as if I had come home with good news.

She was sitting in the garden at the back, under a flame tree, reading a copy of *L'Esprit*. She might have picked it up to vex me; its dandified neo-Catholicism was never to my taste. There was a copy of *Vogue* on the ground by her white wicker chair. Before I could begin to imitate Aeneas and stammer my prepared speech, she said, 'I don't suppose you're going to be surprised at what's happened, are you?'

Had some important world event taken place while I was at odds with Istvan? There had been no new signs of war, but you never knew with the Israelis. I said, 'What now? I was . . . I was shopping.'

She said, 'Look at me.'

She was wearing a cotton dress and a floppy straw hat. She had on wedge-heeled espadrilles, one of which dangled from her bare foot. I hate guessing games. I said, 'New dress?'

Berthe said, 'Have you got any instincts at all?'

I said, 'The fact is, I've got things on my mind.'

She said, 'I'm pregnant, aren't I?'

I said, 'It's not easy to tell. I thought you looked very well.'

She said, 'I've got Greece to thank, presumably.'

I said, 'Well, this is wonderful news.'

'For you maybe. I feel like hell.'

'I've brought you these,' I said.

'Why? What have you been up to?'

'I was in the souks,' I said, 'and I thought of you. Naturally.'

She never used the coasters, although she often had a glass in her hand. Later, when we were due to leave Damascus for B.A., I saw that she had put them in a stack of things which she proposed to leave in the house for the new Second Secretary. I said, 'Don't you want these?'

She said, 'Cheap and nasty, don't you agree?'

XXIII

When I had looked again, and again, at Félix's photographs, I put them on the bed, inserting them in their previous place in the pile of clothes. The whole stack could be returned in an instant to the damson suitcase. Meanwhile, like an examining magistrate who cannot resist exceeding his brief, in the hope of finding traces of a spicier crime, I continued to search through Félix's things. How happy I should have been to find the bloodstained murder weapon! Were he to walk in as I came upon it, I should be able to justify my curiosity in the name of some law or other. In effect, however, the fatuous pretence of doing my duty served only to blight the illicit thrill I might have had; I lacked the stride to transgress with both feet.

I discovered that Félix's clothes were not all sumptuous. At the bottom of the case were a pair of black trousers and a striped waistcoat, the costume of his hotel service. Had his parents given him the money to buy them? In the style of my own father, I ironised on the willingness of the working class to sell their children into any kind of prostitution provided it had a dull enough wardrobe. At the same time, I wondered why my uncle was not married. For some reason, I associated him with prostitutes. Perhaps it was the open car which he drove in the old days and which he had once said, probably to annoy my father, was good for cruising. (It was my mother, however, who clicked her tongue.)

Having unloaded the main contents of the suitcase, I palped the flounced side pockets. Feeling a double lump in one of them, I extracted two mother-of-pearl and gold cuff links. They were in the form of two pairs of 'buttons' linked by a fine chain. There was a tiny seed pearl in the centre of each button. The blood thickened in my face and flushed through my body. I felt an absolute certainty that, when the war was over, I should enter the public service. It was not so much a vocation as a summons. At the same time, I put the cuff links in my trouser pocket.

The damson suitcase lost all interest for me. I had the opportunity to look again at the blonde girl and the cropped man up behind her, but my appetite was gone. Félix's cuff links were all I wanted. I restored everything to its pristine position and gazed at the refilled case to be sure, so I told myself, that my intrusion could never be suspected. I knew, however, that I was also postponing the moment when, with the case refastened, there would be no further chance of being caught in the act by the returning Félix. Did I want to be caught? I am not sure that I wanted anything; I enjoyed the uncertainty of the plot more keenly than any conceivable resolution of it.

Having returned the case to its exact place under the window (where Félix had tightened his laces on it before he went over the sill), I sank into a mortifying depression. I was a thief without valuable booty and a detective without a case. I thought of the lesson with Fritz at which I had first learnt of the knight's fork; I felt that I had a weapon of rare potency which few opponents could match, although I discovered quite soon that it was a standard ploy. I contrasted my ambition to astound Fritz with Félix's merely sporadic interest in my tuition. Having committed a crime against him, I decreed it a punishment: the cuff links were my reward for his sloth and ingratitude.

I could think of no better place to hide them than in the same recess behind the *lambris* where I had put my money. As I put them there, I was inciting Félix to a game of *cache-cache*, if he was up to it. At the same time, by secreting them in a safe place, I had a cover story whereby I could maintain that I had found them, not knowing them to be his, and had put them somewhere reliable. I should thus be able to make a winning move, whatever happened: the knight's fork could ride again! I could already hear myself laughing at Félix's accusation that I wanted such gaudy trinkets for myself. The bourgeoisie, I would tell him, may lack many things, but rarely cuff links!

Where was he? Midnight struck; there was no sign of him. I listened for a car and I watched for masked lights by the gate. If he had been arrested, and had talked, the police would come in the early hours. Thinking that I should pack my things and get away in the countryside before it was too late, I undressed and sat on the bed in my pyjamas. I was resisting the moment when I might, for the first time, get into the double bed before Félix. A sense of imminent humiliation relit the fuse of my anger at his absence. It also kindled a blazing jealousy: what kind of person had he found that was so much more attractive to him than I? I was father and mother, lover and husband, to a despicable little tart for whom, without feeling a vestige of either love or friendship, I was sentenced to endure these pointless torments.

I turned out the light and lay down on the cover of the bed, my head on the chilly bolster and my hands between my legs. Slowly, the darkness beyond the window lost its black uniformity. It took on a mottled, bruised look, like funereal marble. I tried to be asleep, so that I might be unfairly awakened by the returning Félix; at the same time, I was determined to be awake so that he might know that he could not escape my vigilance.

I never intended that this period of my life should occupy so much of my narrative. When I began to write, I thought that I might manage not to mention it at all. Rather like the Procurator of Judaea, in Anatole France's story about Pontius Pilate, to whom the name of Jesus meant almost nothing, I thought my memories of those distant events were too hazy for recapture. I intended to mention Rodecin only as a prelude to what followed. I have gone to the attic of my memory and, opening a case I could have sworn to be more or less empty, I find myself squatting by it, dismayed and enraptured by a mass of material which I am powerless to abandon as quickly as I should like. Luckily, I owe no one an apology; this manuscript is not intended to amuse or to sell. I am writing it because, in my retirement, I have no future but my past. I have no public reputation to defend and none to make. I am, at last, a free man. I do not intend to curtail that freedom with concern for a reader who may well never exist and who, if he does, will have to have sufficient curiosity (and patience) to accept that I am more concerned with what interests me than with what might appeal to him. To be candid, I have lost the appetite for seduction, if I ever had it.

I watched the window and, no doubt, I dozed. My body was a question mark bracketed towards the night. Félix would not be able to get into bed without disturbing me, nor could he pretend to be the master returning from a revel to find his loyal mate in the usual place. The unremoved bedcover announced that I had not truly gone to bed at all.

I was asleep and I was awake. I dreamed and I could not have dreamed. My eyes were shut and they were open when I heard (quite as if I could see it) the sound of footsteps on the stairs. I was trembling with an unidentifiable emotion. Fear swamped annoyance; joy sweetened fear; hope diluted rage. Knowing that the sounds were unlikely to be those of the police – whose noisy arrivals were meant to stun the victim into immobility – I still played with the possibility that Félix had been intimidated or bribed into disclosing the shallow grave in which my uncle had arranged to bury me alive. The door creaked and I was cheated of my treacherous fears: Félix's hair was unmistakable with its cowlick of moonlight from the window. Disappointment and relief made me sigh with realistic shiftiness. Open-eyed, I drew regular, sleeping breaths.

'Are you asleep?' Félix did not call my name. I had the impression he was still more likely to call me 'Monsieur' than Guy. He sighed and started to undress. The moonlight made it easy for him to move around the room. Hammocked in anticipation, I waited for the sweet moment when he found that he could not slide into bed and would be obliged either to lie on top of the bedcover or wake me up in order to remove it. Breathing dreamily, I watched him unbutton and remove his trousers.

I had, of course, seen Félix take off his clothes many times, but I had never watched him do so. Now, supposing that he was as good as alone (so I assumed), he allowed himself a languorous insouciance as he disrobed. By making me an invisible man, he appointed me a spy. I was thrilled less by the disclosure of his moonlit body than by the secrecy of its observation. Did he suspect all along that my eyes were on him? I daresay he often saw himself as others saw him; it was his shame and his pride to be an object of admiration. Narcissus is never alone.

He arranged his clothes on the damson case to which he would return them, carefully folded, in the morning (he always seemed ready to leave at a moment's notice). He then stood naked by the window, basking in the moonlight which silvered his skin. He might have been some polished statue in a dealer's window on the Quai Voltaire. He flipped his penis briskly with his hand, as though it had snagged on some memory, and then stood waist-deep in shadow. Moonlight plated his chest. The sight of him excited such a confusion of desire and disgust that I was not sure whether I wanted to crush or embrace him, if there was any difference between the two. My uncertain feelings alarmed me less than incertitude as to who exactly was experiencing them. How could I want what I did not? I saw someone embracing his pretty nakedness, penetrating the shadows which dressed it in a showy modesty, forcing itself in him, but that someone was not me. I lay on the bed, in my questioning pose, locked in the passivity I had taken to be clever and which now seemed vacuous and foolish. I wanted to do something to Félix, but neither my mind nor my flesh could suggest anything appropriate.

I blamed him for my indecision. I tried to imagine how he could be what he was. I wanted to possess him, not from outside, not by gaffing him like the cropped man, but by crawling inside him. I wanted to know what it would be like to be in every corner of that hairless and enviably proportioned body. As I watched him, I seemed to become his creator. I saw him acting in the light of my presence by artfully ignoring it.

He moved at last into the thicker shadows by the washstand. He poured water and washed himself. His hands played hands which might have held and caressed him earlier in the evening. Rodecin, which had never triggered my imagination, became a warren of hot places. After he cleaned himself, like a piece of machinery on which he must leave no trace of its use, he drifted to the window again in order to dry himself with his Royal-Concorde towel. He frisked his body in a way that made him smile.

So far as I could see through one shuttered eye, my appearance puzzled him. He extracted his big pyjamas from between the bedcover and the bolster (where he had been trained to leave them) and sat on the bed, with his back to me, to put them on. Finding that he could not pull the bedcover from under me, he stood with rewarding helplessness between the bed and the window. The night was cool; he had just washed; he crossed his arms and hugged his shoulders. He cleared his throat and said, 'Are you awake?'

I let him stand there.

He said, 'Because you'll catch cold like that.'

I said nothing. I liked him standing there.

He said, 'You ought to get into bed properly.'

I made some incoherent mouthing noises until, in a discordantly loud voice, I said, 'Hello?' I then affected to realise where I was and, in a quieter tone, I added, 'Are you back?'

He said, 'I'd like to get in, even if you don't.'

As if emerging from a deep sleep, I stood up next to my bedside table, leaning to avoid the incline of the roof and offered him no help as he removed the bedcover. My feet felt the roughness of the boards (Lonchat was certainly no perfectionist). Félix pulled back the covers and got between the sheets. Only then did I climb in myself, thus preserving my unspoken rule of always joining him rather than have him join me.

He said, 'Did I really wake you?'

I said, 'You don't really think I wasn't asleep, do you?' I lay with my back to him, dreading and craving his touch. 'Goodnight.'

He said, 'Goodnight.' Like a scolded pet, he cowered within his own territory. His mute pleading for forgiveness afforded me the luxury of its denial. As I was wishing that he would try a little harder, I heard him say, 'Why are you angry?'

I allowed time to walk down a long corridor before I said, 'I'm not angry; I'm tired. And a little bored.'

He said, 'You need a woman.'

'And where am I to find one? How did you get in?'

He said, 'You tell me, because you weren't really asleep, were you? The downstairs was open; Big Tits left it for me. You can always find something if you really need it, you know. Not least a nice arse.'

'How did you fix it,' I said, 'her leaving the door?'

'How do you fix anything?' He rolled over and I felt the fall of his hand on my shoulder. It was the first time he had ever touched me between the sheets. 'Sorry,' he said. 'If you want me to be.'

I said, 'What have you been doing?'

'I'll tell you a secret,' he said. 'Something better than chess.'

I said, 'You smell, don't you?'

'I'm sorry I woke you,' he said. 'It won't happen again, unless you want it to.'

I said, 'You wake me up . . .'

'Some people would think you were lucky, having me around.'

I said, 'Some people like tarts better than I do.'

He said, 'Oh, haven't we come to bed in a nice mood!'

'This isn't going to go on, you know.'

'Go to sleep,' he said, 'and wake up in a better mood.'

I should have let it go. I waited a few seconds and then I turned and threw myself on him. I did not know what to do once I had launched my first attack. I waited for him to resist and so indicate my next move by baulking it. To my embarrassment, he seemed genuinely surprised and easily overwhelmed. I straddled him and had a knee on each of his arms before he could stop me, if that was what he wanted to do.

'Look,' I said, 'let's get a few things straight, shall we?'

He said, 'No need to crush me to death. I'm not going anywhere.'

I said, 'Because this is going to stop.'

'I wouldn't honestly say it had begun, but go ahead.'

'You're not going to go out at night without my permission and I'm not going to give my permission.'

He said, 'I didn't mean to upset you. I thought you'd appreciate some time to yourself. Like in the old days. *Comme avant la guerre!*' It was a phrase which was tiresomely current among those who pretended that the Occupation, like a bad summer, was something which could be alleviated by nostalgia. 'If you want me not to go, I won't go. Unless you insist on sitting on me all night, of course.'

I said, 'I'd like us to be friends, but you don't seem to want that.'

He said, 'Look, I've offered to suck your cock, but I'm not sure that I can go any further than that until I know you a bit better.'

I said, 'You are the most disgusting little tart I've ever come across. I never even knew people like you existed.'

'Well, now your luck's changed a bit, hasn't it? Do get off.'

I said, 'I know exactly what you're trying to do.'

'I'm trying to make the world go round, sweetheart, but it's uphill work with you, isn't it?'

'You want me out of here, don't you? You want to make it impossible for me to stay. I don't want to spend my nights waiting for you to come home. I don't want to wonder what filthy police spy you've been messing about with.'

Félix said, 'There are things you shouldn't say, you know. No, I don't think you do know. But I think you should.'

I said, 'I'm not accusing you.' I climbed off him and fell rather awkwardly into my half of the bed. 'It's just something that might happen.'

He said, 'Why can't you behave like a normal human being? We could be perfectly happy here if you'd only relax.'

We were no longer touching each other. I said, 'Go to sleep.'

He said, 'Is that what you want?'

I said, 'Of course it is.'

XXIV

I watched Berthe finish her drink without any sense of having been betrayed. Presumably, she had hoped to shock or provoke me by telling me that she had not been a virgin on her wedding night, but since I had approached that occasion with no vivid feeling of privilege or immaculate opportunity, I could not now summon up much indignation. Strangely enough, her revelation convinced me that Pierre had been telling the truth, while at the same time I felt no inclination to disbelieve what she had just told me.

She said, 'What are you going to do now?'

I said, 'I'm going to go home and say goodnight to my sons.'

'No, you're not,' she said.

'Then you don't know me,' I said.

She said, 'Have you got any feelings at all?'

I said, 'For you?'

'For anything?'

I said, 'I don't discuss my feelings with strangers.'

She said, 'Is that your idea of a good one?'

I put money on the table and stood up. 'Are you coming with me?'

She said, 'Have you got another woman by any chance?'

I said, 'Would you like me to have?'

She said, 'To think that I used to think you were kind! Not that that is a term of praise with me necessarily. What kind of a man is it who resents not being a cuckold?'

I said, 'The fact that you lied about Pierre doesn't guarantee your virtue in other regards, does it?'

She said, 'You haven't exactly been an education in pleasure, have you?'

'Is there any evidence that even the best professor would have had a pupil capable of getting good marks?'

'Oh God,' she said.

I can imagine how many marriages would have ended soon afterwards. Mine did not; nor did I wish it to do so. I did not dread losing Berthe, but I had no wish to alter my way of life; its dissatisfactions, being both incurable and habitual, were familiar enough almost to be congenial. I had not been pitched from happiness to despair, nor from complacency to doubt. If I saw very well that Berthe thought me a cold fish, I was quite used to the waters in which I swam. My professional life was, in many ways, more personal than my private; Rome was a city of diplomatic variety which fostered the ruthless courtesies that are so attractive to the scions of Talleyrand; subtlety is more stylish than zeal. My duties involved liaison between different bodies dealing with the implementation of the Treaty of Rome. A colleague was once flattering enough to tell me that I had the reputation of being the kind of dull dog who would chew happily on dry sticks; I was given the unamusing, weighty dossiers to justify his views. If one cannot be a wit, one had better be reliable.

It would not have surprised me if Berthe had proceeded to spring some new surprise, but when she did not, I found myself too busy to force her to conclusions. One of my regular pleasures, when I had time for it, was to deceive her. Pia was not a passion, nor did I imagine that I was punishing Berthe by my infidelity. She was not someone to whom I ever remember feeling faithful. I was not disillusioned because, although I might have misread our relationship, I had had few illusions about it. I lived in a city where the pursuit of pleasure was nobody's business except for those who catered to it; since no one moralised about morals, my arrangement with Pia was less a vice than a banality.

As I write, however, I am conscious of postponing the next thing that I did. I should like to think that it was out of character. Certainly I was puzzled as to why I did it. Although I can construct a logic which, in certain eyes, might account for it, especially in view of its almost fatal consequences, I should still insist, under no matter what examination, that I stole Berthe's white showercoat simply as a caprice, a joke which was more amusing because she would never be given the opportunity to share it with me.

I cannot, of course, claim that I had never stolen anything before (I still use Félix's cuff links), but I am not a thief. Indeed, I am not sure that taking Berthe's coat amounts to theft or even that I did not mean to return it. Had I had the chance to do so, it would not have been out of guilt or a sense of honour, but I can still see myself doing it. I took it a week or two after it became clear to me that, for the present at least, she had no intention of leaving me or of causing me any further embarrassment. It seemed a little thoughtless of her.

I wanted to do something which would disconcert her. I thought of making anonymous telephone calls, but I was not sure that I could manage the histrionics; I thought of sending her flowers, as if from a frustrated lover, but I was not sure that I should be able to find an appropriate reaction to their presence in my living room. And so, on a sort of premeditated impulse, I went back to the flat one afternoon, when David was at the *lycée* and I knew that Patrick was at the zoo with little Maria (there was a dancing bear he loved to feed). Berthe was at the hairdressers' as usual. I was giddy with apprehension, although no one could possibly have questioned any of my actions. It seemed extraordinary that my key slipped so easily into the lock and that the door opened without any alarm sounding. I walked into my own apartment and confronted its familiar objects as if they were priceless. I might have gained access to a tomb unopened for centuries. I saw the evidence of my own family's daily life as if it had been arrested by some Pompeiian catastrophe. I was touched by its details, but I was curiously cold in my survey of them. I did not think of my children as dead, but as dematerialised. I did not mourn or regret them, but it was as if they had been and were no longer part of my life.

I daresay that I am rationalising. Is it convenient to believe that I was helping myself to a souvenir rather than indulging in an act of petty spite. Is it a kind of self-pity to declare that I could look back, as I seemed to be doing, on the disappearance of my children and remain unmoved? At all events, I looked around the flat like a tomb-robber too timid to take anything of real value and too greedy not to take something. Was that damned showercoat already in my head? Did I know what I was going to do with it? Such a charge makes sense only if one bears in mind that we often think that we know exactly what we are going to do, or would like to do, and make that a substitute for doing it. Acting according to plan is by no means the same as planning an action. I was not at all sure that I was going to do what I had come to do, or even that that was what I had come for. I wanted to hurt Berthe in such a way that she would not feel it. I did not steal her mink coat (bought in Athens) nor did I think of taking her jewellery. As if I could not have taken anything else, I took the white showercoat, folded it and put it in a plastic bag from the supermarket in the Olympic village and smuggled it out of the building. Luckily, Nando was not behind his Travertine marble cubicle in the hallway.

I had left my car round the corner (the privilege of diplomatic plates was a conspicious one which I could not deny myself) and I walked to it with a furtive insouciance which was by no means my usual style. I might have committed a murder, so relieved was I to get back to the car. At the same time, I knew very well that the circumstances were so unexceptional that I was immune to challenge.

I drove across Rome to the Via Giulio Cesare, whose broad, tree-lined pavements offered me a parking place from which I could easily stroll to Pia's building. Once again, I was being more cautious than sanity required. I relished the frisson of the illicit, even though I was breaking no law that anyone would be likely to enforce. My encounter with Pia seemed to begin as soon as I locked the car in a street where its presence had no reputable excuse. I walked with my plastic parcel (now openly displayed) as if it conferred an erotic grace on the afternoon. I felt the pulse of anticipation in my trousers.

I had never been particularly interested in Pia's other clients. My habit being a parody of a busy man's uxoriousness, I preferred to play at fidelity, although I recognised that I was the only faithful partner. My lease on Pia, like that on a hotel bedroom regularly booked, gave me the comfortable feeling that she was reserved for me, even if others made use of her from time to time. On this occasion, however, I was uncommonly alert to the possibility of seeing someone who knew her as I did. It was illogical, since I was doing nothing I had not done before, apart from carrying a yellow plastic bag with the showercoat in it, which hardly constituted a flagrant aberration. Why on that particular afternoon did I approach the entrance to her building with such a mixture of caution and defiance?

Since it was a tall *palazzo* with, among other things, a large *pensione* in it, there was a '*viavai continuo*' of people going in and out. It was impossible to be sure who was an insurance agent or a pious tourist and who might have come from Pia's bed. My suspicions fastened on a short man, in a grey belted raincoat, wearing a brown hat. As I approached, he was standing on the steps buttoning his coat, although the day was fine and warm. He wore shell-rimmed glasses and looked a little peevish, as though someone had failed to honour a rendezvous. He had none of the lineaments of spent pleasure; only the absence of a briefcase gave the impression that he was a businessman whose call, in this instance, had nothing to do with business. My interest in him precluded me, typically enough, from looking closely at him as I walked on past the entrance to the *palazzo*. I reached the corner and then stopped to buy a newspaper from a kiosk.

The man consulted his watch and then left the steps and limped briskly in my direction. One of his legs was stiff, perhaps artificial. I continued to read *Paese Sera*; it carried a comprehensive list of the films which Pia might have seen. The summaries of their plots enabled me to make polite comments on pictures which I had not seen. As the man I was watching lurched towards me, I had to restrain myself from walking on down the street. I could foresee an absurd situation in which his attentions would drive me further and further from my appointment and I should lack a plausible excuse to make a half-turn and get back in time to enjoy what honour, so to say, would oblige me to pay for. I need hardly say that he walked past me, as I held the newspaper tremblingly in front of my face, and went on into a tobacconist's.

I was under the lintel of Pia's *palazzo* long before he emerged smoking a small, thick cigar. I had had to wait for a minute or two in order to see him again. He crossed the street and got into a grey Alfa Romeo Spider, which I should have envied him if motorcars had interested me. I watched until he had backed safely in among the traffic, quite as though my attention were a condition of his doing so successfully.

I put my ten lire in the elevator and went up to Pia's floor. I rang the bell quite apprehensively and was relieved when, after the usual tactful delay, she answered it (she never gave the impression that she worked by the clock). She wore her black skirt and her white blouse and there was the cross around her neck, tilted slightly forward by the uplifted promise of her breast. She was exactly the same as usual. A surge of affection interrupted the scenario which I had been revising in the elevator.

We shook hands and I stepped inside the heavy door which shut behind me with a sharp click. It occurred to me that anyone wishing to rob Pia would have to do so while she was at home. I asked how she was, which was well, and whether she had been out at all, which she had. She had seen a film with Warren Beatty in it, which she had found 'too American' for her taste, and another, which she strongly recommended: the new Alberto Sordi, a film of 'sketches' which had made her laugh and laugh. *'Ed anche piangeva, sai?'* She traced tearmarks down her cheeks; she might have been a teacher who feared that I did not understand that she had laughed until she cried. Alas, I said, I did not know that side of her. 'Oh yes!' she said. Her eyes were moist with remembered enthusiasm. I wished that I could do for her what Sordi had managed so consummately, but it has never been my department to amuse people.

'You have to see it, *dottore*,' she said.

'Why do you call me that?'

'Oh, you know!' she said. 'You call people things.'

'Was the last person who was up here a doctor by any chance?'

She said, 'People call themselves things, you never know what they really are. Shall we go in the other room? It's nicer in there.' She was attempting, a little pettishly I thought, to resume our usual ritual, which began in the hallway, with talk of films and the weather, and then proceeded into the bedroom, which she always called 'the other room'. The discussion of her last client was clearly an embarrassment. Was I being cruel or was I only attempting to contrive a new ritual by questioning why she had suddenly chosen to honour me with a doctorate? I hoped she would laugh about it, but she wished only that I should not persist, which is where the cruelty began, even though it did not show itself in persistence.

The bed was quite straight. The room smelt as clean as usual, but the window was open. She went to shut it. When she turned back towards me, having repaired that small deviation from the usual, I was holding out money to her. Usually I paid her in the hall, so here was another unimportant change in routine. I took the opportunity to add an extra note to my usual amount. She said (as I hoped she would), 'It's too much.'

I said, 'I want you to do something, if you will.'

'Tell me,' she said.

I held up the plastic bag. She was jiggling the cross at her throat and tapping her foot. I took out the white coat and shook the wrinkles from it. 'What do you think of it?'

She said, 'That's a nice coat.'

'Try it on.'

'Me? In here?'

'It's for you,' I said.

'You shouldn't buy me clothes,' she said. 'And why the extra money?'

'Because there's something I want you to do once you've put it on.'

'You're too nice to me,' she said. It was not meant to be a compliment. She looked quite pouty as she waited for me to explain what I wanted. For the first time in our association, I felt that she thought I was prolonging things. She said, 'What's all this about, my dear?' She was already removing the white blouse but not the pout. 'Don't you like what we used to do?'

I said. 'We'll get there. That's why I gave you the extra money.'

I turned her around and helped her into the coat. She checked its appearance in the mirror and smiled. Was she pleased or was she being professional? I was happy either way. 'And now what?'

I said, 'You know.'

She said, 'Is that all?'

'I'll tell you when you're ready.'

I was cheated of her usual slow revelation of herself, of course, but I sat on the bed to take off my shoes and watched as she slipped out of her skirt and pants. The coat swirled apart for a moment (perhaps she was a cleverer girl than I gave her credit for); I was gratified with a glimpse of her black bush between the white panels of the material. I undressed with more urgency than usual and showed her why when she came and stood in front of me. She nodded, but without enthusiasm. 'E poi?'

My confidence was waning in the light of her failure to guess what I wanted before I had to make it explicit. While thinking that I was entering what was for me unknown territory, I assumed that what I had in mind was quite commonplace. I did not consider the possibility that Pia derived any pleasure from what happened after she had put her usual foot on the bed beside me; part of my faith in her was based on the assumption that her little cries of appreciation had no involuntary cause but, like the *grissini* on a *trattoria* table, were a complimentary grace. Although I liked and, I hope, appreciated Pia, I should not like to have paid her for anything that she enjoyed.

I said, 'Oh listen, it's something I always wanted to do,' and then I indicated what. 'I feel rather like a film director, do you know what I mean?'

She said, 'Listen, do you want my feet on the floor or should I get on the bed? It's easier for you on the bed, isn't it?'

I was surprised by my own determination to have things a certain way, even though my desires seemed quite arbitrary right until the moment when I would not have them frustrated. At no point, however, was I acting on an impulse which I could not have aborted, nor – so far as I could judge – was I suddenly daring to fulfil a fetish which had always been there. If anything was clear to me, it was that there was some kind of fusion between Berthe – represented, like some absentee head of state at a conference, by her white showercoat – and Pia, who was a sort of civil servant on whom the weight of reality could be laid. What I arranged that she offer me between the spread wings of the coat might, in some eyes, have been a deliberate and humiliating sacrifice of her individuality, but I did not view it in that way. The act I accomplished was not meant to demean the actual woman whose amusement at Alberto Sordi had made me affectionately envious a few minutes earlier; what I did was done more to Berthe in her absence than to the Pia who lent herself to it. What, after all, was so remarkable about taking a woman from behind while she knelt on a bed wearing a white shower-coat while I had my feet on her shaggy bedside rug? Presidents of the Republic, I have no doubt, have done worse.

The effect of what I had contrived was to prolong my possession of Pia until, whether out of impatience or consideration of my extra payment, she reached between her legs and offered me a service which very agreeably accelerated the end of our commerce.

When we had an opportunity to look at each other again, we exchanged rather shy smiles, like a couple who happen to have been paired to go into dinner although they have not spoken before. She then took off the coat and stood there naked, except for the usual cross. Because of what I had asked of her, it was the first time I had seen her so that afternoon. It was strange to have the usual prelude come after we had finished our business; I had no right to her nudity, and little interest in it. I hurried to get dressed.

She said, 'Here, don't forget this.'

I turned round and saw that she was folding the showercoat and was about to fit it back into the yellow supermarket bag. I said, 'It's yours.'

'No, no,' she said.

'I want you to have it,' I said.

She looked at me with more open contempt than I ever wanted to see again. 'It's not new, is it? It's your wife's, isn't it?'

'I don't care whether you wear it to go out in or not,' I said, 'but I want you to keep it. I might want you to put it on again. Put it in the cupboard.'

She said, 'Does she know you've taken it?'

'She doesn't have any idea.'

Pia said, 'They'll say I stole it.'

I said, 'No one's ever going to connect you with her. She won't ever see you in the street in it, and if she did, well, it's a nice coat, but it's not unique.'

She shrugged; she thought about it and then she shrugged again. Her reaction was disappointing, but it seemed to warrant other ideas that came into my head. I could imagine bringing her one item after another of Berthe's belongings until, in a kind of inverted striptease, I had put together a complete alternative to my wife, although my ideas became hazy when I considered what my living waxwork would then be asked to do.

I said, 'I'll always give you what I gave you today, from now on, because I . . . I appreciate your . . . *disposizione*, if that's the right word.'

She said, 'Don't forget the Sordi; it's worth a visit.'

I said, 'I wish we could go together!'

She said, 'Not possible at all.'

At the door, I said, 'Was he rather a short man, with a stiff leg, this *dottore* of yours?'

'Next time,' she said, 'be yourself. I like you better that way.'

XXV

Rain was slashing across the courtyard and rattling our window when Félix woke me with the breakfast. The coffee was a more promising colour and there was a saucer of plum jam, sweeter and better than I had ever had before. I said, 'What have you been doing to La Lonchat?'

He said, 'You make things needlessly hard for yourself, do you know that? You could perfectly well get out of here, if you wanted to. There are no Fritzes in the town at all.'

I said, 'It's not only Fritzes you have to worry about. Did you meet anyone you liked?'

'I met some people *you*'d like. Very nice. Very boring. They probably all play chess.' He grinned and spread jam on his burnt bread. 'They haven't had any trouble here. There's no Maquis, because it's not the right kind of country, is it? You have to go a lot further south – or back north – if you want trouble.'

'If the coast's that clear,' I said, 'why don't you move out?'

He said, 'I don't have the money, do I?'

'What if I gave it to you?'

Félix said, 'Look, it's eight o'clock in the morning. Do we have to start this early? I talked to old Lonchat, by the way, and he says he'll knock us up a chessboard. He's quite a type! Did you open my suitcase while I was out?'

I said, 'What makes you ask that?'

'I can tell if you did. Oh, before I forget: books. I can get you all the books you want. Coco's dad's got an old *remise* that's chock-a-block.'

'Coco?'

'The mayor's son. His dad's got this place organised: bar, hotel, a couple of shops. I can probably get a job once the all clear goes.'

'You've made rapid progress.'

'Why waste time when it's short? One little problem, apart from the war, and that is – would you believe it? – his dad doesn't know about him. He wants him to get engaged to the daughter of the *garagiste* because that would really tie things up. If we want to see each other, it isn't all that easy.'

I said, 'I'm sure you'll find a way.'

He said, 'You know what I'm after, don't you?'

I said, 'There must be a dozen places you can go at night.'

'I'm not thinking about night-time. It's easier during the day. Except that it's also more difficult. I can ask Madame if you can read a book downstairs somewhere. Or in the *atelier*, if the boss isn't in there.'

I said, 'I'm not budging. If you need money, that's something else.'

He said, 'Don't you ever miss a bit of normal human affection? I could easily be fond of you, if you'd let me.'

'No thanks.'

'You think you're moral; I think you're a snob. It's nothing to worry about. Think of it as wartime rations. You can go back to the real thing when it's available again.'

I said, 'I'm just not like that. Did girls never interest you?'

'I worked with a couple once,' he said. 'And one of them asked me to come with her to a room one night. People wanted to watch us do things. I'd tell you exactly what, but you wouldn't like that, would you? OK, so they watched and then a couple of them joined in, you know what I mean. Afterwards Simone – her name was Simone – was upset. One of the men had been rough with her – took the country road, you know what I mean. They pay, they think they can do what they like. So anyway we went into the bathroom – you should see the bathrooms at the Royal, white marble, pink . . . She asked me to kiss her. So I kissed her. She was sore, so what I did was, I took some of my oil – I had this oil with me – and I rubbed her with it. All over. And shall I tell you something? I loved her while I was doing it. I didn't desire her, because that's not me, but I loved her all right. I rubbed every bit of her and the oil, it was like magic, it took all the pain away, and not only that – it made her into something sweet and smooth that I felt like I could hold easily in my two hands, like a baby. Little Simone! Now, is that being "interested" or not? She didn't come or anything, when I caressed her, but she cooed. She liked it and she liked me, so what does that tell you?'

I said, 'Félix, it's not that I don't like you. It's probably more that I don't like myself.'

'Tell you what, give me that money of yours that worries you so much. You'd be richer without it.'

I said, 'Aren't you the smart one? Seriously!'

'I'll be your girl for you,' he said. 'I'm even smarter than you think. What did you do when I was out?'

'I shouldn't really tell you this, but I waited for you to come back.'

'Who are you afraid of, Guy? I sold myself to German officers, is that what bothers you? I'm a little tart, is that the problem? Do you want to know or don't you want to know? I was friendly with this major. Why are you smiling? As if I didn't know! You don't think you can feel anything for someone who buys you, do you? But what about you? You're bought by the money you already have, in the family. At least I *decided* to be bought, and to sell, whereas you . . . you took your mother's titty and you were done for before you knew it. I was his slave, if you like, but I was also free, like you never were, were you? He was a nice man, he gave me nice presents. You should see the cuff links he gave me. I'll show you them some time.'

I said, 'I've seen the shirts, haven't I?'

'He was being blackmailed, that was his problem. Some Nazi bastard with high moral standards. The worst people are the ones who prefer power to pleasure. So that's why I did what I did, if you're interested. I helped them and I helped Rudi at the same time, so now you can call me whatever you like.'

'And who were "they"?'

'I met these people who'd been organising us before . . . you know . . . the Germans came in. Union people. All right, they were Reds. I agreed to help them lay a trap. I was the trap and, OK, I got laid. I enjoyed it, getting this character to fall into it. I probably could've been an actor, because I went to him, this Fritz, and I told him I was being, you know, taken advantage of and he should come to a certain place where he could see what they were doing to me . . . He fell right into it.'

'And what happened?'

'They were waiting for him. Bang! That was it.'

'And then you had to get out of Paris, is that it?'

'Did I not! Rudi warned me. Because, of course, he knew – not what was going to happen, but that I'd, well, had a chat with this Volheim character.'

'He tipped you off to get out when he heard that this other officer had been killed?'

'Are you losing your faith in the Germans? Rudi told me to get out because he couldn't trust himself not to peach. There was this big hoo-ha going on, naturally, and he was bound to be questioned. He wasn't sure he wouldn't betray me.'

'He sounds like a charmer all right.'

'You're a virgin,' Félix said, 'you haven't got any idea, that's why you judge people. Shall I tell why he was afraid he might betray me? Because guess.'

'Presumably the Gestapo . . .'

'Gestapo! He was afraid he'd tell them about me because he wanted to find out whether or not I really cared for him. He could see himself turning me in and then . . . I don't have to spell it out, do I? The more I suffered, and didn't say anything, the more he'd love me because he'd know how much I loved him. He was sentimental, you know? And there's no one enjoys the idea of cruelty more than someone who's soft. So that was Rudi.'

'You talk as if you had some kind of a romance with this bloody man. You sold; he bought. What kind of a romance is that?'

Félix said, 'You're going to have a terrible life.'

I said, 'Didn't they suspect him – Rudi – didn't they put the screws on him when you'd gone? What happened to him?'

'I wasn't around, was I? I didn't love him *that* much. I expect he was transferred. They were busy getting me out of town: they didn't love me one bit, once I'd done what they wanted. Do you think the rain's going to stop? Because I might go out for a bit.'

I said, 'You're pretty practised, aren't you?'

He said, 'Look, suppose I'd been a tough, a real bruiser, and I'd come in here and shared your bed with you. A real apache, with the knife and the gold teeth and the knuckleduster, have you ever thought about that? Because please don't think that just by meeting me you've walked through fire or been in the lion's den, will you?'

If I was startled by the way he had flared up, I was dismayed when he sat abruptly on the bed and looked at me with helpless, unfocused eyes. His white lips shaped syllables too pale for utterance. His whole body seemed riven by a kind of painless paralysis. I said, 'Are you acting? Because you'd better not be.' His mouth made to smile; a tilt of the head was all the denial he could manage. 'Are you ill or what?' A little lift of the shoulder said that he was too weak to explain. 'Has this happened before? Félix! You'd better tell me what you want me to do.'

He said, 'In the case . . . brown bottle . . . tablets . . .'

As I hefted the case onto the bed, rattling the breakfast tray, I said, 'Is it locked?'

The locks, of course, sprang open as they had the previous night. I rummaged through the contents which I had arranged with such punctiliousness, taking the opportunity for their plausible disturbance. If Félix really had a way of telling whether the case had been opened, I had now disturbed things in so flagrant a way that my earlier effort was surely beyond detection. The tablets were in a flounced compartment opposite the one in which I found the cuff links.

I said, 'How many?'

Félix did not answer. I looked up and saw that he had fallen sideways, with his head on my pillow. His pyjamaed knees were drawn up. One of them was in the remains of the jam. I put the tray on the floor and moistened the corner of his enviable towel to clean his knee. I was calm and I was panicked. I believed that he was very ill and I thought he was faking. I frowned at the label on the bottle; the scribble seemed to indicate that he should take two tablets three times a day.

I tipped the dregs of one coffee bowl into the other and poured water for Félix to take the tablets. Hoisting him with one arm, so that he lolled against me, I held the tablets against his dry lips in the flat of my hand. His eyes were open, but they did not seem to see me. His lips nibbled my palm as they bracketed the tablets.

I said, 'Now drink this.'

He said, 'Guy, I'm sorry.'

I said, 'Are you any better?'

He said, 'No. But I will be.' Humour flickered in his face, renewing my suspicion that this was all some kind of a queer joke. Did I almost hope that it was? It would both spare me the need to worry about him and supply a crime that deserved to be punished. Each breath he drew seemed to strain his strength. Yet he appeared to be amused by his own feebleness, and by my reaction to it.

I said, 'Look, do you need a doctor?'

He said, 'I've got you, haven't I?'

After a while, he seemed better. His condition was a recurrence not so much of an illness, he told me, as a curse. Every so often, always without notice, he had these attacks of utter debility. Rudi had been so shocked that he had had him examined by a specialist, hence the very expensive tablets. Félix did not know what they contained, nor how he would ever get more of them, but they allayed the symptoms.

'What's it called,' I said, as I rearranged the bedclothes and doubled the bolster behind him, 'this disease of yours? Did anyone tell you?'

'It's not a disease, it's a . . . condition. It won't kill me.'

I said, 'So what happens now?'

'I get better,' he said, 'but not all at once, I'm afraid.'

I said, 'I'll look after you. Is there anything you want?'

He said, 'Aren't you a Christian? I was afraid you were angry.'

'You can't help being ill.'

'It's always the things that people can't help that make other people angry. If you were ill, I'd look after you too, you know that, don't you? I'm very sorry, but I need to drink a lot. That's what this doctor told me.'

I said, 'Nothing to be sorry about.'

I held the bowl to his lips and he drank like a dry animal, thrusting all his strength at it to get the water into his system as quickly as he could. My suspicions waned; I became the capable nurse. It pleased me to take care of someone for whom I did not care. Once I was dressed, I sat on the end of the bed reading and glancing now and then at my patient, who dozed and woke to smile faintly before dozing again. He gave sense to my day. I wondered whether he would be able to take some soup at lunchtime.

He said, 'Guy, I'm sorry, but I need to pee.'

I said, 'I'll help you down.'

He said, 'I don't think I can do it.'

'Pee?'

'Get down there. Can you find something for me?'

I looked round the room. There was the washbasin. There was the jug. There were the coffee bowls. I said, 'I'd better go and see what I can find.'

He said, 'Don't be too long, all right?'

The kitchen was empty. Madame Lonchat had gone out. I was a righteous thief this time and helped myself to an old mineral water bottle. The morning light came in through the mottled glass of the kitchen door like an invitation: I had only to get my things together and I could be out of there and away.

I went back up the stairs and showed Félix the bottle. He said, 'It's going to be a tight fit, isn't it?'

I said, 'It takes almost a litre.'

He smiled again, too weary to put me right. I helped him up in the bed and held the bottle towards him. He leaned back and tilted his chin to the ceiling. He said, 'Help me, Guy.'

I said, 'Come on, Félix, if you want it, here it is.' I thrust the bottle into his limp hand. 'Do you want to go or don't you?'

He nodded and turned his body slightly. As I tried to help him, his penis fell through the gap in his pyjamas and onto the back of my hand. It was warm and light; its vole-like head fitted neatly to the mouth of the bottle. I had dreaded what now happened so easily. The bottle warmed in my other hand as the yellow slant crept up, faltered, crept again and then stopped. I feared that Félix would be smiling, but his head was back against the humped bolster; he seemed as exhausted as if he had been labouring to express what had leaked so effortlessly from him.

As I took the bottle down to the half-landing I felt a silly pride in my accomplishment. I poured the liquid into the digusting lavatory as if it were too fine for such a destination. At the same time, I was thinking about exactly what I did not want to think about: what would happen when Félix wanted to do something else.

He recovered more quickly than, in some respects, I had hoped. Before it was necessary to conquer the next stage of my squeamishness, he was able to make his way to the half-landing, while I loitered in case he needed me. By that evening, after his third dose of tablets, his skin had recovered its pinkish vitality and his eyes were less chalky. He even suggested a game of chess. I said that that could wait till the next day; he ought to have a good night's sleep. He said, 'Whatever you say, doctor.'

I said, 'If you get out for a minute, I'll straighten the bed.'

He said, 'Who's doing whose job then? What a Samaritan you've turned out to be!'

What would he have said if he had known that one of the reasons that I wanted to get him out of bed was to be able to flush the imprint of his body from my side of the bed, where he had been lying all day?

The next morning, I woke early enough to go down and get the breakfast. Madame Lonchat was surprised to see me, but I explained that Félix was 'tired'. She was putting rubbish into the furnace of the range on which a big black pot was already smelling of the rabbit which Riri had brought in from the country. She was pale and pear-shaped in a pinafore; her breasts were not on show. She put out a scrape of the rhubarb jam; I felt it was for Félix, not for me.

'She missed her pet,' I said. 'I expect she'll be up to see you soon.'

'I wouldn't want her to do the things you did,' Félix said. 'Imagine if she fell on top of you?'

'Well,' I said, 'are you up to some chess?'

He said, 'I'll tell you what I am up to, and that's a breath of fresh air. How do you stand it cooped up here all day?'

I said, 'You'd better not go out until you're really better.'

He said, 'Promises are promises.'

I could have pleaded with him; perhaps I preferred to have a grievance. In any event, having dawdled, as it were for my sake, until mid-afternoon, he opened his suitcase and took out his best sweater. I watched nervously, waiting for the moment when he would discover that his cuff links had disappeared. He took a little while to straighten the things which I had disturbed.

I said, 'I hope you know what you're doing. Because what happens if you keel over in the street or wherever you're going?'

He said, 'I'm all right now, thanks to you, Mother.'

'It's liable to be my funeral,' I said, 'not yours, if they bring you back here and it all comes out.'

He said, 'You're not really worried, are you? Because if you were, you'd know what you could do about it.' His heartlessness was rather convincing. I was taking too much pleasure in my reproaches seriously to imagine that I was in any danger. Although it piqued me to think of him as a brazen little tart, I did not entirely believe that desire was sending him into the town. Vanity told me that he was teasing me as much as anything else: his desire was less urgent than his need to be the centre of attention.

Yet as soon as he had gone down the stairs ('I've had enough of the Tarzan number,' he said), I felt even more violent symptoms of rage and bereavement than I suffered before. I even thought I might have been poisoned. I fell back on the bed, conscious that I was imitating Félix but wondering also whether his condition might be infectious, or contagious; perhaps it was a venereal disorder. How did I know what the tablets were for? Imagine being sterilised for life before I had even had a sexual experience!

I drank some water and lay back on the bed when darkness closed in yet again on the yard. My ears seemed very keen. I heard a livelier conversation than usual between the Lonchats. Somehow my attic was more permeable than before; I felt less secure and more ridiculous. I was hiding in a place which no longer concealed me; my decision not to leave it was less honourable than obstinate. I thought it would serve Félix right if he came back to find me gone. It would also be very convenient to be out of there, with my money and the cuff links, before he discovered that the latter were missing. Did he already suspect something? His intuitions were so sharp that he did not need evidence for them; I dreaded the skill with which he would try to catch me in a contradiction once he knew of his loss. Why did it not occur to me to put the cuff links back in his case? I can only conclude that, for some reason, I wanted the petty excitement, the mixture of guilt and advantage over him, which their possession conferred.

As I waited, I made a decision: whatever happened, in the way of threats or pleas, I was not having him and Coco in our bed. My promise to my uncle had been that I would do as he asked; I was not committed to the humiliation, and possible danger, of hanging about in some corner of the house while Félix and his friend did things which, until his arrival, I had never imagined and which, even now, I could not believe were more than part of a plan to make a fool of me. I was prepared to give Félix money, but not to let him command my whereabouts. I locked the door and took out the slats of *lambris* which covered my hiding place. I had a moment of anxiety when I thought that the cuff links had gone, but they had fallen behind the beam. I could recover them only by teasing the nail of my little finger under the gold chains. I took several notes off my roll and put them, like a shoehorn, behind my heel.

Félix did not come home for supper, but he did arrive soon after I had finished. He came up the stairs and opened the door with a dramatic rattle of the knob. 'Are you all right?'

'Perfectly.'

'Look, something's happened. They're coming to get you.'

I said, 'What are you talking about? What have you done?'

'No one's been round? You haven't seen or heard anything?'

I said, 'What kind of a game are you playing now?'

'Get your stuff together,' he said. 'They'll be here in a few minutes if they can.'

'Who the hell are you talking about?'

Felix said, 'There's been a tip-off, OK? They've got someone inside the Kommandantur and the word is, there's going to be a *rafle.*'

'Who are "they"? Your whole world seems to be full of these people who know what's happening in places they shouldn't.'

Félix said, 'Do you want to go to a concentration camp?'

I heard myself say, 'As a matter of fact, suppose I do?'

'You're in a bad way, in case you didn't know. You've put something out much worse than you know.'

I said, 'Look, I've got some money for you. You can take it and get out of here.'

He said, 'I'm not the one who's wanted; you are.'

'You'd better tell me exactly what you're up to, Félix.'

'You know what a tip-off is? They've had a tip-off.'

'And what about you?'

'No one knows about me.'

'It's not for want of an opportunity, is it? You've been announcing your presence as if you were some kind of a circus. And telling everyone about me, I presume, which is why this has happened in all probability.'

'You'd like to think I was responsible, wouldn't you?'

'And are you?'

'I know why you hate me.'

'Who are these people who're coming?'

'Friends of mine who want to help you.'

'So I'm supposed to be grateful, am I?'

He said, 'You don't want to venture outside your range, do you?'

I said, 'I'm sorry, but I think you've fixed this. I don't think there's going to be a *rafle* at all.'

'Suit yourself, Julien.'

'Who is this damned Julien?'

'Why would I want to panic you?'

'It might amuse you.'

'You'd like to see *me* with the shits, is that it?'

'Evidently, I don't have your tastes, because I can't think of anything I'd like less.'

'Look, for Christ's sake get your stuff together.'

'Where are they going to take me? How do I know I can trust these people, whoever they are?'

'Because I say so, Guy. And because you don't have any choice. It's not that difficult; you said you had some money.'

'Did you tell them that?'

'What do you think I am?'

'What are you?'

'I'll tell you something about yourself, Guy: you don't trust yourself, do you? You don't know who you are and you don't know what you want and that's why no one can ever give it to you. Get your things together and get out of here.'

I said, 'I looked after you when you were sick and you go straight out and do this.'

He said, 'That's what you hope, is it? That I did what? Sold you to the Friedas? What do you think you're worth to them? Shall I tell you what you really want? You want to make me the enemy. And shall I tell you why? Because you think you can beat me, because it would be nice to have a little nance like me as the biggest villain in the world, when you know damn well I wouldn't do anything to hurt you.'

I said, 'All right, all right.'

'I think you're a prize bourgeois shit, a real two-week job, if that's any comfort to you, but I wouldn't betray you. I wouldn't betray anyone.'

I said, 'What about Rudi?'

He said, 'Don't you have any feeling for anyone?'

'Didn't you know that something would happen to him if you did what they asked you to do? You can bet *they* did. They got this other guy *and* they got the major, didn't they?'

He said, 'I wish they were coming for you, in some ways, if you can say something like that.'

202

'You think you're the clever one really, don't you, Félix? But I think they've had you in more ways than you know. You didn't save Rudi, you did him in.'

He said, 'All right, I hate you. Is that what you want to hear? You've heard it. Now get your things together and get out of here before . . . before anything else happens.'

I pulled my suitcase out from under the bed. There were strange tears in my eyes. I was not moved; I was not hurt; I was not unwilling to go – but I felt like crying. 'I don't know why,' I said, 'but I want you to have this.' I reached to the back of my shoe and pulled out the money I had put there. 'It doesn't matter what we think of each other; I can't go and not give you something in case you need it.'

He said, 'Do you think I'm not going to take it?'

'I hope you are.'

'What do you think you're buying exactly?'

'It wouldn't hurt just to say thank you. Or even not to say anything at all.'

'There's nothing wrong with buying things.'

I said, 'In that case, I'll tell you what I'd like: the truth.'

He said, 'This won't buy you much of it. I think that's them.'

I said, 'They can wait, can't they?'

'Truth about what?'

'You want me out of here, don't you? The Friedas aren't going to mount an operation in Rodecin just to catch some kid who did the wrong thing in school.'

'Your name's on a list,' he said. 'It's not the only one, but it's there. It *is* them.'

I said, 'I don't believe you, Félix.'

'I know,' he said. 'So what are we going to do about it?'

I had my things in my case. I had to get my money, and his cuff links, and I could be on my way, although I did not like to think what its destination might be. I bit my lip and then I said, 'All right, I'll show you where you can hide things.' I removed the slats from the *lambris* and reached in for the rest of my money. I had put the cuff links on top of the beam, so that I was able to enfold them in the banknotes and take them out at the same time.

Félix made a little jump and bumped his heel on the floor at the same time, pretending to leap on me. One of the cuff links slipped through the tunnel in the roll of notes and fell onto the floor. At the same time, I heard the tinkle of a bicycle bell. Félix turned to the window and I scrabbled on the floor.

'Come on,' he said. 'Because it's them all right.'

I found it. I got a splinter in my hand, but I found the cuff link and thrust it into my pocket. I said, 'Goodbye then, Félix.'

He said, 'Don't you want this?' He had spotted my father's volume of La Boétie on the shelf by my side of the bed. 'You better have it.'

I said, 'You keep it. It might weigh me down.'

He said, 'Are you serious?'

I said, 'You want me to go and I'm going.'

He said, 'You might write something in it.'

I said, 'You're quite an item, Félix, aren't you?' I took my pencil and opened the flyleaf. I thought for a moment and then I wrote: *'For someone I trust.'*

He said, 'You certainly know how to hurt people, don't you?' He was holding out his neat, clean hand. I shook it with the ends of my fingers. I still had not removed the splinter; that operation was a pleasure to come. 'I expect that's why I'm going to miss you.'

XXVI

Having broken the routine which had given my visits to Pia their untroubling simplicity, I was both excited and uneasy at the thought of seeing her again. I had wished my wife's coat on her, out of a malice I now regretted but which I was powerless to discontinue. My reluctance to make another appointment with Pia had nothing to do with a lack of desire; my little innovation had quite sparked my imagination. Although I was not sure that Pia was the ideal girl with whom to pursue my fantasies, I was disinclined to wound her by withdrawing my custom. The idea of removing various items from Berthe's wardrobe, and from her jewellery case, even of purloining some of her many perfumes, was irresistible.

If I was excited more by the travesty than I had ever been by the real thing, I was also conscious of teasing Berthe. It would be a compensation for the disappointment of my discovery that she and Pierre were not the lovers she wanted me to believe they were. I did not look forward to her becoming aware of the theft of her things – none of them valuable or ever particularly precious to her – but I could foresee that it would give her something to think about. Maria would be the first suspect, but not the most convenient one, since our little Sicilian maid was affectionate with Patrick, competent about the flat, and made a *pasta Norma* which I liked so much that it exempted Berthe from spending much time in the kitchen. To accuse Maria would be to risk losing her; she had a Palermitan *fidanzato* with fiery black eyes and intimidating eyebrows who sometimes went with her and Patrick to the zoo and who might react vigorously to any slur on her honour.

I suppose that most men would have dwelt on the question of who had taken their wife's virginity. Was Berthe offended at my failure to pursue the matter? Certainly she acted, in the face of my sustained courtesy, as though she had a grievance. When I suggested that we go and see a new Alberto Sordi film of which I had heard particularly good things, she said that she thought him crude and that she couldn't always understand the jokes in Italian films. I said, 'You understood the jokes in *L'Avventura* all right.'

She said, 'There weren't any, were there?'

I said, 'Shall we go to a concert some time? The Amadeus Quartet are coming in, I saw.'

'We can go to the Sordi, if that's what you want to do.'

I said, 'I don't want to force you into anything. I just thought you seemed rather bored.'

'What else would you expect me to be?'

'We could ask Pierre to come to the concert with us, if you like.'

'I don't ever want to see that man again. I forbid you to mention his name.'

'Noted,' I said.

'You wouldn't know what a joke was if someone broke one over your head, would you?'

'I should take anything like that very seriously indeed,' I said.

'Do you happen to have seen that white showercoat of mine anywhere?'

'Isn't it in your wardrobe?'

'That's very helpful,' she said. 'I should never have thought of looking there. No, it isn't; it isn't anywhere.'

'How mysterious! You probably left it somewhere.'

'When do I go anywhere?'

I said, 'When did you last wear it?'

'Oh,' she said, 'there's no need to open an inquiry. It'll probably turn up.'

'Is anything else missing?'

'I don't think it's Maria, if that's what you're thinking.'

'I'm sure it isn't,' I said.

The next day, I delayed leaving the apartment until Berthe had gone to the hairdresser whose regular, and expensive, attention was needed to give her once-pretty hair the serpentine appearance of some mythological affliction. When she had gone, I scanned the bedroom for a suitable fetish, which was both typical of Berthe and not readily missed. Although I was not often sexually stimulated by anything to do with my wife, I felt a flutter of excitement. I walked around the room like a diviner, waiting for the twitch of discovery. Only when I had lighted on a long rope of artificial pearls in a half-open drawer did I feel an urgent desire to go and see Pia. The pearls were of small value and they were, I assumed, now out of style, since Berthe rarely wore them. I had them in my pocket when I saw a little lace handkerchief which my wife sometimes used to remove make-up. I took that too, although I felt slightly greedy at breaking the rule of one thing at a time which I had arbitrarily imposed on myself.

Having decided that she would not enjoy it, Berthe insisted that we go to the Alberto Sordi film. She put on a maroon-coloured coat, with a Persian lamb collar, and black gloves. It was a warm Roman evening, but she always carried gloves, which were exceptionally cheap, especially with the *sconto diplomatico* without which she would never consent to buy anything.

The cinema was crowded and hot. Being in a popular quarter, it lacked the luxury which Berthe thought of as her right, not least when its absence gave her a chance to reproach me. However, she was almost immediately surprised by the broad humour of the sketches and by her ability to follow them. Laughter made her warm; she was soon wriggling out of her coat, one wing of which fell across my thigh. I could tell that her gloves were in the pocket on my side. It was easy to extract them while she laughed. I took them across to the side away from her and rolled them together before tucking them into the recess behind and beside my seat. She was in such an excellent humour by the end of the film that she was almost embarrassed. The last sketch was the one in which Sordi played an actor who was attending the funeral of a comedian who had been well-known to all the mourners. What should have been a solemn occasion degenerated into a hilarious reminiscence of the dead man's corniest and most irresistible routines until all those at the graveside were convulsed in scandalously unmournful homage. I did not laugh as much as Berthe, which she found 'typical'. I should, no doubt, have been more diverted had I not been absorbed in establishing a pattern of forgetfulness on her part which would account for the disappearance of various of her belongings.

I held Berthe's available hand as we walked back to the car so that she would not miss her gloves. We were already driving down the Via del Corso before she did so. With patient affection, I volunteered to drive back to the cinema, although I feared it would already be locked. Berthe said, 'Oh, they weren't expensive!'

I said, 'You'd better buy more expensive ones, and then you won't forget them.'

She said, 'You seem to be in a particularly good mood tonight.'

I telephoned and made an appointment with Pia for the end of the week. When, rather impulsively, I told her how much we had enjoyed the film she recommended, there was a little pause; I might have mentioned a topic which was not proper to the telephone. She said, 'Till Friday then.' It sounded like a warning to contain myself.

I had taken the rope of pearls to my office and locked it in the safe. It must now be clear that I am truly not a man of overwhelming sexual appetites; indeed, I am not sure that my sexual desires are primarily sexual at all: they seem to be an outlet for desires more complex, or perhaps more primitive. Nearly always in my life I have chosen from a menu on which there is no dish which corresponds exactly to what I want, not least because I cannot say, even to myself, what it is. It was, therefore, new to my experience that the days preceding my visit to Pia contained not infrequent moments of urgent longing for her. It was all I could do, on the eve of my appointment, not to make love to my wife.

I lunched on the Friday with our Junior Minister of Agriculture who was in Rome for a conference on the free passage of wine across the frontier. He was dismayed by the excellent and inexpensive bottles we tasted at 'Giovanni'; he did not see how they could be allowed into France in bulk without provoking resentment from our own wine growers. I wondered whether it might not be possible to find some Italian wholesaler whose shipment could be revealed to be adulterated with suspect – perhaps even toxic – substances. He said, 'That, my dear friend, is a suggestion I did not hear and which, had I heard it, I should find more than deplorable. In a word, congratulations.'

He saluted me as he got into his car and I hurried to mine. I had no contacts which would make it easy to arrange the coup which the excellent Valpolicella had prompted, but I could see from the minister's relieved face that he credited me with access to all kinds of disreputable circles. As I fretted among the traffic crossing the Tiber towards the Castel San' Angelo, I was aware of the great nexus of credulities which pass for knowledge and on which our mutual recognitions and convictions are founded. I was infected with a recklessness which enabled me to reach the Via Giulio Cesare faster than I had ever done so; I even swerved unhesitatingly into a narrow parking space. In the same mood of exhilaration, I took a soft waterproof hat from the glove compartment and, thinking that I should amuse Pia by my unexpected appearance, I put the rope of pearls around my neck before buttoning my raincoat to hide it from people in the street. Berthe's lace handkerchief was in my jacket pocket. Its soft feel had pleased me all through my lunch with the minister.

The same man, in the same coat and the same spectacles, was standing on the steps of the *palazzo* where Pia lived. My mood changed: the blood pounded in my head and I put a hand to my throat, to be sure that the pearls were not visible. The man was not looking in my direction when I spotted him, so that I had time, before he turned his head, to veer into a *salumeria* where I bought a piece of *mozzarella*. When Berthe had offered me the same cheese the previous evening, I had told her that I no longer liked it.

I left the shop warily. The lame man was talking to another, substantial man, in a blue raincoat and a soft cap of the same material. There was no reason to assume that they had any interest in me or that their meeting had anything to do with Pia. It was more plausible to suppose that the lame man worked in the district and found the steps a convenient rendezvous, yet some trigger had been pulled in me; I was fired with a fear which quite rejuvenated me, like an opportunity which I had not hoped would ever recur. If the two men were policemen, they had no cause to be looking for me; my face could not mean anything to them. All the same, some obstinate vanity wanted to believe in a continuity between them and the same forces, long since disbanded, which had had me on their list during the war. I felt nostalgia for the days when I was a wanted man.

I loitered under the awning of the *salumeria* (noticing things in the window which were considerably more appetising than the *mozzarella* which distended my pocket) and waited until the two men had shaken hands and nodded so often to each other that they seemed to have agreed on every possible topic. They started off in opposite directions still holding each other's hands as if they had forgotten they had them. Brought up short, they refrained from smiling, but appeared to summarise their previous agreement before going their separate ways. Would policemen have done such a thing?

A card was hanging on the handle of the lift: *Lavori in corso*. I had to climb six flights of stairs. I did so as if I deserved the labour. The stairs were inconveniently spaced; they were shallow but too deep to be taken easily two at a time. I arrived at Pia's door with my toes hot from the stubbing repetition of the climb. As I pressed the bell, I was more out of sorts than out of breath. I looked around furtively, with my hat still on my head, although there was no sign of anyone on the landing. I was about to ring again when I heard the click of the lock. How sure can I be that there was something different in the sound from usual? The door swung open, but Pia was not visible. I stepped inside her little hall, ready to shake hands, and was puzzled not to see her standing there.

She was huddled on the floor, in the space behind the door. Sunlight from the open sitting-room door was a gleaming flag across her naked back. One arm was pointing up towards the lock she must have unfastened as she fell. The open palm of her hand was against the door. It seemed to be propped there because it had nowhere else to go. My first impression was that Pia had devised something new to entertain me. Might she have thought, after my performance with Berthe's shower-coat, that I was dissatisfied with her services? Her present nakedness and her huddled position made me think, for a moment, that she was playing the slave. A moment later, I had no illusions: she moaned and fell sideways and I saw the blood. I saw blood in the tracks that came through the open sitting-room door, even though I had been blind to them when I came in. I saw a stripe of blood down the door and I saw it leaking from under Pia as she gazed up at me with the face of a dying clown, on which the only colour was that of her lipstick.

The first thing I did was to undo my raincoat and remove the rope of pearls from around my neck. I put them in my pocket and then I crouched down, with my fingers on Pia's spine. I resembled someone in his street clothes who happens to find himself by the side of the sea where a child has been injured. I was not indifferent, but I was anxious not to wet myself. Was she still alive? I think I may have heard the heave of her breath, like air through a fractured pipe, and then, almost immediately, there was a raucous sigh and silence. I said, 'Pia?' It was as though a telephone line had gone dead.

I was racked less by emotion than by the empty desire to find a suitable one. My situation was alarming, but I was not alarmed. As for Pia, the body at my feet had collapsed into a huddled question mark in the dark corner of the hall. The flag of sunlight now brightened patches of blood I had failed to see before. She was an emptiness, not a presence, in the apartment. The body neither disgusted nor moved me. Its nakedness was pathetic, but lumpish; it was no more erotic than something on a butcher's slab. What should I do? I had to get away before anyone came. Pia was beyond help; there was nothing to be gained, and everything to be lost, by calling the police. Who would believe in my innocence? I hardly believed in it myself. Pia had actually died while I was in her flat; I had seen no one except the lame man and his blue friend, who – even if they came forward – could corroborate my guilt just as well as my innocence. The same applied to the man who had sold me the *mozzarella* and who, I now had to hope, would not connect his customer with the murder.

It would be noble to claim that I was incensed by Pia's death and that I went into her sitting-room in the hope of finding a clue. In truth, curiosity rather than indignation took me through the door. Only as I stepped into the room I had never seen before (being careful to avoid getting blood on my shoes), did it occur to me that the murderer might still be there. For a second I saw someone sitting in the armchair with its back to me by the window; the fat cushions had the form of a sedate, overweight person.

The room was no more than four or five metres square; it was rather prim, with a few china ornaments on the mantelpiece above the little red stove with yellow glass in its cold door. The stiff sofa did not match the corpulent chair. There were two prints of roistering monks. The television was a black and white set on a plastic trolley. I was relieved (and disappointed) to see that I had not been excluded from a more sumptuous or sexier boudoir.

I was careful not to touch anything. On the other hand, I had no notion of how long fingerprints remained legible. Pia's bedroom presumably carried evidence of many hands, but mine would certainly be among them. I had to hope that she was a diligent housekeeper or that she had a maid who was.

The scene in Pia's apartment was not my first experience of blood, although it was the first since I took part in what happened to the Cabannes. There was little similarity between a wartime *réglement de comptes* and the killing of a prostitute but my memory of indifference in the first case sustained me in the second. It may be that I was equally shocked in both instances, but the form which shock took was that of observant frigidity. A quarter of a century separated the two experiences, but they became immediately adjacent; the war might still have been going on.

My indifference was tested by what had happened in the bedroom. It was disgusting, but I had no physical reaction to my disgust. The room had been wrecked, but it had also been defiled, either deliberately or in the panic of the murderer. It was only when I saw the bedroom in which Pia and I had gone through the parody of love which, in some ways, was happier for me than its enactment in marriage, that I ceased to imagine that I might have been her killer. The discovery of Pia's body in the hall primed the illusion that her murderer might have procured himself a pleasure I lacked the nerve to enjoy, like the shooting of the *Miliciens* in the wood behind La Fontaine. The state of the bedroom, and the evidence (and smell) of what had happened there, should have sickened me, but its effect was more to kill my nerves than to excite them. My body seemed to shrivel; I recoiled so thoroughly from the physical that I felt as if I could walk out of the window and fly, like a fleck of cotton, into the white of the afternoon. The bed was a mess of red and black and brown. The cupboard where poor Pia had so carefully hung her things before coming to me was on its side, showing the undressed wood of the back. The man had smashed it, I assumed, to get at the place where she hid her money. The only thing which moved me, after a minute or two, was the memory of Pia talking about Alberto Sordi. I saw again the scene at the graveside of the comedian whose old routines blessed the funeral with hilarity. Who would ever do as much for Pia?

I was delaying my departure, although I knew I should get out of there. As long as no one had been alerted by the sounds of the struggle, and the violence of the assault on Pia's belongings, I was safe where I was. My problem was getting away from the building, and the district, without being remarked. I looked again at the bed before I quit the room. It was then that I saw that what I had taken to be the rumpled top sheet was not a sheet at all. It was Berthe's shower-coat. I could not possibly remove it. It was bloodstained and fouled. I had to be careful not to touch things. It became a game, and not an easy one to play; one's hands are more promiscuous than one normally notices.

When I went back into the hall, it seemed that Pia had moved; her body now lay against the wainscot like a roll of carpet waiting to be laid. Might she suddenly leap up and pretend that she had mounted this whole thing in order to give me a shock? Should I love or strike her if she did? The lustrous ooze of blood, as it darkened on the tiles, killed the comedy which I had devised to postpone my next move. I had to walk out of that door and down the stairs and across the street and get into my car like an invisible man. I went back into the sitting room in the empty hope of finding some sort of useful disguise. Only then did I go round to the front of the armchair and see that there were two knives struck into the plump cushion. They had been driven in up to their hilts and there was a hoop of blood on the material in each case, where the blade had been wiped upwards by the force of the thrust. I could imagine the clean steel in among the horsehair.

I was filled with lassitude. The killing had blighted my afternoon. I had the rope of pearls and the little lace handkerchief and no one on whom to wish them. It is, of course, despicable, but I was less outraged than disappointed to find Pia dead. Although the bedroom was a terrible sight, and I was properly repelled by it, my principal feeling was that I had been cheated; I should now have to find someone else to whom to explain what I wanted and with whom to fabricate the limited intimacy which I enjoyed with Pia. In short, I felt slightly murdered myself.

I had to leave the flat. Its silence was hypnotic; I wanted to sit down quietly in one of the strict chairs in the sitting room and close my eyes. Did I want the police to come and find me there? My innocence was so improbable that I could see myself puzzling and exasperating the detectives who sought to break me. All the evidence pointed at me, but I had done nothing. Tempted by the perversity of the situation, I wondered if I should happen upon a policeman intelligent enough to know that I was innocent. I should rely on his being a chess player for whom the obvious solution would have no charm. If I knew that it was unwise to take the subtlety of detectives for granted, I wanted to observe the change in the man as he came to see that there had to be a clever answer and that he and I had to be accomplices in the discovery which would surely lead to his promotion. Would my status as a diplomat render me immune to prosecution? It would certainly inhibit my detective from treating me like a routine suspect. I was not sure whether the Quai d'Orsay would seek to abstract me entirely from Italian justice, but I could see myself asking them not to do so, since to rely on my immunity would be tantamount to a confession. If it came to it, I should want to be allowed to stand trial. I felt a certain craving for injustice.

I cannot be sure how long I loitered in that reeking apartment. The air itself was soiled. It seemed to thicken like some horrible aspic and to resist my movement through it. I had to go. The longer I loitered the bigger the hole which I had to darn with some plausible account of my afternoon. Not until I decided where to go was I able to will myself into the complicated simplicity of leaving the flat. How was I to make myself go down those six damned flights and out into the Via Cola di Rienzo? I could see myself backing the car out and I felt the relief of changing from reverse into second gear and driving off, not too fast, but towards where?

I waited for the answer as one does for passport photographs to be developed in those automatic kiosks. I waited and, seemingly without my doing anything, the answer dropped into my consciousness. I got up from my chair, careful not to touch its skimpy black arms with my fingers, and went into the hall. I took one last look at Pia's body. She was lying on her wound; I knew where it was but I could not see it. Her back and hips were grey and faintly glistening, as if with her last sweat. I had to go. I had to open that door. I made sure that there was no blood on the brass knob before using the skirt of my raincoat to ease it open. As I stepped out of my apartment, the telephone rang inside it. It might have been me! The sudden shrill regularity of the sound pitched me out onto the landing and I almost shut the door with my naked hand; I smiled as one does when refusing a naive sacrifice.

To my incredulous relief, the elevator was working. I watched the oiled cables and the plunge of the counterweight as it dived towards the basement and I almost fell into the trap of leaving my fingerprints on the handle as I opened the lift door.

No one joined me during my journey to the ground. Having no

means of concealing myself, I elected to consider myself invisible as I left the *palazzo* and walked to the Renault. I did not acknowledge the existence of the world and so hoped to escape its noticing me. There are advantages to being a person of small distinction.

By the time I was behind the wheel, my confidence was so great that I might have got away with murder rather than from it. I regretted that my cool performance was merely that of an innocent man. I wondered whether the killer who had spoiled my afternoon had come only for Pia's money. I assumed that he had found it; otherwise he would have wrecked her sitting room as thoroughly as he had gutted the bedroom. Now that she was dead, Pia became an object of fascination. I was tempted to stay and observe the doorway of the *palazzo* in the hope of detecting her other clients. Even as I told myself to get away, I was thinking that I might come back the next day. It is not only the murderer who feels the urge to return to the scene of the crime; innocence envies the guilty.

I drove to the Villa Giulia. It was on the other side of Rome and it took me longer than I should have liked to get to it; every minute of the journey added to the period of unaccountable time which common prudence told me to make as brief as possible. There was now a lacuna of more than an hour in my afternoon for which there existed no witness who might not be hostile. As I breathed more easily, I saw more clearly how probable it would appear that I had killed Pia. In her flat, I had viewed the matter dispassionately; now I felt impulses both of dread, lest I be implicated and ruined, and of regret, lest I should lose another opportunity to argue for my life.

XXVII

Two young men were waiting for me at the Lonchats' gate. One looked powerful, with heavier shoulders than his unbearded face seemed to warrant. Both were on bicycles. When we had shaken hands, the second young man left me his bicycle. I had a problem with my suitcase, but my companion took it from me and rode off easily with it across the bar in front of him. His steady pace hinted that we had quite a long ride ahead of us. I did not get the opportunity to ask our destination, still less to question the necessity of my departure. My nameless companion was strong enough for his natural pace to seem a punishment to me, especially after having spent so long a time without exercise. He pedalled; I toiled.

He took me along country roads which he clearly knew well. The daylight was almost gone; the last of it lay in beige panels across the hills. The wind seemed to carry it from the west as if it were some fine storm. I watched the thick back of the youth ahead of me and resolved not to ask for mercy. He became my sergeant and I was his recruit. It was quite dark by the time we reached a town, hardly larger than a village, in which there was a railway station.

'There's a train to Agen first thing in the morning,' he said.

I said, 'What do I do till then?'

He said, 'Enjoy yourself.'

I said, 'And where do I go from Agen?'

'Wherever you like.'

He handed me my suitcase, took my bicycle by the handlebars and rode off into the night. The village was dark; the peasants had shut their shutters. There was a café by the station. It too was shuttered, but dotted lines of light showed around the window in the bar. I had no idea what emotions to feel. Had I been rendered a service or had I been evicted from a perfectly safe place in order to give Félix an opportunity for his activities with Coco? Should I be grateful or angry, afraid or relieved? As soon as my escort had disappeared, I had a number of sensible questions to put to him.

I did not knock on the café door. There would be too many questions to answer. As if I were responding to some examination, and the eyes of Félix's friend were still on me, I walked on past the station (the village was called Montrouge-le-Poteau), quite as though I knew where I was going. Dogs barked and an owl swooped from a telephone pole. I passed the last house and saw the high outline of a wooden structure which turned out to be a sawmill. I went in and lay down at the back of a fresh mound of sawdust whose sweet smell and banked heat were almost better than the bed I had had to share with Félix.

I woke with the dawn. Having no notion of when the train would come, I slapped sawdust from my clothes and walked into the village. The little café was open; a few peasants were drinking an early glass of red wine. They looked at me with incurious hostility. When I asked if there was anything to eat, I thickened my accent to give a local impression. The patron set up a glass for me. When I asked if there was an egg by any chance, he looked at me and nodded, less in answer to my question than as if my request confirmed something he had expected. He reached under the bar and brought out a wooden rack with hard-boiled eggs on it. 'You're lucky,' he said.

'You have to be,' I said. 'Good health.'

Unasked questions loitered in the peasants' eyes. My presence turned them into actors who resumed their dialogue without conviction. They soon found reason to go to work.

The patron said, 'You've come for the train, have you? Let's hope it comes for you. You're very early.'

'When is it likely to come?'

He said, 'You never know what's going to come these days. You can't even be sure about Christmas. Where have you sprung from?'

I said, 'I've been in the country. Family business.'

'There's a lot of that at the moment,' he said. 'Another glass?'

'Why not?'

He looked me in the eye as he poured. It pleased him to rehearse intimidations which were not often available to him, I assumed, in Montrouge-le-Poteau. The effect of the Occupation reached us, at the very limit of its influence, in a country village where it was unlikely that any German soldier would ever set foot. The prompt reluctance with which I had been given my egg somehow alluded to the shortage of such things in Paris, yet the *patron* almost certainly had no direct experience of the situation in the north. While I was sipping my wine, he went to the corner of the bar and picked up the telephone. He kept his eyes on me as he flipped the metal flange across the face of the receiver in order to call the operator. He spoke to 'Suzette' in a loud voice, beginning with what I took to be the usual impertinences about how well she had slept, and why. Then he gave a number and waited. It must have been that of a situation down the line; he asked when the train was coming and whether its arrival was certain or provisional. When he had finished, he said, 'You really are in luck. It's coming. But not till ten o'clock. And you know when ten o'clock is, do you?'

'Of course.'

'Then you know more than I do!'

I laughed, but it was, of course, a joke on me, which his usual audience was not there to appreciate; I stood in for them, as he did for the police whose work he had no practical interest in doing. I was his pampered victim until, soon after ten o'clock, his friend called to say that the train was on its way. We shook hands like successful conspirators.

Only as the landscape put on familiarity, once the broad-brimmed rooftops and *terra cotta* tiles of the Lot were replaced by the steep *lauzes* of the Périgord, did I become uneasy. If it were too risky to stay in Rodecin, what would it be like in Caillac, where my return could not escape attention? I began to feel that I was riding into a trap which was conveniently at a distance from those who had set it. All my distrust of Félix surged back; would it not be typical of him to lend himself to my arrest in return for his own immunity? His betrayal of Rudi might have been inadvertent, but what reason had he to temper his treachery to me?

When the train stopped at Sauveterre, I got off. I was near enough to La Fontaine du Noyer to walk home, although it would take me three or four hours. Did I dare to telephone my father? And how would he react? If the line was tapped, or my call reported, I should put everyone in danger. What I really needed was Roque and the donkey; I did not fancy carrying my suitcase along the road towards Belvès, which might well be patrolled. The sensible thing would be to dump my belongings at Sauveterre and cut across country, but that too would leave a hostage to fortune. I went to the post office and asked for my parents' number. I heard Simone's voice, with its habitual suspicious tone, and replaced the receiver. The woman in the PTT was clearly puzzled by the brevity of the call, but made no comment. Aware that I had drawn attention to myself in a way which, in a film, would certainly have consequences, I muttered that I must have asked for the wrong number and left quickly.

I decided to leave Sauveterre without further foolishness. I picked up my suitcase and walked and walked. What season was it? I remember the sweat and the blisters, but my memory is so tightly concentrated on myself that I am not sure how to furnish the landscape. I think it must have been the early summer of 1943; the months passed slowly in those days and even the years themselves were without obvious character; there was nothing to look forward to except an end of what lay beyond my ability to influence. My stay in Rodecin was a long parenthesis which resolved nothing and had not even taught me the easiest lesson in survival; I had been manipulated rather than self-sufficient. I was not even sure what had been done to me. I felt like someone who had something written on his back, but had no way of discovering what it was.

I approached La Fontaine du Noyer over the hills, not along the valley. My only pleasure lay in refusing to rest or to change hands, even though the handle of my suitcase bit my fingers. I had to be my own sergeant. In order to reach our property, I was obliged to skirt that of the Cabannes. They were peasant-proprietors with extensive lands which they cultivated with only intermittent zeal. Their barns lacked tiles; even their animals had a casual air, as if they were not fully employed.

We had no direct quarrel with the Cabannes, but ever since Roque had seduced 'Little Véro', there had been an unbroken frost between our neighbours and ourselves. My parents had never, of course, had social relations with them and did not deign to regret the rupture, but it seemed to deepen over the years. Even the briefest courtesies had now been abandoned. It would not be wise for one of our dogs to stray onto their land. I assumed that I was in no direct danger, but the Cabannes would certainly have been aware of my absence and might make mischief if they knew of my return. Roque said that they were 'Communists'; in that way he could be sure of my mother's righteous refusal to listen to any of their complaints.

Strangely enough, I had observed that Roque himself, although in a state of supposed vendetta with the Cabannes, seemed now and again to enjoy a truce with them, during which he and Baptiste, as a small boy, would attend a wedding, or a funeral, and chat with his enemies, quite as if both sides were glad to repair a breach that would be reopened in the following week. There were no such amiable moments between my parents and their neighbours; we were locked in an inflexible situation, even though, in my grandfather's time, my family had been conspicuously generous to the Cabannes. At that time, the big field below our house was rented to the peasants under terms which, according to some antique formula, could not be rescinded until the death of all the male Cabannes who were alive at the time of the original lease. The field was not important to the running of La Fontaine, nor would its appearance have been

218

markedly different if it had reverted to us, but Roque complained about its unkempt hedges and about the failure to clear the stream which ran through it. In this way, we were recruited to a feud which we had done nothing to provoke and no interest in sustaining.

It is never wise to assume that a landscape is untenanted; to have seen no one is not the same as not having been seen. However, the laziness even of the Cabannes' dogs meant that I passed through the thick oak and chestnut woods (it must have been late May, I think) without any direct encounter. I went wide of a derelict brickyard, abandoned by 'The Belgian' who had bought it after the 1914 war, and was about to climb the unmortared wall up behind the broad field from which we could get our only wide, if hazy, view of the Dordogne valley, when I heard 'Eh-oh!' It was between a challenge and a greeting. I waited until I saw a figure in mustard-coloured hunting clothes loping lumpishly towards me. I could make no sense of him until he was almost up to me and then I realised that it was Martegoutte.

'How are you, old fellow? And where have you been?' He clapped me on the shoulder as though he had been waiting to congratulate me on some news I had yet to receive.

I said, 'Nobody knows I've come back, because I haven't.'

He said, 'You've heard, then? About the *rafle*?'

I said, 'I haven't heard anything. I've been in the Pyrénées, you might say.'

'They got Loubet, and Despinasse, they got a lot of people we know. Hauled them off to Germany. They didn't get me, though, and they didn't get you. And old Picpus is still . . .' He threw an imaginary scarf around his neck. 'Some things never change.'

'What're you doing this side of the river?'

'They don't come this way, unless they're invited, do they, the Fritzes? I've got cousins at Saint Amand; they feed me – and a few others – we're in the woods, we move about, depending where the drops are.'

I said, 'I've obviously got some catching up to do, because who's dropping what?'

'The English. When the weather's right they've been sending us all kinds of stuff.' He opened his tunic and showed me the Sten gun he was carrying. 'I can get you one with any luck. You have to be in the right place, because there's quite a bit of competition. The Reds don't like other people muscling in, and other people don't like the Reds. I tell you, it's not a bad life at the moment. They shot some people the other day, but that was because we got a couple of them, and their girls. Between dances!'

219

'What do you mean "got"?'

Martegoutte explained with a grin and a gesture. 'You ought to join us. I can introduce you.'

I said, 'It's tempting. Only I can't do it carrying a suitcase, can I? I'm only half a kilometre from home, so I may as well dump it. And then I'll see.'

He said, 'Nothing stands still around here these days.'

What would have happened if I had not walked those few extra steps to La Fontaine du Noyer? I had no strong wish to see my parents, nor any expectation of a happy welcome. Perhaps it was my lack of desire which, as so often, impelled me to act as though I were driven by passion. I should not like to believe that cowardice had any part in my decision, although Martegoutte's buccaneering swagger warned me that events had put distance between him and me.

I climbed on over the wall, with a wave to Martegoutte which, a few years earlier, might have indicated that I would come back and play with him if my parents agreed; the small change of life can be spent on all kinds of things. The hill tilted down towards the back of La Fontaine. I came first to the old bakehouse, with its great wig of ivy, and then I could see the open shutters of Roque and Simone's cottage and the dark mouth of the cellar door leading to the *barrique* and the limbo of my childhood.

I had no vision of how my return would be greeted. I could hardly be blamed for leaving Rodecin, but I had no heroic illusions: however justifiably, I had broken my parole. I did not think that my father would reproach me, but I intended to explain that I wanted to go and find Martegoutte and that I did not mean to be a burden, or a threat, to the family.

As I walked round to the left of the house, in order to reach the terrace steps, I met Simone toting a high basket of creaking laundry. She seemed as wide as a cart. Her task gave her no energy for amazement. She said, 'Well, so here he is!'

I said, 'How is everything?'

She said, 'Ouf! You know . . .'

Her laborious but routine movement implied that whatever had happened was of no importance, or at least that it was nothing to do with her. I left my suitcase by the steps and took the first four of them, from the side, in one homecoming leap. I was on the terrace in a moment, but I was still taken by surprise. 'So much for doing what you're told! So much for using your wits!'

I said, 'What're you doing here?'

'Ah, that's the tone we're going to use, is it?'

I said, 'I've come to see my father and my mother. Is that forbidden?'

'Not if you want to put them both in danger.'

'Are you living here these days?'

My uncle said, 'You've had a fright, it seems.'

'Not at all.'

'I think that's probably right. Not enough of one.'

I said, 'Do you know what happened? They said I had to get out. What did you expect me to do?'

'You're not going to stay here, if that's what you want.'

'No, I'm going to go and join some friends of mine. In the woods. I just bumped into one of them.'

'Those cretins,' Jean-Claude said. 'That's one thing you're not going to do. They put everyone's life in danger, haven't you got the brains to know that? They're hooligans having a good time and they're almost certainly going to have to be taught a lesson one of these days.'

'By you? By whom? Rodecin was a mess. I had to sleep with a queer. Was that supposed to be a lesson?'

Jean-Claude said, 'You seem to have grown up a bit. Have you grown up enough to realise that if anyone sees you here, it can be the end for everybody? Who've you been fool enough to say hello to so far?'

I said, 'Are you not still in with the Fritzes?'

'You have no idea who I'm in with, so mind your clever tongue. I'm getting you out of here today. Right away. They've been here once and they can come again. I got everybody out of it, pretty well, last time but I can't work miracles every day.' My uncle's moustache had grown darker and thicker; it had pointed wings now, which made him seem both younger and less impressive. 'I've fixed for you to go to some friends of mine – friends of friends at least – in Villefranche-les-Évêques.'

I said, '*Putain*! Why do I have to go that far?'

'I'm trying to save your skin, that's why.'

'And why is my skin subject to your wishes?'

He slapped me across the cheek. There was something both conventional and intimate in the gesture; it was more a declaration than an assault. He would not have done it, I felt, unless he wished to re-establish an intimacy which had never been admitted between us until that moment; he took a liberty that would not have been available did he not depend on me to appreciate it. In the ancient snapshot I have of him in my head, I see the same air of aggrieved

221

possessiveness that men have when they slap a woman. I think I smiled, in recognition not of my uncle's rights but of the change that must have come over me in Rodecin. I had feared that Félix had made a fool of me, but perhaps he had helped me to become a man. Jean-Claude seemed smaller and less respectable; I actually felt that I had grown taller than he, as perhaps I had, without realising it until that moment. When I straightened up, there he was below me!

Accompanying this sense of emancipation, there came a sort of panic. As I realised that I could do as I pleased, I felt an urge to do what pleased my uncle; I was more afraid of being in command than of being commanded. All I had to do was to say that I was insulted by his action (although I was not) and that I was going to go and find Martegoutte, who would introduce me to his *bande* and that would, I think, have been that. No fear of my uncle or even of the life I should lead in the *maquis* (the thought of the punitive rape of naughty girls was not wholly disagreeable) dissuaded me from an abrupt break with the family. Yet I did not give my uncle the slow, pitiless smile which was ready to sidle onto my face like an actor fully rehearsed and waiting in the wings. I found a slyer liberation in taking no liberties. My freedom was announced by what Jean-Claude supposed was his reminder of my bondage, but now that the way was open, I was in no mood to hurry through the gate; the sweetest of treacheries, I discovered, is fidelity.

I said, 'Who are these people I'm going to?'

My uncle said, 'That's better.'

I was scanning the terrace and the landscape beyond it. Yes, it *was* the spring: cowslips were paling in the Cabannes' field; the chestnuts were tiered with white and purple candles; hawthorn filled the hedges. On the far side of the valley, the pine trees wore buttons of new green. Nothing had changed, it seemed, except for the better. I said, 'Where is Gertrud?'

My uncle said, 'Go and talk to your parents. They're inside. Then we'd better go to the station. I'll drive you to Le Buisson.'

I said, 'Where is she, Uncle? They've taken her, haven't they? Did you give her to them?'

He wished that he had saved his slap. I saw it in his eyes. My own warned him not to fire the other barrel. Today I wish that he had, but I did not wish it then, even though I knew that I should turn and leave at once. I could see myself up in the Belgian's brickyard, volunteering for Martegoutte. My uncle said, 'You say wild things. Be careful: it's not over yet.'

I said, 'You know it is. You know who's won and who's lost and if you don't, you're a fool.'

He said, 'Let us try to be clear. I know who's won and who's lost and I also know, as you seem not to, that the greatest dangers lie ahead of us. The greatest dangers and the greatest opportunities – '

'To make money, you mean?'

He said, 'You think anger is a style – it isn't. It's an excuse as mediocre as sincerity, its dull cousin. Think about that. Money? You think it negligible? You must never have been without it. The danger is simply of death, because no enemy is more dangerous than one who is defeated but not disarmed. In short, be brave if you must, but never be angry. As for me, you look forward to the time when I am powerless, because you think you will be able to judge me, and that judging me will exempt you from owing me anything. I will tell you one thing, Guy, before I get tired of trying to educate you: you cannot have any idea of what I've done, or will do, or – most of all – why. I am unknown to you, do you understand me? Think whatever you like, but not that you have me. Clear?'

I said, 'What happened to her?'

He said, 'Forgive me, but it has no importance.'

I said, 'You want me to strike you. I shan't.'

He said, 'There will always be people who buy and sell other people. In my case, however, the retail trade is of no interest. The little Austrian? They came for her and I had to pull a lot of strings in order that that should be all they did come for. Understand?'

I said, 'Do I believe you?'

'Your state of mind is your business. Go and talk to your parents. I have to get you away from here. Give me your papers. Give me your papers, Guy. I need the photograph.'

I said, 'Who told you I'd be back? I wasn't sure myself.'

He said, 'And how important are you in these matters?'

I said, 'Simone! It was Simone, wasn't it? Who sold her to them? Our own dear Simone!'

He said, 'Was it? And if it was? And if it wasn't?'

XXVIII

The Villa Giulia had few cars parked in front of it. There is an air of desolation about the long hill on which it stands. Tram tracks cut bright grooves in the wide roadway, as if it were a main axis, but there is little traffic. The museum is one of the best stocked and least frequented in the city. I strolled in and made a point of coming back from inside to the kiosk where I asked about a French guidebook before returning to the rather ill-ventilated galleries. The copious exhibits provided a stiff crowd amongst which it was possible to become lost. I tried to see my missing hour merge with the centuries like a drop of water in a bucket; I looked at the grotesque beasts and men who crouched on the shelves and saw myself as no less absurd and insignificant. The famous sarcophagus, on which the married couple recline in pinkish felicity, has never been my favourite item, but I paid a visit to the elusively smiling pair knowing that I should soon be joined by whoever else might be in the museum. I could thus hope to be noticed, if I drew casual attention to myself, and so garnish my alibi.

There was a photographer inside the ropes surrounding the tomb. I had the impression that he was dawdling over his work in order to parade his privilege. He had removed his shoes, which stood together outside the ropes. He wore a plaid shirt and a thick beard. I did not like his teeth.

I said, 'Do you have to pay to do that?'

He said, 'French?'

I said, 'You've guessed it.'

'Only after you told me.'

'And you're American, yes?'

'Yes and no,' he said, 'I'm Canadian. I don't have to pay; they have to pay. The magazine I slave for, OK? Are you enjoying Rome?'

I said, 'I work here.'

'And you don't enjoy it?'

'I like it very well,' I said.

He was taking a reading with a light-meter on a strap around his neck. I thought that I had done enough to establish my presence; it was lucky that I should be able to identify my witness so decisively. The museum would probably have a record of his name. Mission accomplished, I walked through the narrow galleries towards the exit. My next step was to return to the Embassy and display my insouciance to as many of my colleagues as possible. I should make a point of asking how the minister had fared with his negotiations. It would be a good opportunity to suggest that I had been making contact with certain circles who might be helpful to us, although I could not, of course, specify where and with whom I had been involved.

'Guy?'

I had come to the Villa Giulia in order to be recognisable, but I was startled to be recognised. My name sounded like an accusation. Without turning round, I knew immediately who had spotted me.

I said, 'Hello, Pierre.'

He was making notes on a clipboard in front of a case filled with black figure vases. He said, 'You've caught the infection then, have you?'

He was wearing grey trousers and a high-necked sweater under a black cotton tunic. A briefcase was propped against the bottom of the case he was examining. He seemed to be advertising his scholarly standing. Only his new, somewhat military haircut, which seemed cheaper than his clothes, might have indicated that he was a priest.

I said, 'Do I look ill?'

'The Etruscan disease.'

'Oh, that. I drop in here from time to time. What are you up to?'

'The more time I spend in here, the less I like the Romans,' Pierre said. 'They had all the nasty tricks, didn't they? As soon as one culture has reason to admire and respect another, you can be sure they'll soon be at war and that admiration and respect will lead to obliteration. First we kill the thing we love and then we love the thing we killed. That's how we hide what we did. In our hearts.'

'Hence Christianity?'

'How are you, Guy, really?'

'Reality is a supposition for which I haven't much time at the moment.'

'In form, evidently! How is Berthe?'

I said, 'I really have to go. I've got this minister in town.'

Pierre said, 'What a good liar you are, Guy!'

'I've not lacked expert instruction,' I said, 'one way and another, but as it happens what I'm saying is perfectly true.'

Pierre caught my arm as I made to go past him. 'I hoped you might be beyond this kind of nonsense, Guy. But do I sense that you're still in a state of self-induced hysteria?'

I said, 'Pierre, this will do neither of us any good.'

Pierre had always had a tendency to sniff; he did it now. He winced, like a taster on the verge of guessing a vintage, and then he said, 'Are you really all right, Guy? Why are you here? Oh, I'm sorry, that wasn't meant to be an intrusion. I simply had the feeling that . . . antiquities were not your most likely solitary virtue. Am I wrong? You know the great thing about this place, don't you? One can't get a cup of coffee! *Fuori servizio! In permanenza!* All the same, I could do with one, couldn't you?'

I said, 'This is a bad moment for me, Pierre.'

'Who hasn't forgiven whom? And for what?'

I said, 'I don't have time to breathe on dying embers.'

'Then off you go.' He released my arm. I was reminded of the second after one opens a plastic bag and allows fishes to swim free in a pond: they never go at once – nor did I. 'Unless you want that coffee as much as I do, in which case I can stroll with you up to the Borghese Gardens.'

I said, 'Please yourself. I shouldn't like to seduce you from your work. And I shall only have to come back for the car.'

'I never cease to accumulate the dry sticks with which, no doubt, my superiors will eventually construct my pyre.'

I said, 'Come on then, if you're coming.'

I had much the same symptoms with Pierre as I had in Pia's apartment; I both wanted to be quit of him and I wanted to stay in his presence. He was an almost too reliable witness of my visit. Whereas the photographer was suitably anonymous, my meeting with Pierre, although no less accidental, was so convenient as to smack of contrivance. Furthermore, the twitch of his nostrils and the vigilance in those lustrous eyes of his seemed to flay the surface of my disguise.

We walked up the wide steps above the tram park and through an elaborately planned area of low hedges and paths which had failed to live up to its design. We went through a triumphant gateway and into the Borghese Gardens. The familiar alley of trees took us up towards a café where tourists were sitting at metal tables within a hedged perimetre. Over to the right I could hear the thud and scamper of horsemen practising their jumps. I asked for a *capuccino*; Pierre ordered red wine and a *toast*. 'You've had lunch, I take it,' he said. 'I haven't. I was thinking about you the other night. Have you seen the new Alberto Sordi film?'

I said, 'I think everyone has.'

'There was a sketch about a husband and wife . . .'

I said, 'You're very broad-minded, Pierre.'

'You make that sound like a shortcoming. I was just hoping that you and your wife . . .'

'Berthe.'

'Indeed. I was hoping that you'd seen the funny side.'

I said, 'Pierre, it's very strange bumping into you like this. I wasn't ready for it.'

'What would constitute preparedness in such an instance?'

I said, 'Do people ever confess things that aren't true?'

'I've no doubt of it. Are you speaking of crimes or of sins? I'm sure they do so in both cases.'

'This secrecy they all talk about – I presume it's limited to cases when a Catholic tells you about something he's done.'

'He or she. It's a kind of privilege that exists in other forms, of course: a lawyer and his client, a doctor and his. Why?'

'No particular reason.'

'Like chastity, it excites rather morbid interest in lay people. They wonder how we support the burden. In fact, it rarely weighs very much. Their curiosity is considerably more ponderous.'

'Have you had no occasion on which you felt you should have spoken out, because you knew that someone else was being accused of what one of your people had done?'

Pierre said, 'You're constructing a Hitchcockian dilemma which rarely applies. There's usually some way of nudging people into discovering the facts which one already knows. Life is only a carbon copy of the ideal; it's full of inelegant but convenient smudges.'

I said, 'What is the true centre of your life, Pierre? I don't expect you to tell me, but do you know?'

'Is the Trinity One or Three? I only know one thing there: if Jesus were to leave, I should not be able to follow Him.'

I said, 'I was told something that wasn't true about you . . .'

He said, 'Oh Guy, for the love of God . . .'

I said, 'I want to ask you to do something for me, something very important. And, of course, because it's important, I'm not very eager to ask you. What time did we meet?'

He said, 'I don't know – twenty minutes ago? About ten past four, was it?'

'Suppose I said it was just after three.'

'I may weigh heavily on you, Guy, but I can assure you we haven't been together for over an hour. Not a chance.'

'Have you been in the museum all afternoon?'

'Since noon as a matter of fact. Hence . . .' He took a bite from his toasted sandwich. 'May I ask what this is all about? Or have I guessed?'

'I want you to understand that I have done absolutely nothing of which I'm ashamed.'

'As bad as that, eh?'

'No, no,' I said, 'don't play the Parisian. It's not the moment. I swear to you that I'm not asking you to do anything except perhaps –*perhaps* – at some moment in the future, which may well never occur, testify that I've been in your company since soon after lunch – not all the time, but . . .'

Pierre said, 'Are you in some kind of trouble, Guy?'

'Only potentially. I've done something foolish, but not wicked – at least not according to my moral calculus.'

'Are you trying to tell me something or trying not to do so? Why do you want to put yourself in my power?'

I said, 'I had no idea that I was going to see you today, as you must know, but now that I have, well, the chance is too . . . fortunate to be ignored. I had lunch at "Giovanni" with my minister and then I strolled across the park and spent the afternoon at the Villa Giulia. Our trip to Cerveteri gave me the urge to spend more time with the Etruscans. You are my obvious guide, so could we say that we walked together for a while and then went to the Villa Giulia?'

Pierre said, 'Guy, what have you done?'

'*Nothing*,' I said. 'Just like you.'

He said, 'You want me to be a liar without your being one yourself. Is that fair?'

'Is death? My dear Pierre, I want to be able to lie, if it comes to it, as I hope and think it will not, because the truth will not, in this instance, make me free. Far from it. I have a certain taste for the perverse, maybe, but it doesn't go as far as being condemned for a crime I did not commit. That is the simple heart of the matter. I ask you to believe only that I have done nothing – except be in the wrong place at the wrong time.'

'Someone's dead, am I right?'

'Someone is always dead,' I said. 'Our whole lives are lived in the light of that, aren't they?'

'You move in my direction suddenly!'

'Pierre, for the moment, sitting here, this is academic. I hope it will remain so. Either it will or it's bound to become a test of – let's say – everything. When you know, *if* you know, you'll have your doubts. If you didn't, I'd think less of you. Doubts are everything. That's why, here and now, it's so important that you believe me when I say that you are free, of course, to do anything that you feel you must, but that if you commit perjury, as I ask you to, you will not be doing it for the sake of a liar. Only of a fool.'

Pierre said, 'You make doing what you ask seem like an act of faith. But I don't know what faith.'

'Does that make it more or less attractive to you?'

He said, 'Oh, don't worry, I'll do as you ask, even if it is only for the sake of an innocent man!'

I said, 'You may find it much more difficult than you think.'

'You need not make such promises,' he said. 'I won't pretend I'm not glad about this; it gives a sense to our earlier . . . squabble.'

'It has nothing to do with it, I assure you.'

'Everything has to do with everything. If you didn't still think that there was something between me and your wife, would you want to put as much weight on me as you do now?'

'It's in spite of that that I trust you and that I want you to trust me.'

'Then we're agreed,' he said.

XXIX

I was Bruno le Guen. I was suffering from tuberculosis, which required both rest and seclusion. I had not only my identity papers but also a set of X-rays in a buff envelope of the same size as the one in which Félix kept his photographs. I came from Angoulême where, my uncle told me, a large number of records (including 'mine', of course) had been destroyed in an allied raid on the railway junction, which had not been hit. My parents had been killed in the same raid; I was free to invent whatever poignant details I chose. Jean-Claude went through these matters with me hurriedly in the car; I was no longer spoon-fed.

My father had been alone in his study. He had stacks of papers around him. I suspected that they were more to give the impression of industry than its occasion. I expected him to be frailer and a little helpless. In fact, although his cheeks were hollow, there was a new lightness in his bearing. He neither reproached me for my return nor questioned the need for me to leave. It occurred to me that his papers had been spread out for a charade in which I had no part: they were there to make him a dustier figure than he now was. He told me at once that Gertrud had been denounced. He did not think that Simone was responsible, although he conceded that she had been a little too defiant in her denials. 'I am content that it should remain a mystery,' he said.

I said, 'A mysterious contentment.'

He gave a little shrug of distaste. Either he no longer recognised his own style or he no longer found it palatable. 'Your uncle managed to convince the . . . authorities that we had no knowledge of her . . . race, but thought she was a Czech refugee. I can confess to you, Guy, that it was one of the most shameful moments of my life. It goes without saying that I shall not forgive myself.'

I said, 'I love you, Father.'

His eyes shone but he shook his head. 'That's as good a way of saying goodbye as any other! It's inexcusable, but when it came to it, I couldn't be Quixote. Quixote had to ride out of his castle, didn't he, and his library, before he could be the Don?'

I said, 'I'd better go, hadn't I?'

He said, 'If she survives, which must be most unlikely, it will be a comfort, but it will never, of course, be an excuse. I want you to understand that.'

If I had wanted to hurt him, I should have said that I imagined it was a relief to him to have such a refined conscience that what he could not have prevented was what weighed most heavily on it.

I said, 'I don't want to do what I'm going to do.'

He said, 'It's for your mother.'

I said, 'And Louise.'

'Oh,' he said, 'Louise . . . in a sense, but Louise . . . I think Louise can survive, with luck.'

'Is she here?'

'Louise has gone, only this morning, with a cousin of ours, Berthe de Jardin – who seems a very pleasant girl – for a stay with some friends of your uncle's in the Aveyron, I think. She'll be sorry not to have seen you.'

'What a coincidence!' I said.

'Perhaps.'

I embraced him and went to see my mother in her upstairs rooms. She was arranging dried flowers in a large herbarium. Its heavy, yellow prewar pages were interleaved with tissue.

'It's hello and goodbye, it seems,' I said.

She said, 'No one tells me anything.'

'And you know it!' I said. 'Do you happen to have a needle? I got a splinter in my hand. I thought I'd got it all out, but I seem not to have.'

She relinquished her dried specimens with a sigh; she might have been regretting allowing me to play with rough children. 'Look in my basket over there,' she said. 'I have to do all my own repairing these days. Sterilise it first, won't you?' As I watched the tip of the needle redden in the match I held to it, she frowned, but not at what I was doing. 'You're wrong to blame Simone. You always did jump to conclusions.'

'My uncle seems to be of the same view.'

'Jean-Claude will agree with anything,' she said, 'as long as it's wicked.'

'You'll vouch for that, Mama, will you?' I wiped the soot from the needle and picked at the cuff of the wound at the bottom of which I could feel the last dark trace of Lonchat's floorboard. 'Whom do you blame, then?'

'She made enemies. The *strüdel*-maker! I wish she had not, of course, but it's not clever to be proud and weak at the same time.'

I said, 'I'm leaving, Mama. Being too weak to be proud, I'm going where my uncle wants me to. I assume he has your vote.'

'I'm a woman,' she said. 'I have no vote.'

Was it a kind of generosity in her to make herself so dislikable? I should have liked her better for it, had I not detected that element of sincerity in her performance which was indistinguishable from artifice. We recognise with the keenest repugnance those characteristics of our parents which we share with them. My mother's ability to endure unhappiness was due less to religion than to self-indulgence. To be happy requires an investment of will and imagination, and a trusting to luck, of which she was (or had become) incapable. Her Catholicism was an obstinacy, not belief; her endurance was a kind of squeamishness. She once warned Louise against smiling more often than she could afford; it was all right if you were plain, but unwise if you had a face worth preserving.

As the train carried Bruno le Guen towards Villefranche-les-Évêques, I could rejoice in the death of his parents even as I reconstructed them with the tender *bricolage* which only the spy and the trickster find necessary. It proved more difficult than I thought to compose a happy couple. A strong father made a weakling of me; a weak one was too easily defeated. As for my false mother, should she be beautiful, and unfaithful, or strong enough to dominate the man she did not need to deceive? In truth, of course, I was trying to confect an equation whose result – myself – was already known to me. I could not imagine who Bruno was apart from a public version of myself. While I was involved in these specious calculations, I felt the weight of shadows on my shoulder and, looking up, was faced by a man in a black leather coat and a broad-brimmed hat. He said, '*Police allemande*, your papers.' I had not heard him ask anyone and I turned to see how many other people were in the compartment. Two old people were asleep at the end of the carriage. There was another man, in a shabbier coat, with a wide belt and a dark blue beret, behind the German. I fumbled for Bruno's papers and handed them up. What would my first question be, I wondered?

The German took his time. I coughed as if it were something I was trying to conceal. He pointed up at my suitcase. 'Open it up.'

The man in the beret was clearly a Frenchman; a twitch of his psoriatic face seconded the speaker. He combined menace and mediation. I affected anxiety which was not wholly affected: my mother had given me a jar of *rillettes* (part of what remained of our poor Pierrot) and another of truffles in brine. What might be interpreted as evidence of black marketeering was, of course, nothing more than proof of my mother's refusal to admit that the old rules did not have any place in the present.

The German said, 'Bruno le Guen?'

I said, 'Le Guen,' in the manner, I hoped, of someone trying to help him with his pronunciation.

'What do you do?'

I said, 'I'm a student. Unfortunately . . .' I allowed my cough to make its own excuses. 'I've been unwell. I'm going . . . to try and improve.'

'Where are you going?'

'Towards Brantôme,' I said. 'I have an old aunt there.'

He was already handing me back my papers. Having failed to engage his interest, I closed my suitcase with such a mixture of relief and rejection that even I could see the joke. I began to think that it was my destiny to keep my virginity under every circumstance, although my encounter with Félix, and his photographs, gave me the illusion of having had experiences which the crass history of my flesh denied.

Villefranche-les-Évêques lies on the flank of a deep, narrow valley. The palace of the bishops was derelict at the time when I lived with the Poulain family. The rest of the village consisted of simple houses which spent almost the whole day without sunlight. The palace alone caught the morning sun and its soaring façade kept its neighbours in shadow during the afternoon. For a moment, when I first saw the village, I imagined that my hosts were the owners of the palace (my mother's blood was, after all, in my veins). In fact, the Renaissance windows – commanded it was said by a baron returning, via Italy, from the Crusades – were void of glass. The majesty of the building was an illusion, although it has since been restored.

I had no notion that I should spend the best part of a year with the Poulains. As I think again of that time in 1943 and 1944, I realise both that it comprises the heart of what I want to recall and that I shall have the greatest difficulty in writing accurately about it. As I think of those days, which turned out to be months, I am filled with a sense of bereavement which is the measure not only of the pain but also of the joy that memory revives. How can I be smiling when I remember the house in the woods, the curve of the terrace wall which began quite low and then surged above the pinewoods on the reverse side of the hill on which the bishops' palace stood? I smile because that summer was thick with life; during it, I seemed at last to be born, to emerge from the trammels of a long gestation and breathe uncurdled air.

Dr Poulain was a short man, with keenly humorous eyes. He was acting as a *généraliste*, but he had specialised in pulmonary diseases in

Bordeaux; it was he who had 'borrowed' the photographs in my suitcase. When I asked how they had arrived so promptly at La Fontaine du Noyer, he said only that prevention was the best kind of cure: one had to think ahead. He must have been at least fifteen years younger than I am today, but he had an air of assurance which even now I cannot imagine in myself. His amusement was a way of being serious: unlike my father, whose wryness smacked of resignation, Dr Poulain relished the absurdity of the truth and made it a good reason for engaging with life. The accidental did not affront him; I remember him saying that the great thing about biology was that it was never abstract. 'We medicos lack nobility, that's our strength, Guy, you know.'

Madame Poulain was a pretty woman; that is less her description than her vocation. She was short and fair and energetic. Her prettiness did not exempt her from work but it required her to do it with grace. I never saw her angry, because anger would have soured her face. If she was vain, she showed it only in her modesty. It is tempting to think that she and her husband were as they were because they were lovers, but I think that they were lovers because they were as they were. They belonged together because they recognised the same qualities in each other: they were of the same rare race, that of people who can dare to be happy.

The war did not seem to have come to Villefranche-les-Évêques, although it was nearer Périgueux than Caillac; the Germans used the valley road warily; it would lend itself well to ambush. The villagers were apprehensive of the *bandes de maquisards* which operated in the region and the mayor did his best to persuade their leaders not to mount an operation which would lead to reprisals; the Germans, and their French auxiliaries, could be expected to take their hostages from where they could most easily find them. As a result, when I first arrived at the Poulains', the valley was tensely peaceful. I assumed that my new hosts, like the Lonchats, were supplementing their revenues with my rent, but I was soon aware that they were of a different character entirely. Dr Poulain explained that I was going to be 'extremely useful'; my presence furnished proof that he was running a clinic for tubercular patients. Whereas at Rodecin I had been consigned to secrecy, here I was to play a more public part: by going for walks, in not too vigorous a style, I could be useful to my new friends and to others whom they would, from time to time, be able to shelter.

My hosts had two sons. David Poulain was then about seventeen; Pascal, his brother, must have been twenty-two or three, although his physique and his confidence made him yet another of those whose age I felt I should never reach. Pascal did not spend the day in the house, nor was he always there at night. His maturity made him liable to forced labour; it was prudent to practise invisibility. I was soon aware that Pascal did not merely hide in the woods; I asked no questions, but I guessed the answer that he belonged to one of the *bandes* of which local residents were both proud and afraid.

Pascal came in after dark on the night of my arrival. He was taller than his parents; his air of amusement resembled the doctor's, but it hinted at unmalicious pleasure in being so much larger than his father. David had not yet made the leap into manhood which Pascal's broad and stubbled jaw announced, but the younger brother's slimness and the delicacy of his complexion had nothing of Félix's trim effeminacy; he would be a man, but his time had not yet quite arrived. My presence seemed not to matter to him; he accepted me whole-heartedly because he was indifferent. Like his parents, he knew how to be happy and that knowledge was infectious: even that first evening, when we exchanged banalities, I had a feeling of undeserved election. I knew who I wanted to be and that I could never be that person; my emotion was exempt from envy, and self-pity: I was as happy as I could be in the presence of happiness. Is that the feeling which people call 'love at first sight'? Almost certainly not! Yet I was immediately infatuated with the Poulains. My love was both unconditional and without any individual object: I loved the doctor, whom I did not know, his pretty wife, who found it so easy to be glad at my intrusive presence, and I loved the two brothers who joined so effortlessly in the entertainment of 'the sufferer'. They promoted me to an important place in the busy charade whose purpose they did not explain or conceal; they flattered me with a confidence that made no disclosures. When they assumed me to be of the same stuff as themselves, I could ask for no better compliment. Before the meal was over, I had told them about having to share a bed with Félix and of the embarrassment I had experienced. I did not mention the photographs. After we had eaten, Pascal kissed his parents and shook hands with me before going out into the night. Dr Poulain then said, 'You won't mind sharing a bed with David, will you?'

I said, 'Do you have a daughter?'

They laughed. They laughed and I laughed, but I was mortified by what they took to be my boldness. I had asked the question, I could swear, without any of the meaning which they read into it. I had no notion of my question being a response to Dr Poulain's; it was intended to temporise, not to be insolent.

'Do we have a daughter?' he said. 'Alas, not!'

There was a pause between the repetition of my question and its unmournful answer. It may be a convenient excuse for the dryness of my life, but in that momentary caesura, when a girl seemed to exist who proved, a second later, never to have been born, I had a vision of my future in which I should acquire the qualities of my hosts. In brief, but forever, I saw myself married to their daughter and, callow as it may seem, I knew that I should be happy.

It is a measure of what I have not become that I should feel shame at the thought of anyone reading what I have just said. I felt no such shame when I described my afternoons with Pia or my unlovely dealings with my wife, but I can imagine the scornful laughter of those with whom I have spent my life at the idea that Guy de Roumegouse could ever have been so sentimental as to fall in love with a phantom, let alone that he can still believe that, had she existed, such a girl would have wanted him or could have transformed him into a lifelong lover. Do I not know that I have never been of the race which, to my infatuated eyes, the Poulains impersonated and to which no marriage could ever have assimilated me? I know, I know. But what difference does knowledge make?

I did not, of course, have to share a bed or a room with David. I was billeted in one of the three rooms in the wing of the house facing south-west across the forest at the northern limit of 'The Double'. This wing constituted the 'Clinic' in which, as the weeks stretched into months, I was to see a variety of 'sufferers' receiving the brief 'treatment' which they needed before they continued on their way south. These 'patients' were escaped allied personnel or agents who had had to be moved at short notice. Their 'treatment' was to be given plenty of good food, rest and, when necessary, fresh clothing and papers. I was aware of what the Poulains were doing by a kind of osmosis which demanded no overt information.

I woke on the first morning to high heat; it must have been eleven o'clock and the sun was already rehearsing summer. I had slept easy for the first time in weeks. The first thing I heard, through some open window, was an American record: 'Heaven . . . I'm in heaven . . .' The war was over, it seemed, or had never begun.

David Poulain was crazy about America. He had several American records (he particularly liked Duke Ellington) and he had a shelf of American books, including all of Hemingway's. It was uncommon, in those days, for young Frenchmen to be fascinated by America, but David's appetite for jazz made him dream of the United States as the home of the modern; it was not art but life which interested him. Not knowing how long the war would continue, he had made a leap into the future which encouraged him not to escape what lay between him and it but to imagine that he could treat the present as an inconvenient but undepressing parenthesis. The afternoon after my arrival, he took me on a 'useful walk'; its purpose was to show me the ways through the woods which could, in an emergency we did not need to specify, enable me to get away into 'The Double', where Pascal and his friends would be able to pick up my trail. The less I knew of exactly where to go, the easier it would be for me to do the right thing: if I was not told where the *réseau* was likely to have its base, I should not be able to speak under torture. It was typical of the *style Poulain* that I did not need to have this spelt out to me.

My weeks at Rodecin had seemed endless, both in prospect and in fact; as soon as I arrived at the Poulains', I became unaware of time. I dreaded only its lapse or its curtailment. Is it disreputable to admit that I was in no hurry for the war or even for the occupation to end? I wanted to be part of what the Poulains were doing, less because it was patriotic or morally right than because I wanted to be well thought of by them.

Dr Poulain worked long hours. While throughly engaged in his profession, as his crowded surgery proved, he moved around a large practice in the pony cart which gave him a Balzacian agelessness. He went slowly, but without difficulty, into the countryside; justified by his profession, he had a telephone which might ring at any hour, without exciting suspicion at the exchange (provided the message was either medical or anodyne). No one could know whose illnesses or wounds he was treating and, better than most, he was protected from casual informers by the need which the district had for his services; even those who were not trusted by Pascal and his friends had reason to keep their suspicions to themselves.

David indicated that it would be imprudent to keep left at the ruined houses where local legend said that one of the mediaeval bishops kept two mistresses. Whatever the truth of that, the merchant who lived at Le Moulin des Garrigues was 'a little . . .'; I gathered that he was hostile to one of the *réseaux* because it had been particularly demanding about supplies. Before my return from Rodecin, I was naive enough to think that the Resisters who lived in the wild were almost universally admired and supported. I now learned otherwise: they were feared for their exactions and for the pleasure some of them took in intimidating the farmers and merchants who lacked their mobility. The Communists, under 'Colonel Maurice', were said to take delight in promising to 'admit' that their political enemies had furnished them with supplies. They were both brave and unscrupulous; whereas Pascal's group was composed mainly of local residents, linked by wireless to London but acting on its own initiative until a large-scale allied invasion was imminent, Colonel Maurice's fighting strength included a number of Spanish republicans for whom the liberation would be merely preliminary to what they considered the main battle, which would begin when the allies armed them against Franco. The Spaniards had moved up from the camps in Languedoc-Roussillon. Some of them had been on the run from the French authorities before France was overrun; their hatred of Fascists prevailed over any allegiance to the country in which they happened to be fighting them. So far there had been a tactful concordat between Colonel Maurice and Pascal's commander, but trouble always threatened over sources of food and arms. The Communists believed that London was supplying their rivals with a view to an eventual repression of Colonel Maurice and his group.

The outside world was much closer in Villefranche than it had been in Rodecin. David and I would lie in the woods above the palace and watch German columns pass along the valley. Although we had no weapons, we would take note of the strength and defensive vigilance of the Germans by piling pebbles and sticks between us to form a natural abacus. We memorised the results and reported to Pascal. He thanked us generously, though probably he had all our information before we gave it to him.

At the Poulains', not only was I happy but also, through its cure, I became aware of a sickness from which I had been suffering all my life. Although I was only pretending to be 'the sufferer', I had a feeling of recovery from a genuine malaise. I may have been apprehensive of the Germans and of the Milice, whose parody of their masters' brutalities made them more savage than the savages they served, but I ceased to be afraid within myself; this sense of being cured indicated that something had been wrong with me. It could be said that the callow desire which I certainly felt for Madame Poulain was the kind of attachment which Oedipus might have had for a woman who could have been his mother but was not. I did not attach my fantasies to any part of her, as I had to La Lonchat's detachable breasts, but felt for her that kind of untroubled affection one owes a pretty woman who belongs to another man. The idea of seducing my hostess was repugnant to me, yet I gloried in her cleanness and I enjoyed her polite, breathy kisses quite as though they betokened passion and not familiarity; she gave me a brisk share of her son's rations. Her embraces might be meaningless, but that was their charm; they took me, at least temporarily, for granted.

My stay with the Poulains was a function of the war from which it exempted me. Those months were painful with hope; one wished to be a hero, but not a dead one. It would be unendurable, so near the end, not to see the end. I had no urge to be the Robert Jordan who died happily in a hopeless cause. His death was a reprieve from disillusion; mine would be like missing a party. The Poulains were people in whose company I wished to rejoice. I wanted the war to end, so that we might celebrate our victory. I wanted it to continue, undangerously, so that we might always look forward to, but never reach, the moment when I should cease to be Bruno Le Guen, the young man I should have liked to be, 'the sufferer' who felt so soaringly well and happy, and should be forced to return, without any excuse for further concealment, to the character of Guy de Roumegouse, the shadowy person I should never again escape from being.

XXX

We did not have a daily newspaper delivered to our apartment. Berthe considered it an extravagance, since all of the papers were available to me at the Embassy. Maria laid the breakfast on the round glass-topped table by the terrace window. Berthe did not come to the table, where David and I often ate alone. Patrick was not due at the Montessori school until an hour after I had to deliver his brother to the Lycée. Although my sons are not central to my story, they are likely to be my most attentive readers (I cannot think that Maureen will be more interested in me once I am dead than she is now). The thought of my sons going through this manuscript urges me both to frankness – knowing how much I should have appreciated it (I believe) from my own parents – and to dissimulation. If I had been a scoundrel, with shameless memories, I should probably think them lucky to share my adventures, but since I have been more adjacent to the dramas of my lifetime than a leading player in them, I can imagine them wondering whether I ever truly lived at all.

David had started philosophy. His topic that morning was 'Is necessity necessary?' In the absence of his mother, who disliked solemn conversations early in the day, we conspired to be serious about it. I wondered all the time in what terms the press would deal with Pia's death (assuming it had been discovered) and how differently I should behave if I were indeed the man who committed the murder, instead of merely the man who might be accused of it. My enactment of the diligent father was scarcely a fraud – I was, after all, the very thing I was pretending to be – but there was a kind of slyness in my rigorous attention to David's topic. How would my opinions have differed, if at all, had I indeed been Pia's killer?

There had been nothing on the television news about her death. Had it been discovered yet, or were the killer and I still the only men in Rome to know of it? I saw the usual stack of newspapers on the *cipollino* marble slab of Nando's cubicle, where they were awaiting distribution, but there was nothing lurid enough to catch my eye. My son and I went from the elevator towards the street, discussing the difference, if any, between the inevitable and the necessary.

240

Like the condemned man who sees the beauty of the world he must soon lose forever, I caught the freshness of my son quite as though I wanted to take it with me like a memory. My unnecessary pretence to an innocence which was perfectly justified seemed to win me his confidence; our improbable topic filled us with good humour. The unsmiling comedy of philosophy sweetened our drive down the hill and into the city. As David opened the car door at the gate of the Lycée, we threw our last thoughts at each other like players who cannot resist one final rally even though their lease on the court is already up.

The more I thought about it, the more unwise it now seemed to have told Pierre of my need of him. I did not have the nerve to imagine that he would betray me; my fear was rather that I had armed him against me for no good reason and that that was the only reason I had. If I wanted to make him my brother, I had done it in a way which required my ruin in every other respect before our fraternity could be sealed. My confession had been both rational and absurd, necessary and unnecessary.

The murder was on no front page; it was, however, quite large on page three of *Paese Sera* and on the back of *Il Messagero*. The problem probably was that the editors had no spicy photograph of the dead woman. The text took the usual worldly line over the death of 'a respectable prostitute' – the inevitable description of a whore as discreet as Pia. Nothing suggested that the police had found any significant clue. On the other hand, what did I know of Pia's habits? Perhaps when she sat in that prim living-room, waiting for her favourite programme to appear on the television, she wrote detailed accounts of her clients which might already be in some lame detective's hands. One could imagine a prostitute who dignified her trade by the precision with which she analysed its venal transactions. Why should politicians have a monopoly in that department?

My mind was sharp that day. Since it did not interest me, I was able to apply myself with great lucidity to the matter of creating difficulties over the export of Italian wine to France while appearing to be doing my best to eliminate them. As I sought to defeat their interests, my Italian colleagues wondered where they would be without me. The morning went so quickly that I had to accept that the police were unlikely to interview me before lunch. Only while I was eating a *cotoletta Milanese* with Heinz Model, a commercial attaché at the German Embassy, and Anton Van Dijk, a Dutchman of similar rank, did I again remember how Pia had told me of the priest who had brought her to climax; I wondered whether my overture to Pierre had not been an unconscious attempt to tease him into a confession. How delicious, after all, if he had not been at the Villa Giulia any longer than I!

It so happened that Anton van Dijk was the replacement for the Dutchman who had given me Pia's address and recommended her services. He was a young and garrulous person, of almost albino fairness. Knowing that he had a pretty Danish wife, who reminded me, in her neat vivacity, of Monique Poulain, I had no reason to think that he too might have been Pia's client. Heinz, on the other hand, was a shinily bald, dark-bearded man (a Bavarian, I imagine), with busy appetites. He sought to enliven the occasion by teasing Anton about the beauty of his wife: 'Rome is so full of compensations for unhappiness that being happily married seems rather like a misfortune, doesn't it, Guy?'

Suspecting that we had certain tastes in common, I found Heinz extremely distasteful. I said, 'Cassata ice cream is a debauchery which scarcely leaves a trace. I shall indulge. Will you?'

Our lunch had no particular purpose unless it was to enable us to pretend to be friends even when no business obliged it. Diplomatic life in Rome lacked the narrowness of that in Damascus or Buenos Aires; there was enough society of all kinds for us to be dispensed from repetitious soirées. Intrigues were voluntary, though gossip welcomed them. We were eating our cassata when Heinz said that he had heard a story which he looked confidently to me to verify, or embellish: was there indeed a Roman bordello where all the girls were the doubles of famous film stars? Apparently their understudies were younger than the real thing, but he had heard that on at least one occasion a star herself had taken the place of her double and had received encouraging tips.

I said, 'Was her name Messalina by any chance?'

'What would I have seen her in?' Heinz said.

As the ghost of Monsieur Picpus threw his scarf-ends across his chest, Anton said, 'Did you see about that tart that got killed in the paper?'

Heinz said, 'Of course.'

I said, 'What was that?'

'This tart that was stabbed in her flat – she was quite famous, it seems, with some of us.'

I said, 'Tell me more. Who wants *espresso*?'

Heinz said, 'You can tell he knows all about her, can't you, Anton?'

Anton said, 'Of course.'

It was a relief again to have something to hide. I made a neat show of being concerned about my *espressi*; it was a foible of mine to order two small cups rather than one large one; big cups diluted the concentration.

Heinz said, 'You remember Jan Pieters, don't you? Didn't he ever tell you about his top ten?'

I said, 'I remember Jan, of course.'

'I've got a feeling she was one of his. You read between the lines, you can see that she was into some pretty fancy things.'

'You've seen lines I haven't,' I said. 'How is Jan? And where?'

'I'll tell you something,' Heinz said, 'the best time I ever had in my life was in Colombia. I was there for a couple of years and some people out there, they took me to a place – the girls were laughing all the time. Wicked as hell, do whatever you like, they laughed and they laughed.'

I said, 'I'm not sure I should've liked that.'

'You would have, I promise you, Guy, because they had no shame, no shame at all. True whores, they thought they were lucky to be what they were: they danced, but it wasn't the tango, it was the come-and-fuck-me! Fourteen, fifteen years old . . . but ripe like pineapples! Tits to knock your eye out.'

After we had shaken hands on the pavement, I ambled back to the Embassy. Two unconvincing anti-terrorist policemen stood outside the gate. They resembled children in fancy dress who had lost the address of the party. I waited all afternoon for an unexpected call from the police, but succeeded only in offering a useful revision of an agreement about olive oil. After accepting my Ambassador's congratulations, I left the Embassy and walked up towards the Piazza della Repubblica. The area pulsed with the vulgarity common to districts near large railway stations; the promise of the illicit and the transitory dramatised the ordinary. The façade of Termini in the distance recalled the days when Mussolini's vanity seemed a form of efficiency; it was from there that his punctual trains were said to leave.

I bought an evening paper and went into a bar to scan it. I was in one of those moods when caprice and compulsion amount to the same thing. Smoke swirled under the fluorescent lights and there were pin-tables at the back. It was the sort of place I detest, loud and dirty, with surly travellers sitting among their roped luggage with the snotty, overheated children on whom they seemed to have spent all their money. The '*capucc*' for which I had had to pay in advance came in a cracked cup.

There was nothing new in the paper. The earlier report had been fattened with interviews with people in Pia's building, including the *padrone* of the Pensione di Londra who hoped that the next tenant would be more careful about shutting the elevator door.

'*Buona sera, commendatore!*'

A man in a blue raincoat and a pork-pie hat (oh that facetious Tyrolean feather!) was looking down at my newspaper. Could he tell that I was interested in Pia? He had a puffy face and narrow, insinuating eyes; he was used to reading people as if they were as easy as headlines.

'What brings you to Rome?'

I said, 'I'm afraid you're making a mistake.'

'*Ma no!* I have something nice for you, if you want something nice.'

I said, 'You're taking me for something I'm not, I'm afraid.'

'*Francese*, no?'

I said, 'I've got to go.'

He said, 'You're someone who likes clean women, aren't you? Not dull, but clean, and young. I saw you in the street; I saw you come in here. I have the ideal thing. Not more than five minutes' walk. Or do you have a car?'

I said, 'I'm on my way home. I have an appointment.'

'Shall I show you a picture? Because I have a picture. And don't worry, this is not a sulky girl, this is not some tired old trout. This is very nice, from the country, but not too far out, all right? Someone who enjoys her work.'

I said, 'I'm sorry, it's out of the question.'

He said, 'Ten thousand lire, you can do what you like. She's like this. I'll show you the pictures, what's the harm?'

The pimp and the policeman share the assumption that they are rarely wrong. I suspected that the man might be both. Had he followed me from the Embassy? How did he guess my nationality? I shrugged my shoulders and pretended to finish my coffee hurriedly, as if I had a train to catch. The girl in his photographs was plump and shiny with broad nipples of a kind which does not appeal to me. She had crinkly dark hair; she had turned to one side and was pouting at the camera with one hand on her hip and the other between her legs. Hair was springing between the fingers; it might have been coming through a hole in a mattress. I wiped my lips and waved my hand and walked out of the bar. I walked quite slowly, but the man did not pursue me. The girl immediately became more attractive to me; what I had missed excited me more than what I might have had.

I went back to the Embassy to collect my car and saw two women standing by the gate. As I was letting myself into the compound, one of them came over to me. She and her friend were on holiday; both their passports and all their money had been in the bag of the older one, which had been snatched by a Vespa-rider near the Trevi fountain. Could I help them? I explained that the consular section would be open in the morning and that they should be very careful in Rome. They agreed with shining eyes. One was dark and had wide cheekbones and used a kind of fluorescent lipstick, the other could have been Spanish for although she had fair hair, combed very flat and secured by a slide, there was something of the flamenco dancer in her slim body – that arched back, those unblinking dark eyes! She watched the other woman with the deferential disdain of the physically agile for those who have to use their minds. As soon as the dark woman began to talk, I had all the symptoms which I knew from my conversations with whores. The dancer's smile dwelt more admiringly on her friend as my courtesies grew more elaborate.

I said, 'Have you got somewhere to stay?'

They did, but they had no means of paying the bill nor, of course, could they eat dinner. I said it was unlikely that the consulate would give them money, though their papers could almost certainly be replaced; I should be glad to help them. The dark woman, who was wearing a shiny green dress and heels much too high for sightseeing, said how lucky they were to have met me.

'And what are you doing in Rome?'

'We've come to see the Pope.'

'The Pope?'

'Why not? There was a draw and we won. We had an audience with him today. A dozen of us, no more.'

'And what did he say to you?'

'What does the Pope say to people? Be good, goodbye!'

'Perhaps you could ask him to help you out.'

'They won't let us in to talk to him again, will they?'

I said, 'I'm not a rich man.'

'Oh, but Monsieur . . . we couldn't possibly let you.'

'You don't take money from men?'

'It's true, you know. We were admiring the fountain – we even threw a coin into it – and then this man came along and . . .'

'I don't doubt it for a moment. Look, here's twenty thousand lire. Are you of Spanish origin?'

The blonde woman said, 'Perhaps.' It might have been her only word of French; she used it reluctantly, but with *hauteur*.

I said, 'Have you been to the police?'

'The police? No.'

245

I said, 'They open here at ten in the morning. You'd better come then. And don't tell them that I gave you money. Don't tell anyone, or I shall become more popular than my income can support!'

The dark woman said, 'What can we do for you in return?'

I had given them what I usually paid Pia. Whatever they were – perhaps waitresses who had indeed been lucky in some lottery – they would hardly have resented being asked to give some quick return for my generosity. They would probably have enjoyed the meal better if they had earned it. I was neither hard enough to set out my terms and invite them into my empty office nor chaste enough to take comfort in my philanthropy. I said, 'I'm not always as foolish as this. Perhaps it's the influence of the Pope.'

'That's what it is,' the dark woman said. 'We'll say a prayer in gratitude.'

'To him or to me?'

'Both. She can do him; I'll do you.'

'*Bon appétit*. I'm sorry I can't take you to dinner myself.'

'So are we, so are we. Thank you a thousand times.'

I said, 'May I ask you something rather personal? Do you paint your toenails?'

'Of course. I do and so does she. Shall I show you?'

'Not at all. I was just having a little bet with myself.'

'Is there anything else?'

'Not a thing.' I let myself into the compound and closed the solid metal gate behind me. I had even deprived myself of watching them walk away from me. The excitement I had felt as soon as I had the women in my power was slow to subside. It was, however, not transferable; the whores whom I passed on the pavement as I drove up the Via Trionfale would expect to be paid again, and in sordid circumstances, for what I might gladly have been granted. My desire was not for sex but for a transaction in which both I and the woman would get away with a kind of murder.

The Via Trionfale was always lurid with headlights during the evening rush. That night, the traffic was thicker than usual. I saw flashing lights up ahead and wondered if there had been a fire, or a terrorist bomb. I edged closer to our apartment block without connecting the presence of police cars with anything that could touch my regular life; in my experience, the imagination does not prepare one for what actually happens but is an alternative to it. I was only a few metres from the concrete slab which sloped under the building to the car park when I saw the three police cars parked outside our entrance. It was impossible to turn across the traffic; there were no

246

side roads by which one might escape up Monte Mario. Would I have taken one, if there had been?

I drove down into the car park, expecting to find a *carabiniere* in wait. There was no one. I walked to the lit corner from which the elevator could be taken directly to my floor. I still had money, and a chequebook and my passport, and could, I suppose, have found my way to the airport or back to Termini and given the police, as they say, a run for their money. I had no appetite for any such escapade. I feared only that, now that it was imminent, I should give a weak performance as the innocent man in whose story not a single person was ever going to believe. That election at least I was able to enjoy in the seconds before the little sign announced *al piano* and I opened the lift door.

I rode upwards, once I had pressed the button, in complete serenity. I think it true to say that I was looking forward to all the embarrassments, including even my own. My unworthiest sentiment was of satisfaction not only at Berthe's imminent humiliation but also, more succulent still, at the thought of her irrelevance. How delightful it would be when I called on Pierre to be the crucial witness! Would she guess that he had perjured himself for my sake?

The elevator stopped. I could not see any reception committee on the landing. Did they think me dangerous? Would they leap on me from the shadows as I stepped out of the car? I imagined the tension on their faces, the unstrapped holsters with the rehearsed hands on the butts of their guns, the exchanges of silent whispers. Were they ready? I was. Checking the innocence of my expression, I stepped out onto the marble landing. I could hear the breath in my nostrils. I looked round; there was no sign of anyone. There were two flats on each floor; my door was shut, so was that of the Alitalia official who lived opposite. The ambush must be inside my own apartment. I advanced with my key and slid it into the lock. The door was thrown open instantly.

I reared back, expecting uniforms and the hard faces of men whose very complexions would be pitted with the disillusionment of their métier. Berthe threw herself into my arms; she was like a large, rather damp package. I thought perhaps she had been washing her hair, which was more puzzling than alarming.

'Oh Guy,' she said. 'Oh Guy! This is so terrible, it's so frightful.'

I was looking over her shoulder for the heartlessly kind inspector who had been grilling her about my habits while they waited for the culprit's return. I was more concerned about David's feelings than about hers.

247

I said, 'Calm yourself.'

She said, 'It isn't how you think; I swear to you.'

I said, 'I'm afraid you're going to have to explain what this is all about. What isn't like what?'

She said, 'Didn't you see them? The police? Didn't you see?'

I said, 'I just this minute got home. I parked the car; I came up in the elevator. I saw that there were some police cars in front, but . . .'

She said, 'The most terrible thing has happened.'

I said, 'Is David all right?'

'David? Oh, David's fine. It's nothing to do with him. You didn't speak to anyone?'

'Berthe, try and calm yourself. What exactly has happened?'

'It's all in the last hour . . . an hour ago, everything was perfectly calm . . . nothing had happened, no one was . . .'

I said, 'Come into the bedroom. Let's not upset the boys.'

She said, 'You won't want to be nice to me when you hear what happened.'

'You may be surprised,' I said. I led her into the bedroom and shut the door. 'Now!'

She shook her head. Her hair looked too heavy to support. She sat at her dressing table and leaned her jaw on both hands. 'I know you're not going to believe me,' she said.

'You'll have to persuade me of that.'

She swivelled and looked at me. The girl I had first seen at La Fontaine du Noyer was not entirely concealed behind the woman she had become. I was touched, but not by love. She said, 'I suppose they've taken him away already, have they?'

I said, 'Who? Whom?'

'The police, of course, the ambulance.'

'I saw no ambulance.'

'Then they obviously have. Guy, for David's sake . . . you must believe me. I'm completely innocent . . . you won't think so, but I am. I know you don't love me and I daresay I don't deserve you to, but think of the boys.'

I said, 'I'll believe anything you ask of me, but what?'

'I know you,' she said. 'You won't. You can't. I can hardly believe it myself.'

'Dear God, woman, if there's something you want me to believe, at least come out with it. I may be asking the same of you some time . . .'

'Never,' she said, 'never! You haven't any idea?'

'None. Have the police been here?'

'Of course. Of course.'

'And are they still here?'

'Why ever should they be?' She found some tissues and blotted her face before looking at me once again with those large, cow-like eyes. There is very little anyone can do about their eyes; Berthe's were large but they protruded, especially when she was distressed, so that emotion gave her an air of indignation, which immediately dissipated my sympathy. 'In the end, what's it really got to do with us? Except that it's terrible.'

I said, 'I still don't know what "it" is, exactly. But if it's terrible, it sounds as if it might be something to do with us!'

'There you are – you hate me!'

'Berthe, you're my wife . . . and it's time to explain yourself.'

She said, 'He was mad. He was mad. It's the only explanation.'

I said, 'Who was mad and what does it explain?'

'You're cold. You're always so cold. How can anyone live with someone as cold as you are?'

'I imagine it can't be easy, but is that the most important question at the moment?'

She said, 'Miguel. Miguel.'

I said, 'I beg your pardon?'

'Miguel! It's not true, it's not true . . . how am I ever going to persuade you after what I said before? It's not fair!'

I was sickened, as well as baffled. I was sorry for her and I could not, literally, stand the sight of her. I sat on the corner of the bed and took one of her raw hands. 'What is not true?'

'If you loved me,' she said, 'I wouldn't feel like I do. As it is, I have to endure all the pain, all the fear, just as if you really cared for me, at the same time as knowing that it's all for nothing. *Nothing!*'

'Yes,' I said, 'it calls for certain qualities, doesn't it, our situation?'

She said, 'You're a man without pity, Guy. I've always been afraid of you. Whatever happened to your feelings?'

I said, 'They died young. What is this all about?'

She said, 'You want me to be guilty of something, don't you? I'm not. He was mad, that's all, and I would never even have kept his letter if . . . if I weren't so unhappy.'

I said, 'You're a comfortable woman in good health who drinks too much. Who is he and what letter are you talking about?'

'You really don't know, do you?'

'You're very perceptive,' I said.

'It's unbelievable,' she said. 'It's unbelievable.'

'Shit,' I said.

'Where are you going?'

'Who is this Miguel? Is he relevant to all this?'

'Miguel,' she said. 'O'Higgins. Miguel O'Higgins. Who lived upstairs. You didn't see the ambulance?'

'What did Miguel O'Higgins do, or not do, exactly? And what does it have to do with what I believe or don't believe? Just tell me what happened in simple terms, because . . .'

'Did you see about that prostitute who was murdered?'

I said, 'Prostitute?'

'It was in the papers, who was murdered, cut to pieces, in her flat. Do you know what they found in her bedroom?'

I said, 'Not your gloves by any chance?'

'Of course not. Gloves? Of course not. My coat. My white coat. You know the one.'

'It didn't say anything about that in the paper, did it?'

'Of course not. It's horrible, what happened. My coat was – it was all covered in blood and . . . other things – and they didn't even spot it at first, but in the pocket . . . in the pocket they found, they found this letter . . . and then . . .'

'What letter? You know; I don't. What letter?'

'From Miguel. I never encouraged him, Guy. I never noticed him hardly until . . . until he wrote to me.'

I said, 'How did this tart get hold of your coat?'

'That's what's so horrible, so unbelievable. There's only one way that she can have: he gave it to her. He must have got in here somehow –perhaps Maria let him in, though she denies it – and taken it from my wardrobe. Can you imagine a man doing something like that? Taking my coat and then going with it to a prostitute and asking her to . . . to put it on, I suppose and. . . ?'

'It's not easy,' I said. 'But how did they connect it with O'Higgins?'

She said, 'They read the letter and then . . . there was a cleaner's tag on it, which they traced to the people in the Medaglie d'Oro I took it to. You know what the police are like.'

'They came here?'

'Of course they came here. Perhaps he wrote letters to lots of women. It was all stained and disgusting – but it was unmistakable.'

'And you told them who wrote it?'

'Why wouldn't I?'

'You told them it was your lover?'

'He never touched me, Guy. That's what you have to believe. I had no idea what was going to happen.'

'I still don't know what did.'

'You do. You want me to have to tell you.'

I said. 'What did he say when they went up there?'

'Say? I don't know. I only know what he did.'

'Which was?'

She swung her arm and pointed to the window, without looking at it. 'Half an hour before you got home.'

I said, 'O'Higgins? Were you . . . there?'

'They waited for him to get home. They showed him the coat, and the letter, and where they'd been found and . . . he didn't deny it, he couldn't deny it, could he? He went over to the window and . . . they couldn't stop him.'

I said, 'Do they want to see me?'

She said, 'Why would anyone want to see you?'

XXXI

For reasons of security, Pascal Poulain returned irregularly to his parents' house, but when he was there, he showed few signs of apprehension. I was more nervous on his behalf than any of the family. Perhaps they knew the odds better than I; perhaps they elected to discount them. They recruited me to a kind of confidence which was never natural to me but which it became my ardent wish to imitate. Their generosity lay in their willingness to assume me capable of the same grace which made them so attractive to me. For the first time in my life I was able to become a little proud of myself, though I never lost my suspicion that I might fall from grace as the result of some clumsiness of body or spirit. My desire to match the untroubled virility of Pascal went so far as to imitate his walk, his smile, his vocabulary; I shaped my performance on his, just as sportsmen will repeat the superficial gestures of an admired star. I too wanted to have achievements to understate; I too should have liked to embrace Monique and laugh at the little cry she gave at the coldness of her son's cheeks as autumn stiffened into winter. My appetite for some heroic opportunity owed less to patriotism than to a longing to prove what was never the case, that I belonged with the Poulains.

My shyness, which David – thinking that I was homesick for a grander life! – took for condescension, was the pale face of a passion to be worthy of my hosts' trust and affection. In short, having fallen in love with them all, my desire was not directed at any one of them, nor could it be called sexual in any ordinary sense, but it showed itself in moments of excitement which, no doubt on account of my age, announced themselves in physical terms.

When Pascal told me that an operation had been mounted against a convoy of equipment which David and I had monitored from the top of a railway cutting on the line to Angoulême, I shrugged and made a modest face (as I guessed he would have). I repressed the urge to tell him that I was willing to do anything, anything, which would be of use to him. I envied the facility with which he handled the Sten gun which had been dropped by the British and which he would put at the back of the *armoire* when he sat down to table. Was I the same person who had felt such angry fear when Félix threatened to go into Rodecin for a bit of amusement? I liked to think that I had left my old character behind; the Poulains called me Bruno, in accordance with the name on my papers, so that we should all be accustomed to my false identity in case of a visit by the Germans or the *Milice*. I was glad to be someone with so skimpy a history, whose manners and even whose abilities could be a matter of decision rather than of involuntary heredity. It was prudent and delightful to forget my own background and to become an object of pure fiction. Given an exhilarating chance to start again, I was able to emigrate from the timidities which had seemed both natural and oppressive when I had to be Guy de Roumegouse. Bruno le Guen did not have to be saddled with doubts and confused loyalties of which he was suspicious or ashamed (my uncle's shadow did not stretch as far as Villefranche-les-Évêques); Bruno might be callow, but he had a kind of neatness, an ability to travel light, which Guy could not match. There was nothing which I would have hesitated to do for Pascal; my only disappointment was that the latter was reluctant to take me with him into the woods and introduce me to his network.

Should I have asked him directly? I kept thinking that the moment of election would come and that I might blight my chances by pleading my case. I should be brave, I hoped, were I to be conscripted, but I was less certain that I could establish my claim if I seemed to be forcing myself on Pascal and his friends; I might measure up to their expectations, but could I allay their doubts? It may be that Pascal had no need for trainees who would more endanger the security of his group than add to its strength; it is more likely that my presence in the house was a convenient reason to refuse his brother's requests to join the *Maquis*. Since I was slightly older than David, I provided a plausible argument for patience: if I could wait, so should he.

Wanting nothing so much as to do well in in his brother's eyes, David was irked by the small praise which greeted our amateurish spying. Amiable as he was, he began to visit on me the resentment which he did not like, or dare, to show to his brother. Had I not been around, he could have insisted that he was old enough to do more than run occasional errands. For the present, he was willing to be his mother's consolation, but he feared that the war would end and that, partly on my account, he would have only a schoolboy's stories to tell. His father's busy humour promised that we should all come through the next few months – or however long it might take – without difficulty. Dr Poulain knew very well that there were risks, and that it needed only some small accident for something fatal to follow, but he was resolved not to let fear intimidate him; knowing that it was infectious, he set a wilfully scrupulous example. David was both inspired and, perhaps, a little soured by his father's energetic optimism; it confirmed his feeling that he was being unfairly excluded from great events. He wanted no longer to be a child, but he was jealous of the toys – the guns and the wireless sets, the cylinders of money and equipment – with which he saw the adults were being supplied. Once, when a drop had taken place in a clearing not far from the house, Pascal arrived, laughing through the black boot polish on his night face, and put a chinking satchel on the oak dining table; it contained thousands and thousands of English sovereigns.

'We're rich, Mother! You can have anything you want!'

Monique said, 'What's going to happen to it? What's it for?'

'It's for buying people, isn't it? You can buy a lot of people for what's in here.'

'No,' she said, 'What is it for?'

'It's for when we need it.' Pascal's face was all black again; the white smile had gone. 'It's not over yet.'

'And what if it never gets used?'

'My mother wants to be rich!' Pascal said. He kissed her and kept his arm around her; he might have been posing for a photograph. 'It's not enough to be beautiful.'

'Never,' she said.

A few days later, at the beginning of December, Dr Poulain asked me if I would care to do him a service by going into Brantôme to meet a 'patient' who was to spend a day or two with us. There was a café on the far side of the river, facing the *quai*, where I should sit reading the newspaper folded in a special way. He demonstrated it to me as if it were a simple conjuring trick. A man would come up to me and ask whether I knew where 'the one-legged soldier' lived. I was to say that I knew someone who knew him, to which the answer would be, 'I have a message from his aunt.' Dr Poulain rehearsed the exchange with me a couple of times. We might have been cast at short notice in a village play; his smile admitted the artificiality of the dialogue but encouraged me to take it as seriously as I could. If the stranger arrived, which was not at all certain, and if his replies accorded with the script, I was to take him to a peasant's house on the outskirts of Brantôme and wait for transport.

Although Dr Poulain gave the impression that I was doing him a simple favour, I took my commission as evidence that I had reached the stage of being an active probationer. I should have liked to be in danger as I caught the bus which took me to Brantôme, but only so that I should feel more worthy of the Doctor's faith. The small anxiety which rode with me was that my expedition was going to be as banal as I feared and that I should have no opportunity of displaying the courage or initiative which might qualify me for promotion. Hence, when I saw that there was a German reconnaissance car parked under the trees by the Dronne, my reaction was one of gratitude. The apprehension that went through me was closer to stage fright than to any practical dread of arrest.

I set Bruno's face in the mould of Pascal Poulain's – cheerful rather than defiant – and walked with his casual swagger past where a greatcoated corporal was dozing at the wheel of his vehicle. Two soldiers, with rifles, were talking to a girl under the trees by the slow green river on which two swans, knowing no better than to be peacefully beautiful, drifted and paddled in mean-eyed complacency. I looked at the girl without malice but with a trace of envy; her unguarded proximity to the enemy – whom she may have been simply unable to avoid – was a kind of privilege, as if she were exempt, by virtue of her sex, from any cruel response to her pouting insolence. It was by no means certain that her frailty entailed that she was safe from abuse or arrest, but the very shape of her breath on the cold air seemed to declare a kind of soft defiance. I could not help looking back at her from the parapet of the bridge; a blink of pleading apprehension in her dark eyes blessed me with more power than I possessed. I was grateful and a little embarrassed by the urgency with which she wanted me to forget what I'd seen. I felt close to her, in consequence, quite as if I craved the same access to seduction (and rejection) which brought her face to face with the pale young soldiers who were trying to win her favour.

I had come equipped with the necessary newspaper, which I had under my coat; it might have been a hidden weapon. The café was a single high, gloomy room with a fan in the ceiling. I asked the mittened woman behind the zinc bar for a glass of red wine and went to the table by the door; wishing that I had brought a book, I unfolded the newspaper, fumbling in dread lest I should forget how precisely it was supposed to look when my 'friend' arrived. Between the cretonne curtains, I was able to see the bridge and the wide corner he would be obliged to turn in order to reach me. Although I was sure that the man who first came that way was not my contact, I hurriedly folded the paper and set it beside my glass, only to unfold it again, with a nervous glance at the *patronne*, when he waved to her and indicated that he would be back later, before walking on past. She came towards me and I awaited her arrival with blank helplessness; I was nothing more than a hoop of consciousness which she seemed quite capable of stepping through and puncturing without even noticing what she had done. In fact, she went to the corner of the room where there was a small stove; its long metal flue rose halfway to the ceiling before veering towards the wall where it disappeared. She put a couple of splits of wood into its mouth, closed it and went back to the bar. When I again glanced out at the bridge, two men had already crossed it; one of them had his hand out for the door of the café. I folded the newspaper in what I hoped was the prescribed way and sat back, certain that my solitary contact was yet to appear.

One of the men was dark and his face was stippled with beard; the other was taller but more boyish, with a fair complexion and a square jaw which reminded me of the cowboys I had seen in American films. Both men seemed to be walking inside their baggy clothes, as if their bodies were independent of what covered them. They went to the bar and the younger indicated the bottle of red wine.

'Excuse me, but do you know the old soldier?' The dark man addressed me from the bar, in an accent I could not distinguish, though it was certainly not that of a Frenchman.

I said, 'What old soldier exactly?'

The dark man looked at his friend, who came across to my table. He put his hand on my newspaper and leaned down to me. 'Are you the man who knows the old soldier?'

I said, 'It depends who you mean.'

The *patronne* had filled the glasses and pushed them towards the dark man.

'We had a few problems and that's why we're late, so let's get on with it, shall we? Did someone tell you to wait here?'

I said, 'I don't know what you're talking about, I'm afraid.'

'Isn't this your newspaper?'

I said, 'Do you want to borrow it?'

The younger man sat down next to me. 'I was meant to come on my own,' he said, 'but then . . . something happened and I didn't have any choice.' He spoke in a snappy tone, neither whispering nor casual; he bulged his lips at his companion, as if he had offered me a clue which I was being too stupid to accept. 'Can you take us somewhere where we can talk?'

I said, 'I don't have any idea who you are.'

The young man made an impatient face and went to the bar, took his glass and whispered to his friend. I had the impression that they were debating whether or not I was reliable. I could feel the sulky, pedantic Guy de Roumegouse usurping the place of Bruno le Guen, who believed himself capable of handling these situations with flair and instinct.

The dark man came over to me and, in even less fluent French, asked me plainly whether I was expecting to meet someone or not.

I said, 'Who are you exactly?'

He said, 'Let's get on with it, can we?'

I said, 'This old soldier, does he have an aunt?'

His response to my prompt was to slap the edge of the table with my paper. 'Does he have an aunt? He could have.'

The man at the bar said, 'Let's go and see her, shall we?'

I stood up and went to pay for my drink, but the 'cowboy' put money on the bar and with a circular movement of his hand included my bill in his. He left too much money anyway. When we were outside on the *quai*, I said, 'Why are there two of you?'

'Because twice one is two. We had to clear out in a hurry and we didn't know what else to do.'

I said, 'What are you?'

'I'm Australian,' the fair one said, 'and he's English. We're both fliers. Are you going to take my word for it, or do you want to see our wings?'

I said, 'Weren't you told what to say?'

The Australian said, 'Let's get on with it, can we now?'

'Follow me.'

'That's more like it. What's wrong with this bastard? What does he think we are? Jesus F.!'

I was mortified by their failure to honour the formula which Dr Poulain had announced, but I had no serious doubt that they were entitled to my help. I wanted to believe that I was taking a risk in leading them to the safe house where we were to wait for transport and that it had required decisive nerve on my part not to walk away in pretended ignorance. Their failure to appreciate my adaptability wounded my vanity; it seemed not to occur to them that their safety depended on my decision to give them the benefit of the doubt. We were almost at the end of the town when the Australian said, 'The soldier's only got one leg, am I right?'

I said, 'You might have said that sooner.'

He said, 'Two of our guys got caught in Poitiers two nights ago and we had to move fast. A few wires got crossed, I'm afraid. How are things around here?'

I said, 'So far so good.'

'I can think of a few people who'd like to be down here instead of where they are, can't you, Col?'

The Englishman took a few deep breaths, as if he needed them, and ducked into the smoke-browned room of the cottage whose owner, a patient of Dr Poulain, was a small, wrinkled man in a leather cap with loose earflaps who seemed more like a species of incurious insect than a member of the Resistance. He indicated that the Anglo-Saxons should sit by the fire.

I said, 'They've had a bit of a near one.'

He shrugged and sighed and took a bottle from the alcove by the fire and set two small greenish glasses on the mantel. He filled them with *eau de vie* from a clear bottle and left them for me to hand to the men. Bruno le Guen took the drinks to be a restorative for the travellers; Guy de Roumegouse regarded the peasant's failure to pour a glass for him as a sign of disdain. I might as well not have been there.

The owner of the cottage appeared to live alone; having made his single gesture of hospitality, he preferred to act as though we were as good as invisible. He gave a show of solitude, even in the presence of the two men whose foreign whispers, and large presence, might have earned them the friendly interest of another kind of man. Since I had no standing either with the peasant or with those I had been deputed to escort, I elected to remain silent and inconspicuous. The airmen sipped their small glasses and found what occasion they could for mutual amusement. They had loosened their shoes and opened their coats; they might have been visiting a tribe whose ways were mysterious but unalarming. In truth, they were in no particular danger, even if the Germans caught up with them, unless their captors were of an unusually vicious character, whereas the peasant and I would fare much worse, although small glamour attached to us.

I thought that Dr Poulain himself might come by for us in his trap, but no one had yet arrived when the peasant, having lit a small oil lamp, got up and went into the kitchen, adjacent to where we were waiting, and began to prepare himself a meal. A shotgun hung above the shelf in the alcove where the bottle was. It was now quite dark outside. A car or two, certainly in the service of the Germans, went along the main road with the faint hiss of tyres. There was no telephone in the cottage.

The Australian said, 'Looks like we're going to be kipping here, Col.'

The Englishman said, 'Has there been a hitch?'

I said, 'They said someone'd be along.'

'Who said?'

'The people who sent me.'

The Australian spoke in English again. 'This character doesn't look like much of a Jungle Boy to me.'

I said, 'I think you should stay here. I'll go and see what's happened.'

The Englishman said, 'Hold on a minute. What do we do if you don't come back?'

'I'll come back,' I said, 'but it may not be till morning.'

'Do we trust him?'

I said, 'I seem to have trusted you.'

'You've hurt his feelings, Col.'

'What's Jiminy Cricket going to think if he has us on his hands all night?'

I said, 'I'll stay here with you if that's what you prefer.'

'What the hell good's that going to do anybody?'

'If anyone comes and asks you who brought you here, tell them that you forced yourself on –' I indicated the peasant '– and don't say that you're expecting anyone to come for you.'

'We know how to wipe our own arses,' the Australian said. 'On your way, sonny, if you know what you're doing.'

Wanting them to think that I was used to handling crises, I went and told the peasant that I would get the two men away from the cottage as soon as possible and asked him to give them some food, for which I promised him, reproachfully, that I should see that he was paid. He said, 'A little bread, no one has to pay for that. Nor for a bit of *terrine de lapin.*'

'Then why not give it to them?'

I was glad to be out of the house, although I had more than a two-hour walk back to Villefranche-les-Évêques. I had told myself that I should move more swiftly and more safely alone, but I also wanted to spare myself both the burden of their company and the humiliation of being scolded for bringing two men instead of one, if I had been wrong to do so. I walked along the road until I came to a track which David had shown me during one of our scouting expeditions. The winter trees were skeletons in the mist. I walked at an uneven pace; anxious to shed the responsibility for the airmen, fearful of having done the wrong thing, I trotted and then slowed down. I was willing to be reproved, but not to be mocked; I almost wanted the two men to be dangerous, so that my leaving them at the cottage could be taken for intelligent caution. What I dreaded was a great shout of laughter as Pascal told me to go on back and get them. Such a response would turn the resourceful Bruno back into the incompetent Guy.

The countryside was lifeless. Nothing but my own footsteps

259

sounded in the darkness. It was cold and damp; even the farm dogs had abandoned their yapping vigilance. I was as good as nobody and I was happy to be dispensed from creation, an incorporeal message on the night air. Of course I felt the hard breath in my chest as I went up over the hill which then descended toward the Moulin des Garrigues, but my body was a satchel of skin and bone in which my freedom was riding and from which (I could imagine) it might escape, almost without notice, and be lost in the wilderness. I did not desire oblivion but I already enjoyed its irresponsibility: the two airmen meant nothing to me, although I should do whatever I was told to take them to safety. The Poulains' approval was more important than the men's lives.

If I was in any danger as I threaded the woods, it was more likely to be from Colonel Maurice's men than from the Germans; the Communists might not take me for a collaborator, but I had gathered from Pascal's warnings that they were capable of holding any stray members of the 'bourgeois' resistance as bargaining counters when it came to the next 'drop'. It was unlikely that any 'hunting parties' would be out when the weather made air operations impossible, but I approached the wood-merchant's mill with wariness; Maurice was said to have made heavy demands for food and clothing from the man, knowing that this might lead him to ask for protection from the Germans, who could then be ambushed, something which could, in its turn, lead the occupying forces to accuse the merchant of duplicity. It entertained the 'Colonel' (who had, before the war, been the editor of a rather scandalous newspaper) to devise ways of embroiling his enemies with each other.

Pale light edged the locked shutters of the millhouse. I made a wide detour through the woods, hoping that I should find a junction with the track which would take me on up the valley towards the back entrance to the Poulains'. I tried to prepare my speech, and style, in imitation of Pascal. I wondered how he would have described the airmen and whether he would make light of the small suspicion that they were not quite what they should have been. How serious were passwords usually taken? How ridiculous was it to persist in doubts which the men's appearance rendered almost bureaucratic? I resolved to be both light-hearted and eager to do what I least wanted, which was to go straight back to the cottage and guide the men to the 'clinic' where they would be said, like me, to be under treatment.

Having reached the end of the triangular retaining wall from the top of which the Poulains had their long view of the pine-filled valley which pointed the way into the heart of 'The Double', I bent over with my hands on my knees to recover my breath. It was not yet midnight, but it seemed later. A stone path took me up to where the three bedrooms of the 'clinic' stood darkly against the mist. The main house was quiet, but the shutters of the living room were still unlocked. Apprehension over whether I had done the right thing, combined with pleasure at being about to see my friends, so dominated my mind that I did not find the silence significant; one hardly expected music or laughter. Life was generally quieter in those days.

I tapped lightly on the door and then I tried the French window; it was open and I stepped inside. There was only one lamp burning, on the desk where Monique left messages for the Doctor when people had telephoned in his absence. For a moment I thought that the room was empty and then I saw that Pascal was sitting at the dining table; he was wearing a black leather coat and had his head between his hands.

I said, 'Pascal?'

He turned a new face to me. There was no light in it; his eyes were pits of shadows. He said, 'What're you doing here, you damned fairy? Get out of here. Get to bed, you creep.'

I said, '*Pascal*? It's me, Bruno.'

He said, 'I don't want to talk to you, I don't want to have anything to do with you, you damned pansy. I wish you'd never come to this house. You don't belong in here; you're supposed to stay in your room and take your medicines and that's that, so get out of here.'

I said, 'What's happened? What are you talking about?'

'I'm talking about you and I know what you are and what you've been doing behind our backs, you damned coward.'

I could not believe that he had not mistaken me for someone else. I had my little performance rehearsed and wanted only to be allowed to present it; frustration brought tears to my eyes. 'I don't understand you –'

'Get the hell out of here, you sick bastard; this house isn't meant for you – you pay for your treatment and that's all you're entitled to get. You think I don't know what you're after? We all know and we all wish you'd never been sent here. There. Now get out.'

I said, 'Who told you what? Who's been here?'

He looked at me now as if he despaired of my being able to answer the simplest question. I had never seen him so pitiless. With infinite reluctance, my brain responded to the weight of his wordless eloquence; it turned like a millwheel as a mass of water builds against it and presses it into motion. 'Fuck off,' he said, 'and leave me in peace.'

I said, 'Is there anything I can do?'

He said, 'Haven't I told you? We don't need pansies in this house. We don't want sick sods like you anywhere near us, understand?'

I said, 'Fine.'

I turned and walked towards the door, thinking only that I was doing it for him; I was no one but the person whom he wanted me to be. Already with my back to him, I said, 'You've got me all wrong, you know.'

He said, 'I shouldn't be surprised at anything you did, you asthmatic fairy. Not anything. You know what I mean.'

I said, 'I've done nothing.' I sniffed tears which may or may not have been real. 'Goodnight.'

When I stepped through the shutters, I heard the ragged barking of distant dogs and saw the flare of headlights baffled by the tracery of branches in the valley. I was not surprised, but slightly thrilled, by the men who emerged from the shadows and said, 'Keep quiet and come with us.'

XXXII

The murder of Pia was regarded as solved; after Miguel O'Higgins' death, the press ceased to mention it. The Peruvian was no stranger to Roman prostitutes and his panic reaction to the arrival of the police seemed to confirm the guilt which was tactfully left in doubt for diplomatic reasons. I made a painful call on the widow, who did not seem entirely prostrated. There was a bruised hardness in her impatient acceptance of my correct sentiments. The contents of the apartment had already been divided into what was to go with her and her daughters and what belonged to the proprietor. I felt more sympathy for the dead man than for the rich woman whom he had married. It seemed to me that I was, in some sense, his ghost; although I did not regret that we had not gone together in pursuit of the pleasures we had enjoyed singly, I felt that I owed his memory more tenderness than it would find from his family and, during the remainder of my time in Rome, I had intermittent moments of playful piety, when I found myself promising poor Miguel that the case was not closed, for me at least, and that together we might still yet discover who, in reality, had done Pia to death.

The dead Peruvian and I were, it seemed, alone in retaining interest in the case. When the police offered to restore Berthe's property to her and when I suggested that it was a relic worth preserving, she accused me of being morbid; she gave no indication that it might give us something in common. If I was glad to have escaped the mundane consequences of Pia's murder in so fortunate, even fluky a way, I also regretted that the episode came to play no piquant part in my relations with either Berthe or Pierre Salomon. When we happened to meet at a reception for a visiting professor from the Collège de France, Pierre made no allusion, even by raising a questioning eyebrow, to his recruitment as a putative alibi. Whatever crime he thought I might have committed, the death of a prostitute evidently exceeded what he took to be my competence. As for my hopeful suspicion that he had played a serpentine part in the girl's murder, it was a form of unspoken flattery which he refused to honour. If he spent most of the reception in earnest consultation with Professor Dreyfus, it was, I feared, less out of embarrassment at my presence than in the hope (from what I could overhear) of obtaining an academic post if, as appeared probable, he was obliged, on principle, to publish his research against the instructions of his Order. I noticed that he regarded this prospect with doleful glee; he solicited Dreyfus' support with an air of condescending entreaty. Knowing that the professor, whose father had been deported to Auschwitz in 1943, was a socialist in the anti-clerical tradition, Pierre chose to assume that they were men with strong underlying sympathies for whom scholarship always trumped opinions.

Dreyfus – a small man with a shining bald head, which aped a monastic tonsure, and a bristling goatee – became more and more defensive as Pierre insisted on how closely their views converged; while seeking to defer to Dreyfus, he alarmed the other into feeling that he was being pressed to join the Church. How far was Pierre conscious of his mischievous tactics? His blindness to the winces and frowns of his opponents always took him through the smallest openings in their arguments. He navigated with the remarkable verve of a bat; seeming always about to plunge against obstacles, his lurching flight was actually a means of transcending what a more vigilant approach might have led him to hit. His darting questions drew little cries of alarm from Dreyfus which, rather than deterring his interlocutor, alerted him to the next opening. Pierre's rapacious agility rendered assault a kind of compliment; even as I felt sorry for Dreyfus, I was regretting that I was not the object of the Jesuit's muscular importunity. His overheard insistence that he *was* a Jew and he *was* aware of the Church's duplicities, and with *much* more command of detailed instances, seemed to accuse Dreyfus of under-stating his own case and thus of not having any serious interest in maintaining it. Pierre's smile grew more vulpine as his arguments brought the blood to Dreyfus' cheeks.

During their face-to-face, I became aware that a younger – though not a young – woman was expressing a mixture of entertained surprise and sporting solemnity which the rallying couple elected to overlook. She had a coarse profusion of rusty hair; lighter strands sprang this way and that, suggestive more of exposure to a hot climate than of the coiffeur. Her skin was less rough than tough; the lines around the bold eyes gave her an agreeable frown: I guessed that they came of looking into the sun. I watched with unresentful envy as this woman became, by her attentive presence, the prize for which the two men appeared to be competing. I discovered afterwards, from our Cultural Attaché, that she had been Dreyfus' pupil and had now become his research assistant; her contribution to a forthcoming book was such that the professor was to give her equal billing with himself, a gesture appreciated less by his wife (a painter) than by his protégée.

Berthe had come to the reception, although she would be certain to tell me later that she had thought it very boring. I had a notion that she attended in order to remind my colleagues that my promotion would entail her undiplomatic presence at gatherings much more important than this one. Perhaps I flatter myself in supposing that malice, rather than access to the bar and the buffet, led her to accompany me. She was wearing a black and white floral suit with heavily padded shoulders; the skirt was square-cut and I imagine that she thought it made her legs seem slim, or at least less fat.

Stumbling on the dead Pia had shocked me, but I had been reminded by what horrified me that I had a capacity to remain unmoved by it. It had needed a measure of luck for me to escape so completely from the charges which might, under other circumstances, have proved plausible, but I remained conscious that I had stayed remarkably cool: my wiping of the doorhandles, for instance, suggested that I might, with practice, become quite adept in escaping detection. The possibility that, at some indeterminate point, I might make practical plans to murder her somewhat restored my interest in – and even prompted a kind of bleak affection for – my wife. I must have been gazing at her as I considered under what circumstances I might easily dispose of her, so that I should not only escape suspicion but also derive the maximum sympathy from her loss. I speculated on the latter aspect not so much because I had serious careerist ambitions as because it would provide a subtler problem to be solved. There might, Fritz Altschuler used to say, be a certain satisfaction in mere neatness, but true pleasure came from elegance. If I were to find an occasion to despatch Berthe, it would have to be by means on which I could look back with aesthetic satisfaction. In private speculations of this kind, there is no shame; only the public formulation of desires renders them disgusting, like those fish which move with perfect grace in the depths of the ocean but become revoltingly bloated when lifted from their natural haunts. It was a comfort to me to consider that my wife was dispensable; I had no craving to cause her pain (least of all if I had to witness it) but, bereaved at the death of Pia, I was possessed by a sense of grievance at Berthe's unwelcome vivacity.

Since my eyes were dwelling on her with attentive calculation, she may have gained the impression that I was hoping that she was enjoying the evening. Offering a smile as thin as an assassin's blade, she approached me with her glass in her hand and said, 'How much more of this are we expected to endure?'

I said, 'Do you want to go home?'

She said, 'I don't know about home, but I certainly want to go. Is there anyone here who doesn't?'

'Some people are enjoying themselves.'

She looked at Pierre and Paul Dreyfus and at the woman whose expression declared that her silence did not entail that she had nothing to say. 'Those people never cease to gloat over their triumphs, do they?'

I said, 'What people? What triumphs?'

'I'm ready to leave,' she said. 'Those people. Look at them. They know they should be dead.'

I said, 'Are you drunk?'

'Because I'm telling the truth? Probably. They hate us and they smile. They want to win and win and win and that's all they want to do. Luckily, they want to win even against each other.'

I said, 'If you want to go on home, I can always come along later.'

She said, 'Are you so anxious to be rid of me?'

I said, 'Are you jealous?'

'Of your capacity to endure tedium and ask for more?'

'Of that woman.'

'Because you've been looking at her? Look as much as you like. Do anything you like.'

'Because everything that Pierre is pretending to say to Professor Dreyfus he is actually saying to her.'

'That's what's turns *you* green,' she said, 'not me.'

I said, 'Do you think Pierre goes with whores?'

'I shouldn't be surprised. Has he told you that he does?'

'Imagine if your coat hadn't been taken by poor Miguel O'Higgins at all. Imagine if it had got to that girl's flat by another hand altogether. You haven't discovered anything else to be missing, have you?'

She said, 'Pierre has never been in my bedroom.'

'You might have left your coat in the hall on one occasion. You're not infallibly methodical, are you?'

'You're more likely to have taken it than he is. I think it's that little gipsy Maria, or that gipsy she's going to marry. There's a rope of pearls I can't find.'

'Valuable?'

'A couple of thousand francs, not more.'

'Imagine if you knew who'd taken them, what would you do?'

She said, 'It would depend.'

'Why? And on what?'

'Must you be so aggressive? You're only ever aggressive when we're in public. Why is that?'

'Doubtless because on occasions like these, I know that I can rely on your impeccable sense of decorum. A woman of your quality would never get drunk and raise her voice, would she?'

'You've never been very interested in me, have you? For instance, it doesn't occur to you, does it, even in your silliest dreams, that *I* might have been the one to give my coat to that tart.'

'Why would you do that?'

She said, 'There you are: you can't give me credit for anything, can you? Do you have any idea how boring it is to be the wife of a minor diplomat, someone who's completely ruined his career and will never be anything but a sort of glorified secretary – not to say flunkey – for people who really know how to manage their affairs?'

'What about the pearls? Did you give them to her as well?'

'Suddenly that makes them more valuable, doesn't it? You insist on thinking that I'm innocent, don't you – that whatever evidence there is to the contrary, even if I spell it out to you, it can't be true that I am anything but a victim?' Her voice was becoming strident; she showed ominous signs of beginning to have a good time.

I said, 'We can go and have some dinner, if you like. I can easily make my excuses.'

'Of course you can. It's your life's work, isn't it? I wish there was somewhere we could get a decent meal. No wonder all these Italian women get so disgustingly fat.'

I said, 'Not all of them.'

'You don't really like women; is that why you defend them all the time? Are you hoping they won't notice what you are?'

I said, 'And what is that exactly?'

'Exactly!' she said. 'Exactly neither one thing nor the other.'

'And what are you?' I said.

'You always choose public places to become insulting, to get that sneering look on your foxy little face. Why do you have to be surrounded with other people before you can get your courage up and your tongue to wag?'

I said, 'You accuse me of precisely what is true of you.'

She said, 'Do you know that one of your sons is going to be one of them unless you're very careful? Have you even noticed that obvious fact?'

'What are you talking about, and why are you talking about it here?'

'You see what I mean?' she said. 'You don't know your wife, you don't know your children, you don't know anyone or anything.'

I said, 'You'll push me too far one of these days.'

She said, 'And how far is that likely to be?'

I said, 'I think I shall leave.'

'That woman is willing to do anything in order to succeed. You can see it. I expect you wish that I'd been like that. Well, if I had, I shouldn't be here today, I can promise you that.'

'In that case,' I said, 'we both have something to regret.'

'No,' she said. 'No, because I was deceived. I was promised that you were something you weren't.'

'So was I, apparently, and what does it matter?'

'Matter? I never suggested it mattered. For something to matter there would have to be some reason for existing. Now let's go and have something to eat.'

I did not want to leave the reception without a chance to talk to Pierre, or at least to give him the impression that it was a matter of indifference to me whether we spoke or not, but I could find no reason not to do what my wife suggested. I was amused to see that Dreyfus' handsome *collaboratrice* was now no longer silent; in a sudden, torrential but – from the sound of it – admirably structured series of points, she was attacking both the Catholic Church and those who, with a certain smile, implied that its faults were somehow its virtues, since their acknowledgment humanised and chastened its clergy. 'Quite the contrary,' she was saying. 'Why? Because the concession of contingent errors is always utilised to protect the central mystery, to save the most questionable part of the doctrine from intelligent assault. Every admission of human weakness strengthens your theocratic vanity. The process has been going on for so long that the Church can now insist on the solidity of the ground on which it stands which is nothing more than the accretion of its own excrement; your certainties have the consistency and substance of – of – '

'Guano,' Pierre said.

'Thank you!' She put her arm through Dreyfus' and made him her prize.

I said, 'Game over!'

Berthe and I went at a ceremonial pace down the long, shallow steps from the gallery where the reception was being held. It was the kind of staircase designed to accommodate a man on a white horse. The great buildings of the world have become like the costumes of warriors and princes, which the functionaries and surrogates who now wear them cannot quite fill. When Berthe's shoes clacked disquietingly on the inclined treads, she elected to take my arm to mitigate the noise. I might have been an item of furniture.

I took her to 'Giovanni' for dinner, less because I thought she would like it than because I knew that I could be sure of a table. The waiter told us that they had fresh truffles; he suggested an omelette. Berthe said that she supposed that they were *white* truffles, which were good only for flavouring and never for eating. In any case, Italians never made good omelettes. Knowing that I used 'Giovanni' frequently, my wife made a point of being as disobliging as she could; she left most of the food which she had chosen with such prolonged lack of enthusiasm, but drank three large whiskies and, when she was not drawing on it, left a cigarette burning in the ashtray throughout the meal.

I ate everything on my plate, although Berthe's performance deprived it of all savour. As she watched me pretending to enjoy the same food she had pushed away, she said, 'Can you distinguish between courage and cowardice?'

I said, 'Can you not?'

'In yourself, I mean.'

'No,' I said.

She looked at the people at the next table as though they had asked her to prove a point and she had done so. 'Quite specifically, what do you intend to do, if anything, about your son?'

'You seem very confident that something needs to be done. You mean David, I presume, do you?'

'I sometimes think you don't even know their names,' she said.

'I sometimes doubt if I know my own. Let me say this, since you appear to want to pursue this matter: your remarks are beyond the limits of decency. I can understand your disliking me – I can even sympathise with your views – but to seek to destroy your son's character when there is absolutely no evidence of the justice of your conclusions is worse than cruel, it is vicious.'

She said, 'Do you think it matters what kind of meat he wants?'

'If it doesn't, why seek to reproach me for it?'

'Does it occur to you that the way you've treated me is the prime cause for his deviance?'

I said, 'You're making it impossible for us to live together. Is that because you want to help David? If anyone's unnatural, you are; if anyone is making him hate and fear the female sex, it is not me.'

'It's in your blood,' she said. 'And his.'

I said, 'You act as if you have been the victim of some – some assault so terrible that it excuses anything you choose to do. And, although you may despise me for saying so, it is that – and perhaps that alone – which makes you so pitiable.'

She said, 'Your misfortune is to be neither rich nor wicked. Something has made you . . . sensitive without encouraging you to be uncompromising. Quite the contrary, in fact. You've made your life into a facsimile, haven't you, behind which you have managed to remain at some indecisive stage at which everything still seems possible. Are you aware who it was who had my virginity? You shrug because it never mattered to you to possess me; I was your disguise, not your wife.'

I said, 'I've never been a particular believer in conjugal intimacy; only *petits bourgeois* believe in happiness.'

'They also think that doctors are people of quality,' she said. 'Your uncle was the first man to fuck me, as I expect you already know. Some people might say that he was the only one.'

I said, 'I gave that tart your coat.'

She said, 'I hadn't been at your parents' house for more than a few days when he came down in that car of his, with all kinds of luxuries for your mother. I can hardly remember the girl I was then. I was quite slim and I loved music. You never knew that girl. I used to go into the fields and play the flute. Why are you smiling? He hardly spoke to me, your uncle, although it had been at his suggestion that I was sent to La Fontaine. Did you ever read children's books about lumberjacks in Canada? I had a cousin there who sent me one. I loved the way the men were supposed to run out and break the jam by thrusting at the locked lumber with their hooked poles, knowing that once the impasse was broken they would have a dangerous run back to the shore along the twisting logs. I wanted a man who could do that, who had just done it.'

'And that was my uncle, was it?'

She said, 'Your uncle?'

'Then I've missed the point.'

'When I was in the fields, in the heat, I'd take off my shoes and stockings and run through the grass; it was like paddling in the dry. If I'd been a little bolder, I'd have taken everything off, like girls do today, but I think I might have gone mad if I'd done that.'

I said, 'Roque!'

She said, 'Wait, wait!'

I said, 'Baptiste!'

'This interests you,' she said. 'Can I have another whisky?'

'You were attracted by Baptiste?'

'You make a person of him. You do that all the time. He was not a

270

person; he was an object, a creature. His presence made me free. Why? Because he frightened me. I had been deprived of fears and he provided one. I was free in the fields and the woods because he was there. Man was never free before the serpent entered the garden, am I not right? Adam was never amusing until Eve discovered the serpent.'

I said, 'Those literary conceits have never pleased me. What did Baptiste do? How did he approach you?'

'His father made him saw the fallen branches from the walnut trees. I spied on him. I did not care about him in any sentimental way. I was spared that and that was why I liked to watch him. It never occurred to me to think of him as a creature who could speak or be spoken to. He was something out of mythology – a folly!'

'And what happened exactly?'

'Always exactitude with you! I would be in the grass and he would be working with his great empty muscles, muscles with not a thought in them; it was like taking the back off the world's watch and looking at the works! There was no distinction in him between work and existence, between wiping his face and wiping his arse! None of what I saw made me want to be a human being in contact with him. It was wanting *not* to be a human being that attracted me. Just looking at him, now I come to think of it, was a way of being naked. Just looking cooled me; I imagined nothing, I *was* nothing but the air around him, when I got close enough. What am I admitting? That I was a young girl without desires, without modern dreams, but – so it seemed – with a miraculous way of escaping from my virgin self. Divine!' Why did she have to stop and drink more of her whisky? Why did she pull on the cigarette without flicking off the husk of ash at its end? If I had shut my eyes and listened to what she was saying as one might to a testament, should I not have found something almost noble, certainly touching, in her recovery of a youth of which no one could have suspected her? 'You're bored,' she said.

'When did Baptiste start to notice you?'

'You're lurching around like the old toad I found in the orchard one day. I'm not sure that he ever noticed me. He would have lost his grace if he had, don't you think? He would have begun to think things. I couldn't have liked his sweat if he had sweated for me; I couldn't have admired his cock if he'd being showing it to me instead of the wind. He never noticed me except to say "Good morning, mademoiselle" in that clotted voice of his. Your uncle started coming more often to the region after a few weeks. He had grown that moustache, if you remember. He was a flatterer who didn't need to say anything, your uncle. He had the air of a winner, more and more. He asked no one to like him, did he, or to want him? There was nothing nice about him, as there was about your father. Your father always asked me questions about my reading and my flute and he arranged for me to talk to my mother. Jean-Claude had business everywhere, it seemed. As soon as he arrived, men would call at La Fontaine. People came at night. I heard their conferences sometimes, hushed and loud at the same time. The silence when they had all left the house kept me awake. I would hear the drone and throb of aeroplanes and go to my window, knowing that they were searching for your uncle's lights – and other people's – in the meadows. Sometimes I would hear shots; sometimes when I did not I would see the men coming home carrying their wounded. There were fights between various *bandes* – '

'You don't have to tell me,' I said.

'And then there were meetings to try and arrange things between them. Your uncle usually came back smiling; he was an expert at arrangements. One morning, after he had come back very late, with some things the men had stowed in the old bakehouse – your friend was among them – '

'Martegoutte.'

' – that morning it was very hot, and Baptiste was stripped to the waist as he baled the *foin*. He was wearing clogs against the stubble and the *aoûtats* and an apron made out of sacking. He had no hair on his chest and he'd wipe the sweat away with the flat of his hand. It left the brown flesh gleaming like a burn. He was very strong, of course; he'd cut the lengths of wood and then he'd take one under each arm to the edge of the field and stack them. Don't think that I wanted him to take me like that! I didn't want him to take me at all; I should have fought and called for help. I should have spat in his face. That's the mistake people always make. I wanted to be inside him; I didn't want him inside me. I've never wanted that, never. What happened was, your uncle found me in the fields one day and he said, "Well, my little Berthe, what are you doing that's any use to anyone?" I was reading a book. My flute was on the ground. I was doing nothing at all. We can go home if you like.'

I said, 'I'm going to have some peaches and cream. Do you want some?'

'I hate their peaches here. I'll have another one of these.'

I said, 'I think you've had more than enough.'

She said, 'Waiter, another one of these. Quickly.'

'And what happened then?'

'You want to watch, do you?'

I said, 'I'm showing polite interest.'

She said, 'I don't mind you knowing. What does it matter what people know? He said that they needed someone to take a message to one of the villages where they thought there was an informer.'

'And he wanted you to go? What a shit that man was!'

'He said that I was the only member of the choir available. Listen, I don't think it was dangerous in the slightest; if you really want to know, I think he made the whole story up in order to get rid of me for the afternoon.'

'Why would he want to do that?'

She said, 'Your father had gone to a meeting in Caillac. They were planning the civilian administration for after the Liberation. They already had these committees with names and minutes and titles: mad, *mad!*'

I said, 'Did you go?'

'They dressed me very carefully, he and your mother. I was to say that I was looking for the *curé* because an old woman was dying at Fongauffier and needed him. That really was the message; it was the message *and* it was the cover.'

'Neat.'

'Very neat. So I went. I walked there and I walked back and they had the afternoon without me.'

'You think something happened at the house they didn't want you to know about? What do you think it was?'

'Poor Guy,' she said. 'Sometimes I think you're pretending, sometimes I'm afraid you really mean it. That night, your father didn't come back till very late. He came back all right, having walked from the river, but they were afraid that something had happened. They sent me to bed. After your father came in (I heard him on the terrace), I could hear them having a long conversation downstairs – you know what that house is like, the way sounds ride around the place – but I couldn't hear what the problem was, only that there was a problem. When I was almost asleep, your uncle came to my room. He said, "Everything's fine. Nothing to worry about. So now what would you like to do?" He was in a blue dressing gown, with his trousers on underneath, and his shoes. "Are you missing your parents?" I said that I wasn't missing anything. He said, "My little Berthe!" I said, "Did it matter that I didn't see him, the *curé*?" He said, "He came anyway. He had the message another way. He is very brave, that *curé*; he does things you can't imagine. Do you know why? Because he is afraid that God is not all good. He's afraid that, when everything is over (as if it ever will be!), he will never have another chance to be what he is now; his heresy, you might say, is being loyal to a Supreme Being who is not as good as he wants to believe. And here is the comedy, my little Berthe: the damned Communists – Cabanne and those people, who I suppose mean nothing to you – they, who have rebelled against God, they have no such doubts. They think that they have no need to be good, because their cause is good without them. They will die for it because they think they're superfluous to it. Whereas the good *curé* . . . Are you sure that you want to be a human being?" He raised his knees, one after the other as he spoke, and unlaced his shoes, quite casually, as if it was something he always did while sitting on my bed. I said, "Is there something else I can do for you some time? I'd like to do something." He said, "Do you want to be useful?" "Not particularly," I said. "What I want is to do something . . ." "Yes?" he said. "Yes? Something what?" I said, "Something that will prove something. So that I can never go back again." He said, "Do you want to do something for France?" I said, "Not especially, to be honest." That was when he kissed me. Then he said, "Do you know what I am going to do for you, my little Berthe? I am going to tell you something that will make it impossible for you to go back. I'm going to do that for you because you did what I asked you to do and because it amuses me: I'm going to tell you what the world is going to be like after the war. The world is going to be wicked. Because it is only after things are over that they truly begin. Do you agree?" I said, "I haven't any idea what you mean." And he said, "And yet you're beginning to understand. Do you know what I am doing now? What I am doing now is what I have been doing for the last four years: I am trying to make sure that, heads or tails, we win the war. I am very serious. I am someone who is necessary to a family like mine. I know what matters. Nothing matters! But it matters very much, doesn't it? Are you beginning to be with me?" I said nothing and I did nothing to stop him or to encourage him. It was marvellous! "You see," he said, "her husband has come back all right, as I told you, but he had a message for me – " '

I said, ' "Her husband"? Are you sure that was what he said? Why would he call my father that?'

Berthe said, 'A point of detail! I'm sure. Of course. We can go home now, if you want. The peaches *are* hard, aren't they? Rubbery!'

'They're excellent,' I said. 'You're missing something. What was the message – did he tell you?'

'Yes, he told me. He said that I could decide what he was going to do. What do you mean you gave that tart my coat?'

'Just that. It was my little fancy. I took it from the apartment and I gave it to her. Do about what?'

Berthe said, 'All right. Your father was in a café in Caillac, like a fool, in broad daylight, after his meeting, and a man came and sat down next to him, in plain clothes, but a German. Obviously. He was very polite, very philosophical. The war was as good as lost; no – and he smiled then – it was *better* than lost. Better because men of intelligence could rely on the others to continue to kill each other while they made sensible arrangements for the survival of what really mattered – men of intelligence! Europe needed them. This man was apparently quite unguarded, quite fearless; he spoke in a modest voice, because he was civilised, not because he was ashamed of what he was saying. He said he knew who your father was and he also knew the names of the people with whom he was working, locally and nationally. He mentioned some code names. He mentioned your uncle's. Or so your father told him.'

I said, 'He told you all this that night?'

'Of course,' Berthe said. 'I was leaning against the wall of the little bedroom, the one Patrick uses when he comes to the house, and I had my nightdress bunched under my chin, half in my mouth, while he caressed my breasts. He had a way of brushing the pad of his thumbs across my nipples that was quite heavenly. I always wished you'd done it like that. The seconds between his doing it, they were the best, when nothing was happening. Nothing lasts so much longer than anything else.'

'Why didn't you ever ask me?'

'Because that wouldn't have been doing it, would it?'

'So then what happened?'

'The German said that the time had come to make sensible provisions for the future. It was of no personal concern for him whether people were arrested or not arrested, but he had colleagues who were still interested in not hearing the whistle and who might at any moment shoot anyone – your father, his friends, their own people whom they suspected of being able to live in a world in which they would have no chance. Etcetera, etcetera. Your father, so he said, allowed the man to go on talking but made no comment. Finally, the German said that he had a certain position in the police; he came from Périgueux and was in Caillac *en civil* – he had a *petite amie* who was having some problems with a tenant, so he had driven her over. He liked French women; he liked France and Italy. He was a romantic. You meet them, don't you, today? He was in the police because he was a linguist; he didn't have only the flavour of cabbage on his tongue!'

'He said that?'

'So your uncle said your father said. Finally, of course, it was a question of money. The true romance! He wanted a hundred thousand sovereigns or he would have to inform the fools of what only he, for the moment, knew. Your father had forty-eight hours to get the money. Everyone knew there was plenty floating around. He was to bring it, in a sack, to a certain place and hand it over and he had the German's word of honour – oh yes, I promise you – that the entire *fichier* would disappear and never be found again. "I am a man of honour who can be trusted like a Swiss," he said. "The love of money is much higher than the love of women." Your uncle rather liked this man, I think, whom he met only through your father. So, the question was – and it was for me to answer it – whether the man was really what he said he was, whether he really knew enough to have everyone in our corner picked up and shot and whether, if he was given the money, he would not do it anyway. For all your uncle could tell me, he might have been a pretentious clerk who was privy to information on which his superiors, for understandable reasons, were not yet ready to act. What should be done?'

'And all this time my uncle was caressing your breasts?'

'As you might stroke a cat and talk to yourself at the same time.'

'A cat,' I said.

'For example.'

'But cats don't talk, do they? What did you say?'

'I said, "Do you have a choice?" He said, "Alas! Even in an impasse there are always choices. One could, for instance, dismantle the *réseau* of its mobile elements and see what happens. It's not so much a question of morals as of economy. In that sense, wholly modern. War, after all, is the use of men as currency, nothing more. They can be replaced by cash, which aids the recovery that can't be procured so easily by other means. Giving this man the money he asks for may achieve what he promises – a certain immunity for the network – but is that reason enough to let him get away with it? There is always a rate of exchange, my little Berthe! Always, always, always; it is all that man has, a rate of exchange. Do you understand?" He spoke to me like a favourite pupil, while his hand moistened my hairs, you follow me? Did you kill her, is that what you want me to believe?'

I said, 'I seem not to be capable of that. Perhaps it's a matter of not being enough of a gambler rather than, as I thought before you started telling me what you're now telling me, a matter of . . . appetite. I liked this particular tart.'

'She wasn't me,' Berthe said. 'Was that the thing?'

'How could he rely on you to decide what to do? And do you think he really did?'

'You're still a child, Guy, a wrinkled child who has forgotten how to cry but still wants to. Sad! You think there's a difference between appearance and reality; you cannot see that they are both cards in the same tawdry pack. I said to him, "What would be the clever thing to do?" And he smiled then and put his lips to one of my throbbing nipples, the right one, I think, yes, and then he said, "The clever thing, my little Berthe, will be to arrange things in accordance with Laplace's dictum, don't you agree?" I said that I had no idea who this Laplace was or what he might have said. He said that he hoped that that would be true.'

'The mathematician,' I said. 'A friend of Buonaparte.'

'You can see why your uncle preferred my company to yours! You know who he was, you know what he said.'

'But not what you were told he said.'

'How the perfect intelligence would be able to treat the future as history just like the past. How the tenses would lose their sense for such a person and he would remember the future or, if you like, foretell the past. "But," your uncle said . . .'

'Dammit,' I said, 'this person whom you call my uncle, there never was such a person – that is his disguise, isn't it? A pseudonym!'

'It's all pseudonyms,' she said. 'The devil! Pierre! You, me, all of it! She put him in his place, didn't she, that one? He won't let it rest there, will he, if I know anything about him!'

I said, 'But what? My uncle was about to tell you the secret of the universe.'

'Oh, what did he say? I know! He said that since we didn't have access to that intelligence, we're obliged to make bets, to speculate, to improvise, to toss coins – more precisely, to toss sovereigns. It was money and it was not money, this manna that came from the sky. There was no shame in using it to play any game we chose, because it had already bought us; it had already served its purpose. It proved that we had been defeated and would go on being defeated; only by misusing it, your uncle suggested, could we escape its title to us. I said, "Then you know what to do, don't you?" He said, "But I want you to tell me without me telling you, because I want to prove what I know, and what Baudelaire told me long ago, that every young girl knows in her heart *and* just here what is meant to go in here, what will always find a home in here, what she wants and what she deserves." '

'What a swine!' I said.

277

'That sincerity in your voice, Guy – I love it! How rarely you make me laugh this much! How very rarely.'

'What did you say to that?'

'I said, "Is it possible that this man doesn't exist? Is there any way of being sure that her husband is not, after all, cleverer than you are? He's a cold fish, that one." I never liked your father; he was so nice. Jean-Claude said, "Colder than you could imagine. Breathe easily, my little one, and make it last, my pretty. It cannot last, but make it. And now tell me, in a steady voice, what I am to do." '

I said, 'He took your life away from you, didn't he? He took your future away from you. Is that what you wanted?'

'He advanced me my future,' she said. 'I'm not sure that it's quite the same.'

'And what did you say to do?'

'I didn't have to say. He did it.'

'About the money.'

'Oh that!' she said. 'I said to give the money to your father. We thought it would be amusing.'

'Amusing!'

'There you have it,' she said. 'The same reason that I married you.'

I said, 'Did he often come to your room after that?'

'No. Often was not his style. He could never have had the power he did if he had had to do things frequently. He was someone who knew how to make people wait for him. Sometimes weeks, sometimes months. But they waited. Life is divided between those who wait and those they wait for, don't you think so?'

I said, 'And no one was arrested.'

'Some Communists down near Campagnac,' Berthe said. 'You know about that. But I think that was a coincidence. I don't know; I think.'

'There were things he didn't tell you then?'

'Many.'

'Your money . . .' I said.

'Yes?'

'It doesn't all come from your family, is that what you're telling me?'

'My money grew on a tree, Guy, didn't it?'

'You didn't marry me because it would be amusing to you, did you? You married me because it amused him.'

'I need some cigarettes,' she said. 'And her. Don't forget her. Can we walk around the corner?'

'Her? Who?'

278

'My Poor Guy, what a blind kitten you are! What a poor little blind kitten! Some women might almost love you for it.'

As we stepped down into the Via Marche, I said, 'Would you like me to buy you another showercoat like that white one I gave to the girl? I should be very happy to.'

'Why?' she said. 'Do you think it looks like rain?'

XXXIII

I was taken, without violence, down to the front of the house where the track came up from Villefranche-les-Évêques. Two or three cars were parked under the trees, without lights. Tracks in the stiffening mud suggested that other vehicles had been there earlier. I was probably the last of their captures that night. They had lost their fear and with it their ferocity. I was attached by handcuffs to one of the two men who had arrested me. He breathed vigorously through his nostrils. His nose was a beak against the faint light, it looked as though it would bleed easily. He wore a black blouse and beret. He was French.

I was neither frightened nor immune to fear: I was curious. I had no notion of escape or of hope. If I wondered what had happened at the house, and whether Dr Poulain had succeeded in escaping (which I doubted), it was as if the events of the day were already far behind me. As the motor of the Citroën in which I was sitting whirred and failed to start smoothly, I experienced a wince of anxiety, like a child who wonders, without being able to do anything about it, whether the family will get to the cinema in time for the trailers. I had no physical sensations that I can remember: I wanted to know what was going to happen next and I thought it was bad luck that I should be in a vehicle which might be left behind. I suspect that I slightly embarrassed my guard by the little smile of relief which I tried to exchange with him when the motor caught and our driver was able to get away. I might have been trying to give him a present.

Would it be an exaggeration to say that I had a sentiment of relief as we drove through the dark countryside (and how dark it was in those days!)? Certainly I felt remarkably at peace. Perhaps I was in shock, but I do not think so; I was soon able to recover from the impact of Pascal's repudiation. I concluded that it had been typically brave and bold of him to give the impression that he and I had nothing in common; his denunciation made it absurd to suppose that I could ever have been in his confidence. I was a sorry object defined by its want of virility. Pascal had not only warned and repudiated me; he had even proposed what line of defence I should follow and what sort of character I should best impersonate when under interrogation. My admiration was unaffected by the bruise which he had inflicted; I continued to see in him that man of action, of humour, of grace, to whom even Hemingway might give the palm, and I envied, more than ever, the quick genius I should never possess, while fearing that he had misunderstood me. As to my capture, I accepted it not only without resentment but also without any wish that I had – by staying at the peasant's cottage or by taking a more circumspect route – avoided returning to the Poulains' house.

When, for a moment, I speculated on what I should have done, had I been able to avoid the trap, I had a greater sense of dread than I did as the gates of the Gestapo headquarters swung open and we drove into the courtyard before the elegant *hôtel particulier* in which, to say the least, I could expect to pass an unpleasant quarter of an hour. If I had any conscious hope, it was that I might somehow have time to receive a signal from Pascal (who had, I thought, been bundled into the car which left ahead of us) that he was relying on me to play the part he had assigned to me. I hoped above all that I still enjoyed his friendship. Even at that dark hour, there was in me an inability wholly to inhabit my time. What might in others be a source of imaginative strength was, and is, for me a failure to engage with the world. I cannot bring all my strength, of mind or body, to bear simultaneously: some part of me always manages to escape.

Can this fugitive trait imply that even after death some fragment of my being will be at liberty to journey on into eternity? I can honestly, if disgracefully, say that I have no such ambition for the survival of some tattered trace of myself. Even if such a thing were to happen, I am not sure that I should consider it an indication of divine generosity or eventual redemption. It is a tradition, of which Descartes is our national instance, to suppose that the mind is rarer and more durable than the body. The perishability of the flesh, like the scandal of shit, leads philosophers to think that we should be happier and nobler if we were purged of our carnal shell, but is it necessarily the case that our thoughts or feelings, dispensed from practical considerations, are the better part of ourselves or even that they could be sustained, in any recognisably personal form, without the vulgar envelope of the body? I cannot say that I have enjoyed my physical form (I am, as I have often been reminded, neither handsome nor athletic), but what should I be without the limbs I have failed to exercise or the senses I have so clumsily indulged? Intellectually, I am probably among the first one or two per cent of human beings, but my awareness of my mental confusions and defects does not incline me to look forward to keeping company with myself throughout an eternity of sublime cerebration. If I were in more coherent contact with myself, I should almost certainly have lacked that capacity for anaesthesia (it has nothing in common with courage) which enabled me to watch myself being taken into the tall grey building which housed those whose business it was to terrorise me in the interests of a cause which all but a few must have known was as good as lost. They were, in some sense, already dead themselves: they had power, but no hope.

Men like the one of whom Berthe told me in the restaurant in Rome, who proposed to make a premature and profitable peace, may not have been uncommon, but they relied on fools and fanatics who had no prospect of salvation and who would continue to combine brutality with petulance. It seemed unfair to them that all their cruelties – which they could not distinguish from hard work – would soon be rendered futile. The members of the Milice were burdened with a fatuous faith, like racegoers who persist in shouting for a horse that is clearly beaten and who, even in the last furlong, when victory manifestly belongs elsewhere, continue to calculate what they might win and to what worthy ends they will devote the fortune they can never possess. I am conscious that my memory of my captors – and especially of the redfaced, sharpnosed lout to whom I happened to be attached – is softened by the fact that, as this manuscript proves, I survived their attentions. Those who suffered (as I did not) might claim, with justice, that my reading of the torturers as deluded fools, to whom a measure of sympathy cannot be refused, shows only how superficially I knew them.

To speak of their frustrations, when one means that they sweated and swore over victims to whom they behaved as viciously as their derelict imaginations could contrive, is to celebrate one's survival as if it were evidence of innate superiority or a higher destiny. It would be more modest to confess to being very lucky. I have an even less flattering confession to make: I was so fortunate that I have to admit to a sense almost of anticlimax when, after being detached from my sweating escort, I was thrown into a cell and left there with a mortifying feeling of insignificance. I found myself going through everything that I knew about the Resistance, in a panic of shameful recognition that there was unlikely to be anything which I could conceal or reveal that the Gestapo and the Milice did not already know. The other Poulains were clearly either under arrest or (as I prayed, though not to any god) in flight; to give their names was nothing. As for the rest, I had heard of Colonel Maurice (who had not?) and I had, of course, left the two airmen in the peasant's cottage, but even if I could not resist betraying them, I had every reason to think that someone would have been able to warn them before the Milice reached them. This sense of exclusion from important knowledge engendered more depression than relief, although it lent plausibility to the story whch had been so cruelly and so nobly improvised by Pascal. Sitting in that green cell in the basement of the Milice headquarters, surrounded by the mute obscenities and encouragements scratched on the walls by previous occupants, I felt my innocence like an accusation. As for the possibility that Pascal had been serious in his revulsion (did he really think me an asthmatic fairy?), that was an abcess too painful to touch upon.

They had taken my watch and such belongings as I had on me. My cell was at the end of the row; it seemed at a distance from the noises which I dreaded to hear and for which my ears nevertheless strained as they did when I was alone in my bedroom at La Fontaine and did not know what it was that I was sure I should recognise as soon as it became audible.

The memory of Fritz did not come unbidden to me; it required conscious effort to retrieve my 'friend' from the oubliette into which subsequent events had thrust him. I wanted less to see him than to have him see me; my arrest was a painful comfort, like the confession and payment of an outstanding debt. It was as if he had some complicity with my captors, since I expected him to derive some satisfaction from my situation. He had, in fact, never reproached me, or even seemed envious of my immunity from his fate. I realised again that there is no human condition, in which one observes another, which cannot seem a privilege. Imagining that I now belonged to Fritz's school, I wanted him to witness my election. There was an element of vengeance in my wishful renewal of our comradeship. In the event, I was discomfited by the hazy image of him which I projected on the bilious wall. My imagination procured him ineptly; only an approximate ghost came to haunt me. I find sometimes that when I dream, the faces of the cast are not quite right; I labei them with the names of old friends but they are badly drawn and they play their parts sketchily.

I punished myself with Fritz's amusement at my present predicament. I contrived to think of him as contributing to my series of humiliations and concealments. It was as if he had contaminated me; the chess pieces which he left on my desk in Monsieur Picpus' classroom became sinister, like the crucial clue in a flashback. If I seemed to conjure Fritz to my side, it was not for the pleasure of his company, but so that he might see what he had done to me. I should have preferred the company of Félix, whose blonde resourcefulness would, I daresay, have given him the hope of being able to render some service to our captors which would allow him to bargain with them. It had never occurred to me until I was locked in that cell by myself how dependent I should always be on the kudos, however petty, which came from my impersonal utility to others. I realised that unlike Félix (or Pascal) I was in myself almost wholly unappealing; my future, if I was to have one, depended on usefulness to others – even to myself! – rather than on any charm I might have, for them, or for myself. I came to this conclusion without self-pity, as one might the solution to a mathematical puzzle which, at last, one had found the opportunity to finish.

There was a wooden bench attached by chains to the cold wall. How long did I sit there? Time had been taken from me like a possession. Several hours must have passed. I had a sense less of being spared than of being neglected. With a plunge of hope, I once heard the threat of sliding bolts and the clang of a door down the passage, but otherwise I appeared to be forgotten. I lay down on the bench. The lack of a blanket did not surprise me, but I was almost offended by the state of the wood on which I huddled; I could imagine easing a long splinter from the middle plank and using it to open an artery or to inflict some other mortal injury which I flinched from specifying. I had my hands between my bony knees as I lay on the bench. I did not want to fall asleep; I dreaded a sudden awakening, the pain that came from blows I had had no time to expect. My dread was a soporific which came over me like a sweet gas. I remembered the sound of Baptiste being beaten. The absence of a dream was what I dreamed: a velvety blackness swayed around me like a trickster's curtains.

There was a barred window at the top of the narrow wall of my cell; it gave onto a sort of trench which was covered with mesh. A little light showed there, as grey as cheap paper, when I opened my eyes after one of my futile attempts to deny sleep by imitating it. It seemed that I had survived the night. I heard the sound of a car arriving, but I suspected that it was at the front of the building. The voices of the passengers seemed to bounce off the courtyard wall before they became audible to me, distorted but aggrieved; I gathered that they had come further than they wanted on a journey which interrupted more important activities. If they were to be my torturers, they were men who had better things to do.

When I heard footsteps in the corridor, I have to confess that, until the door was opened, I had an obstinate expectation that I was about to be given breakfast. The door was fastened with more locks and bolts than my sorry ingenuity could ever have undone. I was a mouse in a trap for a lion. When at last the tallowed hinges yielded, the two Miliciens slung something in at me. My wishful eyes tried even then to make the bundle on the floor into some kind of an amenity; a bedroll perhaps or a change of clothes. It was David Poulain.

I seem to have committed myself to telling the truth here. Having been a diplomat almost all my adult life, I can say without irony that the truth is something of which I have always been deeply conscious, if only because it has so often been my professional obligation to conceal it. The truth that I am trying to tell here is of a strange character; it reveals nothing that will make any difference to the history of our times, it might as well be buried with me. To a great extent it does not even seem to belong to me; it is like those letters which one discovers in an old dossier, which bear one's signature but are in a style which, at an inquiry, one could swear not to be one's own. The truth about myself is like a forgery; the imposture which I have inhabited for so long is a better fit. What I am reviving in these pages is the youth of someone who is as remote and as unreliably remembered as Fritz Altschuler. I could wish that I had not made this appointment with him, but I am resolved to keep it now, whatever the cost to my self-esteem, whatever the reaction of my sons or my wife, Maureen, should they ever bother to scan it.

Yes, I have been postponing what I have now to confess: when I saw that it was David, I was disappointed. Even the brutal distortion of his face, which looked as though it had been pumped up, like a football, almost to the point of explosion, even the devious and painful wheeze as he tried to draw breath through his broken nose and swollen mouth, could not quite – no, not *quite* – shame me into thinking only of him. The truth is, he was like a parcel which turns out not to contain what one really wants. As he lay there, and as I helped him, with all the tenderness of my shameful insincerity, onto the bench, I was regretting that it was not Pascal to whom I could offer my pitiful attentions.

David had been too badly beaten to be able to speak or even look at me (his eyes were wounds; the lashes seemed to stitch them together). How could it be that in such circumstances I looked to him to console me? How was it that I wanted him to promise me, as soon as possible, that Pascal had not meant what he said, and that I had, by my apparent acquiescence, played my part to his satisfaction? I am conscious of vomiting the truth almost gratefully, even ostenta-tiously, like something which has lain too long on my conscience and is being revealed so shamelessly that it comes up almost with pride. I hope that I can also say that I did everything I could to help David. The obstinate fact is that my very devotion to him was also apologetic: I was making up for my only just unspoken preoccupation with his brother.

There was no water in the cell, of course. I had nothing with which to minister to my friend. The cracks in his face were filled with drying blood. His tongue was thick between his red teeth. I felt that he was looking at me, but I could not see between his eyelids. I sat on the bench and held his hand. It occurs to me now that he had been thrown into my cell to terrorise me with the prospect of what might soon happen to me, but at the time I think that I was quite without fear for myself. The English speak of people being 'frightened out of their skins': perhaps that was my condition. I was somehow disembodied, at least in the sense that what I cared about, almost frantically, was that I should do, and have done, the right thing as far as the Poulains were concerned.

The door had been slammed and locked and bolted behind the guards. I was relieved. Suppose that they had left me some heroic option! How could I possibly have been equal to it? I did not *desire* their brutality but I needed it to continue for my peace of mind. As I sat beside him, listening to his laborious breathing, I tried to think of some kindness I could offer David. Since it was cold and I dreaded being without it, I took off my jacket and laid it across his wet chest (his upper body was drenched). His head moved. A red bubble grew out of one of his nostrils, waned, and grew again. His thick lips came slightly unstuck and I could see that he was trying to find syllables slim enough to make their way to me. I said, 'It's all right, I don't need it.'

Somehow the motion of his head beckoned my ear to his lips. I leaned down over him. His speech hyphenated with effort, he managed to say, 'Don't . . . talk . . . to . . . me . . . don't say anything to me, *ever* . . .'

I waited for a final epithet. I supplied two myself: pansy and traitor. How could I be so ready with them when neither was applicable? Perhaps I simply chose what would be unjust, so that my grievance could have some shred of justification. Perhaps I hoped for an injustice. What is certain is that David's demand that I be silent was beyond appeal. I felt tears in my eyes; he had insisted on the one thing which hurt me. A few months later, he would tell me that he suspected that the Milice could hear whatever was said in the cell; he was worried that, inadvertently, I might give them valuable information. In short, he was afraid of me; I was a danger to them all. The effect of his words (and Pascal's) was to fill me with a sense of rejection and hence of injustice. As I watched the bubble that swelled and deflated in David's nostril, until finally it burst, I went back over my stay with the Poulains like a man searching through an archive for the impossible proof that something never happened; nothing mattered more to me than to establish, as I clearly could not, that Pascal's accusation had been a ruse. Surely, surely, it was because he knew that I should recognise its absurdity that he had chosen to say what he did. He had, after all, been successful. I had not – *had* I? – blurted out any revealing remark; the airmen's hideout had not been given away. By now they (and their indifferent host) would surely have been spirited out of danger. I was not quite a hero, but I was no sort of a traitor, was I? No, I was not.

I sat by my brutalised friend with every appearance of gentle concern. I *was* gentle, I *was* concerned – and yet some part of me escaped the concentration of my emotions and my thoughts and was leaping ahead to a time of inquiry. Comedy and tragedy lost their divisions; I saw the absurdity of my situation, but I could not smile at it, even from the safe perch of the future, to which a part of me had already emigrated. The fact that I seemed to be looking back at the present, alone promised me a future. It was a flimsy kind of faith with which to endure what was about to happen, but it was, fortunately, all I had. My good fortune lay in having no faith to lose: I might be hurt, but I should not be disappointed, unless I were not hurt.

My need to suffer had nothing in common with masochism. My sex did not exist; certainly it had no appetite for pain. My bodily functions were in abeyance; I had no wish to eat or to excrete. My mind veered and soared and plummeted, but cold and fear served in the office of anaesthetic. Even David's sufferings seemed muted. I was confident that he would recover. He was more like someone who had been injured in a rough game than the subject of a murderous assault. In my innocence, it had not even occurred to me to wonder why his hair and upper body were soaking wet: I supposed that they had thrown water over him to revive him. At that stage, the subtleties of the *baignoire* were unfamiliar to me.

Towards the middle of the morning, I heard boots in the corridor. The bolts were drawn; keys turned; the cell-door opened. A single middle-aged man, whose rimless glasses reduced the menace of his black uniform, beckoned to me. His air was not friendly, but there was a weariness about it which made him seem almost inadequate to his part. Only his boots and gaiters armed him with any sinister quality.

'Follow me.'

I said, 'What about him?'

'Leave him. Follow me. No talking.' His words may have been meant to sound intimidating, but they came across to me almost as advice. He shut the door on David and refastened the bolts and locks. He looked through the spyhole and then gestured to me to go ahead of him down the corridor. I glanced behind me as I reached a wider part of the cellar where a young man with fair hair and blue eyes (he reminded me of Félix) was sitting at a table with a machine-pistol and a cup of coffee on it. He had the pettish appearance of someone who had been promised something more amusing to do. He put his hand on the gun as I walked into the room and looked rather guilty; I might have been an inspecting officer. He said, 'You won't be smiling in a minute.'

The man behind me said, 'That'll do.'

'Intellectual bastard.'

I felt a push from behind. I might have been being warned not to take offence; there was more complicity than force in the gesture. I looked back, uncertain where to go; the next push was less ambiguous. I was glad to stumble and be pushed again. Stone steps led upstairs at the back of the building. I wondered what purpose it had served before the war. On the top floor there were three white doors. The man behind me reached past me to open the one on the left. It led into a spacious loft with an unplaned wooden floor. There was a desk under the mansard window with a telephone on it and an old swivel chair behind it. A bentwood chair was alone in the middle of the room. Against the back wall, unpainted trestles supported a table made of three planks. A door was open into a darker room which contained a rusting bathtub with clawed feet. The floor of the bathroom was puddled with water. Instantly, I knew why David was wet; I knew it as certainly now as I was ignorant before. I also knew that the man who shut the door behind me was in an emotional state which, if not fearful, gave him a relationship with me that might offer me a chance of making some kind of deal with him. It would be reasonable to suspect that, after all the years which have elapsed between the event and this account of it, I am reading something into the past which was not there at the time. I can only say that I am as certain as I can be that I am scanning that distant morning with accurate recollection; I am wishing nothing onto it. If I were tempted to put a gloss on it, I should hardly choose to describe anything so ignominious as the events I am about to set down.

My immediate impression was that the grey-faced, unshaved man in front of me, although quite powerful, wanted me to understand something about him. It was this, rather than his muscle, uniform or possible helpers, that caused me, for the first time, to feel a shiver of alarm. I had left my jacket over David; it seemed colder in this commodious attic than it had been in the cell. My jailer's nationality was not yet clear to me; he wore Milice uniform, but the few words he had spoken sounded quite foreign. I stood near the bentwood chair while he looked into the 'bathroom', where there was no one, and then picked up the phone and wound the bell which, presumably, rang somewhere else in the building. He said, 'I've got the little one up here. I'm all alone. What am I to do? Alone? Of course, but . . . Very well. What shall I do? Will you sign the order? Because I don't want to be responsible. I can do it, if I have your authority. At your orders!'

He had spoken long enough now for me to guess that he came from Alsace. He put down the receiver and cleared his throat. Had he been among those who arrived by car earlier that morning? His manner suggested that he was gearing himself up to an effort he hardly cared to make. Gesturing to me to sit on the bentwood chair, he took a pair of handcuffs from his belt and fastened my hands behind my back to a wooden bracket in the chairback. As a result, I was tilted at a slight angle to the right. I could hear his breath above my ear, and feel its heat.

He said, 'Now, is it true?'

I waited for a more specific cue. His face came closer to my cheek. I might have been a corner he was trying to see round. He was less fierce than curious.

He said, 'Is it true?'

I said, 'What?'

He took my ear and twisted it, more like a schoolmaster of the kind I have never had, than like a torturer. I felt my ear grow thick and red, but I was almost embarrassed by the pettiness of the pain. 'Are you one of them?'

I said, 'I am an asthmatic.'

'An asthmatic? An asthmatic WHAT?' The increase in volume was so sudden that I looked towards the door: I thought that some newcomer had impelled him to change his style. 'You will answer me, little one, or you'll regret it.'

I said, 'An asthmatic . . .'

'I know what you are,' he said. 'Are you a Jew?'

'Do I look any more Jewish than you do?' That is what I said.

He came and stood in front of me. I had a notion of what it would be to be a woman. It looked as though his beard had grown in the few minutes I had known him; his jaw was blue-black and bulbous, like an inedible fruit. 'I'm trying to help you,' he said. 'You don't know what happens to people like you, do you? You don't know what happens in there, do you?'

I turned my head to look towards the bathroom and then I looked back at him. I was no longer unafraid. I told myself, as if I had myself on the telephone from some safe place, that I should abandon sincerity or truth or pride; I should be proud if I escaped without betraying anyone. For the rest, any tactics were permitted; I articulated my dispensation from all other morality quite as if I was serving myself with formal notice. I said, 'I'm not a Jew.'

He said, 'How do I know you aren't?'

I said, 'I swear it.'

'But can you prove it?' He walked to the trestle table and leaned against it. What he did then was as unexpected as it was unforgettable: he undid his buttons and took out his penis as if it were a possession, not a part of his body. 'I can prove it. Look. LOOK!' It was a grey article with a tapering end, smooth and quite long but not very thick. 'I am not a Jew and I can prove it. Now it's your turn, isn't it?'

My hands were locked behind me. It occurred to me that Houdini was probably a Jew; I was certainly not Houdini. I said, 'You aren't one and nor am I.'

He said, 'Do you know what they say you are? The people you came here with? They say that you're nothing to do with them, that you're an asthmatic fairy. Well?'

'If that's what they say . . .'

'I say they're lying. I say you're a Jew and you've paid them to say you're an asthmatic fairy because that's what you'd like to be.' He came across the room towards me. He had not returned his penis to its usual place. Its smoothness was surprising. 'I want to know your real name. What is your real name?'

I said, 'Bruno le Guen. My papers – '

When he hit me across the mouth I gasped more with amazement than pain. I had expected violence, but not from him. His grey cheeks grew a little pink; anger and embarrassment worked together. He wiped his hand on his thigh and then, with his eyes looking into mine, he fumbled between my legs. I squirmed and then told myself not to make it difficult for him. He opened my trousers and then he waited a few moments before reaching for my penis. I could do nothing about its size; its tip scarcely protruded from where he had undone my buttons. He stood astride my chair and, requiring rather more effort than perhaps he imagined, he dangled his penis towards mine until I felt its alien chill. I remembered the soft coldness of one of my mother's earrings when, bending to kiss me goodnight before going to the theatre, she allowed it to touch my cheek.

My jailer's behaviour excited heavy breathing from him. His nostrils were above my forehead and his whole body seemed arched around mine. He squatted on and over me like some grotesque bird. I waited for his next move with a mixture of condescension and dread. The absence of a witness made his actions seem hardly more than a bad dream; he had not hurt me and I did not, after all, expect any subsequent contact with him. There was no need for anyone ever to know what he was doing. I cannot say why my being alone with him exempted the occasion from disgust, but it did.

He said, 'How did you like that? I'm trying to help you, do you know that? This is better than Russia, don't you think so? Would you sooner be in Russia?'

I said, 'Not at all.'

He said, 'They say you're what you are, don't they?'

I said, 'I don't know. Where are they?'

'Who are they?' he said.

I said, 'I was in the Doctor's clinic.'

'They're going to shoot them,' he said. 'All of them. They're going to shoot them later today, perhaps tomorrow.'

'Is there anything you can do?' That, again, is what I said. What else could I have said? 'He's a doctor.'

'They're Cocos,' he said, 'the whole lot of them.'

I said, 'Not at all,' and wished that he had not noticed.

He turned his back to me and did up his buttons. Mine were still open. He said, 'You knew about them, didn't you? DIDN'T YOU?'

I said, 'He's not a Communist, he's a doctor.'

'Scum,' he said. 'DO YOU HEAR ME?'

How could I feel pity for such a man? I pitied him. As for myself, I was indifferent. I was not brave. I had, as it were, abandoned my own ship and was observing its drift from a distance. My interest centred on the man who, I suspected, would be my salvation. The more despicable his confusions and the clumsier his attempts to indulge his power over me, the more likely it was that I could at least hope to find an accommodation with him. He became briefly important to me. I felt something close to an affinity with him; contempt bred familiarity. To say that I liked him would be absurd, but my sense of relief was such that a certain scornful affection made me hope that no one came to interrupt our corrupt and secret romance.

'You have to tell me something,' he said. 'You have to help me if you want me to help you.'

I said, 'Are you a good Frenchman?'

He hit me at once, harder than before. I felt my jaw swell and I tasted blood. It was a relief, like an alibi. I should not go unscathed from the place where David had suffered so much and where the rest of his family, for all I knew, had suffered even more.

'You are a traitor,' he said. 'You are a . . . pansy and a . . . a . . . Freemason and a . . . a . . . !' He reached into the poor purse of his vocabulary for some new coinage. 'You like Jews?' He looked down at the disappointment of my penis. 'You call me a bad Frenchman? It's just as well for you I'm all alone up here. Don't say that again, in front of other people, will you? You have to tell me everything you know.'

I thought of the Sullan constitution. The self-pity of the pot-bellied man in front of me was an involuntary generosity; his threats came out as pleas. His fear of what his colleagues would say, if he emerged from our interview without tasty news, blighted his competence to extract it. At the same time, it allowed me a respite in which it became impossible not to consider what crumb of insignificant information I might conceivably offer him. Although I could not (and cannot) credit him with the subtlety of deliberately impersonating both the gentle and the cruel policeman whose alternation of blows and promises is so often used to break down a suspect, the effect of his intermittent bluster and violence was to split him into two characters, to the nicer of whom I had every interest (and a certain pleasure) in pandering. My education in diplomacy was in his hands.

'Do you want me to ring for some help? Not everyone in this building is as decent as I am, you know.'

I said, 'I'm asthmatic. Doctor Poulain is looking after me.'

'They're going to shoot your Doctor Poulain,' he said. 'They'll shoot you if I tell them to.'

My reticence was an effort of will. Clever, stupid answers to his bluster surged in my throat and had to be kept down. One insolent remark could puncture his vanity and my prospects at the same time. I said, 'It's all a misunderstanding. I'm sure of it.'

'You think I'm a poor slob, don't you? You think you can make rings around me! You're wrong. Those days are finished. You're going to tell me something because I need you to. I need you to, my little one. There, do you like that, you little pansy? Answer.'

'Not particularly,' I said.

'They didn't trust you, did they? Tell me the truth. They didn't trust you because you're not a man, are you? Look, because is this what happens to men? Men who are really men wouldn't react as you're reacting. They hated you, they despised you. And you're protecting them! Why?'

'I'm not protecting anyone,' I said.

'They're terrorists, little one! They're Communists. You talk about good Frenchmen! You don't know what a good Frenchman is. Have you seen any foreigners at the house?'

'None.'

'How do you know what a foreigner is?'

'Come on!' I said.

'Do you want me to get a colleague to come up here?'

I said, 'You're bad enough on your own.' It was the most flattering observation I could think of.

'I'd like to help you,' he said. 'Why won't you help me?'

I said, 'I would if I could, I promise you.'

'Promise me! And when the time comes, *if* the time comes, what will you do? You'll tell them I did terrible things to you. You'll forget what you promised.'

'I don't think so,' I said. 'No, I won't. Definitely not.'

'Tell me something,' he said. 'A little thing. You're a clever person, you must have noticed something. They're going to shoot them all anyway, they're possibly dead already. You won't be hurting anyone.'

I said, 'The guy at the mill . . .'

'What mill?'

'I shouldn't say this. The Moulin des Garrigues. I don't know this for certain.'

'Out with it. Out with it!'

'You know this already. He plays a double game, to say the least, doesn't he?'

'I work here,' he said. 'I don't even know where you come from. I'm not from here.'

'I know that.'

'How?'

'Your voice, your accent . . .'

He took my jaw in his thick hand and bracketed my face with thumb and forefinger. He squeezed my mouth open, like a vet with a dog and then he reached in with his other hand and tried to catch hold of my tongue. His face was close to mine; his eyes bulged and dilated until they seemed to swim into my brain. He rummaged in my mouth and I gagged and resisted the desire to resist. His act was a folly; I could have bitten him and, perhaps, kicked him. He was at once raping and tempting me. When, at last, he withdrew his wet fingers, he tried to look at me like a schoolmaster who hopes that a hint of what he might do will serve as a lesson. There was no routine ambition of which he did not offer some pathetic vestige: he had failed to be a doctor, a professor, a vet, a priest and a policeman. Why had someone not had the prudence to let him drive a train?

He said, 'Wait a moment.'

Although it was soured by his assault, a dislocated smile twitched at my mouth. Who but a man ruled by platitudes could have told someone in my present situation to 'wait a moment'? He went to the desk and found paper and pencil. On his way back to me, he stopped and listened; his eyes consulted mine for confirmation that no one was coming up the stairs. I recognised once more how lucky I was that, deprived of a colleague, he found it necessary to recruit me as a sympathiser.

'Now . . . what is the name of this man? And where does he live?'

Having had the idea that it would be clever to betray a traitor, I was now committed to denouncing the wood merchant as if he were a friend. My memory of the light showing behind his shutters as I made my way back to the Poulains' was an irrational justification of what I was doing. I recalled thinking that something unusual was happening, even though I had never before seen the mill at night and had no good reason for my suspicions.

'It's only what I happened to overhear,' I said. 'I don't want to get anyone into trouble. It's the . . . the Moulin des Garrigues . . .'

My inquisitor cocked his head. There *were* footsteps on the stairs. He looked at me as if I had sprung an ambush. As the footsteps reached the landing, he took hold of the back of my chair and threw it sideways. Powerless to break my fall, I crashed onto the dusty planks of the floor and felt my cheek split like a fruit. Was I pretending or did I really lose consciousness for a moment? I was sideways, with the chair clawed over me, my arms twisted. My position was humiliating but also, somehow, comic; rather than being the prelude to further violence, it seemed to secure me against it, if only because I felt myself inaccessible to threats. I was in the wrong place for them.

'What are you doing?'

'You said to start. I started.'

'He's a nobody. He's nothing. You're wasting your time.'

'He gave me a name. A place at least. A mill . . .'

'Get him downstairs. He goes with the garbage.'

'I don't think he knows much more.'

'An hour you've been with him and that's the conclusion you come to! Congratulations! Shit!'

'You never know . . .'

'He's some poor pansy asthmatic and you have to break a chair with him when you could have been doing something worthwhile.' The newcomer had a smart, scathing voice and a complete officer's uniform. His shining feet came close to my face and seemed to stare disdainfully at me; I could see myself in their blackness. 'Now get him off the floor and down to the hall. Where's his coat?'

'He didn't have a coat.'

'He had a coat. Where is it?'

'I haven't taken it. He didn't have a coat when I brought him up.'

'Find it. Where's your coat? You! What happened to it? You can tell me.'

I said, 'Downstairs.'

'What? Get up! Get him up. What've you done to him?'

'I did what I was told to do.'

'He doesn't know a thing.' The newcomer touched me with his toecap. 'They were terrible about you.' He was a handsome young man with a flop of blond hair and a crooked nose which parodied aristocracy. 'You're lucky, aren't you, they wouldn't have anything to do with you? There are some people even scum won't have anything to do with. Disgust, that's something even the Cocos can feel sometimes. Be grateful! Now get him downstairs.'

XXXIV

During the few years of our marriage, Maureen has never failed to honour her conjugual obligations. She has been the facsimile of a loving wife, just as I hope that I have been that of a devoted husband. We play ambling golf and gentle tennis; we attend the cocktail parties of the local *gratin* where my diplomatic status gives me a spurious dignity and leads to invitations to visit the retired Dutch and Scandinavian bourgeois who have come more and more to settle in our region; we listen to music during the late afternoon, and before dinner we watch the English news, thanks to the satellite television which I acquired so that Maureen should not lose touch with what is happening in her native country. We say goodnight in the corridor which leads to our separate rooms and we say good morning, with a kiss, at the breakfast table. In short, we act like a civilised couple, which presumably gives some indication of what each of us is missing.

It is easy, now, to say that my marriage with Berthe should never have taken place or that it should have ended much sooner than it did. Although what happened in Rome led to an exchange of confidences which might have inclined other couples to passionate reconciliations or instant rupture, Berthe and I soon relapsed into the same kind of rancid indifference which was both the cause and the effect of our slow divergence. Did my confession of giving her showercoat to Pia lead her to think that I might have been her killer? She lacked enthusiasm either for a grievance or for the dread that I might be a dangerous man. Her revelation that my uncle had been her lover came too late, and was too unalluringly delivered, to presage a revival of our sexual activity, which had never been very urgent. When, after returning to the Via Trionfale, I sensed that she was restless in bed and turned to honour what I suspected was her impatient desire, she told me that her dinner had disagreed with her. I was unguarded enough to remark that perhaps it was the whisky which had disagreed with the dinner. She said that the trouble was, as everyone except me already knew, that they would make ice with tapwater. She went into the bathroom and was accusingly sick.

Looking back, one might argue that had her father died more promptly she might well have left me sooner; while I assumed her to be doing her duty by her children, she was perhaps maintaining some unspoken contract with the father whose money would emancipate and reward her for keeping up appearances. He lived to a great age in a spirit of obstinate and acidulous resentment. Longevity became his monotonous and surly argument against any suggestion that he had behaved dishonourably or unwisely during the war. Thanks to my uncle's sagacious and serpentine diplomacy, no severe sanction had fallen on a man who had not only allowed his factories to produce war material for the Germans but who had also countersigned the most objectionable of Vichy laws. He insisted at length on the difference between signing (which would have been an endorsement) and countersigning, which was, he argued, evidence only of having read what he could not alter. My father-in-law's dryness and pomposity became more and more pronounced over the years; in the rectitude of his dress and his manners, in the punctiliousness of his vocabulary (one felt that he used no word unauthorised by the Académie Française) and in the severity of his morals (or at least of those he prescribed for others), he became more and more senatorial. That he had been saved from ignominy, and perhaps from the confiscation of the property he had been willing to do anything to preserve, made him the very instance of inflexibility in the upholding of standards which, he argued, were everywhere being betrayed. If he deplored this decadence, he also welcomed it as proof that his Maurrasian views needed no emendation.

Denied influence in the postwar world, my father-in-law became the pitiless critic of every government of the Fourth and the Fifth Republic. His repudiation of General de Gaulle made no reference to the loss of Algeria but was directed at the General's style, which he regarded as vulgar ('St Cyr and water'). Once, when we were alone after dinner, he challenged me to deny that Pétain was in all respects a truer vessel of the French tradition ('including when it came to women'). I asked him whether he knew the story of the Marshal, in the lift at the Hotel du Parc, asking one of his aides, 'Who am I?' He said that he had heard it of a quite different lift – extreme accuracy is always a weapon of dishonest arguments – and that it was perfectly false. In any case, what did it prove? He regarded people who drank wine with their soup as infinitely more reprehensible than those who had acquiesced in, and indeed instigated, the deportation of their fellow-citizens. The former gave proof of an irremediable lack of breeding; the latter had been under the pressure of raison d'état which, however regrettably, lacked the elasticity of sentiment.

I made no effort to insist on the iniquity of the Vichy régime. As my father-in-law grew older, his eyes began to match those of the Marshal and he carried himself with the same air of majestic and dolorous modesty. My failure to challenge him was not due to cowardice, but to something perhaps even less savoury: I was reluctant to do anything which might dissipate the flavour of those years in which eloquent and courteous men could persuade themselves of anything except the possibility of their own worthlessness. The old gentleman became an antique whose fragility I could not bring myself to endanger. It amused me, to the point of tolerance and even indulgence, to listen to his principled defence of the indefensible. It became part of the glory of the French language, if not of the French themselves, that it could be deployed faultlessly, elegantly, and with cultivated references to our finest minds (including both Proust and Bergson!), for the sake of a cause for which a less resourceful vocabulary could not have found a single word to say. France has not only digested the shame of our defeat, she has, thanks to her taste for irony, made it a part of her regular diet, something to be regurgitated and relished and swallowed all over again. More naive cultures (especially the Anglo-Saxon) now seem deficient in subtlety, since they lack an experience of duplicity to match ours. The acquaintance with evil, and a sense of the beauty of certain of its flowers, is an assumed part of the Parisian style. As a diplomat, I have noticed how much happier our statesmen tend to be when in the company of Germans rather than with Englishmen or Americans. There is a complicity between the old enemies like that between a man and a mistress with whom his old quarrels had a savage charm which no rational accommodations can ever match.

I cannot say that I stayed with Berthe purely for the sake of being sweetly exasperated by her father; I never found an apt moment or an urgent need to go through the tedium (and expense) of a divorce. Yet my reluctance to be done with my marriage somehow paralleled my father-in-law's determination to stare down the postwar world. The worse things got, the more skill and calculation were needed to sustain the appearances of normality; joylessness, like defeat, has its consolations. In the event, the years in which Berthe and I maintained our common home, supposedly for the sake of the boys, were not entirely devoid of tepid pleasures which – now I come to think of it – were not very different (though somehow more genuine) from those I now enjoy with Maureen. Berthe played worse golf but better bridge than my present wife; if she had less conversation, she was (inadvertently) more amusing, if only because she made less effort to please. Maureen's lack of malice is like a diet without salt; she is as good to me as she knows how, but I cannot say that she is good for me. Has she any idea how often she makes me think of Berthe? Does it occur to her that she is like an insipid antidote which no one would ever dream of taking except as a specific against a poison that had an altogether more astringent flavour? I have every reason to be grateful to Maureen; her scrupulous attentions reassure me that my possessions, if not my person, can induce a woman to make every effort to please me. I have no sexual desire for Maureen, but the assiduity with which she performs her genteel routine gives me something of the satisfaction which the best protitutes used to offer: I am touched by her decency in honouring her contract just as I was by Pia and a few others who managed to combine shamelessness with dignity. If, as is statistically likely, I die in Maureen's arms, or at least in her presence, I can rely on her sustaining an attitude of tactful tenderness until my very last breath. The last image on my retina is likely to be that of a good wife. How unfair that her presence leads me more and more to think of her predecessor! It is typical of my mismanaged emotions that I am quite frequently tempted to make contact with Berthe and that I dream of her returning to La Fontaine du Noyer, quite as if she liked the place more than Maureen, who is never without plans for its improvement and the click of whose indefatigable secateurs even now comes to my ears as I sit at my father's *escritoire* by the open door onto the terrace. The forsythia has already flowered and turned brown in the spring rain.

I have absolutely nothing to say against Maureen. Does that indicate how marginal a place she has in my life? She is like an excellent secretary whose only failing is that she cannot imagine how one might behave in her absence. She excites no ambiguous feelings in me, since she excites no true feelings at all; my unfailing courtesy to her is the evidence of that. Shortly, I shall shut this *cahier de brouillon* in my desk drawer and pay attention to her plans for renovating the loft. I have agreed to go through the boxes which are stored in it so that we can jettison whatever lacks interest or value; she has an idea that we can pay for the alterations by discovering forgotten antiques which she is quite prepared to sell at the next *foire à la brocante* or, if they are of appropriate quality, to take in to a 'little man' in Bordeaux with whom she has had very instructive conversations. The new room (with bathroom *en suite*) is intended for my sons when either of them comes to visit. The fact that they rarely do so does not disincline Maureen to go ahead; she argues that they will come more often if they have a proper place to sleep. Does it ever occur to her that her existence, together with the likelihood that she will keep them from inheriting the place until after her death, is a much more potent deterrent than the want of a hot towel rail?

Although I am now the master of La Fontaine, I think of altering its structure with a certain apprehension, as if my parents might come back and chide me for my impertinence. The death of my mother occurred while I was *en poste* in Buenos Aires; she went into hospital for the treatment of some minor gynaecological disorder, caught pneumonia and (as my father put it) 'disdained to recover'. He understood her better than he loved her. I was unable to return for the funeral. My sister Louise has chosen not to forgive me for this delinquency. She has had five children and is married to a doctor in Montpellier who, I believe, treats her indifferently; she keeps her troubles to herself, as other women do their lovers. I could speculate quite plausibly on why she has clung to her grievance, to the point of communicating very rarely with me, but I seem to have found it as convenient as she does to reduce our contacts to a minimum. The flare of love, hardly distinct from desire, which I felt for her (and she, I think, for me) on the occasion of my departure for Rodecin was, as they say, without sequel, unless its consequence was to embarrass both of us with its memory. It is one of my rare and well-concealed vanities to think that the banality of her marriage and the loss of her looks, which seemed less the result of natural change than of wilful neglect, were self-lacerating gestures intended for my mortification. In practice, there was nothing I could have done to save Louise from the crassness of her life, but I cannot forget that we spoke, with all the hyperbole of youthful romanticism, of a life together in some distant paradise.

When I did return from Argentina, I found my father much thinner than I expected. He had had many letters of condolence and was answering them, in his delicate hand, at the *escritoire* I now use (and which I shall not, under any circumstances, allow Maureen to sell). My mother's funeral had been my father-in-law's last public appearance. The presence of a good number of men who had been conspicuous in the Resistance had put him in an excellent humour. 'He moved through the crowd,' my father said, 'as if he alone of all of them had a clear conscience. His performance trumped his record, even for those who were least disposed to forget it. His courtesy was indistinguishable from irony. I have to confess to you, Guy, that he was, in his person, and at that particular juncture, when de Gaulle was at the height of his authority, the incarnation of what should have been the true dignity of France. The pity of it was, is, and always will be, that his whole way of being, the very example he set, is as flawed as it is admirable. The discovery that scoundrels can behave even worse than one could have suspected hardly affects one's vision of humanity, but the reminder that nobility is at its purest when it is most pitiless, that it will excuse absolutely everything, except wine with soup, well, that makes one wiser than one would choose to be.'

My father was not markedly bereaved; there was a lightness about him which seemed to counterfeit youth. He had an air of urgency as he went about the house and he promised me that there was no risk of his being bored or lonely. I was not to think of him as a man without plans or pleasures: he intended to spend part of his time in Paris and he had in mind to go to the Far East. His lack of inclination to make demands on me amounted almost to a declaration of indifference, if not distaste. I was more relieved than offended, but I confess that I had expected my mother's disappearance to make him more accessible to me, at least in terms of conversation. There was an element of defiance in his independent manner; he made it clear to me that his appetites and intentions would best retain their piquancy if they remained unquestioned. Yet the way that he spoke of them hinted at the pleasure he derived from my frustrated curiosity. In short, my first meeting with him as a man on his own did not lead to any sudden frankness on any topic. Although he looked different, it pleased him to maintain that he was the same as ever; it was at once a tribute to my mother and an indication of how well he would manage without her.

Did I imagine or hope that, in her absence, he would feel himself dispensed from discretion and able to tell me of the long imposture of his marriage? Perhaps he had a notion that I was still committed to a life which, to some extent, mimicked his and that it would be tactless to confess the rueful exhilaration he felt at the removal of a halter which I still wore. I was probably naive in supposing that the death of my mother implied any absolute caesura in my father's life; I daresay that she took on an added vitality once she was no longer a charge on his time. Death can purify a relationship quite as much as it can put an end to it; one can be respectful and even grateful to the dead in a way that the pettiness of the quotidian makes less easy with the living. My father went on living with my mother, but on better terms than during her lifetime. Something similar has happened to me with regard to Berthe whom I now see as she was when I first came back to La Fontaine du Noyer in the spring of 1944 rather than disguised as the frumpish and alcoholic scold which she was to become.

My father was as polite and articulate as ever during the days I spent with him. At her own request, my mother had been buried in her family plot near Le Prieuré; my father had made plans for his own cremation and, of course, would not have been acceptable in a Catholic cemetery. He and I drove to Angoulême in order that I should see the grave. The road took us past the cottage where I left the two airmen on the night of my arrest. I had had occasion to pass it before, but never in company with my father. To my surprise, I neglected to inform him of its significance; no, I took pleasure in looking at it pointedly enough to provoke a ripple of inquiry on his brow, to which I responded with bland silence. It is possible that the same grudging peasant was still in residence but I had no inclination to shake his hand. As far as I know, the two airmen had not been detected, although my removal from the vicinity made it difficult for me to be sure. By the time I was free to make inquiries I had lost interest in their precise fate.

My father and I had a long and excellent lunch at Brantôme, sitting on the terrace overlooking the slow river where I had observed the two beady swans passing the bank where a girl was talking to two German soldiers. I kept an eye open for her, quite as though only an hour or two had elapsed since her long glance in my direction. From where we ate the Charbonnel brothers' excellent meal, I could see the *quai* and the hôtel-café where I waited for the man who turned out to be two men. Once again, I said nothing to my father; I suspected that I should embarrass him if I tried to make an adventure out of what was no more than an errand. Nevertheless, his lack of curiosity (since he knew that I had spent some time in the area) amounted almost to a reproach, which disposed me, almost casually, to revise my opinion of him. What had always seemed like tolerance on his part, and even a sort of male complicity, now struck me quite simply as a want of feeling even though it was I who had denied him the information which might have kindled his sympathy.

I said, 'Did you ever worry about me during the war?'

He said, 'Your mother was always confident that you would be all right.'

'But she knew absolutely nothing about what was going on, did she?'

'She knew that your uncle would always do everything he could to make sure you were safe.'

'And that was sufficient to reassure her, was it?'

'No greater reassurance was conceivable.' My father had not lost his ability to make a statement of fact into a source of wry mystery. He smiled at me, as if in gratitude for a chance to be himself again. 'What Jean-Claude could not do could not, in practical terms, be done by anyone.'

'But of course,' I said, 'in fact there were areas in which he was completely powerless. It was nothing to do with him that I wasn't shot, for instance.'

'Perhaps not,' he said.

'Nothing,' I said.

'Perhaps not.'

'You haven't told me how he behaved at Mother's funeral.'

'I found him much aged.'

'Did he say anything about my absence?'

'He said very little. He was correct, but extremely reticent. He's not at all well at present, you know.'

I said, 'Why did he never marry?'

'He was a man who had many women. He had a strong sense of family, but mobility was essential to him; he believed in accountants but not in accountability, in the personal sense.'

'You never liked him, did you?'

My father said, 'He had certain responsibilities, certain concerns, certain . . . aptitudes. His relationship with me, though perfectly correct, fell outside what he had time for. He rendered us considerable service, not least with regard to you, but there was always a distance between him and me. It's of no importance.'

'But of a certain interest.'

'Marginal.' He made the single word into a sentence. 'Marginal.'

I said, 'Are you saying that he's dying?'

'He treats his health as a kind of intrigue. He doesn't welcome attempts to uncover its exact state.'

I said, 'Would it be an impertinence, at this late stage, to ask you what in your life deeply concerns you?'

My father gave a more candid laugh than I ever heard from him. 'My dear boy,' he said, 'what concerns me is dead and buried. Dead and buried. But don't worry, there's something to be said for a state of numbness . . . a surprising liberty in having false teeth. The absence of feeling gives one an intimation of the sublime. Our vision of heaven, I often think, is instinct with all the cowardice of which man is capable.'

I said, 'Have you always lived in a logic of lacunae?'

'Oh my dear Guy, how considerate you are of me in your choice of phrase!'

'Curiosity is composed partly of malice and partly of courtesy, isn't it?'

'And hope,' my father said. 'We must never forget hope, must we? The last of our punishments!'

Two small girls with plastic satchels on their backs came skipping along the narrow path which ran below the terrace where we were lunching. They giggled as their white stockings twinkled in the midday sunshine. I had the feeling that they made a habit of leaving it till the last minute before they returned to school. They looked up at us for reproving admiration as they made their kittenish noises and I saw that they were twins.

My father said, 'Your mother hoped that you would be twins.'

I said, 'And was I not?'

XXXV

The blond officer looked at my split face without pity but with a sigh which seemed to solicit my understanding. His attitude implied that his staff was incompetent and unsubtle and that it was, in some way, my fault. Had people like me not been so unreasonable, he might have commanded an efficient service. We all but acknowledged each other as people with whom it might have been possible, under less foolish conditions, to have a sane conversation. I denied him my smile or my respect, as I did any hint of appeal, but I could not deny that I both feared his temper and was a little disappointed not to have suffered somewhat at his hands. It occurred to me that, had I stayed in Paris for the years when I was forced to be at the *lycée* in Caillac, I should have been flattered to belong to his society.

The Miliciens downstairs tried to give the impression of drilled competence, but their efficiency bore the marks of haste, almost of panic. They sought to intimidate by the clash of their boots on the flagstones and to impress by the briskness of their obedience; I had the feeling that our captors were somehow auditioning before those whom they had at their mercy. They were demonstrating how unfair it was that the world did not conform to their orders and how they were impeded from creating something of truly savage beauty by the men of little faith who filled their files with needless paperwork and whose alien masters incited them to acts of disruption.

No doubt I was able to observe the sullen urgency of the Miliciens with such surreptitious detachment because I had, by the standards of other prisoners (not least David Poulain), scarcely been scratched; my cheek was split and bleeding, but my injury more disguised me as a victim of brutality than proved me one. I could almost interpret it as a sign of good fortune; to have been unmarked would have suggested too prompt a divulgence of what my captors wanted to get out of me.

David was carried into our midst at the last moment. The blond officer indicated to me that I would be well advised to make sure that he went with us. Again I felt a twitch of involuntary gratitude; I was almost too ready to exempt the officer from responsibility for the brutality he had caused on account of the confidence he appeared to have in my ability to relieve him of the viler duty of submitting David to further torture. How did I know that the officer was as good as saying that unless he went with us, my friend had no chance of survival? Sympathy, in the ordinary sense, was no part of the officer's style, but some instinct of communication was open between us, or so I was sentimental enough to feel.

The transport was late in arriving. I had again been handcuffed, but my hands were now in front of me. My buttons had not been fastened again, which added an element of farce to my state of mind: at a time when I should, perhaps, have been considering the state of my soul, I was afraid that I might be subject to the most puerile of embarrassments. I did not, in truth, think that we were going to be shot. My earlier jailer, now wearing a greatcoat and a beret and carrying a sub-machine-gun, regarded me with an unforgiving expression (my witnessing his humiliation distressed him more than any other crime I might have committed). He stood next to me in the lobby and found occasion to mutter, 'We'll see how much you like where you're going now.' It did not sound like a sentence of death to me.

It must have been early afternoon before we heard a truck pull into the yard (first came the creak of the metal gates). David was slumped against the wall, with his knees to his chin. I indicated to a swarthy, moustachioed man to help me with him. A steely sun was shining like a knife; it seemed to lance my head as the Spaniard and I hefted David over the tailgate and into the lorry. There were portable wooden benches along the sides. A tarpaulin roof was hooped over metal struts. The driver wore blue trousers and a thick sweater; something in his busy, unaggressive manner indicated that this was not his regular activity and that he wished us to know it. He asked more questions than a disciplined functionary would. The guards who were to travel with us in the back of the truck turned out to be my middle-aged jailer and the same beaky young Milicien to whom I had been handcuffed when they brought me in. I had the illusion of being among friends.

As we were about to drive away, the blond officer and another Milicien, of modest rank, came out of the headquarters. The officer shouted something disrespectful through the door and, when a rejoinder was thrown out after him, like a drunkard's hat, he went back inside and we heard more shouting. When he came out again, he appeared to be in a state of greater rage with his superiors than with the prisoners he had been deputed to accompany. He got in beside the driver and slammed the door. Through the little window of the cab, I could see him delivering tart phrases to the sweatered man who had little taste for them.

I was right: we drove through Périgueux only as far as the railway station where we were ordered to get out. The Spaniard jumped down before I could ask him to help me with David. We were watched by passers-by who had the air of people unfairly accosted by a history which had nothing to do with them. Most of them seemed to resent the need to show us sympathy; it was a charge on their skimpy spiritual purses. Others, I guessed, felt disparaged by not being of our number and did not thank us for the reminder of their impotence. Only a gendarme played the Samaritan: he had the nerve and the licence to help me with David, murmuring, 'The bastards, the swine,' as he did so. The hint of decency was enough to prime a sudden fear that we were on our way to something more cruel than I knew.

We stood there while the blond officer argued with the lorry driver who wanted to be on his way. He had done what was on his slip of paper and he had other missions. The officer drew his pistol and cocked it. 'If you get back into that lorry, I shall shoot you like a dog.' He found the opportunity to use the phrase so exhilarating that he looked round for someone worthy to wink at.

The lorry waited. The passers-by were glad to be gone before they had to witness anything further. The gendarme came back from the station with a cup of water and a rag. His kindness hurt like a brand. I could hardly keep the tears from my eyes as I washed David's face, gently, gently, and saw his eyes respond, with a wince, to the light. The gendarme said, 'Courage! They've blown up the line, I think.'

We were ordered back into the lorry. David groaned as I thrust him once more over the tailgate. It seemed a good sign. We sat there while the officer went to the police office in the station concourse and made a telephone call. He came out making a twisting signal to the driver: 'Start up, turn her round, get us out of here.'

Our jailers' attitude of grievance began to exceed their prisoners'. The middle-aged man looked at his watch; perhaps his wife had promised him some treat which would now have to wait in the oven. Resignation replaced truculence. The mask of militant virtue slipped and was not replaced by any disciplinary reflex. I held the gendarme's wet rag in my hand, as if I had promised to return it.

As we crossed the bridge, the younger guard lifted aside the flap at the back of the lorry and I caught a glimpse of the 'Byzantine' cathedral. Its mongrel style seemed to stand as an aberrant sermon against the notions of Catholic purity which the Milice were supposed to embody. The furtive action of the guard (who perhaps wondered when he would next see the dumpling domes of his home town) gave him a tiny fleck of local colour which both humanised and belittled him, just as he may have thought the silly aperture in my trousers did me. The lorry stopped, with the cathedral still framed in a triangle of sunlight, and we waited again. I heard the approach of a motorcycle and a German shout above its snorting engine. The motorcycle went ahead of us and I was able to sight it, as we took the gradient towards the south; there was a steel-helmeted driver and a soldier with a machine-gun in the torpedo-shaped sidecar.

The road we took led towards my corner of the department. I was exhilarated and alarmed; it pleased me to think that I was again going to see familiar things, but I feared the emotions they might stir. I tried to abate my hopes by speculating on our final destination. David, slumped against me on the rocking bench, required my active attention; I had no time for conversation and in any case I did not wish to test my Spanish on my disobliging neighbour. We might, of course, have been going to Brive to meet the main line, in which case we should avoid Caillac and its hinterland, but that possibility was soon aborted: we left the *route nationale* after Niversac and took the road towards home. We went through the usual villages and smelled the usual smells. This was the true France whose values the Marshal affected to support in his broadcast homilies; his facile antitheses contrasted the vices of the city with the virtues of the village. In fact, the countryside's only value was its indifference: our lorry and the men in it were specks of dust blowing across its face.

By the time we reached the Dordogne itself, I was lost to imagination. Half-dozing, while my shackled hands awkwardly restrained David from toppling like a book from its shelf, I observed the increasing blankness of the lorry's human cargo; even the faces of those who had been maltreated seemed to be more bored than anguished. Wounds and bruises became as numb and unremarkable as a moustache (I saw that the Spaniard's was crusted with blood on one side where someone, I guessed, had tried to tear it from his lip).

We crossed the Dordogne at Le Bugue, ducked past Le Buisson and headed towards Siorac. I knew the road well; it went under a high bluff which had once been a prehistoric bank of the river. The lorry had to slow down to take a steep bend under a narrow railway bridge. The first shots sounded like misfiring from the motorcyle ahead of us. The lorry butted the arch of the bridge and we were thrown to the floor. The two guards in the back with us were as much taken by surprise as we were and obeyed the law of gravity with equal helplessness. They scrambled to sit up, hugging their weapons, and hacking at us with their boots while they tried to stand up. The sound of light machine-gun fire came in sustained bursts. Before our guards (who were in no great hurry) could get out of the lorry, the flap was torn open and there was Martegoutte and a comrade of the same age, wearing their fiercest faces. I called out, 'Eh oh, don't shoot! Don't shoot.'

The Miliciens made it seem that all along their only desire had been to surrender; they held their guns out like presents. They could not have been in a greater hurry to unlock our handcuffs. Beyond my sight, on ahead, there was more shooting and then silence. Martegoutte helped us down into the road and handed me my jailer's submachine gun. 'Keep an eye on them, old man.'

I said, 'We need some help.'

'You'll get it. Don't move.'

Martegoutte ran back under the bridge as the door of the lorry's cab opened and the driver staggered into the road with his forehead hanging down in a flap of red. Blood gushed over his face and stippled his hairy sweater. He held the hinge of skin up against his forehead and said, 'Shit, but shit!' The broken windscreen was badged with blood where he had smashed against it. The blond officer was trapped inside, where the side of the cab had been crushed against his legs. I gestured to the two guards who had been in the back with us to sit against the side of the lorry with their hands behind their necks. They tried earnestly to place themselves exactly where I indicated. I might have been a photographer at a wedding whose time they were anxious not to waste.

A man thin and light enough to be a jockey, wearing a sheepskin jerkin, riding boots and jodhpurs, ran lamely back from whatever had happened on the far side of the bridge (the dip and bend made it invisible to me) and called out, 'Doctor Poulain? Which one is Doctor Poulain?'

I said, 'He isn't here. He isn't with us.'

He said, 'Yes, he is.' He called again. 'Doctor Poulain?'

I said, 'This is his son, David. I'm Guy de Roumegouse.'

He said, 'Be quiet. Doctor Poulain?'

The blond officer groaned for the first time. It was like a small cough to draw attention to himself. I looked at his legs and felt sick. I gave him the opportunity, which he took, to sneer at my green expression. The man in the sheepskin said, 'Why isn't he here, Doctor Poulain?'

I said, 'Who said he would be?'

'Damn,' he said. 'We've got the wrong lorry. *Damn.*' He pursed his lips and looked at his watch. 'Right. Get this thing pushed off the road. Come on, quick, let's get this thing off the road. Fast.'

The late prisoners seemed more stunned by the ambush than our two guards, who were the first to seek some credit by being as helpful as possible. I slung my German gun over my shoulder and went to take the lorry out of gear. The blond officer gasped as the metal of the cab unbent slightly when the lorry was disengaged from the bridge. His courage was all the defiance he could still offer. I said, 'We'll get you out of here in a minute.'

He said, 'I think not.'

The lorry was rolled under the poplars at the side of the road, but it would certainly be visible to another convoy. I went to the man in the sheepskin and said, 'There's an officer trapped in the cab. Both his legs are smashed. What shall we do?'

He said, 'Has he got a pistol?'

I said, 'I suppose he has.'

'Then go and get it and shoot him with it.'

I looked up and saw the Spaniard smiling at me. I said, 'Can't we take him with us?'

'I said to shoot him. Shoot him. I know that bastard.'

'You know him?'

'Shoot him and let's get out of here. This isn't going to work. Shit. We were told Poulain was on this transport.' He turned and ran back under the bridge. Despite his frail physique, he ran with the heavy haste of a lame man.

The Spaniard was watching me as he brushed cinders of blood from his moustache with the flat of his thumb. He said, 'I'll take care of it. Give me your gun. What are you, a schoolboy?'

I looked at the middle-aged guard who wanted nothing more than to do something which would recommend him to us. I was thinking that I was an asthmatic pansy. I said, 'He's a prisoner of war, don't you agree?'

'Give me your gun,' the Spaniard said, 'and quick.'

I held it away from him and turned to where the blond officer was slumped against the bent door of the lorry. He had enough strength to look at me with half-closed eyes; the sunlight caught the fairness of his lashes. I raised the gun and pulled the trigger and nothing happened. It was hard against my finger. People were running around; birds were singing; the silence behind the noise resembled an orchestra that might come in at any minute. The blond officer said, 'You've got the safety catch on, cretin.'

I did not know the model of the gun, but I had been shooting with my father. I bit my lip as I adjusted the position of the safety catch and then, with my eyes blurred with tears, I shot the blond officer, several times. I wished it could have been the Spaniard.

The man in the sheepskin jerkin was back, with another FFI man. My middle-aged guard was looking at me with such a mixture of horror and entreaty that I made a little calming gesture with my hand. The younger guard was leaning against the truck, one leg across the other, with an air of naive interest, like a tourist. The second FFI man, whom I would know later as The Writer, had a clipped moustache, dark brows and a yellow cigarette between his lips. He acted as though he alone were unhurried and unruffled. 'Right,' he said, 'they're not coming, are they? So let's get away from here. Someone somewhere is expecting them. Logic. Marteau?'

Martegoutte came under the railway arch and stood to attention. 'Colonel?'

'Get them on the move. You know where to go.'

I said, 'Excuse me, sir, but this is David Poulain. I don't think he's going to be marching anywhere.'

'You'll have to carry him.'

'I'll help,' my ex-jailer said. 'I know him, don't I?'

I said, 'Why not?'

The Spaniard said, 'We ought to shoot both these bastards. Give me the gun and I'll take care of it.'

The Writer spoke quick Spanish. He was a man who liked to display his abilities. The Spaniard was not happy, but he shrugged and retied his laces. There were about a dozen ex-prisoners who seemed more dazed than liberated by the ambush. I stood apart from them, numb with surprise at what I had done. The only reaction from my comrades was that they moved hastily away from the scene, and from me. I was glad of the company of the middle-aged Milicien who supported David on the left. I said, 'What's your name?'

He said, 'Thierry. Thierry. Thank you.'

I said, 'I haven't done anything.'

He said, 'All the same. Thank you.'

David said, 'Perhaps he's still alive. Dad.'

I said, 'It sounds like it.'

'I think I can walk.'

'Save your strength,' Thierry said. 'We don't mind.'

David said, 'Lose the beret, I should.'

'You think?' The Milicien snatched his beret from his head. He unpinned the Franciscan insignia and threw it into the undergrowth. 'All right like that, do you think, old man?'

David said, 'Up to you.'

'It's my beret,' Thierry said. 'Not theirs.'

When we had passed under the bridge and walked about fifty

metres, we saw the bullet-stitched motorcycle and the sidecar with a dead German lolling out of it like someone attempting some lazy repair. Thierry said, 'The other one didn't get away, did he?'

I nodded towards the side of the road where the driver was lying with his face against the asphalt.

Theirry said, 'Thank God for that. They won't like this very much. I wouldn't want to be anyone who lived around here, that's for sure.'

We marched steadily away from the setting sun. The shadows lengthened and faded into the general darkness. We joined a track I knew which followed the valley behind La Fontaine du Noyer. If I broke away, I could be home within half an hour. Martegoutte was at the front of the group. The Writer and the man in the sheepskin jerkin came with us as far as a fork in the track which would take them up to a hamlet which was famous for its honey. The Writer said, 'You're with us now, whether you like it or not. I hope you like it, but I don't give a fuck, all right? You're soldiers and you're under orders. You'll do what our friend says – ' he clapped Martegoutte on the shoulder – 'and you'll do it first time. I may see you tomorrow. I may see you next week. Some of you may be moved on. Most of you perhaps. Now you're free, do what you're told, all right?'

Thierry said, 'And us?'

The Writer said, 'I didn't hear that. Because you, the best thing you can do is say nothing except your prayers. Understood?'

Thierry said, 'I didn't do anything bad. Ask him.'

The Writer said, 'As soon as we've shot you, I'll ask him.'

'I was in the police. They knew me. They made me. I've got a wife, I've got kids. Ask him if you don't believe me.'

I said, 'Can't you shut up, you cretin, when he says to?'

'Fine,' Thierry said. 'Of course.' He hitched David's arm round his shoulder again. 'All right, old man? I've got you.'

We resumed the forward march. It was getting cold. The first stars stood out like chipped glass. I said, 'Where were we going anyway?'

Thierry said, 'What do they tell us? Absolutely nothing.'

'Was it a camp or were you going to shoot us?'

'Do you think we'd drive halfway across the department if we were going to shoot anyone? I never shot anyone in my life. I was a policeman, old man. I filled in reports. I'm a pen-pusher. I'm fifty-two years old. My daughter got married last month. In a year I'll be a grandfather. In three years my wife and I will have been married a quarter of a century. Imagine, a quarter of a century!' He was filling in the agenda of his future in the hope that it guaranteed that he would have one.

I said, 'Is there a camp this way?'

He said, 'I live in Agonac. I don't know this corner.'

'Perhaps they were going to take us down to the Pyrénées. They've got camps down there, haven't they?'

'The Spaniards,' he said, 'the Reds, those people, what are you going to do with them? No one was going to shoot anybody, that is certain. Frenchmen shouldn't shoot Frenchmen, you agree?'

David said, 'You are a coward and a creep and I'm sick of your whining.'

Thierry said, 'Good. Understood. As you wish. Nevertheless . . .'

The countryside was without lights. Martegoutte must have had a comrade up ahead because after an hour or so he allowed the file to move on past him until he was able to drop in just behind our trio. He said, 'All right. Someone else can take over for a bit.'

'It's all right, sir,' Thierry said. 'I'm not tired. I may be older than the rest of you, but don't worry, there's life in the old dog yet.'

David said, 'Get this fool out of my sight, for God's sake.'

'Anyone can see you're feeling better, sir!'

'Jesus!'

Martegoutte told the man behind us to take my place. We dropped to the back of the file. He said, 'So, someone sold you out, did they, old man?'

I said, 'How are things around here? Everything all right at my parents'?'

'The boss takes care of them, don't you worry.'

'The boss?'

'Your uncle, he's the *gros bonnet* around here, isn't he?'

'Who's . . . with the cigarette?'

'The Writer,' Martegoutte said. 'He comes and goes. He knows people in Paris, Lyon, Bordeaux. Don't feel bad, old man, because you know what they did, among other things? They shot old Picpus.'

'Why?'

'He was a Communist, can you believe it?'

I said, 'No.'

'So they shot him. Old Picpus. Imagine. He wasn't the only one. Lespinasse, he's in Germany. His father stopped him joining us and they shipped him to Germany. Delrieux too; remember him?'

'There were two, weren't there?'

'Two hundred. Arabs, all of them, my father says. This was Jacques I'm talking about. He's gone too, disappeared in an air raid; he may be in the woods somewhere, he may be dead. That's today.'

'You're enjoying yourself,' I said.

'You know me, old man, not someone who misses his books. And if we come through it, we'll be well placed, you have to admit that.'

The indifference of the countryside, which had seemed to mock us when we were prisoners, now became our salvation: the endless folds of its valleys and woods, the gurgling wriggles of its streams and torrents, promised that no hostile force would ever find us. We arrived finally at a burned-out *château* high on the flank of a long and remote valley. It was as if we had retreated to another century.

I have only sporadic memories of what turned out to be the months I spent with the *bande* commanded by Le Sanglier (the codename of the lame man who we all knew was actually Gilles Quintard, a chemist from the Lot). I can remember being happy, or at least forgetting to be unhappy, on several occasions, but my time in the Maquis was blighted by what happened between me and David Poulain. Do I understand it even today? I can construct a plausible account of why he might have taken against me, but I am still not convinced by it. It began before we heard that both Pascal and his father had been shot and his mother sent to Ravensbruck. Can he have imagined that I had indeed betrayed the family? He never accused me; he simply avoided me. When I tried to render him a service, he accepted it as if it were his duty. Did he despise me for shooting the blond officer? He said that he would have done the same thing. Nothing I did or said disposed him to admit or mitigate his coldness towards me.

Thierry and the other younger Milicien begged to be allowed to join the *bande*; they swore that they had been lured into the Milice and wanted to prove that they were good Frenchmen. Justo, the Spaniard, argued for immediate execution, but the moment for it seemed to be past. Le Sanglier said, 'To be candid, I'm sorry we didn't shoot you yesterday.'

Thierry said, 'I understand.'

'If The Writer was here,' Martegoutte said to me, 'they'd be goners. Bang, bang – like that. No problem.'

I both pitied my ex-jailer – to the extent of hoping that The Writer would not have occasion to visit St André – and I resented the claim which he had on my affection. I cared about him without liking him in the least. When I began to realise that some insurmountable barrier had grown up between David and me, I was graceless enough to blame Thierry for it. His endless attempts to ingratiate himself with me were too manifest in their motivations; they made a compromising claim to me. By putting himself under my protection, he flattered me with powers I was by no means sure of possessing: I became an inadequate god. His earnest questions made him my elderly child; I was cursed with a fat, middle-aged son of limited intelligence and, however unfairly, I cursed him with alienating me from the brother whom I desired. David became strong; his agility and energy *were* his fearlessness: he did not have to decide to be brave, it was his nature. When he learned of the fate of his family, his cheerful eagerness scarcely faltered; he wore his true character like a happy disguise. If I sentimentalise him, it is with no conscious exaggeration; if I say that I was in love with him, I have to say also that my love transcended the flesh. I had no notion of embracing him; I wished to be his intimate and, if possible, his only friend. The availability of Martegoutte and the slavishness of Thierry did nothing to alleviate the anguish of David's coldness. My initiation into warfare, which began with the shooting of the blond officer and continued with a dozen and more skirmishes and close shaves, did less and less, during the next few weeks, to persuade me that I had indeed achieved manhood. Despite my machine-gun and my leather coat (dragged from a dead German), desperation made a civilian of me; if I knew very well that it was a luxury, in the conditions under which we lived, to harbour so irrelevant a passion, perhaps that is why I luxuriated so painfully in it.

I am about to describe a disreputable episode. My memory flinches from it, but I am resolved to disclose it. I watch my hand like a jailer who has extracted and now wants written evidence of a confession. I had escorted three of the ex-prisoners from Périgueux to Cahors, where we were met by a girl from Montauban. I had been given quite a lot of money by Le Sanglier ('because you never know'). In the event, the transfer went smoothly and I was able to buy myself an excellent *foie gras*, followed by a *confit d'oie* in a backstreet restaurant. I had killed a man but, in sexual terms, I was still a virgin. It was a disequilibrium which embarrassed me within myself: I had fired the second barrel before the first. However vulgar it may sound, that was how it struck me. I now seemed to have an ideal opportunity to respond to my rejection by David. I should not boast to him of what I was about to do, but I should know, when I looked at him, that I had done it. I realised that even my meal, in a restaurant with a dubious clientèle (too well dressed, too shrill, too greedy), was the first stage in a show of defiance which no one but I should ever know about. I asked the waiter to direct me to a clean brothel.

Can I claim that, had I not wanted to take my revenge on David (even though he would never know of it), I should never have done what I did? It hardly matters; I did it. In the usual sense, the experience was hardly sexual. The woman whom I chose, almost at random, was past her first youth, although she had large, smooth breasts (I gave her an extra note to let me fondle them, although I did so more as a courtesy – and as a sort of homage to Madame Lonchat – than out of urgent desire). I watched what she did quite as though I was not participating in it. When, after a while, she looked up from sucking me and said, 'What do you want that I should do?' I smiled both at the prim pedantry of the subjunctive on the lips of a whore and at the notion that what she was doing might not be quite what I wanted. A few seconds later, I said, 'Get on me. Quick. Please.' She sighed, like a maid asked to scrub an extra floor, and straddled me. The hand she put expertly behind her and between my legs put an end to the occasion.

The woman looked down at me with some consternation and said, 'It wasn't my fault.' She could have been the same servant afraid of being accused of a valuable breakage. 'You were too quick.'

I said, 'It's all right. It's been a long time. Since I last made love.'

She said, 'Good God!'

I left the brothel, having at last fired my first barrel, without any sense of shame or of achievement. I had passed a frontier like a modern tourist, hardly aware of any transition. I had now fucked a woman and killed a man. What remained for me to do in order to be finished with childhood?

I decided to stay in Cahors that night. There was a little hotel by the station where, before the war, I had dined with my parents when we went to the funeral of a local notable who had been a Polytechnicien. I remembered the Murano glass in the leaded doorway and the easy swing of the hinges. It was an anonymous homecoming. I was no longer Bruno le Guen; I had become Pierre-Henri Portas, a character with whom I never felt any easy affinity. It gave me more pleasure to observe how willingly the *patron* agreed to my imposture and gave me my key than it had to have the prostitute slot me under her body and ride down on me as she had.

The next morning I was able to get a lift with a farmer as far as Catus and made my way from there, in the sunshine, to St André, without incident. When I arrived I found that The Writer had been to the camp in my absence. The Spaniard and David Poulain had shot Thierry and his beak-nosed companion 'without anger or regret', as Martegoutte put it. My love for David, whatever its nature, did not die, but it became impossible: the friend I wanted could never have done what he could perfectly fairly say that I had already done myself. In fact, he did make a few gestures of reconciliation (without admitting that we had fallen out), but the willingness with which I responded to them socially was the measure of my inability to do so in my heart. Some weeks later, when we had moved to another camp, and then another, I returned from a drop (where we had had an exchange of fire with another *bande* who took us, they said, for Milice) and, coming in first, with a sack of grenades over my shoulder, I saw David and Justo, the Spaniard, together. They were fully dressed and drinking *eau de vie* by a small fire. The shape of their conversation was as good as an advertisement of what they had become. I cannot remember any emotion, but its absence was irrevocable. Not long afterwards I had an opportunity to go back to La Fontaine du Noyer. That was when I first saw Berthe. Soon afterwards, my uncle promised me that she would make an excellent wife. I had no reason to demur; indifference was now the sweetest of my feelings, and the most common. When I resumed being Guy de Roumegouse, I felt no more convinced by my true identity than I had been by the spurious one of Pierre-Henri Portas.

XXXVI

Maureen and I took the train from Le Buisson to Bordeaux first thing in the morning. I should have ample time for a visit to the dentist and she, so she promised me, had many things she wanted to do. Her reassurances when she was on the point of leaving me, for however brief a period, brought her closer to me than any other display of affection. Her blue eyes glittered and her voice became husky; she leaned her hand on my arm and I felt her weight like a reminder of pleasures to come. Oh she had so many things she meant to do! But she would see me later; we fixed one early and one later rendezvous. As we separated gratefully, it seemed that we could hardly bear to be apart.

My dentist, Professor Delmas, had his surgery in a turning off the rue Judaïque. Realising that I had nothing to read, should there be a wait, I went into a *bureau le tabac* and bought the *Figaro*, although (or because) I have small sympathy with its proprietor or the right-wing centrism of its politics. I have often found it more amusing to read opinions I do not share than to be made conscious of the cant of those with whom I agree.

Professor Delmas did not see many private patients – his main activity was as a teacher at the university – hence the paucity of magazines in his tiny waiting room, for which I made provision. I opened my newspaper to a middle page and almost immediately saw what an observer might assume I had bought the paper to read, despite the fact that I had no notion of finding it: EX-JESUIT TO MARRY. Pierre Salomon declared that his decision was 'at once a breach and a continuation – in the measure that my purpose in life is unchanged, even though my means of pursuing both the Truth and the Ideal of love now take another path'. The hint of parody in his pronouncement came so clearly to me across the abyss of years that when I opened wide for Professor Delmas, I did so in the secret knowledge that it was a smile of a kind.

Pierre had already quit the Jesuits, when they sought to deflect him from publishing his thesis, so that I was not wholly astonished by his renunciation of the priesthood. His statement referred, tactfully, to a wish to strengthen rather than question the Church. He granted that his book challenged the interpretations of certain ecclesiastical scholars, but he emphasised the distinction between disagreement and heresy. As for marriage, the scholar who was to be his bride had been the ally but never the instigator of his dissent. I recognised, in the blotchy photograph, the face of the woman who had been the close collaborator of Professor Dreyfus.

The work on my uncomfortable molar took so long (although Delmas' skill, as he peered through the enlarging lenses which were clipped around his forehead, was almost mesmeric in its unalarming menace) that the professor said that he was very sorry but he would have to ask me to come back later in order for him to finish the other troublesome tooth. He had a class which he had to honour, but he could see me at the end of the afternoon. I greeted this dislocation of my plans as if it accorded perfectly with them. The reason for my eager acceptance of Delmas' suggestion did not become fully clear to me until I had met Maureen at the Café Régence before we walked down to have lunch at a cheap restaurant opposite the Grand Theatre. Her face took on an expression of patient amazement. 'But, Guy, I told you: we *have* to catch the afternoon train. I've got Christophe coming to have a drink and talk about the plans before dinner.'

I said, 'Telephone him. He would certainly telephone you.'

She said, 'But I fixed it.'

I said, 'Then catch the train. I'll take the late one to Bergerac.'

She said, 'He's probably got a little girl-friend, this professor of yours. You Frenchmen! What will you do all afternoon?'

I said, 'There's always the bookshop. And I have several old friends who might be willing to see me.'

She said, 'Do you know how much a taxi will cost you from Bergerac to La Fontaine?'

I said, 'A lot less than your drink with Christophe, if I know anything about his plans. His hot towel rail alone would get me to Bergerac and back several times.'

She said, 'That's naughty! I'll check the train when I go to the station and whenever it gets to Bergerac, I'll meet it there.'

I said, 'You really are the perfect wife, Maureen.'

Several times during my diplomatic career I had the unexceptional experience of knowing that I had an engagement but of being unable to recall it. In practice, of course, there were appointment books and secretaries to second my memory, but the sense of almost missing some crucial appointment – or of having already missed it – has been an irregular phenomenon of my life, with something of the unnerving

319

character of a recurrent dream, in which the content is less menacing than the fact of its repetition.

Having lost contact with Pierre for several years, and having no conscious reaction to what I had seen in the *Figaro* except, perhaps, one of facile derision, my feeling of exhilaration at staying in Bordeaux alone could scarcely have derived merely from the unamazing news that my old friend's sensuality was not a figment of my wishful imagination. It was improbable that he had decided to marry on purely spiritual grounds; I even dared to think that he had found a means to flaunt that Jewishness of which Berthe was so tactlessly conscious in a way which would vex the Church without giving it any tenable grounds for making an issue of it.

Having walked around the shops with Maureen until it was time for her to catch a taxi to the station, I considered calling one of the old friends of whom I had spoken with such enthusiasm, but I could not think of one whose company I truly cherished. Without any deliberate intention, I walked down from the Librairie Mollat, where among the profusion of memoirs there was no shortage of modern equivalents of M. de Norpois and his epigoni. I left the bookshop and ambled down the walkway, unallured by the cashmere sweaters and the bombastic music which advertised the kind of clothing I have always been too old to wear, until I came to the unmodernised quarter where the prostitutes were beginning their evening parade. I had only an hour or so before I was expected at Professor Delmas' surgery; I should have to find a taxi fifteen minutes before that. Since I have lost the appetite for haste of any kind, I can safely say that my visit to the streets where whores could be found was, let us say, purely nostalgic. Had reading about Pierre put me in mind of Pia? In practice, none of the women had the rather prim accessibility which I found so reassuring in my Roman woman. Perhaps my age, and the dread of seeming ridiculous (as if money were ever ridiculous!) made me aware of the crudeness of the lounging whores; perhaps it was simply that it was too early in the evening for the shadows to be deep enough to glamorise what was on sale. I congratulated myself, a little ruefully, on the maturity of my response and turned down a dank lane to cut through to the main post office, where I could expect to find a cab.

'Good evening.' The voice came from a window which was flush with the street. A slim, young blonde girl was leaning out, under the open sash. She had a lightly freckled face and only the low neck of the leotard she was wearing announced that her greeting was professional.

I said, 'Good evening,' but in a dismissive way and I walked on without slackening my pace.

I had to wait for Professor Delmas. If he had been on time, should I have been visited so insistently by an image of the blonde young girl as she leaned over the sill? The odd thing was that my vision of her was from inside the room. I saw her neat buttocks presented to me and I saw myself, as an old fool, moving too quickly past the window. As the professor's enlarged eyes glared down at me, with the mantled quartz lamp at his back, I decided that, after leaving his surgery, I would catch a taxi to the station from the rue Judaïque and have a meal there. What a shame that Clavel had left its old premises!

It was not lust which made me change my plan; it was curiosity to know which of my two expectations would be honoured. If the girl were still there, I should go in to her. If not, I should still have time for a quick meal before getting my train. In either event, so I told myself, it would be the last time that I should indulge myself with a whore. She was there. From the end of the alley, I saw her leaning on the sill, with the darkness around her like a cowl. I stood for a minute, telling myself that I was under no obligation to go forward, and then I walked on down to where she was waiting. She said, 'Good evening,' exactly as before. Was she flattered by my return? Did she even recognise me?

I went in. She shut the street door and the window. I said, 'Are you alone in the building?'

She said, 'For the moment.'

'Aren't you afraid?'

She said, 'Of you? No.'

I said, 'Is this enough?'

'You can give me another one if you want to.'

'Afterwards perhaps.' She took the band from her hair and shook it loose, then she pulled down the straps of her leotard and let the top of it dangle over her waist. It was against the code of the prostitutes I had known when I was younger to reveal the breasts first, but she was either ignorant or untraditional. She was young enough for it not to be unattractive. Nevertheless, I said, 'Just a minute, because there's something I'd like.'

'What's that?'

'It's all right,' I said. 'But – I'll give you another one, don't worry, no problem there – you may not believe this – '

'I always believe anything. Calm down. Are you all right?'

'I'm all right. I had no intention of doing this but you remind me of someone.'

'Yes?'

'I know, you've heard that one before. But the thing is this, I have a feeling that I shall never do this again. With anyone. People always remember the first time, well, this is the last. I can't swear, but I think so.'

'Come on then,' she said. 'What's this you've always wanted to do?'

I said, 'I want you to say something to me. I'm going to call you something and I want you to call me something.'

'If it's all about calling you something, name it, if it's not too complicated.'

I said, 'Can we go into the bedroom? I hope you don't mind this little charade.'

She said, 'Listen, I'll call you President of the Republic if you like.'

I said, 'I'm going to call you Félix, all right?'

She said, 'Help yourself.'

'And I'm Rudi. I'm Rudi. You can decide for yourself when you say it.'

'Félix, am I? Come on then. Let's do whatever you want to do. Is it always the last time?'

I said, 'I'd be grateful if you'd just do as I ask. No questions.'

'If you want a Félix, I can find a Félix.'

I said, 'This is fine. You're a very pretty person. I'm lucky to have found you. I wish I'd found you sooner.'

'Oh Rudi,' she said.

As so often, even before I touched the girl, I had the feeling that I had mistimed the occasion. Already it belonged to my past, as my present so regularly did. Her skin did not disappoint me; she was the colour of a pale lemon, more white than yellow, but tinged with a golden freshness. Her body was firmly fleshed and she displayed it with businesslike pride and even a measure of generosity; with whores, as with other people, there are those who combine a certain avarice with open-handedness. It was a relief to me to see the thicket of brown hair which promised that she was a grown woman (even though my interest had been primed by her almost childish appearance). I have never, in truth, wanted to possess very young girls, but my mind has sometimes been infected by the appetite for them, as it has, in another context, by a wish to learn Chinese or to become an expert skier. It always seems to me that I should be more the man I should like to be, were I to have scholarly or manly competences which, in truth, are not at all my style. Men who desire young girls advertise a domineering callousness, an indifference to sentiment, which confuses poetry with conquest; they are men who do what they want, not what others will approve or sanction or, in the

322

case of women, connive at. Even with whores, I have always relied on a measure of collaboration. I observed with grateful anxiety that my blonde assumed me to belong to a category of men who will take what they want and who expect no geniality from their partner.

I told myself that I had plenty of time and that, since I should never do this again, I should relish my last taste of pleasure. Simultaneously, I was asking myself why I had decided on such an arbitrary renunciation; this conflict of considerations deprived me of the unalloyed joy which I had promised myself. I was too wide awake to dream luxuriously. The naked girl sensed my uneasiness; I had arranged her at the edge of the bed, with her flattish, white heels presented to me (her slim feet looked as if they had stayed in the bath longer than the rest of her) and her rump tilted so that I had easy access to her, but she looked round with quite a public, troubled face and said, 'Do you want me to do something in particular, Rudi?'

I was moved by her pale feet. I put my hands on them, with a certain timidity which she took, no doubt, for the announcement of some habitual fetish, although in truth I had never before been fascinated by female feet. My greedy tenderness evidently struck her as the declaration of a vice. A rougher expression replaced the one which, a moment earlier, had been that of a passenger who fears that something has gone wrong with a machine she may be called upon to repair. She sighed as I sat beside her on the low bed, from which she had not removed the red velvet cover, and I bent, awkwardly, to taste the uncalloused arch of her foot. There was a slightly garlicky odour, which I did not find disagreeable.

As my lips and tongue touched her skin, she gave a little cry and squirmed, torn between indignation and laughter which she repressed, perhaps in the knowledge that fetishists can react violently to those who do not take their desires as seriously as they do themselves. Her apprehensive blurt of laughter was ineptly converted, by her fear, into a gasp which was intended, rather implausibly, to suggest pleasure. This understandable ineptitude had an effect on me quite opposite to that of the tolerance which, somewhere in my mind, I was happy to accord her. Her attribution to me of an obsession which was far from habitual, matched with her fear that I should be enraged by her ticklish response to my caresses, excited in me precisely that urge to violence typical of a class of man to which I most certainly did not belong. This anger was deeply personal; it gave rise to a wish to declare myself more candidly to her, to explain that I was touched by her pale feet in a way which was unlike any that I had previously experienced with any kind of woman.

Hardly had I adopted the name – and attempted to impersonate the character – of Rudi than I wanted to throw my disguise aside and announce my honest and specific affection. However, recognising that things had gone too far for revision, I was obliged to stay silent, although an inner voice was rehearsing a fatuous prospectus in which I invited the girl to come with me to some hazy destination where, as one would expect, I should offer her the freedom to lead her own life, provided only that she found a regular portion of time for me. My inability to remain wholeheartedly attached to her feet rendered my attentions both awkward and unconvincing. Like most whores, she regarded me with a mixture of impatience and puzzlement. She wanted to earn her money in the shortest possible time, but she had a certain brusque honour (indistinguishable, perhaps, from the occupational fear of brutal reproach from disappointed clients) and was anxious that I should complete whatever I wanted to do to her quickly enough to please her and satisfactorily enough to leave me content and, perhaps, generous. Wavering between the urge to re-enact the performance which I remembered from Félix's photographs (as if I had waited all my life for the chance to play the part of the blond beast whom I took, after all these years, actually to be Rudi, despite Félix's denials) and the wish, at the very least, to leave the girl with an agreeable impression of me, I found myself yet again incapable of doing precisely what I wanted to do, or even of knowing precisely what it was. The comedy of my indecision was not lost on me, but it scarcely seconded my virility.

With tentative urgency, the girl did her best to revive me, rolling her blue eyes up at me as she did so in a manner which, I guessed, was usually successful with her clients. She combined delicacy with boldness and her eyes, like independently amused witnesses, solicited approval of her performance. I thought of Berthe practising her flute in the field while she watched Baptiste sawing logs. It was enough to procure the effect for which the girl supposed her diligence to be responsible.

Although I felt considerable sympathy for the girl, and an admiration for her professionalism which quite transcended my role as a client and turned me into an appreciative critic, I was also conscious of a frustration so great that I could understand, and even envy, the man who had done to Pia what I had been the second to see. My little whore, seeing that I was responding happily to her treatment, arranged herself more comfortably on the bed in order to continue it, while at the same time presenting herself shamelessly to me, partly out of politeness, partly in order to encourage me to move towards a conclusion. I observed her with pleasure and with detachment. My mind was investigating Pia's flat and imagining the nature and attitude of the man who killed her. I no longer felt inclined to postulate someone who hated her or who was visiting on her some other hatred he lacked the means to express directly; I saw that Pia's murderer could well have been someone who, in theory, wished her no harm. I saw, belatedly, how it was that murderers could live with their deeds and, contrary to vulgar assumptions, experience no more regret or shame than I did when leaving Pia after one of our routine encounters. I had no sudden insight into the motives for murder, which are doubtless legion, but I understood how it could be both trivial and (in some terrible way) apologetic, the confession of an incapacity to match acts to hopes. I was not making excuses for Pia's murderer, nor did I feel any furtive complicity with him; I simply had an inkling of what he was like. I gave him no face, but I should not have been surprised, if the film of the past had been played in front of me, to have it reveal the features of Miguel O'Higgins, or of a dozen other men I have known and more or less liked. Knowing – or having decided – that I should never again buy a woman, I had, without any such intention, blessed or cursed the present occasion with a finality which made it portentous. I dreaded its conclusion not because I should never do it again, but because I should survive it with – I expected – such unmarked ease. I should leave the blonde girl's room with not even the sweet charge of her blood on my account. I should be like a man whose suicide passes unremarked because, so far as other people can tell, his life continues without interruption. I had a sense of the horror which will be consequential to our discovery, if we make it, that the soul is indeed immortal. Immortality is the recognition that there is absolutely no way out.

My wish to strangle my little blonde, at the same time as I penetrated her, was without malice. It was unarmed with practical muscle less because I am incapable of actual violence than because, in the attitude on which we had finally settled, I could not see into her eyes. Although I am, after all, someone who has killed before, I retain a virginal attitude to murder, as I always have to sex: previous experience, for certain men, does not alleviate the feeling that every time one is about to make love it is for the first time, even if it is with a wife with whom he has been sleeping for many years. We call this fidelity. I have no sense of the accumulation of experience; my inability to believe that I am really the age I am and that I appear, to people in the streets, like a man whose maturity is beyond question, may derive from my reluctance to admit how many years separate me from those hours at La Fontaine du Noyer when I might have done something more positive, more assertive, more honourable, to persuade Fritz Altschuler not to go back to Caillac. My weakness was also that of my parents; it was as if we had conspired to be done with Fritz, whose actual person lacked the charm which might have strengthened our courage. I could neither blame nor fail to blame them for a delinquency whose crucial element was a function of their feelings. As I stood comfortably behind my little whore, my main pleasure came from the way my mind ranged freely, as if it were as naked and wanton as I wanted my body to be. Some unexpected licence authorised me to fly, as it were, over the long landscape of my life and to contemplate it with an unblinking severity which, like that of Monsieur Picpus, became first quizzical and then, if not amiable, at least rueful. Is it a sign of some convenient hypocrisy that I have felt more guilt over the death of my old schoolmaster, in which I had no conceivable part, than over that of the blond officer whom I shot in the cab of the lorry? If I sometimes think of the latter guilt, it is more because I regret not having had a chance to talk with him at greater length than because I think I was wrong to shoot him. I am aware of the absurdity of my belief that we might have been friends, nor do I doubt that my feeling that secretly and somehow (oh somehow!) we understood each other could be interpreted as a rationalisation of my guilt; iniquitous as it may seem, I go further and admit that my killing him has made him precious to me. In other, plainer words, I have become the trustee of his soul; he yielded it to me as I winced and pulled the trigger on the sub-machine-gun which he knew how to handle so much better than I. Do I truly believe anything as grand as my words? Does anyone grant reality anything like the majesty of the words with which we clothe it? The charm and disappointment of the whore lie in the promise which she offers, again and again to our resurgent virginities, that she will in reality be that nameless guide to the quick of life which myth makes her. The misfortune of Pia was (perhaps) not that she fell into the hands of some homicidal psychopath but that she misread the mind of a sentimentalist; wanting nothing more than to please was exasperating to a man who wanted more than pleasure.

How could I know such things as I pumped the hips of my little blonde? I was doing exactly what I had thought I wanted to do as I rinsed the Professor's surplus amalgam from my mouth, but I lacked the hands and other organs to achieve that ubiquitous possession which others, with more time and virility, are said to purchase in series. Oh for the two penises which give the devil his hold on women! I could not even plumb the flesh in front of me as I wished and also caress the almost embarrassingly long breasts hanging from the narrow ribs. In my voracious frustration, when I had everything that I thought I wanted, I conjectured that killing could be an abbreviation, a collapse, of a multiplicity of things one wanted to do over a much longer time, and in a different world. Was there not a shameful frivolity in my speculation? It was certainly frivolous – since I was treating ultimate things in a playful way – but I am not, and was not, ashamed. I do not believe that the killer conceives of death as a finality, because he himself will survive it, which is his great frustration and the reason (in a sense) that he is at least tempted to repeat his acts: his victim's lack of reality means that he is more irritated than horrified by what he has done. The proximity of love and death – *l'amour* and *la mort* – is not only an observed common-place, it is symptomatic of the systematic disappointment they engender. It may be wicked to treat death as something that recurs, like sexual activity, rather than (as it is for the victim) a single, conclusive experience, but human history is an account of recurrent killing, and its more or less successful, victorious, results; we are utterly incapable of any account, except in numerical or sentimental terms, of what has been lost: the dead tell no tales and have no redress. The killer, like the lover, can and often does treat his actions as if they had not only been forced upon him but had also left him with a certain grievance, like an account which the deceased has left unpaid. All this is fanciful and maybe disreputable, but what I fear is true is that *all* readings of human behaviour are as frivolous or, if you will, as solemn as each other. The elusiveness of the truth as to our motives or our purpose on earth is nothing more than the impossi-bility of netting our acts or our ambitions in a formula whose fulfilment can be realised in the world we inhabit. All conclusions, whether sublime or grotesque, are fraught with the impossibility of that final coincidence of hope and reality which appetite craves and nature denies. We remember and we remember; we forget and we forget, until what we recall is only an aspect of oblivion, until what we have lost becomes the only thing we wish to retrieve even if, at the time, we thought ourselves lucky to lose it. My companion on that velvet bed in the Allée Fumel was less Félix's Rudi, whose part I had intended to play, than *my* blond officer whom I had shot in order – was it? – not to lose the right to the gun I handled with such innocence. Does it matter whether or not I realised precisely then, as I thrust myself into the girl's arched body – there was a spread of light fluff in the hollow of her back – and felt the soft bump (almost a kind of splash) of her buttocks against my hips, that my impersonation of Rudi was badly achieved because it was a blind, since the real object of my fantasy was the man I had myself killed, not the one whose death Félix had – I had little doubt – helped to procure? Whereas I owed Félix's victim no compensation, my blond officer – over whose death, I can swear, I have never agonised – was entitled to an outing. Of course, my intimate conviction that I had chosen the blonde girl, against my usual – or at least my admitted – inclination, because I was somehow possessed by the blond officer, is as questionable as any other hypothesis concerning human motives (which are, in my repeated view, never, never, never single-minded). I concede that it could be argued that my naked companion played the part of a man whose existence she could not suspect. Even as I told myself that this was my last opportunity to do whatever I wanted with a woman, I had to derive what wry comfort I could from recognising that neither a woman nor a man, nor any conceivable creature, could answer my desires. I was as far as ever from any notion of why that might be (or even of what 'why' might mean), but I saw the impossibility of knowledge as being as close to knowledge as I could hope to come.

Meanwhile, perhaps because of my lack of attention, I became aware that the blonde girl was gasping and thrusting back at me. Whether it was cause or effect, I felt as though I was bigger and thicker than I had ever been. My reaction was less one of vanity than of alarm: the blond officer, it seemed, was more present than I. The succulent slap of the girl's flesh against me was the proof either of her desire or of her impatience; only a whore, perhaps, is able to divorce what, in less venal women, are aspects of the same urgency. My little blonde's imitation of orgasm was worth the extra note with which I honoured its heat. She took the money easily enough, but there was a touch of pink about her face and even her throat which, if it was wilful, argued for an extraordinary control of normally involuntary responses. I ended my experiences with prostitutes almost more naively than I began, hoping that she might remember me for the pleasure I had forced upon her.

I left her with joyful regret, at once relieved and slightly vexed that I had not signed off, so to say, with some more clinching symptom of finality. I consoled myself with the fanciful company of both the blond officer and that of Berthe, to whose absent presence I believed that I had proved something, although I was sure that she would find a way of holding it against me, should she be conscious of it. I left the little blonde sitting at a little table, one leg laced over the other, entering my contribution in her notebook. I was glad to see her recovered – her breasts were neat and round again, her flesh unblushing – but there was an element of cowardice in my departure; there were other things which I could see myself doing to her, even though I am glad that I never did them.

I did not fear detection by Maureen (who might have been interestingly affected by discovering my capacity for independent pleasures) nor did I decide to buy no more women out of abstract morality; it was a retirement such as sportsmen announce, when the stress of anticipation rather than the strain of performance determines their decision. I walked down a street where more whores clustered; their types varied, as usual, in conformity to the kinds which were traditionally available in the licensed houses which postwar legislation closed, not because the deputies did not approve of their existence but because they could not confess as much. I saw the Jewess and the Bride, the Cruel Mistress and the Timid Virgin and I realised that the joke would always be on men, because they insisted on a humourless response to their devious brutality. The clients imagined themselves conscripted to the office which they themselves chose; even the murderer, I could imagine, could come from the scene of blood with an aggrieved frown: why did she have to make such a fuss or bleed so copiously? How different had I been when, after shooting the blond officer, I turned quickly away and, without pretence, pretended to be the same young man I had been before?

Remembering the two prostitutes on the train, and the 'innocent' girl who had met them with such proprietory courtesy, I was reminded of how far I had travelled, in time and space, only to find that the future was costumed very like the past. Today's girls were dressed in the modern style, but they belonged, without knowing it, to a tradition almost as inflexible as that of tragedy. (Fashion is a way of redressing the invariable in an air of novelty.) My life was like one of those trains in old-fashioned theatres, when the movement of an endless – sometimes rather creased – landscape, rotating around rollers in the wings, gave the illusion that the immobile travellers on the stage were passing through a landscape which only the vigilant or abstracted members of the audience would notice was repeating itself. I had always been too old; I should always be too young.

When I arrived at the Gare St Jean, I discovered that there was no train to Bergerac that night, or any night. Had I known this when I made my arrangement with Maureen? Had she discovered it when she caught her own train? I telephoned La Fontaine. Rosa, our Portuguese woman, said that La Senhora was 'below'. I presumed that she and Christophe were deliberating on how to improve the house with which I found no fault. I left a message to say that I should be staying overnight in a hotel and walked out into the sweet darkness of the city, wondering with fanciful greed what reason chance might supply for some artlessly arranged rendezvous with I knew not what.

XXXVII

I accepted the loss of David Poulain's friendship almost with relief. Only after I saw him with the Spaniard, and recognised the nature of their closeness, did it occur to me, perhaps as a compensation, perhaps because I was now free to see the truth, that our comradeship had been as irksome to me as it was to him. I always took him to be a substitute for Pascal, whom I should never see again. The painfully convenient result of Pascal's arrest, and subsequent execution, was that my only true passion for another male was never more than an aspect of my memory of those days at Villeneuve-les-Évêques. My flesh never participated in my love for Pascal; even in moments of solitary obsession when, had my thoughts been about a woman, I might have risen to the occasion, my flesh was sublimely, even primly, unresponsive.

In fact, Pascal was almost a stranger to me. He is the only untarnished hero in my life. By the time that he was the age of my son David (who should, I suppose, have borne his name, not that of the brother for whom he was never consciously named), Pascal was already dead, yet he had accompanied me through my life as if he remained older than I and, were he to return, would still be wiser and stronger. My vision of him is blessed, no doubt, with something of the force and competence of his father, whose optimism had been both an inspiration and, perhaps, the reason for the unguardedness which had resulted in his death and our capture.

Although no one spoke of it, I knew that The Writer was still angry that the wrong lorry had been ambushed and that I, and my travelling companions, had been rescued. My survival, like David's and the Spaniard's, was the result of incompetence. There was no obvious tension between David and me during the months that we were in the woods. Martegoutte became my cheerful instructor in clandestinity. He was an energetic lout, to whom our activities were an endless adventure; the war struck him as a piece of good fortune, like an unexpected inheritance, which he was determined to enjoy to the last drop. Did he take some pleasure in being my master? His cheerful insolence suggested that he knew very well that I was now as obedient as, in peaceful circumstances, I might have been condescending. He grinned at my panting efforts to match his elastic speed when it came to straddling walls – on one occasion I left my sub-machine-gun cocked and almost managed to shoot myself – or zigzagging across open ground. I became a sort of soldier, and not a bad one, without ever wholly inhabiting the 'uniform' or wholly losing myself in the ethos of my companions. I should like to think that I worked as hard as anyone, and ran as many risks at most, but I lacked that sense of a glorious present, of belonging entirely to the hour, which David and some of the others seemed to have.

The Spaniard fought a separate battle. He had the courage of a man to whom our skirmishes with the Germans or with the Milice (or confrontations with rival *bandes*) were only a prelude. His bravery was mixed with anger, as his passion was with display: he dared anyone to comment on what he did with David, and no one did. He was willing to be brave for us, but not to take us seriously. He knew he could not die here because he meant to die for Spain. His devotion to our cause was the measure of his disdain for us. His courage was an example and a bore.

The Writer came and went with an air of frustrated genius. His anonymity was a form of advertisement. He assumed that we knew who he was, although it was unlikely that either Martegoutte or any of his friends had heard of him, let alone read his books. The Writer delegated his authority, and offered his confidences, exclusively to Le Sanglier, whose lameness had perhaps made him something of a bookworm and who seemed, in consequence, to accord The Writer more informed respect than the rest of us. As it happened, I had read one or two of The Writer's books, which I did not greatly admire, though their virile style, with its hectoring conceits, had somewhat intimidated me. My knowledge of his work disposed me to regard him with more suspicion than faith. He may have guessed that I came from different social circumstances than the others of my age. For whatever reason, he chose me to accompany him on a mission to Fumel, where there was to be a meeting of the 'regional command'.

Credulous as I was willing to be, it was hard to believe that any unified action by the disparate bands in the area would lead to anything but a one-sided, badly coordinated battle with superior forces. As we made our way, in the back of a succession of carts, down the long straight road to Fumel, I found the nerve to say as much. The Writer was wearing what he took to be the outfit of a gentleman farmer, including leather gaiters, a beret and a brown *blouson* with a silk scarf knotted at his throat. His disguise announced him to be someone of consequence. He had a black moustache and a permanent frown; I never saw him smile or laugh.

He treated my scepticism with indulgent disdain. 'What you must understand, my dear friend, is that we absolutely must prepare for a pitched battle and we absolutely must never have one. Do you think that I, who have had some experience of mounting military operations, am incapable of seeing that sporadic and clandestine actions alone have any chance of success? Do you take me for someone with less intelligence than yourself? What we are doing, and what we must do, is to devote ourselves to a massive fraud. That's a word I can use to you because I know who you are. We must prepare a plausible history of an insurgent population, of what is, for all external purposes, a *levée en masse*, and – as with all falsehoods – we must have the evidence of its truth! You smile; you shouldn't. What we are doing, what *I* am and have been doing, is to make straw into bricks! I am creating an army of bumpkins and cowards – I'm not talking of your people, or of those who take brave risks to retrieve and operate wireless sets and all that sort of thing, but of the committee-men and the last-minute warriors who will, I promise you, prove to have saved our national honour and be worthy of leading the new France. What we are doing, my dear friend, is to furnish a myth for the future. It hardly matters whether the Hydra ever existed or whether our heroics are responsible for her death, what matters is that we should be able plausibly to say so. Why have I created my reputation for ubiquity, for working twenty hours a day, for doing without sleep for three and four days at a time?'

I said, 'I didn't know you had.'

'You're in the woods,' he said. 'You're a child, but don't pretend you don't know that men need heroes, they need the superhuman and they will believe in it, if it is artfully supplied, because they need it. They will not forgive a ruling class which has not taken the trouble to create an alibi for the trimmers and the crooks and the traitors, which cannot promptly offer them the promise of acquittal for all the crimes, all the petty cowardice, of which they should stand accused. Who will save us from the Germans? The Anglo-Saxons, the Americans in particular, as they did in Seventeen, the Russians; I know it and so do you. Our little battles, our acts of rustic heroism, they are the *faits divers* of local journalism. No one denies that blood is courageously shed or lives freely given, but what does it matter on the great chessboard of history? Nothing! Why did I ask you to accompany me on this mission? Are you an escort or an encumbrance? Forgive me, but it is my duty to educate someone and you alone have the wit to deserve it. Our whole performance is a charade, a counterfeit, a fabrication, but it is also a necessary, crucial thing, this imposture of ours. Do you think me a charlatan because I tell you these things? It doesn't matter. I am a great man! I am a great man, my dear Guy. (Of course I know who you are!) I am a great man and it is your duty to agree with me. You smile. Smiles are never in agreement. I am great because I dare to look into the abyss without blinking. That alone is my greatness; my response may be hollow, but I can see where others discern only darkness – I can see that we must have a grand plan and that we must do at least enough, if we can manage it, to be able to maintain that our contribution has been decisive. Is there anything more worthy of an artist such as I am, a rhetorician – as I can freely confess myself to be, at least to you, whose words are unlikely to carry any weight against my indignant denials! – and a speculator, in the highest sense, than the promotion of a national myth? To be frank – if only in celebration of this magnificent morning (although I am usually of the opinion that nature is overrated) – I was not among those who responded to the earliest calls for resistance. I have better things to do than risk my life in a prototype! No, no; in war, as in love and other sports, there is such a thing as timing; to go first is to come last! The battle we are fighting is a battle which will take place in the future. The present is taken care of; nothing we do or do not do – nothing – will affect the outcome of the war in the least. In this sense, Pétain's position is quite rational: he sees no sense in risking French lives, and property, in a war which we have already lost, and won! Hence the spurious present we are living. Limbo! Mantegna depicted men entering it quite voluntarily – *choosing* the inevitable is the mark of the intellectual! *This* is limbo, my friend. If our freedom can be restored, as it almost certainly will, it will be thrown at us like a bone to a mangy dog. So why fight? You're not shaping your lips to form the word "patriotism" or anything of that kind, are you? The only reason to fight – or to appear to fight – is to establish an option on that damned bone. We are a bunch of curs sharpening our teeth for each other. Do you follow me? Pétain is wrong not because he is wicked, or senile, but because he is reasonable. He is a soldier who saved lives in nineteen seventeen and believes that his mission is the limitation of damage; he has no notion of politics – he thinks himself Lear and he is, of course, the Fool! He can't see that bluff and imposture are as much the stuff of history as hot air is of a *soufflé*. We are going to Fumel to recruit the hot air which will enable France to rise again. We are to be present at the resurrection of a *soufflé*. Remember who told you that! One day you will put my words in your memoirs, and I shall no longer be available to deny them. You will, I daresay, imagine that you are puncturing my reputation, but sincerity has nothing to do with reputations or with art or with politics. What I am doing for France I am also doing for myself, but I too, like it or not, am part of what France is, a country where philosophers outlast kings!'

I said, 'I thought you'd be a Communist.'

'Do you think that the Americans will ever allow the Cocos to win? Why kick against the pricks? The future doesn't lie in that direction, not in my view. War, not God, is the father of all things, as Heracleitus told us, and hence Our Father has no time for morals; there may be a place for princes, in the largest sense, because they are born and schooled to lead, but to give opinions a place in strategy is to accept that defeat can be honourable. The Germans are losing not because they are wicked, even if they are (I leave these evaluations to *petits bourgeois*), but because they are opinionated; their army was governed, quite literally, by the wrong ideas. How do we know they are wrong? Because they are losing! The battle that I am pretending to fight is a real one, and that is why we must treat these pompous idiots in Fumel, if they turn up, as if they were valiant captains and why, if they don't, we must concoct the minutes of a meeting which never took place but which, in due course, everyone who is said to be present will swear that he remembers well. Cynicism? By no means: ideas are facts too, and they fail or succeed like athletes, for whom victory justifies everything, and is everything. Read the world correctly and you will always be accused of pragmatism; read it correctly *and* swiftly and the charge is superficiality, the price of seeing through the mud to what is clear, clear, clear at the bottom! My view is of a future in which, as almost always, energy – in the largest sense – prevails. Energy here includes, and depends on, power. To gain power one must seem already to be in possession of it. Do you know the decisive moment in my life? When I walked out on the woman I loved. It was when I did that that I became the master of my fate, because whatever I did, from that moment on, was pure speculation! Philosophy as action, do you follow me?'

I said, 'Certainly.'

'You have your doubts then!'

I said, 'I don't know you, sir. I've read only one or two of your books.'

'I hope you didn't like them. I cannot believe that they are so bad that a child can like them.'

I had never, and perhaps have never, been in the presence of a man whose charm was as detestable or whose derision as seductive. I

335

knew that he was practising his methods on me as a champion might his backhand on a side court before a big match. His nervousness was all vanity, in the strict sense of the word: he was big with emptiness. Yet his claim to greatness, although preposterous, was not foolish. He was rehearsing an act of will; he juggled expertly with sacred ideas and recruited contradictions to his service by never handling them at the same time. The juggler is a more common figure in our national pack than the joker, who is always discarded when the game grows serious. The veering from left to right, of which The Writer made no secret (it was to be his postwar pride), the faith in art and the refusal to see it as differing in time from 'other forms of fraud, intimidation and imposture to which, quite rightly, we grant the supreme accolade of belonging to The Beautiful', the preference for sexuality as against love, with all its debilitating anxieties, the respect for the mask and its designed hardness, for the gnomic rather than the candid phrase (as a result of which speech became oracular and was as bleached of personality as an ancient statue which has survived too long to be seen in its true colours), all the styles and attitudes, the gestures and false frankness which The Writer rehearsed in my presence were soon to become his credentials. His lack of fixed principle was accepted as the proof of his originality; his capacity for bluff recommended him to those who had used the same means and who thought it wise to make common cause with him in a cartel of self-made heroes.

The Writer fell silent when, on our last cart, we lurched into Fumel, where the cattle market afforded us convenient cover. By that time, I was stunned and outraged by the force of his personality, to which bombast and opportunism lent all the allure I had assumed to be the province of sincerity. Was there something female in the fascination which his every repulsiveness evoked in me? I was unable to oppose what dismayed me; my wish for his approval was an aspect of what I most detested about him. He was, or managed to seem, a tower of blood; his reddish face and thin lips (only just curtained by the bar of his moustache) were deliberately brutal. His whole body was like a gorgeous cudgel, but something in his eye promised me – and, it seemed, *only* me – that all his feelings had been supplanted by calculation. He was like one of those international machines which are capable of adapting to any source of power without so much as the flick of a switch. His ability to blend with the more prosperous farmers was, in my eyes, distinguished by the scorn with which he regarded those who were taken in by it. I was there, I felt, in order to be the silent applause which, for the moment, was all he could expect but which foreshadowed the fame that he would soon be putting on, like the colonel's uniform which was waiting in some cupboard or other. His disguise was so close to a declaration of his importance that as we clopped into town, I was reminded of Palm Sunday, although our high wheels passed over nothing more welcoming than cabbage leaves.

The market was a facsimile of itself. There were some old horses and a few oxen for sale, but otherwise only guinea fowl, pigeons, chickens and rabbits were on offer. The forcible 'purchase' of meaty animals had made the peasants wary of parading their healthier beasts. The country itself was more and more a masquerade; deception was the diplomacy of the defeated, allowing them to make normality a bluff and dissimulation a form of honesty. Some of the men in the market may have guessed that The Writer was a famous person, a major piece in whatever game was being played for or against them; they looked at him as if they recognised him, if only because his walk, his scornful gaze, his – for the moment – laconic diction claimed their deference. I was both proud and ashamed (being young enough to resent *and* savour my servile role), but shame too has its pride, as I was to discover in the diplomatic service when I derived more satisfaction from being congratulated on prevailing in cases where, on merit, I should have been unsuccessful than when I had, as the English say, fought the good fight. My ride to Fumel with a man of whom I still think only with revulsion, was a plodding yet accelerated course in the unedifying wisdom necessary to a Parisian career.

The Writer allowed no difference between bravery and bravado. He insisted on going for lunch to a hotel in the centre of the town which was notorious for its two sittings: at the first, soon after noon, the 'Resistance' had one hour for the *plat du jour*, cheese, fruit and 'coffee'; at the second, any German officers in town, and those who craved or accepted their company, had access to a rather more expensive menu. The Writer insisted on our going to the second session: we should, he said, never miss an opportunity for effrontery and it was our duty to notice the local faces which chose not to smile at the enemy. He ate a full meal – 'Truffles? Why not?' – while telling me that we had chosen the rockier road; he instructed me that ostentation was the best method of hiding in the open. For him, life had no 'days without'. There was, he could assure me, from repeated experience, a kind of immunity in fame which could be valid even among those who did not know precisely who you were. He had had successes with women – conquests was the right word – simply as a result of looking like someone with whom it would have been a mistake not to make love. He could, at some point, demonstrate to me the efficacity of a certain

337

hard stare. He was, he said, like one of those 'cruel' menus, without prices, which are given to women in three-star restaurants; it was a commonplace that most women were drawn to expensive luxuries. He himself was irresistible because women knew that they could not afford him; they yielded to him as they might to a priceless temptation.

It occurs to me as I recall The Writer's sententious arrogance that I may have taken him more seriously than he did himself. Quite possibly I disappointed him with my want of asperity; had I spent my schooldays in Paris, at the Lycée Louis-le-Grand or Henri IV, I might have been more apt in my responses. As it was, I recognised a sacred monster, but I showed it more respect than it deserved or, quite possibly, desired. It never struck me that all his whispered stridency might be part of a show mounted for my amusement or even seduction. His interest may not have been sexual, but – now that I think of it – I felt embraced by him, suffocated by his insistence that the air I breathed should come directly from him: he wanted almost literally to inspire me. There is no conceit in my belated reading of our long, loud lunch; he was a man whose belief in himself required the submission of other people, regardless of sex, and whose dread of a meaningless world could be allayed only by allegiance to whoever represented the Future. His earlier Communism (he was never a serious Marxist) was a snobbery which had little in common with the populism to which the naive assimilated it. He thought that he was gaining a privileged place in a new, international élite which, until the defeat of the Spanish Republic he assumed to be the vanguard of History. He then lost confidence in it, lay low for some years, only to emerge, when the Allies were certain of victory, not as a 'pro-American' – of which there were hardly any French instances – but rather as someone who, with furtive clairvoyance, saw that France would survive thanks to 'Atlantic' forces which could be acknowledged only with ingratitude, which was as near independence as the French could come for several decades. Fortunately, he argued, it would suit the Anglo-Saxons to be reviled (it would establish how successfully *their* schemes had worked if they were apparently frustrated), just as it would suit those who owed their power to them to give the impression that they had wrested it from them. 'The history of France after the war,' The Writer predicted, 'will be one of sustained, preferably subtle, imposture. Shall we go?'

Our rendezvous was at a dentist's house – where comings and goings were unremarkable – in a surburban section of the town far below the citadel. Armed with a revolver which had been slotted under the cart when our papers were checked on the way into and out of the town, I was to wait in a *café-tabac* across the road. After the meeting, The Writer and I would go to a certain farm where we would spend the night; its address would be given to him at the meeting. As usual, I was less nervous than uneasy. I was a willing witness, but what kind of bodyguard – let alone rescue force – could I provide, in the event of serious trouble?

We arrived at the dentist's house, walked past it and round the fenced block. The Writer strutted with a defiance at odds with our show of caution. His fearlessness celebrated a victory which had yet to be won; it belonged to a parade not to a campaign, unless the campaign was itself a parade. Later he would say, for my ears only, that de Gaulle was never so lucky, never so manifestly blessed by 'the Mandate of Heaven' – The Writer was famous for his orientalism – as when he was fired upon, in the heart of Paris, by those unidentified snipers whose bullets were 'better than confetti in the marriage of the French with their self-elected prince and deliverer, their inverted scapegoat!'. The Writer's military stride around those empty suburban pavements was a foretaste of his eventual master's haughty march into Notre Dame de Paris. I am almost tempted to believe the stories, which as a diplomat I always denied, that The Writer himself organised the sniper fire which gave his master such a clinching opportunity to display his fearlessness.

Our joint tour of the quarter ended at the dentist's metal gate, from which I crossed, feeling somewhat naked, to the *café-tabac*. The longer I loitered there, under the complaisant eye of the woman behind the bar, the less prudent the rendezvous appeared. The arrival of first a car – with two passengers – and then a bicyclist, and then a pair of pedestrians (*all of them* suffering from toothache?) declared a convergence which amounted almost to a reunion. My office was that of lookout and backup man, but I had no way of signalling to those in the dentist's house when danger threatened. I drank a glass of gritty white wine and tried to imagine how I could create enough of a diversion, if the moment came, to allow The Writer and his 'O-Group' to get away. My reluctant imagination could hear the eulogy which he would deliver, in my father's presence, at the dedication of the monument which would one day be erected over my grave.

What happened, when it did, took place both quickly and, it seemed, in a sort of slow motion. I was sipping at the chilly glass, listening to the sarcastic babble from the radio (on which the collaborators had adopted a more and more moralising tone, where previously they had gloated and threatened), when a black *traction-*

avant, of the kind we had learned to dread, slid into the empty area in front of the *café-tabac*. It cruised slowly across my line of sight and I could observe two men inside, leaning down and looking up, in the manner of those who look for a particular address. The woman behind the bar narrowed her eyes, as if in sympathy, and went through a glassed, curtained doorway into a back room. Had the men come in response to her call? I took out my revolver and looked at it, quite as though this inspection were itself a military move.

The driver opened the door of the Citroën and went to the metal gate of the dentist's house. He was not in uniform, but that was quite usual with Gestapo or Milice officers. He wore a suspicious overcoat and a hat. The other man was huddled in the passenger's seat, looking out in the same way as before. Should I run out and shoot one or both of them? If I was to do it, I should do it at once; another car was almost certainly close behind. I did nothing. I decided (I think) that the car's arrival and the tentative manner of its occupants must have been observed from inside the house. From our circuit of the block, I knew that there was a passage down which The Writer and his more agile companions could make their escape. It occured to me that, since I had no address for transport, I should now probably have to find my own way back.

The driver was now inside the gate, which he left wide enough open for me to see the steps and the front door with the glass canopy over it. The driver had pulled the bell and was lighting a cigarette when the door opened and The Writer appeared with a pistol in his hand. If I say that I was both astonished and unsurprised, it may give some idea of the clarity with which I saw what I could not quite believe. Panic and courage had an identical appearance. The driver shook out his match and turned, with a polite manner, towards the man whom he may well have expected to be a nurse. He began to ask a question and The Writer shot him twice. I cannot say by what means I knew at once that his action was both unnecessary and melodramatic. The reaction of the man still in the car may have indicated as much: he raised his body, with painful reluctance, and twisted to look out of the side window. He held something in his hand against his jaw. Unlike me, he could not see directly through the gate and up the path to the dentist's house, but the sound of the shots alarmed him sufficiently to make him get out of the car. His frown did not originate from what had just happened – he had been wearing it from the start – but it deepened now, more in puzzlement than horror, as he leaned round the gatepost of the dentist's house. What he saw gave him sudden energy. His feet stuttered on the roadway and then he came straight

340

across to where I was watching him. He burst into the *café-tabac*, where I was now alone, and said, 'Melephone. Wick!' His voice was both urgent and muffled by what I now saw to be a lumpy, wet cloth which he was still pressing against his distended jaw. Resentment, rather than fear or dismay, was in his face: it matched the tone of the newscaster who was still scolding the Allies for their 'terrorist' attacks on French civilians who happened to live near military installations.

I said, 'I don't think they've got one.' He seemed to be unarmed and not even to be thinking of defending himself. I could not bring myself to the tactlessness of displaying the revolver which I had in my right hand.

He said, 'There's a maniac over there. Did you hear?'

I said, 'No.'

'You didn't hear shots?' His eyes were wild with dismay. 'Are you deaf?'

Behind him, I could now see The Writer, whose eyes were hardly less wild, as he looked with furious apprehension out of the gate at the empty car and the empty square. If there was a backup force on the way, it must have got lost or delayed. The Writer ran, in a crouch, to the back of the car and peered inside. He tore open the door and then he said, 'Shit!'

'He's a maniac. He shot my friend. I need the dentist.'

Only after The Writer had looked left and right and left and right again did he glance across the square. 'Guy!' he called. 'Guy!'

I said, 'Lie down on the floor, fast!'

The man looked in vain for some sane solution. Then, with speedy reluctance, he used a table to help him on his way to the floor. He sat there for a second, wincing up at me with an air of obedient incredulity; he was less afraid than appalled. I had shown him the gun, in order to hurry him, and he continued to stare at it with amazement.

I said, 'Are you German?'

He said, 'German, yes,' quite as though it might be in his favour. 'I'm a German wine merchant and I have a very bad toothache, very bad.'

'You're in the army?'

'The *army*?' He seemed to be winking at me. He had only one eye. 'A wine merchant?'

Somehow we had time for this conversation before The Writer, who had been waiting for me to respond to his call, came scampering across the road and banged with the flat of his hand on the window.

'Is he in there?'

341

I saw the man's fear now and I pitied him as much as I regretted his failure to be as frightened of me as he was of The Writer. I saw the plea on his face and glinting from his live eye and I said, 'Yes, he's in here.'

'Kill him,' The Writer said, 'fast. And let's fuck off out of here.'

'My God, you're barbarians! Barbarians!'

I had killed already; why did I hesitate to do it again? My virginity had been as good as restored; the previous occasion gave me neither taste nor licence. I said, 'Crawl down to the end of the room . . .'

He said, 'You want me to crawl?'

'. . . and get out the back, cretin.'

He said, 'I wanted to see the dentist.'

'Kill him and let's go, let's go . . .'

'For the love of God,' I said, 'do as I say.'

He started to slither between the tables. The Writer made urgent signals and then ran back to the Germans' car and got into it. The crawling man, curious despite himself as to whether I would shoot him, could not quite look where he was going and clattered against a chair. The impact caused him to yelp (perhaps he jolted his jaw) and he went crabbing on, hating the indignity, I dare say, more than the fear. I had an image of him, as soon as he was out of sight, standing up and brushing sawdust and muck from his nice overcoat.

I had time to see the *patronne* at the curtained window behind the bar and then I ran out into the street as the Citroën made a wide circle and came round to where I stood. I am not at all sure that The Writer would have waited for me. He leaned across and opened the door and I scrambled inside. He said, 'We were betrayed.'

I said, 'He had a toothache. He was a wine merchant who had a toothache.'

'And you,' he said, 'what are you?'

'You called "Guy",' I said.

'No, I didn't. You *heard* Guy. Did you finish him off?'

I said, 'No.'

'What? You disobeyed orders?'

'I do not obey cowardly orders,' I said.

'Are you teaching your superior officer his duty?'

I said, 'They're going to be after us.'

'We're ditching this car as soon as we can. Never presume to teach me anything. Do you want to be court martialled? We were in a trap. I had to think quickly.'

I said, 'You're going to kill us without their help if you drive like this. Take it easy.'

'He got away? You let him get away? Did you fire at him?'

I held my gun to his nose. 'Does it smell like it?'

'You little whore, aren't you?'

'I've been called worse,' I said, 'by people I like better.'

'You've grown up a bit since lunch, haven't you? Don't outgrow your strength, my friend.'

I said, 'What do you think will happen to the people in that quarter?'

He said, 'Listen to me. We were ambushed. Someone gave us away.'

I said, 'Is that an order?'

'We shall never know for sure, but that's war. Yes, that's an order. And a request, if you will.'

'What about the others? How are they going to get away?'

'You should have thought about that before. I don't care if he was a princess of the blood, you should have shot him.'

'Probably.'

'They got out the back while I covered the front. Which you should have done. What were you doing – groping the barmaid?'

'Certainly not.'

'You're someone who will always miss his opportunities, aren't you? A man who will take refuge in morality like everyone whose hand shakes when it should be steady.'

I said, 'Why wasn't there a backup car?'

'We shall never know.'

'Because the man had a toothache. Why would the Gestapo pretend to have a toothache and keep up the pretence even when I was going to shoot him?'

'Because that's all there is to keep up, ever.' He had slowed down and was looking out of the side window in a way that reminded me of the man whom he had shot. He came to a turning which led towards some woods and twisted the wheel in that direction. We went along a track and were soon under cover. 'A green cathedral, wouldn't you say?'

'Not just now,' I said.

'You have no proof, remember that, my friend. You have no proof of anything. It is a green cathedral – the columns, the light, the tracery of the branches.'

I said, 'Shit.'

'Listen to me,' he said. 'Listen very thoroughly. The man was a German, and a German is always suspect and almost certainly an agent. It doesn't matter whether they stumbled on us or whether they came expressly for that purpose. I had to make a decision and I did, at once; it is never wrong to be decisive, do you understand that? He *was* a German agent and I killed him. Perhaps your man was different, but he's not different now. Thanks to you, you poor idiot, he was able to go back and report what happened. He's got eyes – he can describe us both . . .'

'He's only got one in fact. One eye.'

The Writer slapped my face. He was wearing pigskin gloves. The driver must have left them on the seat. 'If I was wrong, you were wrong. But what I did doesn't matter, whereas what you did . . .'

I said, 'Let's get going, shall we? We've got a long march and the sooner we start the better.'

He said, 'I like you, Guy, and it's just as well. I'm not going to tell your uncle the whole truth about this.'

I said, 'I can imagine you won't be telling it to anyone very much, will you?'

He said, 'You talk as if I'd made you do something disreputable or as if I did something disreputable myself.'

I said, 'We were surprised by the Germans, is that it, and it was a case of *sauve qui peut*?'

He said, 'I told the others to get out the back, I went to hold them at the front. No one could know how many of them there were.'

'Wasn't anyone looking out?'

'Remember the backup car.'

I said, 'Is that an order?'

'I can be a great help to you, Guy. When this is all finished. A great help, in whatever you want to do. Ask your uncle when you see him.'

I said, 'I'm not sure there is anything.'

He said, 'Do you know the way – the way back?'

'Yes,' I said, 'don't worry.'

He said, 'I'm only in this region by chance. I had to choose where to operate; I chose here.'

I said, 'Weren't you sent?'

'I was consulted as to where I should be the most use.'

'Follow me,' I said.

After a while, I heard him say, 'Why do civilians die in air raids? Is there any difference? War is war. That's the beauty of it, the terrible beauty – are you familiar with the phrase?'

XXXVIII

As I walked down the long street which leads from the Gare St Jean to the centre of Bordeaux, I realised that I had never, in fact, called my little blonde whore by the name Félix. Did I lack the nerve to announce her the boy I fancied it would be amusing for her to be, or had I never seriously wanted her to be him? To seek a single answer was to assume myself a simpleton, which – for all my faults – I felt no obligation to do. As I have indicated, my sexual desires have never dominated my consciousness; hence I have often been delegated the most tedious jobs. When I am congratulated on my persistence, it is assumed that my modesty is a blind, but in fact it has the implausibility of all innocence: it is no effort for me to make an effort, but it is very difficult for me not to do so. Holidays are more of a strain on me than long hours at the office. Now, with nothing between me and the morning train but a whole night for which I should never have to account, I was plunged into a sense of nullity which did not even have the character of a depression. I recalled no grievances; I entertained no fantasies. Nevertheless, had I known that there was no train, I might have arranged my evening differently. I should have eaten first and then chosen my whore and taken my time with her, perhaps even stayed the night. As it was, I had no great appetite for food, I had spent my desire, and I should have to find a hotel which would either be expensive or uncomfortable.

If I hoped for some involuntary encounter which would give a sense to the evening, I was disappointed. I went into a *brasserie* and ordered something I did not want from the thin menu. A television set was bracketed above the bar at the far end. The place was quite expensive but the owners had spent a good deal of money giving it an air of cheapness. I ate my *faux filet* and some of the flaccid chips and drank some suspect wine, all the time behaving as if I expected someone to come in at any moment and join me. I thought again of the college friends who lived in Bordeaux and, lacking the will to telephone any of them, still hoped that one might answer my unspoken call and appear in the doorway.

As I drank my coffee, my attention was distracted to the coloured

345

flicker of the television screen, from which only a faint sound was coming. They were showing a news flash, one of a series at the end of a programme: a woman was lying on the pavement outside an apartment block on the Avenue Montaigne, her body covered with a gendarme's white mackintosh coat. It seemed that she had been the victim of a freak accident (why otherwise would her death be newsworthy?). Some workmen had allowed some bricks to fall from the scaffolding where they had been repairing the façade and one of the tenants, Madame Berthe de Jardin, a widow, had had the misfortune to be walking underneath. She had, it seemed, ignored a warning sign, but an inquiry had been set in motion. The announcer's voice became more and more distinct as he spoke, until I had to cover my ears against the shrill statistics of the number of people who, each year, find accidental death on the streets of the capital.

I continued to watch after the long, brief moment of Berthe's fame was displayed on the television. My mind tried to make what followed on the screen relevant to the casual image of the woman with her feet showing from under the white décor thrown over her. The advertisements, and the loud announcement of the winning numbers on the *Tapis Vert*, more advertisements (including one in which a woman wearing only a swirling white robe walked upstairs towards an assignation with some bath salts, shedding her garment as she went, so that her naked loins and ostentatiously turned back struck one as a snub) and then the weather report, delivered with an excess of winsome gestures by a posturing creature with his hair fastened at the back in a pigtail, although his high forehead shone with its absence – all these discontinuous elements seemed to compose a pattern and to imply further information, if only one's mental key could turn their lock and disclose the solution.

I drank my coffee and then a glass of smarting Armagnac and tried to discover what my emotions were. Berthe's death seemed to be linked to Pierre's marriage. Indeed, as I kept looking again at the television (where footballers were now moving up and down some South American pitch), I acted as though I was waiting for someone to make the connection. Could it be that my ex-wife – my wife! – had sought her death, that it was not an accident at all? I had to confess that she was an utter stranger to me. I could construct a plot which would have her consumed by jealousy at the marriage of a man whom she had never liked and with whom she had once pretended to be having an affair, only to appreciate, some two decades later, that she had been pretending to pretend and that the desire she attributed to him was immanent in herself. It seemed an unduly elaborate scheme to suppose that she had committed suicide by accident, so to say, but then again, what prettier bet could she have taken with the unknown? The elusiveness of Berthe's purposes overwhelmed me with pity; the 'love' which eddied around me was for nothing tangible, but who will say that it was not genuine? The body under the white coat seemed to be there for my benefit and to my despite. Her stillness could never mean as much to anyone else as it did to me; only for me was her accident not accidental. In that sense, I felt that she had died for me, although I recognised very well that it was unlikely that she had been thinking of me or, if she had, that she was thinking kindly. My possession of her body, in the past, had never been particularly enjoyable. Yet the mind and body which knew me were now mindless matter and I was flayed by their abrupt withdrawal. I did not suffer exactly, but I did *not* suffer: I felt the absence of pain like pain. I waited for it, as if for a lover who does not come.

I ordered another glass of the despicable Armagnac and swirled the oily, spirituous stuff in the bottom of the tight glass. The waiter came with the bottle and ministered to what he presumed to be my needs. I said to him, 'Is your name Félix by any chance?'

He said, 'Bruno.'

My thoughts composed themselves around Berthe. I could believe that I was destined to be alone in Bordeaux and that I had fabricated that nonexistent train in order that I might savour and grieve over my wife's death during that lacuna which, until a few minutes earlier, seemed so misplaced. I had never had any interest in those who try to account for coincidences or seek, by reference to them, to construct theories of divine purpose or secret systems by which the universe conspires to tease, amuse, mortify or redeem us. All conclusions in such cases are either perfunctory or the result of a circular argument in which modesty and conceit share the intellectual amenities. We all know very well either that God does exist or that, if He does, He is literally inconceivable to us. His good is not ours, nor ours His. Those who argue for Him seek to ingratiate themselves, as The Writer recommended, with the power that may command the future. They make the same bet as Blaise Pascal, whose thought in arguing that we might as well believe in God (since He was our only hope of immortal dividends) was precisely as base as it was noble. I admire his invention of the wristwatch more than his metaphysical salesmanship. Even as I mourned, quite genuinely, I was comforted by the intimate conviction that I had now seen the last of Berthe. Only an exceptionally cruel God could ever contrive for us to meet again in another life.

Had I been a regular and responsible parent, I should have gone to telephone my sons, but my contacts with them were infrequent (though perfectly cordial) and I did not know exactly where either of them was. No doubt David would have heard the news – he is the kind of person who always hears and deals admirably with bad news – while Patrick (so far as I could remember) was not due back from Canada, where his bank had interests, for several days, perhaps weeks. In the privacy of the ugly *brasserie*, I was happy to be dispensed from the need to explain or reconcile the sweet contradiction of my feelings; in silence, they consorted without difficulty. The idea of Berthe seemed to be delivered to me in a wonderfully clean form, like a legacy which, coming from a dubious source, proves – against all expectations – to be quite untainted by its provenance. She enriched me, as I sat in the tight, hooped booth in which my plastic table was fitted, a step above the jostling crowd at the bar, and I was like a sated miser who is quite content with the luxury of the wealth in his wallet, without the smallest disposition to disburse, still less to share, it. Berthe was close to me, part of me even, as she had never been during the years of our physical proximity. I sipped the Armagnac as if it were the essence of the woman herself; I was a prim cannibal, without anyone suspecting it. Did I have specific memories or thoughts? Yes, I considered, without rancour or relish, whether she had continued to be my uncle's mistress after our marriage. Unless there were letters, how would one ever know? And if she was, did it not lend a certain piquancy to my life? I wondered, yet again, why I had married her, why the marriage had seemed inescapable. I realised that The Writer, and our melodramatic expedition to Fumel, contributed more to my decision than I had cared to notice. His notion that a man could not be free unless he wilfully broke with the woman he loved had struck me as sufficiently repugnant to be compelling. I had not, of course, honoured it properly in choosing to marry a woman whom I did not love; I had avoided the salutary pain of such a rupture by electing to embrace what I did not want and hoping, fatuously, that I should discover liberty by this act of inverted renunciation.

Was that really my hope or my purpose? Could I have behaved with such callous folly and could I have allowed myself to make Berthe into my sacrificial victim in order to honour the 'morality' of a man I despised quite as much as I stood in awe of him? My lifelong duplicity – that inability to match my actions to my appetites – has made rebellion and docility into much the same thing with me. Did The Writer ever truly renounce the love of his life, or was he romancing in order to amuse himself with my solemn reaction? I have small faith in the singlemindedness of men, nor yet do I believe in the relevance of logic – any single logic – to the shape of one's life and motives; by trading on each other's craving for simplicity, we become each other's romances. I was, I concluded (thanks, perhaps, in part to the Armagnac), one of The Writer's less successful works.

No, I do not blame him, or anyone; I do not even blame myself. I simply see that I have been, and that perhaps everyone is, a *creation*. It is our sense of being made, of being as it were postulated, which makes our lives provisional, which gives us that sense of eternal uneasiness on which Pascal traded when he sold us death in the guise of the divine. No man is capable of being the sole author of his own life. We cannot contrive a language within ourselves which could enable us to have the autonomy which The Writer affected. Our most intimate impulses, supposedly finding their origin deep within us, are reprinted and edited from a stock of ideas and presumptions which we can no more refuse than can subscribers stem the flow of books from those clubs, advertised on the back of television magazines, once they have paid their first easy instalment. Berthe was not my victim; she was my mistake, and my misfortune. I had no Edenic memories of her – even her virginity was an imposture – but the knowledge of her corruption was now as touching to me as any innocent recollection. I loved a woman who was dead and who, in the biographical sense, was untrue to life; I loved what Berthe had never been to me and what we had never been to each other, but what *only we* had never been to each other. My romance with my dead wife was not morbid, or sentimental; it was almost brutal in its recognition of our failure to be true lovers. Its tenderness sprang from that brutality.

I am not used to alcohol. My thoughts were eloquence and wind combined; grief and inertia kept me in my uncomfortable place and sponsored the garrulous silence of my solitude. The voices in my head, at once pedantic and a little smug, recalled the Vichy radio commentators who, as the sand ebbed from their hourglass, tried to substitute dignity for opportunism by elongating the sentences in which they complained that the wrong might was proving right; one observed, with vindictive pity, the process by which the vulture took on the lineaments of the dodo. So now, though with no thorough correspondence, I felt the transition in myself towards a state which was both dreadful and welcome, like an old tram in a childhood story which has gone back and forth over the same tracks and whose last journey is indistinguishable from preceding ones, but for the fact that it *is* the last. My renunciation of whores had seemed a caprice, but it now took its place as the first 'logical' stage towards my acceptance that the old rails of my life were being uprooted. What I had supposed to be an economy, or an act of medical prudence, now appeared to be the presentiment of some inevitable closure. It was as if the news of Berthe's death had come to me, like a letter that is already in the box at the end of the chestnut alley, although one has not collected or opened it, and I had acted in the light of what I did not yet consciously know.

I left the *brasserie* after the next news bulletin, in which there was no mention of Berthe's misfortune, rather as though once I had received the message it had been pointless to repeat it. The night air cuffed my cheeks and I turned up my collar against it. People were coming out of the opera. I told myself, quite falsely, that I wished I had known of the performance, even though Gluck's *Orphée* has always struck me as remarkably insipid; perhaps I was entertained by the ironic fact that it was only now, when Berthe was definitively lost to me, that I could summon affectionate memories of her. What warmed me, above all, was not the hope of recovering her, but the certainty that she was gone forever; neither her personality nor her flesh attracted me any more now than before, but the liveliness of what I remembered, including our lack of rapport, the sudden conversion of what had seemed negative into something positive, gave our chilly marriage its retrospective poignancy. I could love her rage and even her drunkenness; her mean greed and her overdressed, overweight body became touching, since I should never again be obliged to endure them. I understood the nostalgia of old soldiers whose eyes fill with tears as they look back on days spent in the horror of the trenches or in the charnel house of battle as if those were the sweetest moments of their life. Can one say that only what is lost is truly ours?

I was free. Happiness was no longer my concern. I was dispensed of the need to act as though it were attainable; Berthe's death had relieved me of the urge to live in her and allowed her to live in me. I am not unaware of the malign interpretation of what I have allowed myself to say; there was always something inappropriate in her femininity, which was less reliable even than that of the ravishing hermaphrodite I used to go and admire in the Villa Borghese. Now that she was dead, Berthe's thick legs and clumsy hair were volatilized and irrelevant to the purity of her presence in me.

I walked to the cathedral and pretended to be disappointed that the waiters in the café opposite were already swabbing the tables and stacking the chairs adjacent to the few clients who chose to ignore them. One of the waiters was quite bald, but he had a pale moustache; a rim of fair hair, clipped short, encircled his head. He went through his routine manoeuvres with a certain balletic elegance; he was not young, but he was as spry as a retired juggler who had settled for something easier. I turned away and walked round the cathedral, giving it the perfunctory, polite attention of someone who goes to see a house and recognises, in a second, that it is not what he wants and yet continues his tour. Nothing about the grey stonework as it yearned ponderously for the sky excited worthy thoughts or reverence; it made a grim claim which I disdained to honour and which made me want to believe in God only so that He might observe my disbelief.

The great tomb of the cathedral, with its mossed gargoyles and its bleak shadows, was less intimidating than ridiculous; it was somewhere I never wanted to live. As I completed my tour of it, the bald waiter, with his limber competence, was adding a top chair to the little edifice he had compiled, and I looked in at him with the admiration which better minds have offered to the anonymous masons whose beaked gryphons and spiteful devils adorned, and perhaps satirized, the House of God. I have always been touched by the mystery of those who are loyal to duties which bring them neither fame nor renown. Unlike most people, I respect the repetitious functionary whose habits I mimicked for so many years; when, after a long interval, I visit a provincial town and happen to be served by the same waiter, who, years before, warned me that a plate is 'very, very hot' and hear him once again do the same thing, although he shows no sign of recognising me, I am moved by his impersonal solicitude, just as I was by Pia's mercenary reliability. The aristocrat is closer to such people than his usual affectations allow; his blood enrols him in a métier whose courtesies and routines he must observe and which, while making him part of the landscape, recruit him to a certain regularity. I have no notion of nobility, on account of my petty *particule*, but I have always known when I was departing from the code which no one has ever spelt out to me but which, like the unread instructions one always puts back in the box with the medicine one occasionally takes, is nevertheless respected. Why had I shot the blond officer and recoiled from killing the 'wine merchant'? I did not kill the former because he was a traitor, but because I could not endure the shame of being disarmed on the field of battle; I spared the latter because, although my orders came from the same source, I could not submit to the commands of a posturing clown, even though the 'wine merchant' was no better than a looter in need of dental treatment.

The balding waiter looked around for more chairs to stack, saw none for the moment and looked through the glass towards me. As

351

our eyes met, one expression took the place of another on his face. I cannot say that he recognised *me*, but he substituted a general sort of recognition for its lack. I was a possible client, who merited politeness even if he was too late for service; if I was to be denied the chance to tip him now, I was not therefore to be deterred from doing so on a more timely occasion. The pale lashes, the almost jaundiced freckles across the low saddle of his thickish nose, the lips that twitched but did not smile, stunned me with their distant proximity: behind the glass, he was like Félix in a bottle. He made a gesture of denial, and I took it, out of politeness, to indicate that I could not be served. As if flattered and reprimanded at the same time, I turned hotly away and walked to a hotel down the street, where I took a room, underwent a drizzling, tepid shower and dreamed many dreams which I allowed to drift from my memory as soon as the breakfast arrived. Since it was not the kind of hotel which supplied a newspaper, I dressed and walked to the corner.

Berthe's death was mentioned in a short paragraph on an inside page. The 'comedy' of the circumstances was implied by the dryness of the report, which said that the dead woman was the divorced wife of a 'distinguished retired diplomat'. I derived no satisfaction from the putative distinction of a man of whom none of the newspaper's readers was likely to have heard. Nevertheless, I read and reread the paragraph, standing in the exhaust of the morning traffic, and pitied Berthe not least for the lack of emotion which accounted for the tears that salted my cheeks.

XXXIX

I did not telephone Maureen until I had bought my ticket and had only a few minutes before the departure of my train. I gave the impression that I was calling only in order to have her meet me at Le Buisson station, if that was convenient.

She said, 'Guy, I've been wanting to be in touch with you. Why didn't you say where you were going to be?'

I said, 'I wasn't sure. I hadn't got a hotel when I called. What's the matter? How was your meeting with Christophe?'

'Oh,' she said, 'that was fine. It's about Berthe.'

'What?'

She had pronounced my first wife's name 'Birth', as she always did. 'Berthe. Your ex-wife.'

'She's been in touch with you?'

'Oh Guy,' she said, 'she's . . . I'm afraid she's dead. Guy?'

'I'm here. Are you sure?'

'It was on the news. It'll be in the papers, I daresay.'

I said, 'I see. When . . . when did it happen?'

'Guy, are you all right? It was an accident. A thousand to one chance. She had something fall on her from the building she lived in. I don't think she suffered. I wish I was there, with you. Maybe I shouldn't have said anything till you got here, but . . . Your son called – David called – he's on his way to see you. He's flying down.'

As I have made clear, I have rarely experienced desire for Maureen. I accepted her place in my life as one might that of a servant who makes herself indispensable and of whom, with a measure of honesty, one is able to say that one 'loves' her, without meaning that she is admitted to one's confidence or one's bed. Now, however, all alone in the plastic cabin where I was listening to her tactful attempts to break the news which I already knew, I experienced all the symptoms of desire. If she had been there, I should, I daresay, have been more embarrassed than zealous in bringing matters to the usual conclusion; it was her absence, and my ability to deceive her and to prompt her sympathy as I did so, that allowed my flesh to stiffen for a woman who, had she been present, would never have stimulated me.

What Maureen was it that I was ready to embrace? It *was* Maureen, and not some casual instance of a woman, who caused me to alter my stance and wonder how I should get to my train without looking ridiculous, but it was also only *a* Maureen, a creature whose overheard tenderness was at once touching and fatuous. The effort to be my true wife, when my true wife was dead, seemed to disrobe her soul and it was that – the thin, naked, vulnerable nothingness of the woman who, for whatever reason, had decided to link her life with that of a man whose language she could not speak and whose mind and body were equally alien to her – which inspired a lust which was a parody of what I assumed other people to enjoy in reality. Maureen's willingness to be attentive to a shadow, to show consideration for an unknown man, was as touching as Pia's and inspired the same mixture of cold affection and involuntary heat.

I said, 'I must go, Maureen. The train . . .'

She said, 'I'll be there at the station. Have a drink, if you have time, before you get on the train.'

I said, 'I'm all right. I'll see you soon.'

She said, 'Was I wrong to tell you? I couldn't not, could I?'

I said, 'You were quite right.'

My excitement had wilted before I was out of the booth. I went down the steps to the underpass which would take me to my platform and had to dodge the passengers from a train which had just arrived. I heard a voice say, 'Roumegouse?' It came from a man who had just passed me; my name was thrown back at me, rather sharply, like a pass from a rugby player. I looked round, expecting a younger face than that of the traveller who had turned and was frowning at me as he lowered his wheeled suitcase to the damp floor of the underpass. 'It *is* Roumegouse, isn't it?'

I said, 'I'm afraid not.'

He said, 'Guy de Roumegouse? Aren't you Guy de Roumegouse?'

I said, 'Bruno le Guen, Monsieur. I'm sorry.'

'We were together in Damascus. Damascus. Istvan Kovacs. Moroccan Ali's . . . surely you remember Moroccan Ali's?'

I said, 'I'm very sorry, but I've never been to Damascus. I have an excellent reason never to have been there. Good morning.'

He said, 'Forgive me, but . . . the resemblance, even after so many years . . . it's perfectly extraordinary. I was at the Czech Embassy and we . . . we played tennis on several occasions. I'm living in France now. I teach at the university – at Bordeaux Trois. Slavic languages. Do you have a brother?'

I said, 'I had one, Monsieur, but he died during the war. In Germany. Forgive me – my train . . .'

He said. 'I could have sworn . . .'

I said, 'Bruno le Guen. I must go.'

He said, 'I can hardly believe it.'

I said, 'Those are so often the things we have to believe.'

He made me remember the Indian coasters which Berthe gave away when we left our posting in Syria. The persistence of things and the evanescence of our own identities made me smile and I seemed to drift up the stairs and onto the train like a wisp of casual fluff.

Maureen was wearing a narrow red coat and a little black knitted hat. Of course she had her white gloves on. As the little train made its snorting approach, I saw the sensitive creases on her face and the woeful anxiety in the wide blue eyes. What a nice welcome! It put an end to any vestige of desire I might still have had for her.

'Oh Guy,' she said, 'I felt so helpless! I didn't know what to do.'

'There was nothing you could,' I said. As so often, speaking English made a happy, nameless counterfeit of me. 'When is David arriving?'

'Oh Guy,' she said, with the usual heavy hand on my sleeve. 'He wasn't certain, but he's flying to Bergerac and he'll be with us tonight at La Fontaine du Noyer. I'll drive, shall I? How are you?'

'I'm perfectly all right,' I said. 'Less affected than you might imagine. I saw it in the paper.'

'Was it in the paper?' When I held it up for her, she took it and scanned the indicated paragraph as if it were quite a long article. 'I like the way they call you "distinguished"!'

I said, 'I thought you might.'

'You deserve it.'

I said, 'I deserve better than that, don't I?'

She said, 'Oh Guy, I wish I knew when you were being serious.'

I said, 'So do I, Maureen; so do I.'

We drove along the road towards Siorac. It took us beneath the limestone bluffs and under the railway bridge where I shot the blond officer. They were widening the corner, to improve the visibility; the column against which our lorry had crashed, after the ambush, was being replaced.

I said, 'I once shot someone just here.'

She looked at me with a twinkle. 'Now whatever do you mean by that?'

'I was Bruno le Guen in those days and I shot an injured man, right back there. The safety catch was on and he told me it was and I let it off and then I shot him, with my eyes more or less closed. Rat-a-tat!'

355

She said, 'I don't believe you.'

I said, 'Quite right.'

While we were waiting at the roundabout, below the *château* of Siorac, she said, 'How many people did you shoot altogether?'

I said, 'Alive or dead?'

She said, 'It's upset you. I can tell.'

'I shot dead people too. I promise you.'

She looked at me as if my accent amused her. We drove along the valley which I knew so well; they have recently built a narrow golf course, of only nine short holes, in the section before the branching of the roads which I always took to be halfway, although I recognised that it was not. How many thousands of times had I gone along the same road, before and since it was asphalted and garnished with the neat signs to Circaud and the other hamlets and farms hidden in the hills? I observed once more the green reservoir where a plastic duck floated lopsidedly and I waved, as if I were returning after a long absence, at young Delrieux who had recently lost his father (and his own youthfulness) in a terrible accident which he himself had witnessed; a button on the father's cardigan was caught in a threshing machine and, before he could escape, his arm was dragged into the machinery and torn from its socket. The farmer bled to death in front of his son, who now ran the farm alone. He did his work with admirable efficiency, but he never joined in any of the activities of the village, quite as if he had something in common with the 'other' Delrieux, who was no relation but who lived, in utter seclusion, further down the valley. The other Delrieux had been a child when his father was shot by Martegoutte during the *accrochage* in which Cabanne and his wife also died. It was on that occasion that The Writer, who had organised the operation, ordered me to fire into the corpses which Le Sanglier and the rest of us were then told to arrange as if they had died in battle and not, as happened, while they were sitting at table. The Writer refused to regret that there had not been a fair fight. 'In war,' he told us, 'a fair fight is one that has been inexpertly planned by one side or the other. I make no apology for saving your lives. Now do as I say.' After the Cabannes and their friends had been dragged outside and festooned with weapons, all of us fired some more shots and the The Writer took photographs. As soon as the inquiry had confirmed that the Cabannes had been playing a double game and had tried to betray our *réseau* to the Germans, their property was put up for sale and my father was able to acquire the big field to the right of our chestnut alley and so complete our possession of the whole 'corner'.

As we drove past it and up to La Fontaine, I said, 'Did you come to any decision with Christophe?'

'He left a few rough drawings. It won't be as expensive as you think.'

'That I can easily believe.'

Maureen said, 'Naughty!' Altering her expression, she looked earnestly at me. 'He wants to talk about the funeral. David.'

'Couldn't he telephone?'

'Among other things. He didn't say what. Do you want me to come?'

I said, 'To the funeral? Do they want me to go?'

She said, 'Guy, I don't know, but if you want me to come, I will. I don't want you to be alone with all of them.'

'Everything will be done in exactly the same way, whether you're there or not.' We got out of the car and I said, 'Do you know – that's where I saw her for the first time. Right there.'

She took my hand. 'I wish she'd made you happy, that's all I can say.'

I said, 'I wonder what David wants.'

'Perhaps he wants to comfort you.'

I said, 'David?'

When he telephoned again, I left it to Maureen to take the message that he would be on the plane arriving at La Roumanière at half past nine. I did not want either of us to be embarrassed with the obligation to express regret, even if it was genuine. Maureen told me that she had cancelled her arrangement to go to a meeting of her Gardening Club, but I insisted, with what she took to be typical unselfishness, that I should be perfectly all right on my own. I promised that I should look at Christophe's plans and let her know of any improvements which occurred to me (she twinkled at the possibility of my supplying them). As soon as she had left the house, I went up to that part of the *grenier* which would be affected. The floor had been cleared, probably by Maureen, before the architect's visit, since she always liked to give a neat impression. Old trunks and boxes had been pushed against the wall and then (of course) dusted. Without any urgent wish to check the plans, I had hurried upstairs, as though my wife's departure had given me a secret opportunity. The rearrangement of the relics in the attic was, I daresay, to be expected, but my purposeful haste had nothing consciously to do with what I thought I should find. It was as if I were visited by some detective urge and did not wish to lose a moment of Maureen's absence in order to indulge it. So far as I know, no distant memory, no nagging inquisitiveness, no curious instinct drove me to haul out an old tin box and open it (I was a little disappointed that it proved to be unlocked). Berthe's death seemed to give me a licence to do something I had never done before, but the box had never belonged to her and there was no connection that I can think of, however remote or fanciful, to account for my decision to rummage in that particular place on that particular afternoon.

Naturally enough, the box was dirtier inside than out. There were bundles of old bills and papers, tied with officious string; there were old cotton reels, one or two with needles stuck through them, which appeared to have been put in such improbable company only temporarily and had, in the event, never been removed. I sat on a ribbed trunk and, without any sense of discovery, untied some of the dossiers. Most of the papers were as frail as old leaves, veined with writing or figures whose ink had faded to brownish purple. How can I convey the mixture of indifference and impatience with which, for no reason I can supply, I continued to investigate the dossiers which slumped this way and that as I removed their neighbours? (I thought of the slippery fish which were being unpacked the morning when I walked from the *lycée* in Caillac up towards the apartment where I saw Fritz's parents for the last time.)

In the end, of course, I found what I was not looking for. The dossier was not at the bottom of the box, but wedged down the side, as if it had been thrust there in some final, provisional attempt to find a safe place for it. The most accessible papers were bundles of essays which I guessed at once were part of my father's work at the 'X', when he was in his early twenties. They were the kind of thing which I might have written myself, had I not spent the equivalent period of my life in the *Maquis*. I had no sense that I had been doing something more real than my father. On the contrary, even when I was running, firing my gun, possibly killing the figures I aimed at through hedges or over hard walls, I had no impression of baptism, of admission to some brotherhood which certified my maturity. I can remember coming back to St André-le-Fort after a skirmish in which I think I hit a German sergeant (and perhaps saved Le Sanglier's life) and then noticing that I had torn a flap of skin from my thigh and that my trouser-leg was crisp with dried blood. How shall I explain that I felt more shame than pride in my 'wound'? I was pretty sure that it had been caused by my clumsiness in vaulting a wall with wire along the top, but even that unglamorous recollection seemed to be borrowed from the memory of a fighter whom I was impersonating rather than my own property. I insist that there is no false modesty in this account. In fact, I am perversely rather proud of it, as one might be of having the sort of silly symptoms which might stump a doctor, although he was sure that they were negligible. Perhaps more people than I know have much the same impression of having a memory which is stocked with elements that are undeniably 'theirs' but which seem to have been picked up by chance. My wartime adventures were undoubtedly my own but like the German industrialist's coat which I took from the cupboard in the British embassy in B.A., they were not quite my size; even now I cannot take them from the depths of my memory without wondering to whom they might more properly belong.

When The Writer, as my commanding officer, decorated me with the Medal of the Resistance, long after the events which it supposedly honoured (not least the 'battle of La Chapelle', rescripted by The Writer's history into a close run thing), I accepted his congratulatory kisses with all the emotion of someone who receives an award for valour on the secret understanding that he is taking the place of the proper recipient but that he deserves it, if only for the brazenness of his impersonation.

Inside the dossier of faded work from the Polytechnic was a fat, yellowing envelope which had been thoroughly stuck down. The glue had cracked like the glaze on an old picture. I eased the flap open simply by rolling the long envelope over the rounded top of the trunk on which I was sitting. I relished the fragile crepitation and was sorry when it ceased and I was able to take out the pages which had been sealed for so long.

Life, like chess, is full of surprises that are no surprise. The news that is broken to us with tactful hesitation, like Maureen's when she told of 'Birth's' death, is sometimes already known to us, but even when it is truly new, it turns to old dust almost as soon as it is revealed, like ancient bodies in freshly opened tombs. The moment of amazement or of consternation is almost simultaneous with the feeling that we have always known what has just come to light, so that our show of dismay or astonishment is both genuine and wilful.

Certain of the sheets were on the same lined paper from a *cahier de brouillon* as the essays among which the yellowing envelope had been inserted. The lack of superscription indicated that those particular pages had been drafts which it was never intended to send. They were written in a hurried, yet unexcited hand. What drove the pen to snag on the cheap paper was less passion than impatience. My father might have been drafting notes for a minister who cared more for thorough-ness than for elegance. Do I hesitate to repeat what I read? I do, but not out of prudishness or shame or the fear of seeming a fool for being surprised even by what did not startle me (it seemed to come as a confirmation of what I had always known); I hesitate because my discovery seemed to pinch me in an identity which it had always amused me to slip on and off like a glove that gets easier and easier as the years go by. My freedom to speculate was lost as a result of what I found. I heard my father's voice, not as I had ever known it but as it was when he was silent and spoke only to himself.

'What does this love mean which cannot say what it is, not because I am ashamed of it, but because it is *not* what any language can convey or speech embellish? It is neither a desire nor a hope; it is a kind of obstinacy, a sweet affliction whose pleasure derives from its futility. I have no illusions about it. I lack the temperament which might make something perverse or rebellious from it, something in the least practical. If I were another kind of person, I should know how to domesticate – or eroticise? – yes, eroticise undoubtedly! – what, in my actual case, cannot be, let us say (clumsily, but truly) dis-ennobled. Every painful development in our story is foreseeable and even, in a way, what I want to hear, but only because it proves that what I feel is *not* a story, not part of what is happening in your life or in mine, but something in a different dimension altogether, something which, unlike a mundane lover, it is inconceivable for me to consummate, to arrive at the peak of, and hence to imagine *having been*. Only what will never be always is.

'You ask me – as I ask myself, in a certain voice – how I can consider marriage. You ask me if I know what I am doing to myself and to her. I know *and* I do not know; I know that *I* as a decisive entity, will somehow cease to exist once I have accompanied myself to the ceremony. What I cannot know is how well, how honourably, I shall be able to impersonate what I shall cease to be, or never was. I think that I shall do it very well. I can even say that I am looking forward to it. I should not take this hectic, frigid line if I did not recognise that *they* suppose me to be ignorant of their design. The only pleasure that they cannot understand is that their concealments alone impel me to agree to do as everyone wants. If I were not being deceived, I should lack the nerve to go forward; their cruelty is a kindness I cannot decline.

'Am I lying? Your face comes to me and I can see the light glinting on your lashes and the golden gloss it brings to your cheeks just above the line where you stop shaving (though, one day, I suppose, you will have to soap yourself there). I do not pretend that my love is unalloyed with desire, but nor do I pretend that it is not: it can survive your kisses, after all, and the coarseness of your little laugh when I gasp and wonder whether we are really doing what, I suppose, you have done or will do with others. I crave your kisses and your embraces, but they are not at the heart of what you are to me, even if you want to believe as much. They are approximations, like these words, for something intangible which neither derision nor satiety can dispel. Am I perhaps welcoming, in this doleful way, something which will fix me forever in a style that is not quite mine? What expresses the human situation better than something which fails fully to express it? Who shall I better be than someone correct, since what I am is what I cannot be? I shall build on what amuses you when I am least like what will please you. What better tribute can I pay you in your absence than to behave as if you were always there? You wonder why I have decided that this particular girl, woman, female, should be my wife. You write from where you are as if you were at my shoulder and I look over it to ask why it should matter if it is this or another creature with whom I am to link my life (or its simulacrum), since it cannot be with you? We are, I know, I know, incapable of being together what we shall always be apart, at least for me, who am less able to take our love, if that is what it is ("It is, it is!" the lamenting myth reminds me), for something with commonplace *succursales* – oh those suburban shops which advertise the same wares as one can find in Paris, but somehow do not supply them with the same *élan*! Do you really take such delight in your provincial adventures as you say? I hope you do; I hope you don't. (I hope the first as one who loves and the second as one who believes in you.) There is – I quite confess it, if in a whisper – something parental in my affection, something which is neither sensual nor of the same age, although I cannot deny that I am both. I crave and dread the voluptuous things because, in the first case, they would purge what is beyond time and, in the second, because they would do exactly the same thing! My contradictions are indistinguishable from my singularity, you see? Will it hurt or affront you if I say that what is irreplaceable in you, for me, is also, in some respect, nothing to do with you? I love you by accident and yet your love – which is what I feel for you! – is now the very essence of what I am and will always be: someone who cannot have what he wants and who, if he had it, could not be what he is.

'When you said that you were going to Indo-China, I had some idea that you were going to take a holiday and I felt a sense of dread and impatience; I wanted to come with you, or at least to be invited, but when you said that you were taking a post there and that your absence would be as good as permanent, I felt a great relief, such as a condemned man might feel, I suppose, when he learns that he had misunderstood the prison governor's message and that there is not, after all, to be a reprieve. For an ironist, I need scarcely say, the only elegant form of suicide is to go on living, which is what I shall do.

'Our kisses, which would seem to mocking spirits to be the "truth" to which all our fine words supply nothing but a spurious skirt, are indeed perverse, and always seemed to be so. You are not "like that" and nor am I; it is not a matter of morals, but of nature. What made your lips sweet to me was not what I always wanted but what I always dreaded; it was the absence of revulsion, not the presence of delight, which made them seductive. It amazed me that we could do something so untypical and that it should become typical of us. Do I lie? What is the truth? To speak of *the* truth is to accept the judgments and categories of other people, whoever they are – Aristotle or your man who drinks Dubonnet! When I had said goodbye to you and you had promised me that you would not remember me and that, at the first opportunity, you would visit a *succursale*, I wept with gratitude and did not disbelieve you, yet what you said made no difference: you will always be the same to me whether you are faithful (which is absurd, but possible) or whether you sleep with a million boys or father a further million. You cannot escape me by being absent forever nor could you lose me by losing yourself in other people. I need no news of you, for I have it all with me, and forever. You may call this selfishness, even a kind of kidnapping, and you may be right, but there is nothing you can do to change it, since there is no rate of exchange – no ransom – which can have the least appeal for me. I do not deny – I should not even *try* to deny – whatever accusation might be levelled at me as someone who is worse than an "immoralist"; I might as well be said to be "very unique"!

'I am writing this at such length (and can imagine writing all night), not least because it postpones the moment when I must seal it in the tomb of some silly envelope and send it, like a flimsy ambassador, across the water. No, that is not the only reason I delay: I delay also because when I reach the end – when I choose to stop and call that an ending – I shall have to add to the very beginning of what I have written, or write out again, some superscription "Dear P." or "my love" or even "Monsieur" (to have the last small pleasure of imagining that frown of yours which is better than a smile, more to be provoked and enjoyed) and, when I have done that, I shall reduce you to a formula, like some stupendous crystal which, for all its specific rarity, belongs to a well-known group. The love that has no name is better on that account than those the poets cover with their phrases.

362

No, what I feel for you is not forbidden, it is unbidden because no formula can describe it, for better or for worse.

'I can imagine you sighing; I can see you shifting your seat not (I like to think) because you are seriously bored but because it entertains you to observe how mortified I am to think it possible that I am becoming sentimental. The unforgettable thing about my love for you (I use an approximate term, rather as mathematicians posit "x", using an old term for what is generally unknown to betoken what is unkown to them alone) is that – unlike x! – it cannot be rendered in other terms and is the equivalent of nothing but itself. So I come to the great equation of my life, the sublime discovery that x equals x, of which there can be neither proof nor contradiction.'

Below the sheets with my father's words on them I came, as I knew I should, on a piece of writing paper from Raffles Hotel in Singapore. On it I read:

'Old man,

'How are you? We have had a quiet crossing, the highlight of which was, according to your taste, either the Purser's dance or the false alarm which almost cost the lives of two antique sisters via simultaneous heart attacks. These were so realistic that it was decided not to take to the boats after all. I have met several fascinating people whose conversation one would not welcome necessarily on a wet afternoon in Nantes but who, in the present circumstances, have all the allure of Confucius-he-say at the top of his form. I shall not pretend that I miss your company, for fear that I should give you grounds to feel sorry for me, or for yourself. I regret only that I shall not be present at your marriage, since I know that the champagne will be good enough to mitigate the horror of the speeches.

'Two weeks later! Now safely in Saigon! I was glad to find your letter waiting for me and to hear that you are fit and happy in advance of The Great Adventure with our beautiful Mireille. Should I offer you advice as to her treatment? I will be brief: do not let her beauty make you read her for an angel. Remember that she is one of my family and do not credit her with too much sensitivity! You remember the old phrase (Valéry's, is it?) about the profundity of the surface. Don't, above all, look below it: that's all tripes and plumbing, remember!

'Well, old man, I've got a thousand things to do, all of them in this damnable heat and humidity which they say I shall get used to in twenty years or so! In between eating my heart out for one of our outings together – the Alps seem much further away than you do! – I shall take comfort in the hope that you will be a proud father by the time you hear that I have made my first million or caught malaria or been run through by a jealous choirmaster. One day I shall come back to France and you will walk right past me without recognising the jaundiced old colonial with his dated tie and mothballed suit.

'So listen, I shake your hand with my very long arm and I shall clink glasses with you on The Day and think of you – courage, courage! – on The Night. You are marrying a treasure, but be sure that you don't fail to take mean advantage of her!'

The signature was 'Your D.' Clearly it was an answer to a quite different letter from the one my father first drafted. At the bottom of the envelope, there was another sheet from the same squared *cahier* tightly folded, like a wedge one might use to steady a café table. I unfolded it and tilted its tight writing towards the skylight.

'You have more power than you know. What I see in you is an ability you cannot recognise in yourself. Do you want to be a victim or do you think that you can escape by victimising another? Do I take a tone of hostility? It is because I think so well of you, of your possibilities, and because I fear that you underestimate yourself. You are beautiful and for that reason, I fear (since I cannot quite understand) you abase yourself – you allow others to arrange what you should do and, out of the despair which is your vanity, you elect not to resist. Do you look to me to resist? (I should call you "my love" but I love you as I do only because I cannot!) I cannot resist, perhaps because I am too weak, perhaps because I am strong enough to think that only by accepting what has been arranged, by draining the cup, can I escape from *my* predicament (which has nothing, of course, nothing whatever, to do with yours, which – maybe – you do not even recognise). I am surrendering because it is the only way I can show any sort of courage. Yes, truly. But you – you are capable of something better than this marriage; I feel like someone who goes on bended knee to a beautiful woman and asks her, with tears in his eyes, "Please, please, will you not marry me!" I am making love to you by saying that I want you to know that I cannot love you as you deserve. I am a siren who begs you to keep away! My beautiful M., I am afraid that you do not see that my willingness to be your husband is the same thing as my inability to be what you want, what you need, what you deserve. I fear that we shall succeed with dignity, even with a kind of pleasure, in being what they would like. We will give our families a family, our servants their orders, our houses their roofs and extensions. We shall be everything that is required of us except ourselves, which no one will miss, perhaps not even you and I. I will miss you, my dear, but only if you are with me! I shall see you, with all the pity and (I fear) politeness in the world, as someone who cannot be what she should be and who might have had the strength not to be what duty calls strong.

'Cowardice is also the willingness to be brave in the wrong cause. I will not, I cannot, explain to you why I feel that I have given my word to be such a coward. I want only to say to you that my life cannot be what I want it to be, and that I must take what pleasure I can (it may well be quite considerable) in the irony of my situation, but you – you, my beautiful M. – can escape, should escape, *will* escape if (as I pray) you can find the strength to open an unlocked door. Understand that I cannot open that door; neither for myself nor for you. You know why.

'Have you heard from D.? I have, so probably you have too. He is well and sends you a thousand kisses and the sort of disreputable messages I refuse to pass on! He loves you, and so do I, which shows how many things a thing can mean.

Your

Two long ink lines made an X across the surface of the text; they resembled the marks which artists make when they are displeased with an etching and deny its publication. I have seen ministers do the same with sheets of official photographs when they embargo the prints which display their baldness (which everyone knows) or their paunches or their uneven dentures. We all take infinite trouble to conceal what is perfectly obvious.

I replaced the pages in the envelope, which I tried unsuccessfully to reseal (the glue on the flap would not take moisture from my tongue), and then I put the envelope back in the box and piled the other dossiers on top of it. Why should I deprive one of my sons, or their children, of the amusement to be found in discovering them once again?

I went out onto the terrace on which I remembered being passed around as a baby. I looked up at the window from which my mother had looked down on the evening when Jean-Claude drove me to Caillac station, on my way to Rodecin. Manuel was in the field which once belonged to the Cabannes and was now ours. I never think of the house and the land as 'mine'; it is as if I had a brother I did not know or as if my parents might yet return, like 'dead' actors when the final curtain has fallen, and claim what I should be happy to yield to them, like a minor actor who hands the principals forward to receive their deserved applause.

Manuel came up from the Cabannes' field and straddled the fence which still separates it from our old land. He gave me a little wave, which announced his foreignness, and called out that the rabbits were running around in broad daylight now. 'Shameless!' He used the French phrase, *sans gêne* with a certain shyness, as though he hesitated to speak disrespectfully of rabbits whose nationality he did not share. He looked down towards the road along which Maureen would soon come, and gave a little shrug. I suppose he took me for an anxious husband.

The Cabannes' field had been planted with walnut saplings. Each was ticketed with a little white bandage where it had been grafted by the local woodman whose name happened to be Bois. Manuel had been putting wire-mesh 'gaiters' around the slim trunks to prevent the rabbits chewing the bark. They did not venture up the hill but used all their energy and ingenuity to attack the saplings nearest their burrows at the bottom of the valley. When, after a snack for which Maureen had returned in good time, I took the car to go and meet David at La Roumanière, the little airport at Bergerac, my headlights picked out several rabbits at the end of the drive. I had the intention of taking my gun down there first thing in the morning, but I could not bring myself deliberately to run over a single one of the rabbits, even though they bobbed temptingly under my wheels.

XL

The Paris flight was a few minutes early. The passengers came into the little terminal with that air of inspected indifference which is discarded in an instant when a familiar face is seen. Before he came in, I found myself wondering what David looked like and how I should describe him to the police with sufficient detail to convince them that he really existed. It was a relief to have a moment to prepare the spontaneous reticence with which I greeted him and in which to be sure that this slim, dark-chinned, balding person, in his Parisian overcoat and holding his rigid briefcase (he had a canvas bag in his other hand) was indeed the same man as the one to whom I had last said goodbye. His complexion was a little sallow; I did not associate his appearance with grief, even though I adapted my manner to appear sympathetic. After we had embraced, I reached to take his bag, but he took both handles in one fist and gestured to me with his empty hand to go on out.

In the car, I said, 'It's very good of you to come down.'

'Not at all.'

I said, 'How goes it?'

'Business? Extremely well.'

'And other things?'

He said, 'The death of my mother simply closes a chapter, I suppose, so far as you are concerned.'

'It closes a chapter that is closed, if you want to put it that way.'

He said, 'You're unmoved.'

I said, 'Have you come down here to take my emotional temperature?'

'Very well,' he said. 'I understand.'

I said, 'Do you want my sympathy? I offer it freely.'

'She meant nothing to you.'

I said, 'She wanted a divorce; I have married again. What should she mean?'

'Her disappearance, in other words, simply effaces something you wanted to forget in the first place.'

I said, 'My dear David, I recognise that anger is the easiest form of grief and I am sorry that you feel it. I feel none, perhaps because I am, as you suggest, without any residue of feeling and perhaps – a hypothesis! – because I refuse to mount a performance for your benefit. I regret your mother's death because she was your mother, and your brother's. And because the loss of a mother is more poignant than that of an ex-wife, I defer to your feelings as I hope you will to my lack of them.'

He said, 'I wondered how quickly we should arrive at this situation, but I did not think it would be as quickly as this.'

'It's a kind of liberation, is it not, immediately to be on bad terms? The proof of a certain facility!'

'You won't be coming to the funeral then?'

I said, 'Is that the purpose of your visit? My absence will be appreciated, is that it?'

He said, 'It will be on Tuesday. I am assuming that your attitude is due to the same "anger" you attribute to me.'

'Have you eaten?'

'A snack. It's quite sufficient. I eat little; I drink not at all.'

'You take care of yourself.'

'It's long been my habit.'

I said, 'And what is your pleasure? Apart from your business.'

'I've taken up archery. I joined a club at Versailles and I find it very relaxing.'

'It doesn't look it,' I said.

'One knows exactly how well one has done, and why. That conforms very much to the way of life I favour.'

I said, 'And personally?'

'I'm very happy,' he said.

'Good. You have friends?'

'I have friends. I cook quite well. And quite frequently.' He seemed embarrassed at my smile, and his own. 'I have a life that suits me.'

'And you're very happy.'

'And you?'

'La Fontaine is always La Fontaine. One is never bored. If you ever come to live here, which perhaps you will, if you want to, you'll discover that there is nothing like a simple rural life for consuming whatever fortune you may have.'

'You find your pension sufficient?'

'What government pension is ever sufficient?'

'Do you want me to look at things for you?'

I said, 'Save the bad news for when you receive the good.'

He said, 'You mustn't imagine that I have come down here in order to reproach you for anything.'

'Is there a purpose yet to be disclosed?'

'You speak as I sometimes do.'

I said, 'Perhaps I inherited my style from you.'

He said, 'As if you were speaking for the secret amusement of some invisible companion.'

'Is that uncommon?'

He said, 'Did you never love her?'

'I often loved her and, if I must be truthful, which I should prefer not to be, I as often did not. What about you?'

'Our situations are completely different.'

'I'm counting on it,' I said. 'Nevertheless . . .'

'When I did not love her, I preferred to think that it was you who was responsible.'

'As may well have been the case.'

'I share that view.'

'Then we are one,' I said. 'Your failure to marry, is that to be ascribed to my credit also?'

'Credit?'

'I supplied the word, on approval. Have you a better?'

'It has nothing to do with you.'

I said, 'Perhaps you imagine that I have no interest in being your father. Perhaps it's a little late to say so, but it's not entirely true. I should be glad if we were able to be friends. In the circumstances, however, I thought you might be happier not to be burdened with painful choices.'

'Your frigidity is a form of generosity, is that how I'm to take it?'

I said, 'I understand you spoke to my wife. She'll be at the house. Would it be better if we stopped somewhere? I shouldn't like our intimacy to be compromised by the obligations of courtesy.'

He said, 'Have you any notion of why I wanted to see you?'

I said, 'You inherit something from your uncle – *my* uncle – his capacity to arrive importantly, even when your visit may be nothing more than a politeness.'

He said, 'How long did he continue to be my mother's lover?'

I said, 'Are you implying that it came to an end? I was unaware of that.'

David said, 'Yes, I can see now – there's something almost saintlike in your acceptance of what you are.'

'And of what I am not,' I said, 'which is very close to the same thing, is it not? This is the last café where we can stop. They play billiards here and they have a baby-foot table. I hate the place. What do you think?'

He said, 'Let's go home.'

'If we take our time, perhaps she'll have gone to bed, but I fear not. She has the tact of those who only *just* step on one's toes.'

'It's kind of you to disparage her to me. Why did you marry her?'

'I've always found it easier to do things which do not greatly appeal to me than to go to the trouble of discovering what might. Did my uncle contact your mother in the period before he died?'

David said, 'Are you serious?'

'If I'm smiling,' I said, 'I usually am.'

'She nursed him for several weeks, months even. That was why she never came back to London. Surely you knew.'

I said, 'I was simply wondering if you did.'

He said, 'It was after that that she told me.'

'That they had been lovers?'

'And everything else.'

I said, 'Of course. I'm glad you know. Has it been a liberation? Perhaps you should have been told sooner.'

'You were thinking of Patrick,' he said.

'In all probability.'

'Who isn't really all that concerned. But maybe that's only because of what you decided.'

'One hopes so. It's never easy to get these things right.'

He said, 'I misjudged you.'

'It can be a kindness to do so.'

David looked at me as one does at an opponent whose shot, one has to admit, has touched the line. Then he looked out at what he could not see. Our headlights were flashing on the trees in the valley. Night aged the landscape and made it once again a place of secrets and ambushes. I tried to feel nostalgia for the deep darkness of the nights when we – Martegoutte and the others – would take sacks of walnuts to Fongauffier's press and extract the oil before first light when the Germans, or their surrogates, such as the bad Delrieux (also known as 'The Arab'), would come to confiscate whatever was still available. We distributed the oil to farmers who left food for us, not so much in recompense as to prove the power we had over the region. It was that sense of power which I had never regained, although even in the days when I wore it with a certain swagger it never quite fitted me.

I said, 'He saved my life, Jean-Claude.'

'He saved everybody's, didn't he?'

'He saved it, but in some respect I always felt that he saved it for

370

himself. Lives were things he collected. He had many of them. I always had the feeling that he had been behind the "mistake" that was made when they ambushed the lorry I was in and not the one with Pascal and his father. After the Liberation, I went to him and I challenged him. He denied it.'

'The truth is not only what is denied, you know.'

I said, 'My challenge was very polite: it took the form of saying thank you, but with a slightly interrogatory inflection.'

'I can hear you doing it now,' he said.

David sat in the car for a few moments after I had drawn up in front of La Fontaine du Noyer. Once again I could imagine that he was a stranger and that he was giving himself that moment or two to acclimatise himself. I was looking up at the lights, hoping that Maureen might have gone upstairs, but nothing showed on the first floor but the glimmer of the shutters in the moonlight.

I said, 'It looks like another frost.'

David stood on the raked area below my mother's brace of steps. His shoes were not suitable for the country. Was it a prim courtesy on his part to give such an impression of being a stranger to where I had chosen to live? 'I never watch the weather,' he said.

I said, 'They called it the Liberation, but I was freer before it than after. I think perhaps that's why I married her, your mother – because . . . And then again, perhaps not.'

He said, 'You knew she was pregnant, did you, at the time?'

I said, 'Of course.'

He said, 'There was something heroic in it. I quite recognise that.'

'But certain heroisms are repellent, is that it?'

'It's neither comic nor tragic, is it?' he said. 'What we are. In the past it would have had to be one or the other; today, things are both, and neither.'

I said, 'Had you come in a month or two, you would have had a new bathroom. As it is . . .'

He said, 'You must not be so kind that you allow me to replace what I feel for you, whatever it is, with something so palatable as contempt.'

I said, 'Is your brother going to come to the funeral?'

He said, 'Isn't that the reason I'm here? To discover that?'

I said, 'Is there an outcome to this? Is there some proof, some payment, some apology – surely not an apology – which will give you satisfaction?'

He said, 'I want to be sure that my parents are dead.'

I led him between the half-open shutters and into the flagged vestibule. Maureen appeared in the living room doorway. 'David!' she said.

He said, 'Good evening.'

'What can I get you?'

'Nothing at all,' he said. 'How are you?'

'As you see me! How about a drink at least?'

'Nothing at all.'

She said, 'I'm very sorry about your mother.'

'So you said on the telephone.'

'But I wanted to say it in person. Your English is almost as good as your father's!'

He said, 'I never knew that he spoke English.'

Maureen touched David's arm, as if to indicate, in her usual way, that he was being both charming and provocative. 'I only wanted to welcome you,' she said, 'and now I'm going to leave you to talk. You can show him upstairs, Guy, can't you? I shall see you in the morning. Would you like your breakfast downstairs or shall I have Rosa bring it to your room?'

David said, 'May I come down when I'm ready?'

'Whatever you please.' Maureen gave me a little squeeze of a smile which suggested that, if David had not been there, she would have been more affectionate. She touched my arm on the way out, implying that she knew that David and I were getting along very well. 'I'll say goodnight.'

The fire sighed and blazed with new wood. Maureen had recently persuaded me to buy a new patent cast-iron grate, with a built-in motor which blew the heat into the room. I said, 'She must think that we have a lot of things to discuss.'

He said, 'I shall never live in this house.'

'Perhaps Patrick will. He has a family, after all.'

'I don't know about Patrick.'

'But you know all about yourself. Do you talk to him?'

'Talk? Yes.'

I said, 'Well now, what do you want to tell me?'

He said, 'About Mother's estate.'

'Ah,' I said. 'Are you hoping that I am about to make some unjustified claim on it? You misjudge me. Which is, of course, entirely your right. But there it is. I refuse to deserve your indignation. Can I be forgiven?'

He said, 'It goes back to Grandfather, doesn't it?'

'And further, no doubt, but we must allow for the curvature of time as navigators do for that of the earth. Things drop out of sight. The imagination too has its horizon.'

He said, 'Did you always know that too? About him?'

I said, 'Always is too wide a term. I was a child at one time, you know; if it knew, *I* did not.' Once again I saw myself, but not quite as I did before, being passed along the line on the terrace while I, whoever I was, watched with wise bewilderment from a kind of exile from which I have never fully returned. 'What goes back?'

He said, 'It began there and it ends with me. Please understand that I don't blame you.'

'That seems needlessly cruel of you. But of course I understand. My problem perhaps is that I *only* understand.'

'You know one of the things which always puzzled me with Americans. Not with the British, but with Americans. In certain films. The way they say "Brother!" What is the origin of that?'

'Brother!' I said. 'Who knows?'

He said, 'So there it is.'

I closed the vents in the patent fire and switched off the electric motor. 'Maureen's idea,' I said. 'It's supposed to be economical. It's certainly hideous.'

David said, 'Didn't she ask you before she installed it?'

'Oh yes,' I said. 'She does nothing without asking me. I'm going to get up quite early in the morning and try and shoot some rabbits. Do you want to come?'

'I should miss,' he said.

There were many things that I wanted to say to him, or at least to someone, but I watched him leave the room in his slim, self-possessed way and I kept the flavour of the conversation which I wanted to have with him on the tip of my tongue, to give me an appetite for the morning. I was looking forward to taking my gun into the Cabannes' field.

'Brother!' I said. 'It is strange, isn't it?'

A translated extract from *Le Monde*, 12.2.92.

M. GUY DE ROUMEGOUSE

M. Guy de Roumegouse, who died early on Saturday morning in Caillac Medical Centre, after a shooting accident, was a distinguished diplomat who saw service in several important posts. He never achieved the highest ambassadorial ranks but he was often charged with missions of a particularly delicate nature, requiring the tact and patience which were his mark. His speciality was prolonged negotiation like that involving the restructuring of the British contribution to the CEE. His command of English and his unusual sympathy for Anglo-Saxon culture (his second wife was of Irish origin) enabled him to gain the confidence of Whitehall and to engineer an agreement which gave all the parties the feeling that they had been successful, if not triumphant.

The local police say that M. de Roumegouse, who won the Medal of the Resistance during the war, was an experienced shot and that the accident – which seems to have happened as he climbed a fence in his land – appears to have occurred through overconfidence in failing to apply the safety-catch.

Frederic Raphael has written twenty novels, as well as many story collections, biographies, screenplays, and translations from ancient Greek and Latin. A native of Chicago, Raphael divides his time between London and southwestern France, with forays into the United States.

The front cover artwork is entitled *A Member of the Family*. It is by **Sarah Raphael**, a well-known London painter who also happens to be the author's daughter.

This book was printed by Quebecor Worldwide in Fairfield, Pennsylvania, and the jacket was printed by Strine Printing in York, Pennsylvania.

Catbird Press was founded in 1987. Its specialties include American and British fiction, Czech literature in translation, and quality humor. For a copy of our catalog, call us at 800-360-2391, fax us at 203-230-8029, e-mail us at catbird@ pipeline.com, or write us at 16 Windsor Road, North Haven, CT 06473-3015. Or visit our website for even more information, including first chapters of our books: www.catbirdpress.com.